Demon's Desire

A
Legends of Shadow Earth
Novel

Stephanie Kayne

Acknowledgements

Thank you to all who have helped me in this fantastical, wonderful journey that is writing. I've had a tremendous amount of fun creating my worlds and characters. I'd like to thank my husband, Bobby, for all his love and support and 'is the book done yet?' Thanks to my weekly writing groups for ideas and inspiration, with Special thanks going to Denise, Diana, and Kris for keeping me motivated when I wanted to throw in the towel. Thanks to my editor, Anya Kagan for wading through it all.

Cover by SelfPubBookCovers.com/Mystic

Copyright

Stephanie Kayne

Demon's Desire

Prologue

Demoni Homeworld

How am I going to get out of the stew pot this time?

Deidre stood outside the tall wooden doors that led into the throne room. A shiver set the cold, heavy chains wrapped around her clanking in musical accompaniment to the beat of her heart. She and her fellow prisoner stood in a dimly lit corridor. The torches on the wall did little to dispel the gloom.

They were surrounded by guards to ensure they didn't escape. A wall of scarlet skin filled her view. Leather belts and sashes denoted the ranks of the guard. A tail twitched as one of the guards looked her up and down. With the body of a human, ebony hooves and furred legs, the Demoni reminded her of satyrs in Earth mythology.

What was going to happen now?

Hzine, the other prisoner, collapsed in a blubbering heap on the floor.

Sneers and looks of distain crossed the faces of the guards as they jerked the male from the floor. His crying and whining grated on her nerves. "Silence! Take your punishment like a real Demoni."

A rumble in her stomach.

"Quiet, you!"

Deidre's head jerked to the side as blinding pain radiated from her cheek. Biting back a gasp, she bit her lip and concentrated on not showing weakness.

Tendrils of her power, desperate with the need to feed, twined from her body seeking male sexual energy. The nearest guards twitched with interest as their flesh rose between their legs.

"Bring the condemned."

Deidre pulled her power back, stomach cramping with hunger.

Two Demoni pushed open the double doors. A sharp point in her back, and Deidre hobbled into the throne room, the chains not giving her enough movement to walk. The guard stopped inside the entrance and stepped to the side.

The prisoners took two steps forward and stopped.

Deidre looked around the cavernous space. It was filled with naked Demoni. Those in service to the Overlord were granted the right to wear clothing. The guards, the Councilors and the Magicians were the ones she knew of.

On the walls, between tapestries featuring gruesome battles, spears jutted from the walls, each adorned with rotting heads.

The air was filled with the scent of pungent spices and rotting flesh.

At the far end of the room Khan, Overlord of the Demoni, sat on his throne. The one she'd been summoned to please.

"Approach" ordered the tall Demoni standing at the side of the throne. He held an ornate staff taller than himself and wore an embroidered tunic clasped at each shoulder and falling to the floor.

Another poke in the back and she began to hobble down the center of the room, matching the cadence of the guards.

A clattering of hooves and chains made Khan growl. The guards picked up Hzine and carried him the rest of the way.

They stopped before the throne. Whispers filled the room and Deidre felt as if she was on display. Steam hissed from the Overlord's horns, and the guards took a step back, leaving her and Hzine to face Khan's wrath.

8

The Demoni struck the floor with his staff. A deep tone rang through the throne room and all whispering ceased. The Demoni unrolled a scroll, and in an imperious voice, read the charge.

"Hzine and Deidre, you are guilty of conspiracy. For plotting to overthrow and kill Overlord Khan, you are sentenced to death. Do you have anything to say in your defense?"

Hzine trembled in his chains, the acrid scent of fear a stench in her nose. "I didn't know what she was, Your Merciless. I thought only to procure a pleasure slave for you."

Khan drummed his black claws on the arm of his throne. "Who do you work for?"

"N-n-no one Sire. I'm loyal to you."

"Who ordered you to bring her to me?"

"No one Sire. She came through a spell."

Gasps filled the throne room and everyone shrank back as Khan stood. His black and gold pleated kilt, reached his knees.

"A spell?" Khan asked in a soft tone, sending shivers of ice down Deidre's spine. "Where did you get a spell? Are you a magician now?"

Hzine stammered. "I didn't... I'm not... "

"What creature did you bring into my world?" Khan's voice boomed through the room.

Hzine cowered before him. "She's a p-p-pleasure slave, summoned to p-p-please you, my lord."

Khan looked at Hzine for a long moment. "The Pit."

Hzine screamed in denial and thrashed against the guards. Two additional guards rushed forward to subdue him. They carried him away, his pleading cries echoing through the room after he'd gone.

Deidre flinched as the screams grew faint and cut off, mid-wail.

The Vizier asked. "And your defense, female?"

What could she say? Neither Khan nor the Councilors had believed that she hadn't been sent to kill Khan.

If my last master hadn't starved me…

The spell that gave her form rearranged her looks to please her masters, however it couldn't change her gender. Her last master had a male mate and was interested in her as a symbol of status. While the assignment hadn't been bad, the sexual energy she needed hadn't been enough to live on.

Khan raised an eyebrow at her silence. "Why?"

And still she didn't answer. It hadn't been on purpose. She drained too much of his energy during their first sexual encounter.

Sparks crackled from beneath his hooves as he stalked down the three steps and circled her.

A small smile touched his lips, causing gasps of fear from those watching. In a soft voice he threatened, "You will suffer as none before. Your death will be so horrific that future generations will look back and shudder with dread. No one conspires against me."

Ice filled her veins at the promise of torture. Sweat trickled from her temple and slid down her cheek. He leaned forward, licked the drop, his tongue like sandpaper rasping against her cheek.

She sensed his lust igniting, his aura permeated with sexual anticipation. Deidre inhaled and tasted a tendril of his energy. It helped ease the hunger, but she dare not take more.

"Who do you work for? Why did you try to kill me?"

Hzine's screams echoed in her head. She shook her head once and looked into his face; a face that held torturous death.

Dying seemed unreal, something that happened to others, not herself. But then again, she couldn't die, not by her Master's hand.

Tension left her. She wouldn't die today, but with the look in Khan's eyes, she'd pray for the sweet release it would bring.

J'akala. Khan was not her master, Hzine was.

Heart pounding and palms clammy, the spell wouldn't protect her.

I'm dead.

10

Her life hadn't been great. Not what anyone would call good, but it was hers, mostly. Damn that bastard Mage and his liking for curses. Because of him she was trapped in this half life.

"The only way to gain your liberty is if your master or death free you." The Mage's words mocked her from beyond the grave.

Death free me. Maybe that wouldn't be so bad after all. But looking at Khan, she knew it would not be a peaceful descent into the abyss. It'd be filled with torturous agony.

Khan stepped in front of her, close enough to touch her chain-wrapped body. He grabbed the hair at the base of her neck, jerking her head back.

"Why did you try to kill me?"

Silence was her best defense. Anger flared deep within his midnight gaze.

"Bring the rack." He ordered

Hell. A rack. Lovely.

Out of the corner of her eye, Deidre saw movement. The guards rushed from the room as murmurs of anticipation swept through the crowd.

Khan turned her toward the doors and smiled. She sensed anticipation and lust rolling off him in waves. She inhaled more energy, not too much, not enough for him to notice.

Careful, that's what got me into this mess in the first place.

She drew the lust into her, feeding her hunger until a high pitched screech of metal against metal shattered her concentration; the sound piercing her brain like an ice pick.

A large wooden and metal contraption was wheeled into the room. As it came closer she could see the places where the wood was stained black.

A few strings of what looked like leather hung from various metal pieces.

Wait. That wasn't leather; it was bits of dried flesh.

Bile rose in her throat and instinct demand she flee. Deidre took a step back, but Khan's hold on her pushed her forward toward the machine.

"Answer me, slave. Why did you try to kill me?"

Slave. It rang through her head, flowed through her body like an ocean of acid. She lost all rational thought and became a creature of instinct. Deidre jerked away from Khan's hold, turned and growled low in her throat. His hand came toward her and she sunk her razor sharp teeth into the meaty flesh of his arm.

Her head was jerked back, his face inches from hers as he snarled at her.

She snarled back, snapping her teeth. A red haze fell over her vision and all she could see was thousands upon thousands of men, her former masters, mocking her, taunting her. *"Slave, slave, slave. You're no more than a slave, slave, slave."*

Tilting her head back, she screamed. "NO!"

A stinging slap that made her ears ring brought her back to the throne room. She shook her head to clear it.

Khan and death, right.

A sadistic expression on his face and she knew she wouldn't meekly submit. The spark of life within her demanded she drain him dry as he killed her; taking him with her as they left this mortal coil.

A small flash from her feet drew her gaze to the flagstone floor.

Could it be? Salvation?

As the golden glow of the light beneath her feet brightened, tension fled..

"What have you done?" he demanded.

His arm jerked and she felt her hair being pulled from her scalp. Tears gathered behind her eyes, but she refused to let them fall, refused to show him weakness.

Twinkling lights encircled her; starting at her hooves and rising upward, enveloping her body.

12

Deidre raised her head, looked him in the eye and gave him an insolent smile before the light encased her.

The throne room was gone in a flash of brilliant light and inky blackness surrounded her.

"You won't escape me, Deidre, no matter where you hide." Khan's voice followed her into the void.

Chapter 1

Transition hurt like a bitch.

Each time she was summoned to a different dimension, pain screamed through her body as her essence was stripped of its form. Traveling through the void left her disoriented; the lack of light messed with her sense of time and distance. When she arrived on the other side, it felt as though something was missing, as if some part of her hadn't made the transition.

It wasn't until a few days into each incarnation that she felt at home in her new body. Awakening into a new body and new dimension, left her drained. The first encounter with her new master resulted in extreme energy drain for him, but after a full nights' rest they'd recover. With Khan however… She shivered. He was in the past.

A thin glowing rope appeared, leading from her chest through the darkness of the void, pulling her to her next master.

Where to this time?

Her attention turned to her next destination. In her thousand plus years of existence, she'd been to many places in different dimensions. Some for a single day before she was summoned away, others for as long as a month.

The damned curse was responsible for her perpetual nomad-hood and she was getting tired of it. Hopefully she'd stay in the next location for the maximum time, a month.

Information inundated her brain.

Earth. Home.

Thank Dar'kirm for a familiar place.

Created and condemned by male belief, she'd been blamed for the sins of man since her inception. Despite that, and one or two small incidents, Earth was her favorite place to visit.

Memories of times past flitted through her brain. New York on New Year's Eve; Paris in the spring; summer in Australia. Over the years, she'd been to every country, every continent. Each time she was summoned, advances in technology amazed her. It was fascinating and scary at the same time. The flood of information helped, but it took her a week to fully acclimatize to the changes.

As she neared Earth, the rope grew to a river and encapsulated her. The light faded to a dim glow before winking out.

At first her vision blurred and jumped.

Shit.

Was something wrong? Had she been damaged in the void somehow? Her focus narrowed to a dancing light, and it took a few moments to recognize the flame of a candle, one of the many lighting the oppressive room.

Stone surrounded her, ceiling, walls, and floor. Against one wall, a scarred wooden table held candles, papers, and glassware scattered across its surface. On her left was a wooden door with metal bands that glowed with magic.

A medieval dungeon. Lovely. But wait, had she gone back in time? Checking the information in her brain, confirmed that she was in the modern era, where women were treated better than mere chattel.

Why couldn't her summoners perform the ritual on the beach, or in a garden? Even a backyard would be preferable. But no, in their secrecy, they chose the most horrible out-of-the-way places they could find. At least there were no insects or vermin around… at the moment.

"You won't escape me, Deidre, no matter where you hide." Khan's voice rang in her mind.

A shudder of fear shook her. *Khan can't find me now, I've escaped.*

She was safe on Earth. To her knowledge she was the only being able to travel between dimensions.

Magic flickered on the floor. Her gaze traced the white chalk lines of the containment drawing. Not one line was out of place. *Damn.* She was trapped in the diagram until her summoner completed the ritual.

Habit forced her to double check the lines. No one had forgotten a key pattern, ever. But she knew the one time she didn't check, her summoner would make a mistake.

Murmuring from the summoner, her new master. The short man had stringy brown hair that looked oily in the flickering light. His beady eyes darted around in quick jerks, as if scanning for danger. The black robe he wore was stained with residue. Of what she wasn't certain she wanted to find out.

He gestured and the smell of- she racked her brain to identify the sour, rotten scent- body odor, wafted around her. She wrinkled her nose, breathing through her mouth. His aura flared and the hope of an uneventful incarnation fizzled out.

Dar'kirm save me! Not another Mage!

The last time she had run across a Mage, the bastard had cursed her into eternal servitude.

Damn! Damn! Damn!

She'd never been summoned by any of the Paranormal Races, and she'd been careful on her previous visits to Earth not to draw their attention. The few run-ins she'd had with them left her wary of all the Races. She'd been chased by the Shifters, cursed by a Mage, psychically attacked by Vampires, and now this?

J'akala, I'm in trouble. But where am I? Real or Shadow?

Shadow Earth was the alternate world where- she consulted her downloaded knowledge- the majority of Paranormals lived.

16

Having never been in Shadow before, she didn't have a concrete way to determine her location.

The Mage gestured with both arms and she bit the inside of her lip trying not to laugh at his pose. Arms upraised, sleeves falling to reveal pale, skinny arms, and green sparks leaping from his fingertips, fading as they fell to the floor.

It had taken a few centuries, but she'd learned the magic of her summoning was contained within the spell itself, so the summoner didn't have to know magic to be able to perform the spell and gain her services. A "perk" the bastard Mage had included in the spell. But to be summoned by a magic user?

I'm screwed.

A book floated in front of her new Master at chest height. He looked at the book, repeated a phrase, and drew magical patterns in the air with a wand in one hand. She bit her lip, swallowing the giggle as she recognized the glowing sigil. *Potency of a stallion.*

If this little man was that good in bed, why summon her?

None of the gestures or patterns had anything to do with the actual spell. For the most part they were nonsense words - fancy window dressing.

Now, if she could get her hands on that book, she'd be able to erase that damned spell!

Unfortunately, Mages were fanatical about their tomes and grimoires.

He spoke the final words and brought his hands down in an abrupt gesture. The glow surrounding her winked out.

His eyes widened as his gaze wandered over her from head to toe and back again. A splotchy redness infused his face. He looked her in the eye.

He cleared his throat. "Is this what you really look like? Why are you naked?" His voice was higher pitched than most human males, and something about it grated on her nerves, causing goose bumps to rise on her skin.

She rolled her eyes. *Dar'kirm protect me from idiots!* Too bad she couldn't hex him. The spell prevented her from working any harm, mystical or otherwise, against her summoner. She'd learned that the hard way after one abusive summoner had beat her bloody. But it felt good to curse even without the effects. *Hounds of Dar'kirm, feast upon his genitals... no wait, wrong dimension.*

The spell built pressure in her head, compelling her to answer. *What was the question again? Oh yes, naked and form.*

"This isn't my natural form."

He frowned. "Then why do you look like a younger version of her?"

His gaze moved down and locked onto her breasts, watching as they rose and fell with each breath. He jerked his eyes up and met her gaze. The splotchy blush returned to his cheeks as if he were embarrassed to be caught staring.

She'd answer his questions – anything to delay his plans, whatever they were.

"My form is determined by your ideal female. The spell does not summon clothing."

He nodded, looking thoughtful. "A perfect version of Elaine."

She remained silent.

His eyes narrowed "How do you know what she looked like?"

"The image of your ideal female was taken from your mind and the spell used it to create my form."

He paused a moment. "What did you look like before?"

Before what? The Demoni? Or before, as a human?

It was best to give the easy answer.

"I don't remember."

"Ah, I see." He cleared his throat and spoke in a formal tone. "I have summoned you from beyond the ether. You will serve me in whatever capacity I desire. In return, at the end of your term of service, I'll set you free of your containment."

Wait, what? No one had ever bargained with her before. He was treating this like a normal demon summoning. She bowed her head, to hide her grin.

"Is there any point you'd like clarification on?" he asked.

Deidre nodded. "How long will you require my services?"

"No longer than two weeks." He paused. "Do you agree to the terms?"

She took a deep breath. "I agree." And waited. Even the most untalented of her masters had known how to finish the summoning.

He tapped his foot. "Well?"

"I'm waiting for the last part."

He frowned. "Last part?"

Was it too much to ask for a competent master?

"Check the book."

He looked down and flipped to the next page. He stared into her eyes.

"I name you Deidre."

She bowed her head in acknowledgement and to hide her expression of disgust. *That's original.* All of her summoners had given her the same name. It appeared she was stuck with it. She'd been Deidre so long, she'd forgotten her real name.

A rustle of fabric brought her head up. He pulled a medallion the size of her fist out of his robe and tossed it to her. Candlelight glinted off the jewels. She caught it and a shiver of energy shot through her. The light was too dim for her to identify the markings carved onto the surface.

What in Dar'kirm?

It felt like a power sink of some kind. She could feel a trickle of energy being pulled from her. Energy she could not afford to lose. She let it drop to the floor.

"Wear the medallion," he commanded.

A shiver of dread raced up her spine. She tried to fight the compulsion but pain pierced her skull, distracting her, and her body bent to retrieve the necklace. Her arms rose to drop the chain over her head. It took all the strength she had to halt the movement. Her arms stopped halfway.

She gritted her teeth with the effort. "Why? I don't understand."

His voice changed, becoming sinister in its softness.

"You aren't here to understand. You're here to obey. Wear the medallion."

Deidre fought the compulsion. A bead of sweat rolled down her cheek. Something inside her rebelled at wearing the spelled metal. Her arms jerked higher, before she regained control.

"Elaine would have obeyed immediately."

Well good for her. Thank Dar'kirm I'm not Elaine.

"Perhaps this will convince you to comply."

He looked down at the book and flipped a couple of pages. Stepping out of the drawing, he paced in a circle and muttered under his breath. As she had already accepted her name, he was free to leave the diagram. Deidre was forced to stay inside until he released her.

Whatever he's going to do to me couldn't be worse than wearing the medallion, could it?

He paced back and forth, alternating shouting and muttering as he read the spell from the floating book. She sighed in relief as the compulsion to wear the medallion stopped. Her arms drop to her sides, and the medallion hit the floor with a dull clang.

A tingle along the bottoms of her feet had her looking down. A red mist rose from the floor inside the drawing. It swirled around her feet and crept up her legs. Excruciating agony followed the path of the mist. It felt like millions of tiny daggers peeling the skin from her bones. A cold sweat broke out all over her body and did nothing to stop the burning pain.

Guess I was wrong.

She rubbed her clammy palm against her thigh to wipe the mist away, but it made the agony worse. The beat of her heart thundered in her ears, the rhythmic pounding sped up until it was too fast to count. The mist entered her mouth and closed off her airway. Her lungs felt as if they were immersed in liquid flame. Her eyes watered, and the ichor flowing through her veins burned like acid.

Khan's punishment was preferable to this torment. At death the searing torture would end.

A jolt of pain had her focusing outside herself. Her legs gave out and her knees slammed into the stone floor. The sharp pain radiating up her legs seemed pleasurable compared to the torture caused by the red mist.

Unable to stand it, she relented.

Her arm shook as she reached out to him to stop the mist.

"Do you yield?" His voice was terrifyingly pleasant.

Deidre nodded once, shivering at his tone.

He slashed his hand down, and the red mist vanished taking the agony with it. She drew in a deep breath, then another. The medallion clutched in her right hand, she rose to her feet, on shaky legs. Standing upright, she saw him staring at her.

Bastard. Deidre lifted the medallion over her head and let the gold disk fall between her breasts. His eyes followed the motion, an expression of smug satisfaction crossing his face.

"I'm the only one who may remove the medallion."

J'kala! So much for the idea of taking it off.

He held out his hand.

Now what in Dar'kirm did he want?

"Take it."

She took his hand, surprised when he helped her out of the diagram

Once she left the containment drawing she felt better. She went through the normal motions of breaking in her new body. She bent, stretched, and waved her arms around. She did side bends and hip flexes and learned her body's range of motion. The popping sound of her joints filled the room as she moved.

Deidre caught a glimpse of his face as she stretched. He looked dumbfounded, and she had to fight hard to keep her laughter contained. It was obvious he hadn't expected that. A sigh of relief left her. *Better, much better.*

She stood facing him. "How may I address you?"

His gaze narrowed as a frown creased his face. "I'll not give you my name. You'd have power over me."

She shook her head, the explanation tumbling from her lips.

"The name you are known by is not your true name."

"Are you sure?"

"I am unable to speak an untruth to my summoner."

Though I don't have to tell you everything, just enough to satisfy the compulsion.

"I see." A flicker of fanatic glee in his eyes made her wary. The next moment it was gone.

Perhaps I imagined it?

"I'm Clint, Clint Douglas. But you will address me as 'Sir'."

"Yes, Sir." *Bastard son of J'kala!*

Deidre took a deep breath and let her body sink into its seductive state. She took two steps toward "Sir" and in a breathy voice asked, "Are you ready to begin, Sir?"

He took a step back and held his hands palms out. "What the hell are you doing?" A hint of panic flared in his tone. "Begin what?"

She stopped and tilted her head to the side. "Fornication, of course. That's why you summoned me."

Please let that be the reason I'm here.

The splotchiness returned to his face. "N-n-no! Not for me!"

Her forehead wrinkled in confusion. *What the hell?* "Then why have you summoned me?"

"You're to drain males on my command." His voice was higher pitched in alarm.

22

Well that was different. Most males couldn't wait to get her into bed. She shivered. *I've got a very bad feeling about this.*

Her fingers twitched, thumb tapping each finger in turn and back again. The repetitive motion calmed her.

"Who shall I drain first?"

He turned and snuffed the candles, leaving the diagram on the floor.

Dar'kirm, it looks like he knows better than to erase the design.

"None of your business."

Oh-kay. Deidre backed off, not wanting to piss him off to the point of being red misted again.

He paced back and forth in front of the table, mumbling to himself. She didn't interrupt. Something about him didn't feel right, perhaps because he was a Mage. The fanaticism she'd glimpsed from time to time in his expression did nothing to reassure her.

Deidre hoped she would find out who her victim was. J'akala take it, she was starving. She needed to feed soon.

He reached under the table, withdrew a black item, and tossed it to her.

"Put it on." Once again the command in his tone had her obeying before she thought to resist.

She donned the floor-length black coat. It had been so long since she'd worn clothing, she'd forgotten how comforting it felt. Which made her wary and off balance. This was not proceeding in the normal manner.

His gaze assessed her. "That'll do for now. I didn't know you would be arriving naked."

You'd have known it if you'd done the proper research.

She looked around the darkened room to give herself time to control the sarcasm that leapt to her lips. If this was going to be her prison, it left something to be desired.

"Sir," bowing her head, and infusing her tone with subservience, "Do you have somewhere for me to stay?"

"I need to house you?"

"My summoners provide housing."

He frowned again. "Hmm, I didn't think about that. You can't stay with me. I thought you'd find your own place to stay."

Was he serious? She wouldn't have to stay with him? Excitement filled her. Perhaps this wouldn't be such a bad incarnation after all. But she had to move carefully. One hint of how much she wanted to be on her own, and he'd likely force her to stay in this basement for the duration.

In the most diffident tone she could manage, "You don't have to find housing for me. If you'll provide the funds, I'll take care of it."

Sir narrowed his gaze, and she held her breath. *Please let this work!* A long moment later he nodded. "I have no choice."

The watch on his wrist beeped. Glancing at it he shook his head. "Time to go."

He snapped his fingers and the book began turning in place. Each rotation caused it to become smaller and smaller until it disappeared.

He led her out of the room and through a dark passageway that ended in steel stairs leading upward. Holding the coat so she wouldn't trip, she climbed the stairs. The grate on the stair treads gouged her soft unprotected feet. Wincing at each step, she stopped at the top and checked her feet. Good, no blood.

He opened the door and entered the main level of an abandoned warehouse. The high windows were covered with dirt and grime, letting minimal light into the cavernous room. Broken machinery littered the space, and the scent of grease and metal was overpowering.

At the far end of the room she detected three male auras. Two Mages and an Elf.

What in Dar'kirm was he going to make her do now?

24

Chapter 2

Sir led her through the maze of machines to the far end of the room where the three males waited. A Mage and the Elf held the other Mage slumped between them. The Mage's wrists were bound in front of him with magic-smothering cuffs. He'd been beaten, with blood dripping from multiple cuts along his face and arms and from the rips in his black uniform. She could see the multicolored strands of magic that held him captive.

What in Dar'kirm is going on?

Sir stopped in front of him. "Tell me, Earl. Did you get the information you were looking for?"

The Mage, Earl, lifted his head and smiled, "All I need to send you to prison."

Sir turned and ordered, "Drain him."

Damn! She was afraid of this. "Yes Sir, but…"

He raised an eyebrow. "Are you refusing?"

She shook her head. "He's not healthy enough."

A frown formed on his face. "What do you mean?"

"He needs sexual release; he's not healthy enough for that."

And he doesn't have enough energy to feed a child let alone a demon after transition.

Hunger pangs gurgled through her midsection, the urge to double over was difficult to resist. Somehow she remained standing. Small tendrils of lust teased her senses. The wisps came from the two holding the prisoner. She winked at them and inhaled the small amount of smoky energy. A tasty appetizer, it appeased the worst of her hunger. For the moment.

Good to know her internal defenses were working. Too little energy and her body produced extra pheromones to draw her prey. Lust was growing in the males before her. Perhaps she should take a little bit more. Smoky tendrils thickened and she inhaled. The amount of energy wasn't enough to fill her, but it allowed her time to seek healthier prey.

Sir moved in front of the prisoner and shook his head as if trying to clear it. He made a sweeping gesture while muttering under his breath.

Cuts closed and bruises faded. The Mage, Earl, appeared healthier, but not well enough to overcome the magical bonds holding him.

Sir turned to her and gestured. "He's all yours."

Deidre bowed her head in acknowledgment and waited. They remained standing in place.

"Are you going to watch?"

"Watch?" the Elf asked.

"Fornication releases the energy I need." *Better nip this in the bud now.* "Do you need to monitor him?"

Sir shook his head, taking a step back, a look of distaste crossing his face.. Perhaps he wasn't a voyeur after all. He motioned and the two guards released the Mage who fell to his knees. They followed Sir until he stopped and turned back to her.

"Do not release him. You are to drain him dry."

"Yes, Sir."

Deidre waited until the three left, and turned to the bound Mage. He looked up at her approach and his eyes widened as he saw her for the first time. She knelt in front of him.

"Save me," he whispered.

She shook her head. "I can't."

Deidre reached out, touched his forehead and let her power flow into him. Touching his cheek, she saw his eyes glaze over in sexual hunger. She traced a finger down his neck, over his collarbone, and down the center of his chest, keeping her touch light, teasing. He sucked in a deep breath as her hand passed below his belt.

Her magic was in full working order judging by the condition of his erection. She lowered his zipper with a gentle hand and removed his hard cock. Soft skin, heated flesh. A pulse of her power had the grip of her hand feeling like a hot, wet mouth. He groaned and thrust into her hand. At his hiss of enjoyment, she increased the strokes, giving him what pleasure she could before draining his energy.

"Please…" he whispered.

"What?"

"Harder," he begged as his hips thrust into her hand.

Deidre smiled and tightened her grip, stroking him faster as his body moved. Sweat dotted his forehead and he groaned with pleasure. She squeezed her grip, wanting to build his lust as high as possible. She needed to drain him fast. Who knew when Sir would return.

Deidre increased her pace, keeping time with his ragged breathing. His body arched and his hips slammed into her hand, once, twice before semen shot from Earl's erection.

The purple wisps of his energy release, hovered above his body. She inhaled the tendrils along with the scent of spent passion. She took enough to fully sate her hunger. Checking her levels, they were at normal. She should have tried a Mage before. Oh, wait, she had, and the bastard had cursed her.

Earl rolled to his side and smiled. "Thank you," he whispered expelling a final, shuddering breath. A moment later, his heart stuttered to a stop.

28

"You're welcome" she whispered back.

Deidre cleaned off her hand on his ripped uniform. *Males...*
they were so messy!

She savored energy. It swirled through her system like
decadent dark chocolate. A twitch and all that lovely energy
drained away.

What in Dar'kirm...?

Standing she looked around in confusion. A thump on her
sternum reminded her of the jewelry. Opening the top of the coat,
she saw the medallion glowing bright in the dark warehouse.

The purple tendrils were being sucked from her body into the
medallion. She touched the disc with her finger and a snapping
spark stung her hand. Her body grew weak and she collapsed to the
concrete floor. Was this what her victims felt?

Deidre knelt facing Earl and the smile that lingered on his
face. She gave him pleasure, but this, this was not fun.

The sound of footsteps approaching had her turning around
but it felt like she was moving in slow motion. She sat back on her
heels and saw the Mage draw his sword and plunge it into Earl's
heart.

Deidre looked up at Sir. A frown crossed his face. "What's
wrong with you?"

"Energy drain." The words were difficult to say.

Sir leaned over, grabbed her arm, and pulled her to her feet.
"Why the stabbing?" She put a hand to her head to stop it from
spinning.

"As a Mage, there's always a chance he could be reanimated
if found in time. Now, he'll stay dead."

A shiver of dread raced up her spine. She didn't kill her
victims, even the first draining after summoning, while significant,
didn't kill the males. It was like killing a cow that gave milk.
Deidre had a feeling this wouldn't be the last time Sir ordered her
to kill.

Heat radiated from the necklace and a dark tendril of power rose from the medallion and snaked its way toward Sir. He jerked when the tendril touched him, and his body began to shine as he absorbed the energy.

J'kala take it! That's mine!

His eyes glowed as power arced in the depths of his gaze. The snap and pop of electricity crackled around him.

He smiled and fear raced through her. Her instincts screamed at her to run, but his hold on her arm was too strong. Her fingers tapped, index to pinkie and back again.

"You've done well." His voice oozed powerful menace.

She nodded, unsure of how to respond. He tugged and led her to a side door before dropping her arm.

"Are you aware of Shadow Earth?"

Deidre nodded. Thanks to that son of J'kala Mage who cursed her, she knew all about Shadow Earth, and how to avoid it.

"Can you enter?"

She nodded again. *Please don't tell me, we're going there.*

He turned to the others. "Get in touch with our Elite contact and tell him to confiscate all information regarding Mage Earl's current investigation."

The Elf and Mage nodded and disappeared into the dark shadows.

Sir turned to her. "Phase into Shadow Earth. Now."

Sherva ne dela... son of a bitch. I've avoided the place since it was created, and now he plans to drag me there?

It was the absolute last place she wanted to go, but she had no choice. Looking into the hardness of his gaze, she knew he'd red mist her if she disobeyed.

Fingers tapping double time, she closed her eyes and reached for Shadow.

A tingle traveled over her body, electric and disconcerting. Even though she'd known how to get to Shadow Earth, she'd never done it before, wanting to stay far away from the Paranormals.

Her eyes opened and the world had taken on an odd sort of glow. Not quite dark, yet not quite light. It was a haziness that lingered on the edge of her vision.

Sir popped into phase next to her and nodded. "Much better."

Better for whom?

They left the building and she squinted against the bright daylight. Blinking to clear her vision, she looked around the unending sea of concrete and plaster. Sir pulled her to a waiting car and held open the door for her. She clutched the coat around her and sat in the passenger seat. Looking around at the luxurious interior she had to shake her head. Technology had come a long way since her last visit to Earth, back in the 1960s.

Sir got into the driver's seat, started the car and drove through the deserted streets.

Where was everyone? The information she'd downloaded told her Paranormal numbers were a fraction of the human population. And while many lived in cities, others, like Shifters and Elves, preferred natural surroundings. Vampires only came out at night.

Severe cramping sent shards of pain shooting through her system. Taking a deep breath, she tried to relax her body, but it wasn't working.

"What's wrong?" His expression was puzzled as he glanced at her.

Sweat beaded on her brow and shivers raced through her. She wanted to remain silent, but compulsion forced her to answer. "I need energy."

"You'll get that soon enough."

Concentrating on the view of the passing city streets, Deidre rode the wave of pain, breathing deeply as it passed. It receded for the moment but it'd be back. She needed to feed, soon.

"Sir, where are we?"

"The warehouse district." His tone didn't encourage further questioning, but she needed to know. "I mean, what city are we in?"

"The greatest city in the world of course, San Francisco."

Of course. The greatest city in the world. As if.

She thought of Constantinople, London and Paris and other great metropolises. But who was she to judge? Maybe San Francisco had indeed become a great Mecca. After all, the last time she'd been in this city, it was the early 1900's.

Sir drove until they reached an area where the grand homes indicated wealth. The buildings were taller, made of glass and steel rather than wood and brick. Nothing looked familiar. She wanted to ask about earthquakes and if the buildings would collapse, but held her questions, not wanting to aggravate him further.

The powerful aura surrounding him dimmed as his body absorbed the energy.

He parked in front of a grand house and led her inside, to a room off the main hall.

"Wait here."

The room was small. A desk and chair sat opposite the door, and a fancy chaise faced the fireplace. The room had the feel of a formal receiving room. Not a place to promote comfort. Portraits lined the marble mantle, and she walked over to take a closer look.

"My family."

Deidre jumped, his voice startling her.

"They're lovely."

"Thank you. Here." He thrust a pile of clothing at her.

Deidre accepted the bundle and separated the items. The pants were a faded gray and looked huge. The top was dull orange with long sleeves; voluminous and shapeless.

Sweats. *It's better than being naked, right?*

He watched her every move as if expecting her to steal the silver candelabra in the corner.

A phone rang in the hall outside the door.

Sir left to answer it and she strained but was unable to hear anything until his voice rose in anger.

"What do you mean, he let them go? Damn it! They're experiments; they haven't been trained yet... Don't give me excuses... Tell Adolfo to round them up, and get them back to the lab. Now."

The sound of the phone slamming down echoed through the hall and into the room.

Deidre jerked the clothes on to hide the fact she'd been eavesdropping. She pulled the pants over her hips and cringed at the bagginess. The waistline was elastic and kept the pants from falling down around her ankles. She had to roll the hem of the pant legs up so she wouldn't trip over the length.

The sleeves of the top hung down past her hands. Pushing the cuffs up her arm got the material out of the way. The bottom of the sweatshirt hung past her hips.

The phone rang again. This time she wasn't able to hear anything of the conversation. Sir hurried into the room and shoved a cell phone at her. "You need to leave. Now."

She looked down at the phone. "What...?"

He grabbed her arm and tugged her toward the front door. "I'll call when I need you. Now go."

Deidre plastered a smile on her face. "Thank you for the clothing, Sir."

Sir opened the front door and pushed her through it, slamming it behind her.

Mages, were they all this strange?

Closing her eyes, she popped back into Real Earth. Deidre opened her eyes and took a deep breath of the cold, crisp air. Time to find some energy.

§

Clint slammed the door behind the demon and took a deep breath. Master Marshall Dean, Mage Council Representative for North America, was coming to visit.

He rubbed his sweaty palms on his robes. Master Dean couldn't have found out about the theft, could he?

Shit! Theft… the book. Damn it, how the hell was he going to hide the aura of the Book? His boss would be sure to sense an item that powerful.

Heart pounding in his ears he paced in front of the door. *What to do, what to do?*

A bright spot on his robes brought him up short. Damn, he had to change. He rushed through the house and entered the guest room that he'd been using since his wife died. Elaine, his love. He pulled off the robe and looked in the mirror to check over his sweater and slacks. None of the residue of his experiments stained his clothing. Running a comb through his hair, he tidied up and took a deep breath, calming the rapid beating of his heart.

He should have attached the book to the demon, but no, there was no guarantee he'd get the Tome back. At the thought, the Tome appeared in front of him, hovering at chest height.

"A Master Mage is coming. You need to hide and douse all auric traces." He thought for a moment. "Hide the demon's aura as well." A wave of hostility emanated from the book. Clint walked toward the kitchen, the book keeping pace with him. "If you don't hide, Master Dean will find you and lock you back up."

The hostility waned and a sensation of resignation replaced it. Clint put his hand on the book, stroking the leather. "Only until he leaves." The Tome of Magic shuddered once, emitting a small pulse of magic that spread in a wave. Two seconds later it vanished. Using his magical senses, Clint looked for any trace of residue from the book. Nothing. His aura and home were clean. Breathing a sigh of relief, he jolted at a demanding knock on the door.

Clint rushed to answer it, slowing as he reached the door. Taking a deep breath, he opened it and bowed low before the High Mage in front of him.

Master Marshall Dean looked like a more distinguished version of his boyhood friend. Generous laugh lines and silver hair at the temples gave him a trustworthy appearance. But Clint knew a that was a mask which hid cold calculation and ambition.

"Welcome, Master Dean. Please come in."

"Thank you, Clint." Marshall extended his hand and Clint emptied his mind for the surge of power that came when they shook hands. It was Marshall's favored method of ferreting out secrets.

They entered the library, and Marshall sat in one of the arm chairs in front of the fireplace.

"May I offer you something to drink?"

Marshall waved his hand. "Whiskey, neat."

Clint busied himself at the small bar next to the fireplace.

"To what do I owe the pleasure of your visit? I was surprised when I got your phone call."

Clint handed him the whiskey and placed his own on the small end table next to his chair.

Marshall took a sip and closed his eyes. "Sorry, it was a hellishly long trip. Noisy humans and their stuffy crowed airplanes."

Marshall kept his headquarters in DC.

"Cross country travel is never fun." Clint replied

Marshall opened his eyes and a sad expression crossed his face. "I'm sorry about Elaine."

Clint caught his breath and looked toward the unlit logs in the fireplace. She'd been gone only a few months, but the yawning chasm of grief, grew day by day until there were times, he couldn't breathe from missing her.

"Thank you." Clint looked back to Marshall. "But that's not the reason for your visit."

Marshall smiled. "Always looking past the obvious. And that's why I'm here. You've been chosen to assist in the Shadow Earth Renewal Spell."

Stunned speechless for a moment, it took Clint's brain a few moments to absorb the news. And then a frown wrinkled his forehead.

"It's a great honor to be chosen. However, I have to ask, why me? My power peaked at mid-level on the scale and while I have the ability, there are more accomplished Mages out there."

Shadow Earth was stable for short periods of time before it frayed around the edges. The spell that created Shadow had to be renewed every fifty years, otherwise the instability would leak into Real Earth, destroying both realities. To generate the astronomical amounts of power needed, a festival was held, the Festival of Lern, named after the group who created Shadow Earth.

The original spell had been deemed too dangerous to be housed in one tome of magic, so it was separated into sections and added to the Five Forbidden Tomes of Magic. One of which was currently hiding somewhere in his home.

"You've not been chosen for your power, but for your attention to detail. I remember how precise you were in school."

"Yes, but…"

Marshall raised a hand stopping his words. "And I feel this may be the thing to get you out of the funk you've been in since your family died."

Clint couldn't argue with that, however, "I don't need pity. I'm working through things on my own."

"This isn't pity. It's a chance to take your life in a new direction."

Clint didn't argue. He wouldn't admit his life had a new purpose, making Detective Alexander and his precious Elite, pay for killing his family. He bowed his head, hiding his expression.

"Thank you for the honor. What do I need to do?"

"My assistant, Jeffery, will get in contact with you in the next day or so. We're still hammering out assignments."

Marshall drained his glass, put it on the side table, and stood. Clint escorted him to the front door.

Marshall took two steps outside and turned back. "You have a long life ahead of you, don't waste it."

Clint nodded in acknowledgement and closed the door behind Marshall, leaning back against it. "Justice for my family is not a waste of time."

Standing straight with renewed purpose to see his plan fulfilled, he walked into his work room. Step one was complete. The demon was here and her draining ability worked as expected. Step two - create the Focus Orb using the power from the medallion.

"Tome of Power, I summon you."

Chapter 3

Deidre walked through the streets, marveling at the wonders this time period held. The fog hid and revealed tall buildings in a bizarre game of hide and seek. Her breath puffed out in white clouds as the temperature fell. Grateful for the fact she wasn't bothered by the cold, she continued to wander toward the heart of the city. Downtown.

A rumble in her belly reminded her she needed food as well as energy. It shouldn't take long to find what she needed.

The variety of humans that wandered the streets, fascinated her. From young people dressed in dark clothing with piercings and tattoos, to businessmen in suits, to scruffy, dirty, people, waving signs saying everything from "Will work for food," to "Vet looking for a meal" Ah, people, the heart and life blood of the city.

Everywhere she turned, technology abounded. Flickering signs with changing adds, touch screen ordering at a deli. It was fantastic. But underneath the glitz and glamour, people remained the same. Full of greed, envy, apathy, selfishness and neglect. It was good to know some things never changed.

A man wearing jeans and a hooded sweatshirt stepped into her path, blocking her as she tried to move around him. Pheromones filled the air as her survival mechanism lured her prey to her.

"Hello," he leered.

How to get him alone? "Hi, I'm new here. Can you tell me where the nearest coffee shop is?"

"No problem, follow me," he turned and led her across the street and into an alley.

Deidre kept up the pretense of being lost. The back of alley ended in a wall. "Where's the coffee shop?"

He leaned against the wall. "You don't need coffee, all you need is me."

Deidre turned her head and hid her eye roll. Time to feed. She leaned close and whispered into his ear. "Let's have some fun."

A shudder raced through his body, and his eyes glazed over.

Deidre inhaled the lust rising from his body. Not enough to sate her, but enough to still the worst of the hunger pangs. Her power twirled and twined about him, feeding his lust, driving his desire higher.

She put her hands on his shoulders and turned him back into the wall. Leaning into him, she pressed her body full length against his and rubbed back and forth. His erection was hard against her belly.

His hands grabbed her ass and she pulled back. "Sorry stud, it's my party."

A frown crossed his face, Deidre leaned forward and whispered, "Don't you want to play?"

He nodded, drugged with desire. A small flash in his aura and she paused. J'akala, he wasn't healthy enough to give her all she needed. *Damn it.* Using her hands and voice she captured him in a dream of desire.

She undid his pants and released his hard cock. Stroking him while building the fantasy, it only took a few moments for his rush to completion. The purple haze of his release was tinged with a sickening green, indicating disease. While she couldn't contract any human illnesses, she didn't want to drain him so much that the disease overwhelmed him. She took a snack amount, enough to get her to the next target.

Once he'd spent himself, she tucked him back into his clothing and lowered him to the ground. She left him sitting there with a satisfied grin on his face and a dreamy look in his eyes.

A thump on her chest reminded her of that stupid medallion. Would the energy she'd siphoned be sucked away? She waited.

Nothing.

Had it been a fluke? She touched the medallion, expecting a jolt, but the metal remained dormant. Did Sir have to be around for the transfer to work? There was no way to find out until he summoned her.

Deidre stepped back out to the street to continue her journey. Closer to the heart of the city, she saw a male runner jog by. She snagged his attention and drew him into an alley for a quick draining. Once again she used her hands and encouraged his imagination to fill in the blanks. She inhaled the purple haze of sexual energy and left him grinning and panting.

Crossing to a bench, she sat, waiting to see if she kept her energy. Perhaps the first time had been an anomaly. Nothing happened.

The energy was hers.

Daylight waned as afternoon turned into evening. A nearby sign listed the time and temperature. It was dark earlier than expected, but as she watched the sign scroll through its information, she realized it was the middle of winter.

She needed one more donor to top off her energy levels.

Finding the male was easy. Dressed in a suit, he'd stepped from the building right in front of her and gave her a condescending sneer. The sweats weren't attractive, but that didn't seem to be the reason for his attitude. Deidre smiled and took two steps toward him, unleashing the pheromones to draw him to her. Dawning interest replaced the sneer. He held out his hand palm up.

"Shall we take this somewhere private?" he asked.

"Of course." Deidre turned and led him around the building to the back loading dock. Turning around to face him she built the fantasy, giving it a bit of an edge, which pushed him to a rapid completion. She inhaled the energy, and lowered him to the ground, leaning him against the wall.

A throat cleared behind her. "Is he still alive?"

Caught in an ungainly squat, she turned and fell back on her butt. About to scold the man for sneaking up behind her, the words stuck in her throat as she looked at him. Her power, which had subsided after filling up on energy, woke with a curl of anticipation. It had never done that before, ever.

There was something about him, something that drew her as no male had done before.

Deidre felt small sprawled at his feet. What was it about him that made her hormones sit up and purr? His tall frame was wrapped in black pants and a skin tight black t-shirt that showed every ripple of his six-pack abs. The only color came from an embroidered patch on the left side of an ankle-length duster. In the dim light she wasn't able to make out the words or symbol.

He held out his hand and she allowed him to pull her to her feet. A jolt of heated desire screamed through her system awakening her libido. *What the hell?*

Deidre tried to get her mind back on track. What had he asked?

"Is he still alive?" His deep voice curled her toes. He could talk to her anytime. His smile revealed a dimple and the tip of a fang. His interest felt like the stroke of fur against naked flesh. *Wait. Fang?*

"Of course he's still alive." *Think, Deidre, think!*

"Why aren't you using Parabank?"

"Huh?" Absorbed with the strange sensation of small creatures dancing around in her stomach, she ignored the question.

"Why aren't you using Parabank?"

"Um…" Parabank, what was that? The cache of information provided the answer. Parabank was where Paranormals donated blood to feed the Vampires.

"You must be new to the city."

Deidre smiled. "Yes, I arrived a few hours ago."

"Here for the Festival?"

"Festival? What festival?"

"Festival of Lern?" he sighed. "You can't go around feeding on people in Real Earth. Either use Parabank, or find a donor in Shadow."

A musical tone rang from his hip. With his free hand, he pulled out a phone and tapped the screen with his thumb.

His attention elsewhere, she shook her head trying to clear it of lust. It took a moment for his aura to register. *Dar'kirm take it!* He's a Vampire! *And he thinks I'm a Vamp as well.* His questions now made sense.

Deidre tugged, attempting to free her hand from his grip. His fingers tightened around hers. Looking up into his face he winked and continued his conversation. "Let me know if you hear anything." He pulled the phone away from his ear and tucked it back into a pocket.

"Where were we?" his whisper brushed over her skin, causing goose bumps.

"I need to use Parabank."

He gave her a grin that caused the creatures in the stomach to flop about like landed fish.

"Don't let yourself get so weak that you have to resort to humans. Their energy doesn't last."

He was right about that, but right now she didn't have much of a choice.

Deidre felt her eyebrow go up. "Are you volunteering?"

Eyes filling with heat and desire, he tugged on her hand, pulling her toward him. The back of his fingers stroked her cheek. "I'd be more than happy to give you whatever sustenance you need."

He tilted his head to the side and his expression shifted from playful and flirtatious to neutral.

Deidre heard a low humming noise. She narrowed her eyes. It appeared to be coming from the Vampire. *Strange, very strange.*

He sighed, stepped back and released her hand. "I've got to go. What's your number? Where can I find you?"

The question was as good as a splash of cold water. She gave him a practiced smile and gestured to her surroundings. "I don't have a number." *Not that I can share.* "I'll be around."

"I'll see you around." He winked and walked away.

Deidre leaned against the building, hand on her chest as she tried to calm her racing heart. What the hell had that been about? Flirting with a Vamp? Was she nuts? Her power subsided, generating more questions than answers.

This incarnation was going to be a pain in the ass.

§

Damien Alexander walked away from the woman and sighed. Captain Jor'dan's order to return to the office had come and the worst possible time. He turned and glanced back at her leaning against the wall, hand held to her chest. A dazed look crossed her face. Once the final report was turned in, it was vacation time. And then he'd have time to find her again.

Lust sizzled through his veins. Damn she was hot. Her blonde tousled hair brushed her shoulders, and looked as if she'd spent time romping between the sheets. Standing, her head came to his collar bone, which made her above average height for a female Vamp. He preferred a curvier figure, but that didn't stop his cock from demanding attention during their brief conversation. She'd be the perfect hook up for the end of Festival. A long night of fucking was just what he needed to get over the bitch who'd tried to remove his heart. It'd be therapeutic, even.

Plan in place he dodged the humans littering the sidewalk. He hadn't spent much time in Real, preferring the quiet of Shadow, but with Paranormals spilling into Real for the Festival, he and the rest of the Elite were spending more time in the human world, trying to prevent humanity from learning of the existence of Paranormals.

A few blocks later he entered the building housing the offices of the Elite Magical Protection Force. In Real, it was called Elite Protection. The building itself was one of the very few locations around the country that bridged Real and Shadow. It existed in both realities at the same time. The Elite needed a presence in Real, a way for humans to report strange or unusual happenings Paranormal in nature. It was against Paranormal law to reveal themselves to the human population. However, there were a few humans who were gifted with the secret.

Damien nodded at the Mage receptionist, chosen for his ability to blend in with the human population. Mark nodded back. "You're expected in the Captain's office."

"Thanks."

Damien took the elevator to the fourth floor. Walking down the corridor, he exchanged nods with his fellow Elite. A sense of pride and accomplishment filled him. This was right; this was what he was meant to do. Help make a difference. As a member of the Elite Magical Protection Force, it was his job to protect humans and Paranormals from magical threats.

And with the Festival in town this year, magical crime rates rose.

Festival was also an opportunity for the Elite to recruit new members. He enjoyed watching the games of strength and endurance. At the end of the competition, those who won were sent through rigorous training and became the best of the best, the Elite.

He knocked on the door of Captain Jor'dan's office and entered. His Vamp partner, James, was waiting, seated in front of the Captain's unnaturally neat desk. The Fae, and Fates save those who had the poor manners to call him a Fairy, had a fixation on neatness that bordered on OCD. The blotter was centered in the exact middle of the desk, the monitor tilted at a specific angle, and the phone was precisely ten inches from the edge, with nary a file, nor paper to be seen.

Captain Jor'dan looked up as Damien closed the door. "Results?"

"The human found a bafflement charm and used it to rob the bank. The charm has been disposed of and the human dropped off at the SFPD along with the bank recording showing everything."

"Anything that would lead back to Shadow?"

Damien shook his head. "Detective Alejandro knows how to take care of the situation."

Captain Jor'dan nodded. "He's a good man."

James stood. "If that's everything Captain, we'll head out."

"Sit down, gentlemen."

A small apologetic smile crossed the Captain's face, and Damien got a bad feeling in his gut. Damien sighed. "Let me guess, vacay is cancelled."

James mouth popped open.

"All leave and vacations have been cancelled until further notice." Captain Jor'dan's expression was somber.

"What? Why?" James demanded.

Damien sat, keeping an eye on his partner. James was easy going, until he got mad. But after a few deep breaths, James regained his equilibrium.

"Okay what's going on?" he asked in a much calmer tone.

"I've received several phone calls from the Mages and Elves saying there was a tremendous power surge this afternoon. Mage

Earl called to report suspicious behavior in the warehouse district. He stumbled on a delicate situation and was going to check it out. He's an hour late."

The Captain paused letting that information sink in. Damien spoke up. "Do you think he's in trouble?"

Captain Jor'dan looked out the window, the clenched fists on his desk the only sign of his anger. "He's not answering his phone, or telepathic pings." He turned back to look at them, his expression grim. "His life force is gone, he's dead."

James was quiet for a moment. "What was his last assignment? If we know what he was looking into, it may lead us to him."

The Captain waved his hand. "I'll take care of back tracking his case load. I need you to check out the area of the power surge, find out what happened and see if you can find any trace of Mage Earl."

James sat forward like a kid expecting a treat. "And then vacation?"

"It depends on what you find. Dismissed."

Chapter 4

Hidden in Shadow, Damien and James arrived in the area of the reported power surge.

Damien stilled and let his Vampire senses flare out.

James' low whisper confirmed the feeling. "We're being watched."

Damien nodded. "I feel them. They're only watching at the moment."

"Can you tell who they are?" James looked around trying to spot the watchers.

Damien let the information flow into him. "A few young Paranormals. An Elf and a Shifter. The others are out of range for positive identification."

"What do they want?"

"Who knows? As long as they stay in the shadows, they can watch."

Damien looked at the chipped paint and crumbling mortar of the building. "Are you sure this is the correct address?"

"Yeah. Hard to believe any Paranormal would slum here."

"Who owns the building?"

James pulled out his phone. "Real or Shadow?"

"Both."

"In Real, Elaine Inc. Shadow, Conner Corp."

"Do we know anything about either company?"

"Searching records… interesting, the files are restricted." James tapped a few more keys before looking up. "Retrieving information." He paused. "That's funny."

"What?"

"The Elite codes aren't letting me in."

Damien turned to him. "That should be public record."

"It's not. I'll get the Captain to override." James tapped the screen.

Damien took two steps toward the building and stopped. *Warning* skittered along his nerves as a tingle ran up and down his body.

Bugs.

It felt like thousands of bugs crawling over him. He looked down at his arm. Nothing. Brushing his hand over his leg, he didn't feel anything more than the rough denim of his jeans.

"Hey James, feel that?"

"Feel what?"

Damien looked back at his partner. James' head was down, attention focused on his phone.

Shit. Damn. Fuck.

He took a deep breath and tried to take a step back, but couldn't. He hit a virtual wall. Reaching out to feel the barrier, his hand didn't encounter any resistance. The wall wasn't physical then. The longer he stood there, the more the feeling of creepy crawlies intensified. The bugs were pinching and clawing at his skin.

He felt pain in his scalp, but felt nothing with his hand. They climbed into his ears, brushed his lips.

"James? You wanna help me out here?"

48

James looked up and put the phone away. "Captain's looking into it. What's wrong?"

Damien started at him. "I can't move."

"What? Not even backward?" He narrowed his gaze and moved closer. After a couple of steps the other Vamp brushed off his jacket. He stopped a few feet back.

"Bugs? That's creepy."

"Crawly too." Damien held his chuckle at his friend's expression of distaste. "Get me outta this."

He held out his hand, and James grabbed it, jerking hard. Damien felt his feet leave the pavement, and he flew through the air. Pebbles and rocks gouged into him as he landed on his ass in the street.

"Thanks." He stood up and brushed off the loose gravel and dirt from his black leather duster, glad that they were in Shadow, or he'd have been hit by traffic in Real.

"I enjoyed throwing you on your ass."

"It won't happen again."

"You just keep telling yourself that." James looked at the building. "How do we get in?"

"Let's try the back."

Damien led the way toward the side alley but was once again stopped by the warning skittering over his senses. He exchanged a look with James. "Let's go one building over."

James led the way down the block, and up a side alley. A long, narrow street ran through the center of the block behind the buildings. They headed back to their target.

Damien approached the rear entrance. The tingling sensation began, and he stepped back before he was trapped.

"That's not going to work. Ideas?"

James glanced up at the building. "If we can't get in, in Shadow…"

Damien grinned. "Let's try Real."

He closed his eyes and popped into Real Earth. James appeared next to him. Rotting garbage from a nearby dumpster and car exhaust made for an unpleasant perfume. And the noise! Car horns, engines revving, shouts, and sirens filled his ears with a cacophony of sound. It was jarring after the peaceful silence of Shadow.

The back of the building didn't look any different from the front. Garbage and peeling paint littered the area.

Damien approached the metal door, all senses alert. The virtual wall of bugs appeared to be active only in Shadow. He motioned James closer.

Footsteps echoed in the short alley leading to the rear of the building. Damien froze, grateful for his dark clothes.

A bum walked by, his gait uneven. He stopped before the dumpster and started rummaging around. Damien had to hold his breath at the stale scent of unwashed human. The search yielded nothing and the bum left, off to ransack another dumpster.

James let out a breath. "That was close. Shouldn't humans be asleep?"

Damien didn't respond, turning instead to the two locks on the door. Flimsy padlocks that posed no challenge to his Vampire strength. How to break in without alerting the owners?

James placed his hand on the door and bowed his head.

Damien also stopped and listened. He wasn't able to pick up sounds of breathing or heartbeats due to the traffic noise coming from the street. It was a competition. James had better hearing but Damien couldn't resist trying to out-hear his partner.

James lifted his head and winked. "No one's home. Let's go." With a flick of the wrist he pulled out his tools. Two picked locks later, they were in. James closed the door behind them, and they both stilled. Damien's eyes adjusted to the dim interior of the large room within a heartbeat. Windows set high in the walls were covered in dirt and grime, and shed minimal light through the room. Pieces of broken equipment and trash were strewn about the floor. The building had seen better times.

Damien took a deep breath and let the mustiness of the interior seep into his brain. He frowned at the trace of copper and... flowers? What the hell?

James motioned to the left and Damien nodded. They fell into standard search protocol. Damien took one side of the building; James took the other. After a careful search, the only thing Damien found was footprints in the dusty floor. Footprints other than those made by him and James.

A low whistle pinpointed the other Vamp's location. Damien found James down on one knee. He pointed to rusted drops clustered in the dust.

Damien inhaled. "Blood. Can you tell how old?"

James shrugged. "It's sticky. In this humidity, there's no way to tell."

"A ritual bloodletting?"

"No. There's not enough. No drawings or spells either."

James stood and brushed the dust off his jeans. "Something heavy was dragged away. Probably a body."

"It could be a human crime then."

"That's my take on it. Did you find anything on your side?"

Damien shook his head. "Nothing to indicate Paranormal activity. But there's a door leading down."

"Let's go."

Damien led the way and stopped at the open door and peered into the darkness. He tried to pierce the depths but his night vision couldn't make anything out. Who knew what lurked below?

James waved his hand toward the stairs. "After you."

"Thanks."

"Anything for you, buddy."

Damien removed a flashlight from one of the many pockets in his coat and led the way down. A long stone hallway extended from the base of the stairs, and metal sconces held torches set into the walls at regular intervals.

"Very Goth. Think they have Halloween parties down here?" James asked.

"Who knows what crazy things humans do?" Damien stopped at a heavy wooden door at the end of the hallway.

Damien waved his partner ahead. "After you Mr. Kirk."

James pulled his weapon, a modified stun gun, and prepared to enter the room. Damien did the same.

"Why me?"

"Going where no-one has gone before is your thing." Damien chuckled at James' glare.

James opened the door and peered in. Damien swept the light around the area.

An elaborate diagram filled the center of the floor.

"Shit. Damn. Fuck. Is that what I think it is?"

"If you think it is a containment drawing, you're right."

James looked at the chalk on the floor. "Damn it, we need Earl for this."

"He's gone. Do we have anyone else at HQ familiar with arcane knowledge?"

"I've been trying to get someone, anyone, to come and replace that Mage, but none of them want to relocate."

The relationship between James and Earl had been antagonistic at best and hostile at worst. Damien never found out how two friendly rivals had become such bitter enemies.

"Can you do your thing and find out what happened here?" Damien asked.

"I'll try." James closed his eyes and went into the usual trance. Damien waited. It could take anywhere from a few minutes to a few hours for James to read the auric events of the room. The Vamp was out for about twenty minutes before blinking his eyes open. Damien caught James as he slumped and leaned him against the wall.

52

"You okay?" Damien asked.

"Yeah, give me a minute." James leaned his head back and took a deep breath. "Aura is complex. Almost too complex..."

"What was the last thing that happened?"

"Two people left the room. Mage, and..."

"Mage?"

"Yes the power is consistent with spell magic."

The magic wielding races had different forms of magic. Elves and Fae used earth magic, where as Mages used spell magic. Each Race was insistent that their method of harnessing the power was best.

"What was the second person?"

James frowned. "I don't know, I can't tell."

"Why not?"

"I've never seen this type of aura before." And that meant the second person was a rare being.

"Do you know what the drawing contained?"

"The second being"

"Shit. Damn. Fuck. You're telling me a Mage summoned something and let it loose in the city?"

"That's what it looks like. The creature is under the Mage's control, not running amok."

"How sure are you about that?" Damien asked, skeptical.

James shrugged. "Think of it this way, we'd have heard by now if some creature was on the loose."

Damien nodded. "But what if it wasn't the right time? And he wanted to get the spell out of the way?"

Dawning horror crossed James face. "Oh shit. Festival starts in a couple of day."

"Bingo."

James took a shaky step away from the wall. "The spell residue indicates it was done here in Real not Shadow."

"Why would a Mage go through all the trouble to cast a spell in Real, unless..."

"He didn't want to get caught." James finished for him.

"Can you get a fix on the identity of the Mage?"

"No. Too many people have used this room and I can't pinpoint the specifics of his aura."

"Are you positive a Mage was involved?"

"That's the only thing I know for sure." James paced around the diagram, steps stumbling at first then strengthening as he recovered from the psychic exertion. The effect was temporary and would wane soon.

"Anything else?"

James closed his eyes again. "There is a faint trickle of energy coming from it."

"Do you recognize the energy pattern?"

"Nope."

"Could you recognize it if you run into it again?"

"Yeah. Damn it, we need an expert." James removed his cell and took a few pictures. "I'll check with a couple of contacts to see what they can dig up."

"Unless you can get someone from the Library of Magic to speak with you."

James snorted. "Those elitist bastards? They'd make me jump through so many hoops, I'd be dust before the deigned to help."

If there was one constant in the universe, it was that Mages didn't share any information with anyone they deemed inferior. Which meant all races but their own. It took an act of the High Chancellor for the Elite to get what little training they could in magical detection and recognition.

Damien took a deep breath and the scent of flowers filled his lungs. "Why the flowers?"

"It's from the creature." James continued to snap pictures.

Something about the scent was familiar, as if he'd smelled it before. But he couldn't place it.

James stumbled and Damien grabbed his arm, draping it over his shoulder. "We need to get you some blood."

54

Damien pulled the heavy door closed behind them and they staggered up the stairs as if drunk. At the top Damien hauled James over his shoulder and carried him to the car. The fact James was not complaining meant the Vamp had pushed his abilities beyond the limit.

"Can you Shadow?"

"I think so," came the weak reply.

They popped into Shadow and Damien placed James in the front seat, grabbed the cooler from the trunk, and put it in James' lap.

"Drink," Damien ordered.

"Yes, Mother."

Three bottles later, and James perked up.

Halfway to the office, James grabbed Damien's arm.

Damien tensed, body alert, sending out his senses. When he couldn't detect the threat, he looked at his partner. "What is it?"

"Pull over. I sensed something. Let's check it out."

Damien pulled to the curb and parked the car. James got out and stood on the sidewalk with his head tilted.

"There's an echo."

"Of what?"

"That strange energy signature from the warehouse."

Extending his senses, Damien focused on the beings within in a moderate distances. "The creature is here?"

James nodded. "Yeah, but the echo is funny. Fuck. It's in Real."

Not wasting any time, they popped into Real. Damien tensed, ready for anything.

§

A cold breeze slid through the thin material as Deidre walked through the shopping district. Clothing was more colorful and there was less of it. Stopping in front of a window display she felt her mouth pop open. Look at those gorgeous shoes. Heels and boots, shiny and sparkly, they called to her. Looking at the small sign in front of a magnificent pair of shoes, it took her a moment to register their cost. Holy Hounds that was a lot of money!

How did one earn money in this time? Perhaps she should have taken some from her victims. The one in the suit would have been the ideal donor.

With great reluctance, she turned from the display. Finding a place to sleep was next on the list of things to do. But without funds how was she to rent a room?

A half a block ahead of her three males emerged from a dark alley.

They were dressed in chains and silver. Hair spiked and pants hanging halfway down their legs. Something wasn't quite right about them, other than their clothes. On the surface, they appeared to be human, yet... they weren't. Their auras were muddy, hard to read. Human and... other? It didn't make sense.

Auras emanated from all sentient beings. She'd quickly learned to differentiate between the different Paranormal Races and non-magical humans.

But these males were something she'd never encountered before.

One of the three turned toward her, menace pervading his stance. A devious smile crossed his face.

"Well, well, well. What have we here?"

Deidre stopped as a shiver of fear raced through her.

Fear? She hated the pounding heart, the cold clammy palms, and the desire to flee. Standing tall, she faced the men. She wouldn't be weak, easy prey.

The other two turned toward her. She heard a muffled grunt from the alley and turned to look. A near silent battle waged between six other strange males and a female dressed in form fitting leather from neck to boots.. The female appeared to be holding her own.

56

The female's aura flashed blood red. What was going on? Vampire week in Real Earth?

Deidre focused on the auras of the men the Vampire fought. Grey with flashes of blood red veins.

A click of chain had her glancing back at the original three. They moved in front and around her, forcing her to enter the alley. *Dar'kirm take it!* They were herding her toward the fight. One of the males hit the woman over the head and the Vampire went down.

A hand caught Deidre's arm, pushing her toward the group. "Move, bitch."

Deidre tried to twist out of his hold. He was stronger than a normal human. She managed to break free, heart pounding in her chest. Damn Khan and these newfound feelings of fear!

"Hey Charlie!"

One of the males fighting the Vampire growled and jerked his head around, eyes flashing red. "What the fuck?"

"We found us a curious little she-cat. Hotter'n hell too."

Charlie and his friends turned to her dismissing the Vampire on the ground.

Deidre glanced at the Vampire out of the corner of her eye. She appeared to be okay except for the few small bleeding cuts.

Charlie stepped forward. A tattoo covered his shaved head and spilled onto his face to join the multiple piercings decorating his features.

"Well now. You're lookin' mighty fine. What say you show me an' my boys here a good time?"

Deidre shook her head. "Not interested."

Charlie stepped forward, a flash of anger passing over his face. He raised his arm and she jerked back, but not far enough. The back of his hand connected with her face. Her head snapped back as pain seared her cheek.

She felt herself falling, then an abrupt jolt as she hit the concrete. Stones and rocks dug into her hip and shoulder.

They wanted to play, did they? She wasn't going to be their whipping girl; beat up, and raped, just so they could prove their manhood. Time to change strategy.

Deidre glanced over to find the female Vampire close to her, playing possum.

A soft whisper reached her ears. "You shouldn't be here."

Deidre whispered back. "Too late. How many can you take?"

"Five."

"Leaving four for me."

Charlie snapped his fingers, and two of the males jerked the Vamp to her feet. She broke their hold and crouched in a fighting position.

Two others pulled Deidre to her feet. She knocked their hands away. "Don't touch me."

Charlie laughed in her face. "I can do what I want, bitch. Who's gonna stop me? You?"

Oh if only he knew. Time to get to work.

Deidre looked down shielding her eyes and softened her stance. She leaned toward him and gave him a smile. In a seductive whisper she answered, "Yes I am."

Deidre took a deep breath. She had never tried to drain this many before. But it was either that, or she and the Vampire would be beaten bloody and raped, then killed.

J'kala please let this work.

She placed a trembling hand against his chest, looked into his eyes and sent a pulse of sexual energy swirling into his body. His lust ignited which fueled her power. She felt it bubble and grow within her.

His eyes glazed over and he began to pant, moving into her body. Something was off… his energy, unnatural. It felt slimy, like nothing she'd encountered before.

Can't stop now; it's too late.

She swallowed back the rising nausea and continued to manipulate his energy.

58

"Hey Charlie, what's goin' on?" One of the others approached and put his hand on Charlie's shoulder. He jerked as his energy was subverted into her loop. The new sexual energy was slimy as well, but she had to continue. She had them both trapped in a cocoon of raw lust. Sweat rolled down their faces, their erections - disturbing.

Careful.

Too much power and they'd try to rape her; too little and they'd escape.

Out of the corner of her eye, she could see the Vampire kicking ass. *Good.*

Deidre kept the power flowing between them. A body flew through the air and knocked the last two to the ground at her feet; one draped over the top of the other. She put her bare foot on the back of the man on top and pulled their energy. They jerked.

A heady tonic of slimy lust swirled in the air above them. Like a sponge, she inhaled the smoky green tendrils. Her skin felt oily, nasty, and the scent of rotting meat filled her lungs.

Energy draw complete, she stepped back and Charlie and the others tumbled to the ground.

A flare of heat and the bodies in front of her turned to ash.

What in Dar'kirm was that? What was going on?

She looked over to check on the Vampire. Those she'd defeated also disintegrated into ash.

The woman stood over the ash, hands on hips, arms akimbo. "Strange. I've never seen that before."

"Me either."

She looked at Deidre and held out her hand. "Thanks for the rescue. I don't know what I'd have done without you. I'm Cyn."

Deidre smiled and took the Vampire's hand. "Deidre."

A wave of dizziness crashed over her, and she had to hang onto Cyn's hand to keep from falling.

Whoa. The world was tilt-y. Was it supposed to do that?

"Are you all right?" Cyn was speaking but her voice sounded far away. Echo-y.

Deidre nodded. Her head kept going. The world blurred. Up, then down, then up, then down. If it weren't for the feeling of nausea, it'd be cool.

Cyn pulled her to the back of the alley.

"Hey, where we goin'?" Deidre stumbled along, not sure where to put her feet since the world kept jumping around.

"You need to sit down. You're glowing."

Huh? Deidre lifted her hand. Her fingers were pulsing glow sticks. She waved her hand around and made light patterns in the air. "Cool." But why was she glowing? "J'kala! Too much!"

"Too much what?"

Deidre slumped against the building. "Energy."

Cyn pulled her down to sit on the concrete, back resting against the rough brick wall.

Maybe the medallion would take it? After a few moments it was clear the energy was hers. *Dar'kirm take it.*

She had to do something and fast. The tainted energy made her feel ill. If she didn't get rid of it soon, she was going to be sick. A first in her thousand plus years of existence.

The medallion thumped against her chest. "Wait. If it drained me before, can I force it to take it now?"

"What?" Cyn sounded confused, but Deidre wasn't going to explain. Frigid air blew through the alley, causing her to shiver. Medallion in hand, she closed her eyes and concentrated on the slimy energy pulsing through her. She imagined gathering it into a ball and was surprised when it conformed to her will. She pushed the slimy ball of energy into the cool metal in her palm. A flash of cold, and the slimy ball of energy was absorbed into the medallion. Opening her eyes, she was relieved to see the glow gone. The breeze felt refreshing against her skin, tinged with the scent of the ocean.

An image blossomed in her mind. A dark bedroom. A figure tossing and turning on the bed. Sir. A shout, sexual release. Deidre released the medallion to drop back to her chest as she looked at her hand. No glow. It worked!

"So you're okay now?" Cyn's voice was shaky, yet Deidre could hear the genuine concern in her tone.

Deidre looked at the Vampire and smiled. "Much better."

Cyn fiddled with something on her head and soft brown strands fell into place around her chin. The Vampire rubbed her fingers over her scalp. "Much better." She turned to Deidre, her electric blue eyes alight. "That was a good fight. But what happened?"

Deidre looked at the piles of ash. "I don't know."

A heavy exhalation left Cyn.

"Are you alright?"

Cyn leaned her head against the brick wall. "Yeah, just drained."

"Oh." What would help Cyn? Vampires needed blood to survive. "Can you Shadow?"

Cyn shook her head. "Don't have the energy."

Deidre took a deep measured breath and let it out. She was the last person anyone looked to for help, but the feeling of gratitude and liking for the Vampire rose within her. She wanted to help Cyn. Shaking her head at all the strange things she'd been feeling lately, she reached over and placed a hand on Cyn's arm.

"I can pop you over." Deidre offered.

"No!" Cyn jerked away from her.

"Okay." Deidre pulled back, a small dart of hurt pierced her.

Cyn grabbed her hand, held on tight, and took a deep breath. "I… they… I just can't. I can't appear weak in Shadow."

Oh. A movement out of the corner of her eye jolted Deidre. *Damned fight or flight response.*

Deidre pointed to the runner jogging by. "How about fast food?"

Cyn chuckled, but it sounded weak. "No. Humans are like potato chips. Good at the time, but no nutritional substance. Only Paranormal blood will do."

"Got it." Deidre wasn't sure what problems Cyn had in Shadow, but she had to do something. Cyn was paler than before, and the strength in her grip was fading.

She'd have to go into Shadow after all.

After a deep sigh, Deidre stood up. "I'll be right back."

Cyn closed her eyes. "You don't have to..."

Deidre held up a hand stopping her protest. "It's not a problem. What do you need?"

"Parabank is too far. If you can find a live donor that would be great."

Deidre popped into Shadow. Even though it was late at night, there were a few Paranormals walking around.

She wiped her sweaty palms on her sweat pants and approached a likely candidate; a young Elf with a backpack over his shoulder.

"Excuse me. My Vampire friend is in Real Earth and she needs blood. Can you help her?"

He stopped and stared at her. She saw his gaze run up and down her body. Deidre held in a sigh of exasperation, touched his arm and batted her eyelashes at him. "Pretty please?"

He gave her a dazzled smile. "Sure. I'd be glad to assist."

Deidre popped back into Real Earth with the Elf. He smiled at Cyn and knelt down by her side. "I offer my blood to you free of coercion. Wrist or neck?" he offered.

"Thank you for the offer. Neck please." Deidre saw Cyn capture his gaze and hold it. He leaned forward as if to give the Vampire a kiss. At the last moment he tilted his head, giving her access to his neck. Cyn closed her eyes and bit. Deidre looked away, oddly embarrassed by the sensuality of the act. Deidre turned when Cyn thanked him.

The Elf stood on shaky legs. Deidre grabbed an arm to help support him. With great care, he bowed his head to Cyn and spoke. "It was my pleasure to assist you in your need."

He stepped back from Deidre and nodded again before popping back into Shadow Earth.

Deidre turned to Cyn, her interest piqued. "Do they always respond like that?"

Cyn nodded. "It is part of the ritual. It protects the donor from the Vampire's psychic power."

"Interesting."

Cyn shrugged. "It's a precaution. When Shadow was set up, so were the spells and rituals protecting each race. The others know we need to feed on their blood. They donate at Para-Bank, and we don't use our psychic abilities to enslave them. Some are also willing to feed us in an emergency."A frown crossed Cyn's face. "How is it you don't know all this?"

"Um... I..."

Deidre held out her hand and helped Cyn to her feet.

"And what are you?" Cyn asked. "I've never seen an aura like yours before."

Deidre hesitated. "I'm not sure I can tell you."

"Why not?"

How to explain without giving herself away? While she liked the Vampire, would the woman would turn her in if she learned the truth? Best to stick with the easy answer.

"A spell prohibits me from revealing my nature."

Cyn pointed to the medallion. "Does it have anything to do with that?"

Deidre nodded. "Yeah."

Cyn was silent for a moment. "What's Jakala?"

"What?"

"Jakala. You said it earlier."

"Oh, that. I've been to many...places and sometimes the local slang stays with me."

"What does it mean?"

"There's no real translation into English. The closest is a deity I think."

"Fascinating," Cyn smiled. "I'd be interested to hear about your travels sometime. Come on, I'll buy you coffee."

Deidre sighed in remembered bliss. "Coffee. I haven't had coffee in such a long time."

Cyn looked at her. "Where have you been that you haven't had coffee?"

Deidre grinned and led the way from the alley. "Out of touch."

As they walked toward the coffee shop, Cyn's cell phone rang.

"Hello?" the Vampire's face lightened. "Hey Hans, what's up? Huh? What were they doing there? I hadn't heard that. Okay, I'll check it out. See you in a few."

She put the phone away and frowned. "I'm sorry, I've got to go. Thank you again for saving me. If there's anything I can do to repay you, let me know."

Deidre hesitated. "There is one thing. Can you tell me where I can go to get some rest?"

"You're homeless?"

Deidre tilted her head and thought about it. "I suppose, technically, yes. I arrived today and haven't found a place to stay."

Cyn looked at her for a moment. "And what about funds?"

Deidre snorted. "My employer has conveniently forgotten to pay me."

"Bastards."

Deidre agreed. "So is there someplace you'd recommend?"

Cyn bit her lip. "I shouldn't do this… but what the hell." The Vamp gave her a narrow look. "Are you on drugs?"

Drugs? Info flooded her brain. "No, I don't do drugs."

"Do you plan on staying in Real or Shadow?"

Deidre jerked. "I'm planning on staying as far away from Shadow as I possibly can."

Cyn nodded. "Come with me, I think I can spare some room on the couch."

Cyn turned to walk the other direction. Deidre stopped, stunned. "Cyn…"

The Vamp turned. "Yes?"

Deidre shook her head. "I… it wasn't… you don't have to do this." How to articulate? Happiness and gratitude swirled within her. She was turning into an emotional mess. Things were so complicated this time around. Deidre wasn't comfortable, but what could she do? "Thank you."

A soft smile crossed the Vamp's face. "You're welcome, now come on and let's get you settled before I figure out what the Elite are looking for."

§

Car horns and loud music from a nearby club filled the air, as Damien and James appeared in an alley in Real. James motioned to the street and Damien followed.

Damien scanned the streets using his psychic probe to filter out possible threats. Nothing registered as they wove through groups congregating in front of a club. One man stepped in front of Damien. He had shocking orange hair, wearing a skintight, glittery, bodysuit.

"Hello."

Damien bit his lip to keep from smiling. "Sorry not interested."

The man gave a dramatic sigh. "You're too handsome to be let loose for long. I hope she treats you right. If not give me a call."

With a flourish the man presented a business card and a wink.

Damien took it and nodded once as walked away.

James leaned against the wall with a huge grin on his face.

"Not one word." Damien warned.

James led the way around the corner and doubled over in laughter. "H-h-hey big boy."

"Are you done yet?"

"No."

Damien crossed his arms over his chest, and leaned a shoulder against the wall. Detective Alejandro needed to get in touch. That was what the exchange had been about. The information was too sensitive to go through normal channels.

A few minutes later, James wiped the tears from his eyes. "Are you done?"

James grinned. "Yeah. I have to admit, I didn't know you swung that way. Was Sienna's betrayal enough to have you seeking solace in another man's arms?"

"Ha. Ha. You're funny. Alejandro wants to talk."

That sobered James up fast. "How do you know?"

"The system was set up a while ago."

"Why didn't I know about it?"

"You were busy setting up your own contacts."

Damien straightened from the wall and looked at piles of ash on the ground. "What's this?"

James turned to look. "No idea."

"Is the creature responsible for this?" Damien asked, searching the area for evidence. If it were a fire being, there'd be scorch marks, and the area looked clean.

James knelt by one pile and rubbed some ash between his fingers. "Looks like ordinary ash, but I don't know for sure." He took out a small baggie from his pocket and filled it.

"It could be someone emptying their barbeque."

James shook his head. "I don't think so. There are traces of the creature here, along with Vampire."

"Did the creature do this?" Damien tried to probe the ash, but there wasn't anything there to lock on. *Shit*. If they had a fire elemental on their hands, this close to festival, the city was screwed.

James stood. " I think so, but I'm not sure. There weren't any fire traces in the aura, but I don't know what else it could be. We need to track the creature, fast."

Damien's cell vibrated at his hip at the same time James' phone chirped. It was a text from the Captain. "Get back to the office, now."

They arrived at the office an hour before dawn. Damien entered the office first and stopped in shock. The Captain was in the same clothes from yesterday. The Fae split his shift to straddle the night and day shifts. Lines of stress bracketed Captain Jor'dan's eyes.

Captain Jor'dan replaced the phone receiver and rubbed his hand over his face. While Fae were known for their easy going demeanor and ability to handle stress, it was obvious the Captain had reached his limit.

Jor'dan left his chair and paced behind his cluttered desk. Wait. There were papers and files scattered all over the pristine surface.

Shit. Whatever was going on, was big.

Captain Jor'dan took several deep breaths, each one instilling a measure of calm."Report."

Damien sat back while James began, detailing everything they'd found out about the creature that was summoned. He presented the baggie as evidence.

"I wonder if this has anything to do with the Vampire attacks." Captain Jor'dan commented.

Damien's jaw dropped. "Vampire attacks? You're kidding, right?"

Jor'dan ran a hand through his blonde hair. "Yes. Reports have been coming in that a small group of young Vamps have been attacking Paranormals in Real."

Damien frowned. "That doesn't make sense. The youngest Vamps are here for the Festival games. Why would they jeopardize that?"

"Your guess is as good as mine."

"They're not. It's a different group. The ones here for the games have been in training at the time of the attacks. This is a new group of Vamps who are not part of the community."

"Rogues?"

"We think so."

"Shit. Damn. Fuck."

Jor'dan gave them a weary smile. "Oh and it gets better. I received a message from Regina today."

Damien groaned. Messages from Regina were confusing at best and incoherent at worst. "And what does the lovely Empress of Air, Oracle of the L'dan have to say to us mere immortals?"

Captain Jor'dan snorted. "Mere, indeed. Here's the message." He turned toward his computer screen. "Hell is coming. Don't piss off the femme fatale. She's your only hope."

"So what are we supposed to do, 'use the force Luke'?"

"Who knows? When I asked for clarification, she told me that was all I was going to get." Jor'dan once again ran a weary hand through his tousled hair. "Sometimes that woman drives me nuts. Ready for the rest of it?"

James sighed. "You mean there's more?"

"Of course, there's always more. The Mages are demanding answers about the magical surge this afternoon. Of course, they want us to make it our top priority."

Damien snickered. "Yeah right, during Festival?"

Jor'dan gave them a look. "You need to focus on finding the creature, and finding out who is responsible for the surge.

The alarm on Damien's phone went off. "Time to head home." He rose and walked to the door.

"One more thing," Jor'dan called out. "I got a complaint from Bar'ella. She says to stop snacking on her girls. A couple of them are getting romantic ideas about the two of you." He chuckled as Damien groaned. "If neither of you are ready to settle down, I suggest ordering from Para-bank."

§

Fear solidified in the pit of her stomach. She recognized Khan's throne room. Torches burned in sconces ringing the throne, with the rest of the room dark, and sinister. Deidre flew through the air toward the figure at the far end of the hall. Khan was sitting on the throne and didn't look up at her approach. He didn't notice her. His gaze was locked on an item in his clawed hand. She peered closer. A lock of hair rested on his red palm.

One of the Demoni raced into the throne room. "My Lord."

Khan clenched his fist hiding the lock.

"Forgive me, Sire. We've located the scroll Hzine used to summon the creature."

Khan leaned forward and Deidre sensed his rising excitement. "Where is it?"

His advisor swallowed and presented the unrolled scroll. "Here sire, but..."

Khan took it and glared at the man. "What?"

"If I may draw your attention to this clause here?"

The advisor's claw shook as he pointed to a section near the top of the scroll.

Khan read the section indicated. "The demon may not be summoned to the same dimension within a single moon's time."

Khan sat back, a thoughtful look on his face, which sent tingles of fear through her.

"Break it."

"Y-y-yes Sire." The Demoni scrambled from the room.

Khan picked up an item from the arm of the throne, and she saw a metal disc. He triggered a catch and it popped open. With great care, he placed the lock of hair inside and snapped it shut.

He stroked a claw over the metallic surface, and she felt a sharp object rake her spine. He whispered to the locket. "You won't escape me, Deidre. Soon you'll be mine."

Chapter 5

Clint Douglas settled into his chair behind the desk in his home office. The Succubus performed well yesterday. He was pleased with the energy she drained from the Elite, though it did take a bit to get used to.

The door burst open and Adolfo stalked in.

The young Mage nodded in greeting before flinging himself into the chair opposite the desk.

"What now Adolfo?" Clint ground his back teeth together trying to hide his impatience.

"The experimentation with human conversion is coming along. We're running into problems though. Half of those converted go mad within a couple of hours. It takes the other half at least a day to reach that point." Adolfo sat back and looked at his fingernails and in a deliberate bored tone said, "I wonder if you gave us the wrong spell."

Clint glared at him. "You have the correct spell."

"Are you sure?"

"Yes, it's the one for Transmogrification. Didn't you study basic magic in college?"

Adolfo shook his head. "I was busy getting The Underground started and rebelling against the men who think they run this place."

The men who run this place. Ha! Looking at the younger Mage's designer jeans and sweater, how would this group of idiots fare without their monthly allowance from their parents? It was easy to rebel when the availability of funds was never in question.

Clint let out a controlled breath. "Speaking of the experiments, what the hell were you thinking releasing them into Real? They weren't ready yet."

Adolfo sat up and looked a bit sheepish. "Well yeah, that was an accident. One of the guys forgot to lock the door."

Clint narrowed his eyes. "And what was done to him?"

Adolfo shrugged. "Nothing why?"

Clint shook his head. "Mistakes are to be punished. What if his actions had brought the Elite down on your operation?"

Adolfo sat back, unconcerned. "Like those idiots could find us."

Temptation whispered in Clint's ear. This cocky young man would be singing a different tune once the Elite imprisoned him. Perhaps an anonymous tip? But no, not yet. Clint still needed him and his idiot friends, for the moment.

"Now when we get into power…" Adolfo began.

Clint held up his hand to stop him mid rant. Once the younger man started, it was impossible to stop him. Instead of learning about society and a way to fight The Man, Adolfo and the others wasted time and energy on something that would have failed in the first six months, had Sienna not gotten involved. What had she seen in the blonde-haired, blue-eyed, idiot?

For his baby girl, Clint had stepped in and saved the floundering movement.

It was times like this when he wondered if it was worth it. The top leaders, like Adolfo, didn't have a single gram of common sense among them. Of course Clint took over and was in the process of turning it into the subversive group it was meant to be.

He let out a controlled breath.

"What you'd have learned had you taken the class is that humans can't be successfully turned into any of the magical races unless they have the recessive magical gene. The Elven scientists found the specific genetic indicator when they assisted in mapping the human genome. Of course they kept it from their human counterparts."

Clint shook his head as Adolfo's eyes glazed over. *Incompetent ass.*

He cleared his throat, bringing the younger man's attention back to him. "The spell I gave you works; you just have to find the right humans for it to work on."

Adolfo nodded."Yeah, sure." And waved his manicured hand around in an effeminate gesture.

The younger Mage surged to his feet, stalking around the office, picking up various things and putting them back down again in a slightly different place. Fidgeting as if he was excited. His normally blasé attitude, subsumed by frantic excitement.

Annoyance surged through Clint and he clenched his fists on top of the desk. Disarranging his space was one of his biggest pet peeves. *Breathe. Calm, remain calm.*

"Anything else?" Clint tried to resist the urge to get up and put things in their proper places. He would do it as soon as he got the idiot out of his office.

"Uh yes." Adolfo turned and tugged at the cuff of his sleeve.

Clint waited. And waited. He leaned back in his desk chair and steepled his fingers. He was going to wait the younger man out no matter how long it took.

Adolfo looked all around the office before staring at his twitching fingers. "I've heard from a couple of the guys that you've summoned a demon." An unattractive red blush covered the young man's face. "I was wondering if she was summoned for the Underground."

Clint sat up, shocked. How had they found out about her? In a nonchalant tone, he asked. "Where did you hear that from?"

Adolfo shrugged, ignoring Clint's rising anger. "I don't know."

"And you didn't think to check?"

"Nah. It wasn't important." The young man sat in the chair, leaning forward, elbows on knees, excited anticipation on his face. "So is she for us?"

This was a happy little bubble, Clint was happy to burst.

"No. She has nothing to do with you or the Underground."

Adolfo's eyes lit with lust. "But we can have her, right?"

"No. She's not for you...." But perhaps... she was the answer to his dilemma. He could use her to get rid of the Underground and grow his power at the same time.

A calculating look crossed Adolfo's face. "Has she been tested?"

Clint stared at the young Mage in disbelief. "Tested? What the hell does that mean?"

"You know tested, so you know her power is working."

"Trust me, she's draining them. It's who she is." Clint narrowed his eyes. "Why?"

Adolfo's excitement was palpable. "Some of us are curious about her and a couple of the guys want to try her out."

"Adolfo, she's a Succubus."

"So?"

"Don't you know what a Succubus is?"

Adolfo tilted his head to the side. "Some demon chick?"

Patience, must have patience. Clint took a deep breath, then another. "A Succubus is a female demon who drains energy from males using sexual intercourse."

Clint was about to continue when he noticed the lust filled look on the younger Mage's face. He rested his head in his hands and stifled a groan.

What had his baby girl seen in this idiot? All the males in the Underground were similar. Young, rash and full of grand ideas with no practical ideas on how to put them into action. Living at home with their parents, never having worked a day in their lives, they were the epitome of spoiled lazy, wannabes. They wanted others to do everything while they basked in the glory of success. Hmmm… It was time for The Underground to cease, he couldn't take their attitude anymore. Their purpose was to serve as a distraction for the Elite and the Alliance, to keep heat off him and his plans. But they were more trouble than his orderly life could handle.

He'd have the Succubus drain them, adding to his power, while getting rid of the young hotheads who refused to follow orders.

Adolfo cleared his throat. "So when can we meet her?"

Clint sighed, "Very well. Let me know when would be best time for your group and I'll introduce you."

"Thanks Clint, that'd be great."

"It's Master Douglas to you."

"Yeah, whatever. I'll go and let the guys know. I'll call you when we've finalized a time."

Adolfo jumped up from the chair and hurried through the doorway, leaving the house.

Clint shook his head and took a sip of cold coffee. "Damn that idiot."

Control. Calm. Breathe. He'll be dead soon.

Control. Calm. Breathe. He'll no longer torment me.

He made a note on his to do list. Find the leak re: Succubus. After making a fresh cup of coffee, he walked around the office putting all the misplaced knick-knacks back to their correct places. He paused as he passed the bookshelf and the leather bound Tome of Power. He grinned. The best way to hide something was in plain sight. The book sat on the shelf right in front of him. He reached out and ran a finger over the spine. An electric tingle of power rushed through him. Once enough energy had been drained from the Elite, nothing in Real or Shadow Earth would stop him from

destroying Detective Alexander, the Council, and their Elite
Magical Protection Force.

A few minutes later his phone rang. He set up a meeting with
Adolfo, his group, and the Succubus for the following night.

Soon the Underground would cease to exist.

§

Deidre woke in the afternoon, in an unfamiliar location. It
took a few moments to figure out why she was on a couch instead
of a bed. *Oh yes*, she was on Earth, her Master wanted to use her
for some dastardly plan, and she was crashing on a Vamp's couch.

She stood and stretched seeing a note on the end table.

Good Day Deidre,

Hope you slept well. Feel free to use the shower. Towels
are in the hall cupboard.

Clean clothes are in the bathroom, along with a pair of
shoes.

Sorry about the lack of food in the house, I wasn't
expecting company. Here is some money for you to get
something to eat.

If you need anything, here's my cell number. Let's meet at
Angelini's at 7 pm to chat.

Cyn

Her eyes filled at the kindness a stranger had shown. Cyn
didn't have to open her home, provide money and clothing for her.
That was something her Master should have seen to. That a
stranger, and a Vampire at that, should show her such kindness
boggled her mind.

Deidre resolved to do anything within her power to help her
new friend. Filled with anticipation of the coming evening, Deidre
showered and donned a skirt and low cut sweater. And there on the
floor, was a pair of heels, the most beautiful she'd ever seen. Tall

with a spiked heel, in shiny black. They were more beautiful than the ones in the window yesterday.

Putting on the shoes she walked down the hall, confidence filling her. With her cell phone and money hidden in a secret pocket she headed out the door.

§

Night fell over the city as Damien left his condo and headed to work. His normal shift didn't start for another three hours, but due to the chaos of Festival, there was too much to do. He met James in from of the Elite building.

"Any word on Earl?" Damien asked.

James fiddled with his phone. "No one has found anything so far."

"And Captain is sure he's dead?"

James raised an eyebrow and gave him a look.

Damien held up his hands palms out. "Just checking."

"You should have seen the look I was given when I asked that question."

Captain Jor'dan did not appreciate his abilities being called into question.

"What did he threaten you with?" Damien asked.

"Guarding the Elite hopefuls," James grumbled.

James was easy going and amiable with everyone, except younger Paranormals. His patience wore thin at their attitudes and lack of respect for authority. But it made great teasing fodder.

James' phone beeped. "Captain said there was evidence of someone tampering with Earl's case file. All info regarding his current case was deleted from the system."

Damien frowned. "Then how did they find out about it?"

James leaned in after looking up and down the street. "They forgot about the backups."

Damien clicked his tongue. "Sloppy."

James' smile faded. "But that means it's one of us."

"You don't think it's an outside job?"

"Security is too tight."

The security protocols involved made it impossible for anyone other than a member of the Elite to break into the data files. Not only were they encrypted with the latest human technology, they were seeded with multiple spells that no one could hack. It was much easier to get a mole on the inside. *Fuck.*

"Does the Captain know who it is?"

James tapped his phone. "He didn't say, but he's investigating this himself."

"What is our task today?"

"We're to track down the creature from yesterday."

Damien's phone buzzed. It was Roger. "Isn't it late for Elves to be out?"

"Suck it, Vamp. That techno-Mage was all over the place. Klaus has sniffed out a new lead, but we need you to check out a coffee shop."

Damien couldn't help but grin at the low growl from the Shifter Wolf in the background.

"Send me the address."

"Will do. Thanks."

The address appeared on the screen.

"Where to?" James asked.

"A place called Angelini's Coffee Roasters."

In Shadow, Damien drove through the streets filled with revelers.

James grumbled. "There're so many people here, it's almost as bad as Real."

"Yeah but they'll be gone in a week, and we'll get our peace and quiet back."

Damien pulled up in front of the building, and parked. No one was coming or going from the building. They walked to the door.

"This place is deserted. Are you sure it's the right address?" James asked.

Damien cupped his hand to the window and looked into the heavily shadowed room. On the floor, a layer of dust lay undisturbed. Damien glanced at his phone. "It's the right address."

"Let's check inside." James frowned, trying the door and finding it unlocked.

"All right, but there's nothing here. Trust me."

James opened the door, and they both looked inside. Empty. No hint that anyone had been through the room. The musty smell of stale air permeated the enclosed space. The dust was inches thick and settled evenly across the floor. James took a step in and the dust puffed around his foot.

A tickle in his nose, had him sneezing in rapid succession.

"Fuck," said James.

"Angelini's is in Real."

"Yep."

"Why would Earl hang out in Real?" Damien tried to puzzle out the Mage's strange behavior. All the magic users he knew preferred Shadow to Real.

James shrugged. "Coffee, I guess."

Damien followed James around the corner and into an alley. A blink later, they appeared in Real.

Damien led the way to the street and the storefront teeming with people. He looked in the window and couldn't see much. He scanned the coffee shop as he entered. No sign of Earl. Pulling out his phone, he brought up Earl's picture. James did the same.

Entering the coffee shop, he was hit with the earthy odor of freshly ground beans. They canvassed the room, showing the picture around. No one had seen Earl in the last two days.

One more table to go, and Damien grinned. It was the attractive blonde from last night. Time to learn her name and find out if she'd be willing to celebrate with him.

Damien took a single step forward, before a hard grip on his arm stopped him.

James hissed. "That's the creature from the diagram."

"Which one, the blonde or the brunette?"

A sinking feeling in the pit of his stomach. *Please don't let it be her.*

"The blonde."

Shit. Damn. Fuck.

Chapter 6

Deidre arrived at the coffee shop at the same time as Cyn. A smile lit the Vampire's features. "You look great."

Deidre twirled. "Thanks."

"You're welcome. Let's get coffee."

They stood in a long line and Deidre looked at the menu. The sheer variety of choices overwhelmed her. What was a latte? Mocha? Espresso? Cappuccino?

"Um Cyn?"

"Yeah?"

"I don't know what most of the choices are."

Cyn turned and gave her a look of disbelief. "You have been out of touch, haven't you?"

Deidre bit her lip. "Yeah."

"Okay, what do you want?"

"Coffee."

"With or without milk?"

"Without."

"With or without chocolate?"

"Oooh chocolate? That sounds interesting."

Cyn grinned. "It's very tasty." She stepped to the counter and placed the order. A short time later they collected their drinks, found a table and sat down.

Deidre tried the concoction.

"So, what do you think?" Cyn asked.

Deidre took another sip. "It's good, really good."

Cyn took a sip of her own drink.

Deidre tilted her head to the side. "I didn't think you could eat or drink?"

"Contrary to popular belief, we can eat and drink, but most choose not to bother. I refuse to give up coffee or chocolate or potatoes or hamburgers… hmmm I guess there are a lot of things I still eat."

Deidre heard the tinkle of the bell over the door of the coffee shop and felt a wave of Vampiric energy wash over her. She glanced over her shoulder and became captivated.

By him. The Vampire from last night.

Anticipation coursed through her. Would he remember her? Would he give her the same wicked smile? Would she drool over him like an idiot?

Her power woke, stretched like a contented cat, and focused on him, ready to pounce. What the hell was going on with her magic? It never reacted to any male without her directing it. Was he somehow manipulating her? She checked his aura again. Vampire, not Incubus.

She reached out and grabbed Cyn's arm, stopping Cyn in mid-sentence.

"What?"

"Check out what just walked in."

Cyn looked. And looked some more. "Wow."

Cyn turned back to Deidre. "Did you see the blond? Hot, hot, hot!"

Deidre shook her head. "Blond? What blond?"

Cyn snickered. "The gorgeous one next to the bad boy."

"Oh him." Deidre gave him a quick glance; another Vampire.

Cyn glanced back at the two and tensed.

Concern filled Deidre. "What? What is it?"

Cyn slumped down in her chair, trying to hide from view. "We're in trouble."

Deidre had to tear her gaze away to look at Cyn. "What are you talking about?"

"Look at their clothes"

Deidre stared, letting her gaze roam up and down his yummy body. "Mmm sexy."

"Very, but that's not the point. See that patch on their coats?"

"Yes. What does it mean?"

"They're Elite. Members of the Elite Magical Protection Force, and off limits. "

The full meaning dawned on Deidre. "J'kala... they're cops!"

"Exactly. A male-only organization that's tasked to keep everyone safe from Paranormal threats." A hint of bitterness laced Cyn's tone.

"No females?"

"Nope."

"Why not?"

"It would recklessly endanger the breeders." Cyn made air quotes.

Deidre frowned. "But you fought well."

Cyn nodded once and leaned forward, an intense look of concentration on her face. "And they must never find out."

Deidre felt the push of Cyn's mind against her own and thought it might be easier to let her friend believe the psychic command worked. After all she had no reason to tell the cops anything. She thought about the Mage that she'd drained. He'd worn an outfit similar to the one the two hunks were wearing. Realization dawned.

J'kala! She'd killed a cop. She was an accessory to the crime.

Dar'kirm, I knew working for Sir would be trouble.

She'd learned to never piss off local law enforcement. They never wanted to help her out of whatever situation she was in, so throwing herself on the mercy of tall, dark, and deadly over there wasn't a good idea.

"Sherva na dela!" Deidre cursed.

Cyn gave her a funny look. "What's that one mean?"

Deidre thought for a moment. "Similar to son of a bitch, I think."

Cyn tilted her head. "I wonder why they're in Real."

Deidre held up a hand. "Wait... are you saying they don't frequent human Earth?"

Cyn shook her head. "It's not off limits or anything. It's just that most of the Paranormal Races prefer to live in Shadow."

Deidre was about to respond when Cyn's face drained of color. "Shit, they're coming this way, what'll we do?"

"Can they arrest us for being here?"

Cyn shook her head. "Not unless we do something to alert the humans we exist."

"Then we finish our drinks and get the hell out of here." Deidre gulped the last of her drink, and put the mug back on the table. Cyn did the same. They stood and turned toward the door. Now to get past those two Vamps.

Cyn led the way, taking them on a circuitous route between the tables. She came to an abrupt stop.

Deidre stopped herself in time to keep from running into her friend.

Looking over Cyn's shoulder, she watched the dark one. A shiver of arousal pulsed through her. She had a feeling she'd enjoy playing with this one. Which fascinated, frustrated and frightened her. What would it be like to feel real pleasure instead of faking it? Considering she used sex to survive, she'd learned to distance herself from the act and from males.

This one called to her on a deeper level. Temptation whispered. *Take a chance.*

Deidre shook her head, trying to rid herself of that thought. He was a cop, and a Paranormal one at that.

84

His head tilted down and piercing green eyes observed her over the tops of his sunglasses. Her breath caught. Time froze.

No one existed except the two of them. His eyes held her prisoner, promising heat, promising lust. Her breath stilled in her lungs, desire pulsed through her veins and small creatures danced in her belly.

A bump and a mumbled apology broke the connection.

He spoke, his voice wreaking havoc with her nerves.

"Excuse me ladies, have either of you seen this man?"

Holding up a cell phone with a picture, Deidre felt the blood drain from her face. *J'kala*. It was the Mage from yesterday.

The Vampire's gaze narrowed. "When did you see him?"

Shit! "Um a couple of days ago I think."

The shorter Vampire shook his head, and gave her a smile that didn't reach his eyes. He took Cyn's arm and led her back to their table.

Deidre tried to take a step toward the open door, when Mr. Sexy grabbed her arm in a surprisingly gentle grip. "I don't think so lovely. I have a few questions for you."

He escorted her to the table and sat with his back to the wall. The blond sat across from him, with Cyn across from her.

The dark one pulled out an official badge. "My name is Detective Damien Alexander, and this is my partner Detective James Kirk."

Cyn bit her lip, and Deidre thought it looked like she was hiding a smile. But she didn't get the joke.

Damien raised his eyebrow. "And who are you?"

"I'm Deidre."

"I'm Cyn."

Damien put the cell phone on the table, with the picture still showing. "What can you tell us about this man?"

Cyn frowned. "I've never seen him before."

Detective Alexander turned to Deidre. "When did you see him?"

Her mouth dried to a desert. She licked her lips; fingers tapping against each other. "I think I saw him a few days ago."

James clicked his tongue and shook his head. "That's a neat trick considering you arrived in the city yesterday."

Deidre froze. How in Dar'kirm did he know that? Was he trying to trap her into giving information about Sir?

Cyn frowned. "How do you know she arrived yesterday? You don't even know who she is."

James smiled at her. "I don't need to know who she is to know that she was summoned yesterday by a Mage."

Cyn's head tilted in question. Deidre took a deep breath and shrugged. They were fishing for information, and she wasn't able to give them any due to the constraints of the spell.

Damien covered her hand, stilling her fingers. "What are you?"

Tingles flooded her system from the touch of his hand on hers. Shit, she needed to concentrate. "I-I can't answer that."

"Can't or won't?"

"Can't."

"Why not?"

She didn't want to answer, but unless she gave them something, they'd lock her up, and she'd have to deal with that red mist when she didn't appear for her master.

"The constraints of the spell prohibit me from sharing information about myself, my purpose or my Summoner."

"Interesting," James said.

"I think so." Damien leaned forward. "Now where did you see this man?"

"I can't answer that."

James sat back. "Meaning it probably has something to do with her."

Damien stood and pulled Deidre to her feet. "Let's go."

"Wait. What?"

James leaned forward, his pleasant voice filled with menace. "You're coming back to the office with us, where a Mage on staff will break the spell constraints, and then you'll tell us everything we want to know."

Shit! Her gaze met Cyn's.

The Vampire bit her lip. "Are you sure that's a good idea?"

Both males turned to look at her, frowning. "Why wouldn't it be?" asked James.

With a sugary sweet smile, she replied, "Don't you think that if she was summoned by a spell, breaking it would send her back to wherever she came from?"

Deidre grinned at her, and Cyn winked in return.

"I don't..." James began.

A loud commotion in front of the coffee shop had both Elite turning.

Outside on the street, a small gang of men attacked a tall man with silver at his temples.

"Shit! Let's go." Damien let go of her arm took two steps and glared back at her. "Wait here."

The two Vampires hurried through the humans that had gathered at the windows to watch the action.

Deidre snorted at the order. *I don't think so.*

Cyn grabbed Deidre's arm. "Let's get out of here, while they're distracted."

Deidre glanced at the fight outside. "I'm right behind you."

They hurried through the growing crowed and made their escape. Blocks away the found a bench and sat.

Deidre sighed. "I suppose I should find other accommodations?"

Cyn gave her a puzzled look. "Why?"

"I'm sure I'm suspect number one right now. It wouldn't be safe for you."

A grin spread over Cyn's face. "Au contraire. What better place for you to hide than with me?"

Confusion filled Deidre. "I don't understand."

"How can they find you if you're not registered at a hotel?"

"I suppose they could track me somehow."

"Maybe, but that would take time and manpower that they don't have, with the Festival starting tomorrow."

Deidre looked at her. "Why are you helping me?"

Cyn looked away and in a soft tone replied. "Because I know what it's like to be friendless in a hostile city." She bumped Deidre's shoulder with her own. "And I'm not the most law abiding citizen you'll meet."

Deidre laughed. "I'm in excellent company then."

"Oh and I meant to give you this earlier." Cyn dug around in a zippered pocket, pulled out a key and handed it over. "There you go, a key to the apartment."

Tears filled Deidre's eyes. "Thank you."

"You're welcome." She hesitated a moment. "Will you try to answer some of my questions?"

Deidre shrugged. "If I can. I'm really not sure what I can share."

A phone rang and it took Deidre a moment to figure out it was hers. She glanced at the screen.

"Who is it?" Cyn asked.

"Someone I'd rather not talk to."

"Then ignore the call."

"I can't. It's my boss." Deidre answered the call. "Yes Sir?"

"I've got a job for you…"

§

Damien and James rushed out into the street. Randall, one of the Elite Mages, was being attacked by seven young punks. Taking quick stock of the situation, it was clear the attackers were inept humans. He was about to pull two of them off Randall, when James cautioned, "Wait. Check their auras."

The auras were muddied. He'd seen this once before as a young Vamp.

He turned to James. "Fuck. Don't tell me…"

James nodded. "Looks like we've got a rogue."

A rogue attempting to convert humans into Paranormals. And by the rabid way this group had attacked, they were poorly trained.

Randall went down overwhelmed by their numbers. Damien went over and pulled off the attackers and threw them to James, who easily subdued them using his modified Taser. When all seven were twitching on the ground, they seized and began to foam at the mouth.

Damien helped Randall up then turned to help James. "Fuck. What the hell is that?"

James looked up from his crouched position. "No idea. Get help."

Damien punched the code into his phone, but he knew it'd be too late. Once the seven stopped seizing, they disintegrated into ash.

In front of the humans gathered around. *Fuck.*

Randall stepped over and clapped Damien on the shoulder. "Good work. I think we got it all in that take."

Damien relaxed his posture and saw James get up, tucking a small bag into his jacket.

One of the bystanders shouted. "What the hell is going on?"

Randall turned to the man and approached the group that had come out of the coffee shop to watch. "We're filming a documentary about emergency response during a zombie outbreak."

Damien suppressed a chuckle as the humans' eyes widened. "No shit? That's cool. But what about those guys that just vanished into dust?"

A lady standing next to the shouter, hit him in the arm. "That was all special effects, dumbass. Probably some remote control device with a covering that made them seem lifelike. With the introduction of electricity it changed the structure of the material and turned it into ash."

Damien was impressed. The stories people came up with to explain strange happenings bordered on the fantastic. He nodded at the woman and gave her a wink.

Two vans rolled up and his fellow Elite began to disperse the crowd.

Damien walked up to Randall. "What happened?"

Randall shook his head. "I don't know. I was meeting a contact and these thugs jumped me. Yelling something about destroying the freaks."

"Hmmm."

James came up. "The creature escaped."

Damn. He'd figured she'd make a break for it. Though he'd been hoping she'd stick around. He looked forward to finding out all he could about the creature, and why she had such a fascinating hold on him. "Shit. Can you track her?"

James shook his head. "There's too much activity." He pointed to the dispersal unit.

"Let's head around the block and see if we can pick anything up."

Randall clapped Damien on the shoulder. Thanks for the assist. See you back at the office."

Damien followed James around the block. "Pick up anything?" he asked.

James frowned. "With growing numbers of Paranormals walking around Real, it's hard to get a reading. I can't tell if she was coming or going."

"Let's follow the trail."

James' cell phone rang. "Yeah, boss?"

Damien watched James' expression turn serious. "We'll be right there." He hung up and turned to Damien.

"Earl's body was found by the human police in Golden Gate Park shortly after sunset."

90

§

Deidre recognized the Elf and the Mage from yesterday at the warehouse. Today they introduced themselves.

The Elf bowed. "I'm Antwon and this is Alexi." He waved to the Mage.

"Are you ready for your assignment?" Antwon smirked.

"Sure," she replied.

They led her to a waiting car and ushered her into the back seat. Alexi rounded the hood, and Antwon took the passenger seat.

"Where are we going?" Deidre was curious.

Antwon answered, "Your targets are currently at a warehouse on Fisherman's Wharf."

Deidre frowned, "Isn't that a popular tourist area?"

"Yes, but they're in Shadow, not Real. You are to drain them to the point of death, but do not kill them. Understand?"

Deidre nodded, wondering about the orders. It seemed strange that Sir didn't want them dead after she'd killed the other Mage, but who knew the workings of the male mind? She wasn't willing to risk the Red Mist if Sir found out she'd disobeyed.

A short time later, they crested a hill and Deidre could see what looked to be fluffy cotton filling the bay. The car headed downhill and they entered the thick fog bank.

They came to a stop in front of an old building on a pier.

Antwon got out of the car and held her door open. She stepped out and took a deep breath of salty air.

The Elf; grabbed her arm and escorted her to the building. Once inside he leaned over and whispered. "Pop into Shadow. Your targets are an Elf and a Shifter Wolf. Let me know as soon as you're done."

Deidre nodded and rolled her eyes, entering Shadow. Males had always treated her as a second class citizen, until she had them begging for sex. Their eagerness to submit to her sexual call was a delicious irony she savored every time she fed.

How in Dar'kirm was she going to drain both of them? If she did them one at a time, the other would be suspicious. And although she'd drained that group yesterday, it wasn't normal for her. And she didn't think she'd be able to trick a Shifter and an Elf as easily.

The answer came to her. Threesome.

She ventured deeper into the maze of crates and boxes. Two shadows at the far end of the warehouse, matched the auric signatures of her targets. One Elf and one Shifter Wolf.

How to approach them?

Males underestimated her intelligence, not bothering to look beyond her body. Perhaps that'd be the best way to deal with these two, playing the role of empty-headed fuck toy and see what happened.

Deidre walked toward them, high heels tapping on the wooden planks of the pier, making enough noise to announce her presence.

"Hello? Is anyone here?" Her hopeful tone rose enough to be heard in the cavernous space.

"Stop!" A deep voice commanded.

She stopped and held her hands out to her sides, palms facing front.

Deidre put a small tremble into her voice when she replied. "Please. Can you help me? I'm afraid I'm lost."

The two males loomed out of the darkness in front of her. A flashlight clicked on and the brightness blinded her. Blinking her eyes against the glare, the light beam roamed up and down her body. The light was tilted toward the ceiling which let her see the Elf and the Shifter Wolf

"Well, well, well, what do we have here?" The Elf raised an eyebrow and his gaze traveled up and down her body, stopping at her chest and low-cut shirt.

She clasped her hands between her breasts, pushing them up with her forearms.

"I am so lost." She lowered her eyelashes in a coy manner. "Can you help me?" she looked up at him and thrust her bottom lip out in a pout.

The Shifter Wolf moved toward her and took a deep breath, then growled low in his throat.

Deidre took a step back and brought her hand up to her throat, making her eyes wide as if he scared her.

"P-p-please?"

She manipulated her power to secrete pheromones to lure them in. And from the looks of the erections tenting their black pants, it was working. Wait… those emblems on their shirts. Crap these two were Elite. Sherva na dela! That's all she needed. But she'd come too far to stop now. On with the charade.

She licked her lips and both gazes locked onto the motion of her tongue.

The Shifter Wolf spoke, the sound close to a purr. "What can we do for you?"

Deidre smiled to herself. *Here comes the fun part. Let's see if they're as gullible as I think they are.*

"I'm new to the city. I arrived early before my friends and thought I'd get some sightseeing in. But I can't find my way around."

She summoned moisture to her eyes, projecting the image that she was near tears.

The Elf reached out and patted her shoulder.

"No need to cry little one. My partner and I will help you. What are you trying to find?"

"The way to Alcatraz."

The Shifter Wolf grinned. "In Real follow Embarcadero to Pier 33. You can't miss it."

Deidre widened her eyes and began to smile.

"Oh, you're the best!" Then she let a frown wrinkle her forehead. "But how can I thank you?"

The Shifter Wolf grinned. "How about a kiss?"

She licked her lips. "Okay."

The Wolf leaned forward and brushed his lips against hers in a gentle caress.

If these two were going to be gentle about it, this was going to take a while. She needed to speed things up.

She parted her lips and sucked his tongue into her mouth. A flicker of surprise caught his face before he closed his eyes and groaned into the kiss. He pulled her against him, her soft curves pressing against his hard flesh.

And now to incite him more.

She let him control the kiss as she undulated her body in a sensuous wave.

He groaned and tore his mouth away from hers.

"Damn little girl, you sure know how to tempt the wolf."

The Elf cleared his throat. "My turn."

The Wolf's arms around her, the Elf leaned into her back, turned her head, and captured her mouth. His kiss was deep and exploratory. She used her tongue to duel with his as she wrapped her power around both of them.

The Wolf growled. "If you want to stop, tell us now."

She pulled back from the kiss. It was sweet of them to offer, but not what she had planned.

Deidre dropped her gaze and pouted her lip. In a small voice she asked, "Don't you want me?"

The Elf clenched her shoulders and she looked up at him.

"Ever had a ménage?"

She shook her head and made her eyes big. Breathless she answered, "No, but I've always wondered…"

The Wolf tightened his embrace and rubbed his erection against her belly.

"Now's the perfect time to show you what it's all about."

94

Both Wolf and Elf stopped, and then she realized they were waiting for her answer.

"I'd like that."

The Elf ground himself against her hip and groaned. "Over by the wall."

The Wolf lifted her in his arms, and carried her to the side of the building around a few broken pallets and a small stack of boxes. He set her on her feet in front of him, leaned back against the wall and looked down at her.

"Are you sure?"

She nodded and licked her lips. "Oh yes."

He smiled and lifted her shirt over her head, eyes glued to her unbound breasts. "God, you've got pretty tits."

Deidre took a deep breath, moving her breasts up and down. Hands reached around from behind her and fondled her nipples. The Elf pressed against her back. She shifted her head, resting it on his shoulder.

Her power prepared her body while she played her part. Over the years she'd become an expert at manipulating her body's physiological responses.

The Elf held her breasts up for the Wolf, who bent his head and sucked on her nipple, pulling it deep into his mouth.

Deidre sighed, and wiggled against the male body pressing against her back.

The Elf leaned forward over her shoulder and whispered while playing with her other nipple. "Does it turn you on to have the two of us worshiping your pretty body?"

"Oh yes." Her breathing hitched. "Please!"

The Wolf chuckled and released her nipple with a pop. "Please what?"

"Please, I ache."

The Elf ran his hand down the front of her body, down her leg, catching the hem of her skirt and lifting it to bunch around her waist.

The Wolf looked down and smiled. "Well now, what have we here?"

His hands roamed down her hips to her bare flesh. "Naughty, naughty girl." He cupped her mons in his palm and moved his fingers in a tickling motion, teasing her clit.

Deidre could see the surprise in his eyes when his fingers encountered her wet flesh. A finger slid deep inside her, and she arched her body and moaned at the touch. With a single thought, she manipulated her pulse rate and breathing to match.

The Wolf chuckled and looked at the Elf. "She's a bad little girl, teasing the wolf by not wearing underwear." He paused, and for a moment Deidre thought he'd broken her sensual hold.

The Elf reached around her and ground himself into the small of her back. "I need to be inside her. Now."

The Wolf nodded and removed his fingers. He undid the button and zipper of his pants, withdrawing his hard erection. He stroked it a couple of times while looking at her body.

The Elf grabbed her hips and lifted her, taking a step forward.

Deidre parted her legs and wrapped them around the Wolf in front of her.

"Ready to be fucked?" the Wolf asked with a raised eyebrow.

Instead of answering, Deidre sank down onto his hard cock. Physically she felt the penetration, but emotionally it was all an act. An act she sometimes enjoyed, but not this time. Deidre resorted to something she'd always done. She faked it.

"Oh that feels soooo good."

The Wolf closed his eyes and leaned his head against the wall. "Damn she's hot."

Deidre fluttered her muscles and pulled a moan from him. *Finally. Now to get the other one into position.*

She turned her head and licked her lips, aware of his gaze following the motion.

"Are you going to come and play too?" Her voice was deliberate in its breathlessness.

"You couldn't stop me." He leaned forward and gave her a deep kiss.

She felt hands on the cheeks of her ass and wiggled, dragging another moan from the Wolf.

Cool fluid was rubbed around her rear entrance. Then she felt the blunt head of a penis, and pushed out as he sank into her.

The Elf rested his head on her shoulder. "Damn she's tight."

Deidre shifted a bit more, pushing him further in.

The Elf's arms embraced her from behind. "Slow down. I don't want to hurt you."

"You won't," she moaned, adding a touch of breathlessness.

The Wolf growled. "I think our girl likes a bit of pain with her pleasure."

Deidre nodded. "Oh yes. It turns me on so much!"

She felt the Elf take a deep breath then pushed until he was fully inside her.

"Oh you both feel so good. So deep." She lifted her arms to encircle the Wolf's neck. "Now take me, hard."

The Elf chuckled from behind and began to withdraw before surging back in.

They began thrusting in an opposing motion. When one thrust in, the other pulled out. They were careful to keep their thrusts from going too deep.

She couldn't believe it. They were trying to be careful of her more fragile feminine body. It was very sweet of them, but she could take anything they could dish out.

"Oh please, harder. I want to feel it so badly. Please fuck me harder."

The Wolf growled. "Are you sure? This can get pretty rough."

She smiled and winked at him, and leaned up to bite his lip. "I can take it."

She turned her head to the side to look at the Elf. "Fuck me. Make it hurt so good!"

Deidre sensed when the reigns of their control snapped. The Wolf braced his hand on her hips, and the Elf grabbed her shoulders. They moved faster and faster, their speed almost a blur. Deeper, harder, faster they went.

Deidre moaned as she began to clench and release her inner muscles. It took a few moments for them to reach their peak. The Wolf came first, followed by the Elf.

Two for one, fun.

She'd have to remember that in the future.

Smoky tendrils of sexual energy flared around them, and she inhaled. The amount of energy they gave off was significant, more than she'd ever consumed before. *There must be something to these Paranormals.* Watching their auras, she monitored their levels. Too much and she'd kill them; too little and they'd recover. *There.*

The Elf staggered back, his flagging erection slipping from her body. He tripped and crashed to the ground.

She disengaged her body from the Wolf as his legs collapsed from underneath him and he slid down the wall.

Deidre used a few tissues from the Wolf to clean herself, straightened her skirt, and put on her shirt.

The medallion flared bright in the dark warehouse nearly blinding her. Once again, the energy she'd absorbed from the males trickled away.

The medallion began to dim. So the necklace only worked when Sir ordered her to drain someone. Interesting.

Time to leave.

Deidre kissed each male on the cheek. "Thanks for the great time guys, you made my fantasy come true." They both gave her sleepy smiles before closing their eyes.

Deidre walked to the side of the warehouse where she could sense Alexi and Antwon waiting. She waved at them, and they approached.

"Do you have any further instructions for me?"

98

They shook their heads, and she left, not wanting to see her targets killed. After all, they'd been nice to her.

A rumbling in her tummy reminded her she needed to feed to recover some of the energy that damned medallion stole from her.

Deidre popped into Real. There was a greater chance she'd find what she needed. She saw a pan-handler approach and smiled. *Perfect.*

§

Damien and James arrived at Golden Gate Park and saw Detective Alejandro standing to the side, supervising his people.

Damien motioned to James who went to speak with the crime scene techs. Damien walked up to the human detective. "I got your message, what do you have for me?"

Detective Alejandro, looked around and lowered his voice. "Other than the body, there have been reports of increased violence among the mid-twenty crowd."

"Gangs?" Damien asked.

Alejandro shook his head, brushing a lock of dark hair out of his eyes. "It's not any of the established gangs. And there's going to be a turf war if these newcomers don't back off."

"So why tell me?"

Detective Alejandro looked him in the eye. "Because these are your people."

"How can you tell?"

"They're stronger, faster, and can take a couple of bullets before disintegrating."

"Fuck."

"No thanks."

"Ha. Ha. You're quite the comedian."

Alejandro grinned. Apparently the Latino had a way about him that the ladies loved. Speaking of which. Damien reached into his pocket and pulled out a handful of sticky notes, handing them to Alejandro.

"What's this?"

"Your fan club asked me to pass those along."

"You've told them I'm not interested?"

Damien rolled his eyes. "Repeatedly. They won't take no for an answer."

"I'm sure my man will be amused."

James walked toward them. "I've called for the clean-up crew."

Detective Alejandro nodded, his posture stiff.

Damien didn't know why the two were hostile toward each other, and neither would tell him. Giving a mental shrug, he watched the Elite Medical Unit arrive.

They transferred the body to a stretcher, covered it with a sheet, and put it in the back of a van. One of the techs walked over to them.

"Preliminary cause of death is unknown at the moment."

James frowned. "But his heart has more holes than Swiss cheese."

"Administered after death. There are no other wounds or visible marks except for old scars and bruises. We also found magical residue. We're taking him to the lab for further analysis."

"Take the body to Luna Clinic and ask if Healer Bar'ella can determine the residue," Damien ordered.

A sour look crossed the Tech's face. "With all due respect, sir, we can handle it."

Damien looked at the Tech. "I want the Healer to look at the body."

"Yes, sir."

Healer Dragon Bar'ella was the preeminent healer in the world. She could diagnose and treat the rarest of maladies. The fact she was female was something many, including the Elite Med Techs, didn't approve of. However there was no one Damien

100

would rather work with than the healer. She'd be able to figure out how Earl died.

Damien's phone beeped. "Klaus and Roger need help."

"Where are they?"

"Fisherman's Wharf."

"Let's go."

They drove to Fisherman's Wharf and after finding a parking spot, popped into Shadow.

They arrived at the large building on Pier 45 in time to see two males sneaking inside.

"That can't be good." James muttered.

They entered the building and followed the sound of footsteps on boards to the far end of the pier.

Damien looked around a stack of crates. The two males they'd followed were dragging Klaus and Roger toward an open door.

A shout of rage left Damien's throat and startled the two males into dropping their burdens. The two men looked at each other, turned, and ran toward the nearest exit.

James took off after them. Damien lost sight of them as they left the building.

He ran over and knelt next to Klaus checking on the Elf's vital signs. Heart beat weak, but discernible. Breathing shallow.

Damien checked for wounds, but didn't see any obvious reason for their unconscious state. Their uniforms were in disarray. Shirts un-tucked, belts loosened, and what bothered Damien was their cocks were out, as if they'd just finished having sex while in uniform. And despite appearances, Damien knew both males were straight.

A squeaky floor-board had Damien jumping up and drawing his weapon, ready to defend his downed friends.

James appeared around the corner, out of breath and shaking his head.

"Bastards popped into Real and got away. Blended in with a bunch of tourists. How are they?"

"Klaus is weak. I haven't checked Roger yet." Damien pulled out his cell phone.

"I need medical assistance for an Elf and Shifter Wolf. Location Pier 45." He hung up and was about to speak, when Klaus stirred.

Damien grabbed his shoulder. "Klaus. What happened?"

Klaus opened his eyes. "Damn…she's… best ever." He closed his eyes and sunk back into unconsciousness.

James looked at Damien. "They don't look good. Medical better get here soon."

They waited with Klaus and Roger until medical personnel arrived. As they were being loaded into the emergency vehicle, Damien caught a scent.

He turned and looked around at the empty street, but the unique aroma of flowers faded in the breeze. There was something familiar about it, but it was elusive, like a vision floating on the edge of his periphery.

James bumped his arm and brought Damien back to scene.

"We need to get back to the office." Damien led the way to the car.

"No time, look." James pointed to the lightening sky in the east. "Find shelter, fast."

Chapter 7

Deidre opened her eyes and looked around, heart sinking as she realized she was back in Demoni. The well-lit throne room showed a group of Demoni gathered near the throne. They were dressed, which was odd. Most Demoni remained naked. These were dressed in pants, not court kilts. Tattooed symbols covered their arms and torsos.

A force pushed her forward toward the group.

They gathered around in a circle with Khan on one side and the five Demoni on the other. In the center of the circle was a scroll that looked vaguely familiar. The five Demoni had symbols tattooed into their arms and chest. The marks emitted a glow. Pungent spices filled the room from braziers placed around the scroll.

These Demoni were magicians.

One held a small wand with a horned skull on the end. Leather strips hung from the base of the horns, with blood red jewels on the end.

He shook the wand over the scroll.

Peeking closer, she saw arcane symbols and words. "Succubus, I command thee…" Ja'kala! It was her summoning scroll.

What in Dar'kirm were they trying to do?

The Demoni with the wand muttered in a guttural language she didn't understand. The other four began to chant, lifting their arms as their voices rose. A shouted word at the end and their arms dropped to their sides.

She felt a tingle throughout her body. Whoa, what were they doing?

Her spirit shifted and it felt as if she was being pulled through the eye of a needle.

Once the pain died, she opened her eyes. Khan grinned at her. Holy fuck. He could see her.

"Welcome, Deidre." His grin caused shivers of dread to course through her.

Khan turned to the magicians. "Leave."

The court magicians scrambled to gather their supplies and ran from the room.

Khan approached, reached out with his claw, and ran the black tip over her cheek. Pain, razor sharp, sliced through her. Wetness dampened her cheek. Tears? Show no weakness. She wiped the wetness away. Black blood smeared the back of her clawed, ruby hand. She was in Demoni form.

No, no, no! This couldn't be happening! This had to be a dream, had to! Wake up! Wake UP!

Khan leaned forward and licked the blood from her cheek, the sandpapery feeling of his tongue adding to the pain.

WAKE UP!

Deidre blinked awake. Darkness surrounded her. Where was she? It took a few moments to recognize her surroundings. Couch, blanket... a sigh of relief left her. She was at Cyn's apartment.

§

It was early evening and Deidre roamed the streets. It took a few males willing to share their energy before she was full.

Stopping in front of a window display, she ogled the revealing clothing and the shoes.

"Hello again," said a deep voice to her right.

She turned. Ja'kala, it was the Vampire cop.

"H-hello. Detective."

"Please call me, Damien."

"Damien then."

He leaned against the wall beside the window with his arms crossed over his chest, a small smile teasing his lips.

"We never got a chance to finish our discussion yesterday."

Deidre bit her lip, unsure how to respond.

Damien straightened from his relaxed pose and held out a hand.

"Come with me."

Deidre swayed toward him, wanting nothing more than to place her hand in his and let him take care of her. *Wait, what?* Deidre shook her head trying to clear it from the cloying fog. Her eyes narrowed and she glared at him. "Stop trying to manipulate me."

He gave her a wicked grin that lit her hormones. "Why would I do such a thing?"

"To control me." She leaned forward. "And I dislike being controlled."

He shook his head and leaned closer, hand still out. "I just want to ask a few questions. What's the harm in that?"

If he only knew.

"If I don't come with you, what will happen?"

Damien's eyes flashed red. "You're coming with me, willingly or unwillingly. Your choice."

With great reluctance, she placed her hand in his, jolting at the touch. His firm grip sent a shudder of desire through her. What would those smooth hands feel like as they roamed her body?

Whoa. Where in Dar'kirm had that come from?

She controlled her body, not the other way around.

He tucked her hand through his arm, with his other hand on top, securing her to his side.

"We're only a few blocks from the office. Come on."

They entered the Elite offices, and she couldn't help but stiffen. Dread formed in the pit of her stomach. This wouldn't end well. But short of running out the door, nothing she did would help. And if she ran, she'd have all of these Elite males after her. In different circumstances, that'd be fun, but not now.

Damien led her to the elevators and after a short ride, he led her through a maze of cubicles.

He knocked on a door, opened it, and ushered her inside.

The first thing she saw was the Fae. He rose from his seat behind a desk, with a grin blooming on his face. He had short, dark brown hair that complemented the sharp angle of his jaw. The dark chocolate eyes took in everything at a glance. He was dressed in a dark grey suit with a crisp white shirt.

A gasp came from one of the chairs in front of the desk. This was the one Paranormal Deidre recognized.

"Well, well, well, look what the Vamp dragged in." Bar'ella's pleasant voice caused a grin to blossom on Deidre's face

"How many virgins have you eaten in the past month, Miz Scaley?" Deidre bantered back.

The Dragon, Bar'ella, wore her short white hair, curled. Her careworn face had generous laugh lines framing metallic gold eyes. Deidre knew Dragons could change their human appearance and had asked why Bar'ella had chosen to look grandmotherly. "Because humans and Paranormals respect the wisdom the appearance of age brings." Bar'ella had answered.

Bar'ella came forward with a grin on her face and enveloped Deidre in a bone-crushing hug. Out of the corner of her eye, she saw jaws drop.

Damien sputtered. "You can't speak to her like that."

The Dragon pulled back and shot the Vampire a look, shutting him up.

Holding onto Deidre's hands, Bar'ella held them out. "Let's get a look at you. You look fabulous, as always, but there's something familiar this time."

Deidre shrugged. "I can't help that."

Bar'ella pulled her into another hug. "It's so good to see you again."

Deidre returned the embrace, fighting the liquid trying to escape her eyes. "You too, old friend."

A throat cleared. The Fae resumed his seat, a friendly smile on his face.

"If you'd care to introduce us, Bar'ella?"

The healer sighed. "Very well. Deidre, this is Captain Jor'dan DuŠan. Captain, this is my old friend, Deidre."

The Fae held out his hand, and Deidre shook it, letting go as soon as polite. His aura radiated kindness layered with steel. Not someone she wanted to get on the bad side of.

The Captain gestured to the chairs. "Ladies, please have a seat."

Deidre chose the chair closest to the door, easier to escape if it came to that. Bar'ella took the other chair, leaving Damien to stand.

"I'm assuming this is the creature?" Captain Jor'dan asked Damien.

The Vampire nodded. "According to James."

The Captain turned toward her. "What are you?"

Deidre rolled her eyes and shook her head. "I can't answer that."

Beside her, Bar'ella also shook her head. "Jor'dan, I can't believe you don't know this."

The Fae looked confused. "Know what?"

"Deidre is unable to answer any direct questions regarding herself or the reason she's here."

"Is this true?"

Deidre nodded.

Jor'dan turned back to Bar'ella. "Then how do we get information from her?"

Bar'ella gave him a small smile. "You don't. There is nothing powerful enough to break the spell that holds her silent." At his look of disbelief she continued, "And believe me, others more powerful than the current Council have tried."

"I find that hard to believe."

Bar'ella shrugged. "It's the truth."

"Do you know what she is?"

"Yes and no. But I can tell you with one hundred percent certainty that she has nothing to do with whoever is attempting to turn humans into Vampires."

"How do you know?" Damien piped up from his spot over by the window.

"Because that is not the nature of her magic." She held up a hand, "And before you ask, I can't tell you what it is. Let's just say she's incapable of causing irreparable harm."

"Do you know what she's doing here?" Damien asked.

Bar'ella shook her head. "Not the particulars, but it has nothing to do with your investigations, that much I'm certain."

"Not even what happened to Earl?"

Bar'ella shook her head.

Deidre cringed on the inside. Why was she lying? The Healer had to have found traces of the smoky energy she'd drained. This incarnation was one cluster fuck after another.

"Is there anything else?" Bar'ella asked.

Both Damien and the Captain shook their head.

"I'd like to catch up, if you don't mind."

Captain Jor'dan stood. "Use my office." He motioned to Damien, and the two left the room.

With a negligent wave from Bar'ella, an iridescent bubble grew until it encompassed the area around them.

"So we're not overheard," the healer explained.

"Very nice bubble of silence."

108

"Thanks. It took a bit to get it just right." Bar'ella turned a frown on her. "Now what the hell is going on?"

Deidre slumped back into her chair. "I have no fucking idea. This incarnation is so unlike any of the ones from before."

Bar'ella frowned. "Are you sleeping with your master?"

Deidre shook her head. "No and it's confusing the heck out of me." She paused a moment. "Why did you lie to the cops?"

Bar'ella tilted her head. "How did I lie?"

"About the irreparable harm bit."

She grinned. "Do you really want it known that you can fuck men to death?"

"No, but…"

The healer reached over and patted her knee. "Don't worry about it. I do have a question though, did you kill Earl at the behest of your summoner?"

Deidre bit her lip. She couldn't say anything but a single nod was all she was able to manage before she froze. The spell against giving information had seized her, stopping her from everything except breathing.

Bar'ella sat back and waited for the spell to release its hold.

The iron grip on Deidre's muscles relaxed and she rolled her neck, stretching each limb. She hated the loss of control when the spell froze her, but Bar'ella had helped her many times before and she might need her help again.

"Let's change the subject," Bar'ella suggested.

Bar'ella cleared her throat and gave her a penetrating look. "Now what is going on with your aura?"

"I can't see it. What does it look like?"

"Pink tinged with gold. If I didn't know better, I'd say you were falling in love."

Deidre jolted upright. "What!? That's impossible! I'm a demon for Dar'kirm's sake! We're not able to fall in love!"

Bar'ella sat back. "If you were actually one of the Hell crew, I'd agree with you. But we both know you were created differently."

"Out of the belief of man."

The healer nodded. "And don't you think that since you were created to sate man's lust, you'd be able to feel all the emotions that went along with it?"

Deidre shook her head. "That's the most ridiculous thing I've ever heard." Her shoulders slumped. "How did this happen?"

Bar'ella tilted her head. "Attraction is based on pheromones."

"So it's all chemical?"

The healer shook her head. "Attraction is chemical, yes. But the emotional attachment grows and changes until love is there."

If she continued to be around him, she'd grow to love him? Deidre shook her head. Not an option.

"So who is he?"

"Who is who?"

"The one who makes your heart pound, your palms sweat and your feminine heart tingle?"

"You're not going to let this go, are you?"

Bar'ella shook her head with a twinkle in her eye. "Nope."

"That meddling Vampire, Damien. My power wakes on its own whenever I'm near him."

Bar'ella clapped her hands in delight, gold eyes sparkling. "Oh this is delicious! Mr. I'm-never-settling-down himself."

Deidre held up a hand. "Before you get too busy planning the mating ceremony, just remember one thing. It can't go anywhere."

"Just because you're cursed, doesn't mean he can't break it."

"True, however I don't see him sacrificing himself for me."

"You might be surprised."

"And I think you're doomed to disappointment. Besides I'm not the most law abiding citizen, now am I?"

"True," Bar'ella paused. "Where are you staying?"

"With a Vampire of all people. She lives in Real."

One of Bar'ella's eyebrows rose. "How did you meet?"

In a few succinct words, Deidre related the tale.

Bar'ella sighed. "Leave it to you to find trouble. Though I'm glad you're staying with Cyn. She's the perfect roommate for you."

"How do you know her?"

"Child, I know everyone."

Deidre raised an eyebrow. "Child? I seem to remember you're younger than I am."

"My appearance suggests otherwise."

A knock on the door and Bar'ella dissolved the bubble. They both stood as the Fae poked his head into the room. "Damien will see you home, Miss Deidre."

Deidre followed Damien out of the building and into Shadow Earth. He held her hand as they walked through the crowded streets.

She watched the various Paranormals as they went about their business, uncomfortable at the stares she was receiving.

"Why are you nervous?"

"They're staring at me."

"Can't they appreciate a beautiful woman? Aren't you stared at in Real?"

"Yes, but that's different. Humans are safe."

"They're just as violent as Paranormals."

She nodded her head. "Yes, but they don't cause irreparable harm."

He stopped and turned her to look up at him. "Who hurt you in the past?"

She snorted. "Too many to count."

Damien stroked her cheek with the back of his fingers of his free hand. "I'd have protected you."

"You're the one who scares me the most."

He seemed to take affront at that. "I'd never hurt you."

Deidre gave him a sad smile. The physical hurt wasn't what she was afraid of.

He cupped the back of her head and pulled her forward, flush with his body. His lips brushed hers.

Deidre let the wariness go; she wanted this moment for herself, wanted to pretend he was hers, if only for a moment. She leaned into the kiss; her eyes drifting closed. Nothing existed except the feel of his sculpted muscles under her palm and the gentle caress of his lips.

Need filled her, hot, urgent and uncontrollable.

She opened her eyes and met his lust-filled gaze.

"May I?" his request brought a smile to her lips. *How polite.* Deidre licked her lips. "You may."

His mouth pressed against hers, his tongue surged into her mouth, and aggressive invasion. Intimate, powerful, elemental.

Her tongue dueled with his, the taste of coffee, chocolate, and male spice a potent combination. His kiss seared her, heating her flesh. Her heart raced, and tingles of desire flowed through her system, igniting her lust. She felt her power rising and fought to keep it down, to keep it under control.

The ringing of her phone jolted her back to reality. It was Sir's ringtone.

Deidre pulled away from the kiss and stepped out of his embrace. She longed to step back, to feel safe, but the real world called. "I've got to go."

He nodded, placing a lingering kiss on the inside of her palm, and slipped a business card into her hand. "Call me later."

She popped into Real, accepting the call. "Yes Sir?"

"I need you to come to the following address." He rattled it off.

"I don't know where that is."

"Where are you?"

Deidre looked at the sign-posts on the streets and gave him the location.

112

"That's a very dangerous area. Only a block from the Elite offices."

"I know."

"And how do you know that?" She heard the rising anger in his voice.

Deidre took a deep breath, not wanting to answer, but the compulsion forced it from her. "I was taken in for questioning."

"You didn't say anything, did you?"

"No Sir, I can't. The spell prohibits it."

He was silent a moment. "Alright. Antwon will pick you up. Be ready." He hung up.

Deidre walked over to a low retaining wall and sat, waiting for her ride.

§

Damien watched Deidre disappear from Shadow. He should follow her to find out what was going on, but the kiss they'd shared, knocked him on his kiester. When the Captain had suggested getting to know her socially, to find out the information they needed, he'd thought the Fae had been smoking something. "There's more than one way to storm a castle, Damien. We need to know why she's here." And so he kissed her. And she melted against him. And he forgot about the mission, forgot about everything, but the feel of her in his arms. *Shit. Damn. Fuck.*

He needed to get his head together. He had to keep the mission in mind, no matter how much he wanted to sate his growing thirst for her.

Unable to fight temptation, he popped into Real and searched for her. She was gone. He needed a long walk to get his head back in the game. His route took him through a section of town he wasn't familiar with. Her kiss was a mixture of innocence and passion. Lust and sweetness. The more he found out about her, the more he wanted to know.

A tingle alarm at the outer edge of his psychic sense had him stopping and performing a more thorough scan. The streets were deserted, which was odd for Real. The tingle faded away. *Must have been a leftover reaction to Deidre.*

Chapter 8

Clint Douglas drove in Real to the subterranean meeting room of the Underground. His phone rang. *What is it now?* Taking a deep breath, he reached for his patience before answering.

"Hello, Adolfo. What do you want?"

Adolfo's excitement was clear in his tone. "We've captured two Elite!"

Clint rolled his eyes. How had that group of incompetent idiots captured two dangerous warriors?

"What happened?"

"We were prepping for the meeting, and they walked right up to us! I was shocked, but I ordered the others to get them. And we did!"

He paused, and Clint could hear another voice in the background.

"Oh, Antwon says they're the same ones from the Wharf."

"What? They should be dead. Let me talk to Antwon."

"Sorry, he had to go get someone."

"Fine. I'll be there in a few minutes."

Clint found a parking spot on the street and took the stairs down to the entrance where Antwon and the Succubus were waiting. He glared at her. "You failed at the Wharf."

She looked confused when she answered. "Per your instructions I was to drain them to the point of death, but not kill them."

Clint's forehead wrinkled in consternation. He turned to Antwon, who shrugged. "It was too soon."

"Explain." Clint felt the beginnings of a headache pound behind his eyes.

"Killing the Elite so soon after the other would have drawn too much attention."

One... two... three... four... breathe. Calm. Control. "Do not override my orders again. Take the bodies to Hans and tell him to make sure to mask the cause of death."

"Yes, sir." Antwon bowed from the waist.

Clint turned to the demon, "Forget this place exists."

The Succubus nodded.

His phone rang. "Yes, Alexi?"

"Sir, a group of newly converted humans have escaped again."

"What? When?"

"Adolfo released them before going to the meeting."

What was that stupid idiot thinking? Adolfo's blatant disregard for Clint's orders made him livid. Clint clenched his fists, and took deep breaths through is nose. Tonight would see an end to Adolfo and the others. In a few hours he'd be free of the idiot and his friends.

Clint pinched the bridge of his nose, headache piercing his brain with each heartbeat. "Do you know where they are?"

"Adolfo sent them after the Elite, Damien Alexander."

"Keep an eye on them." Clint ended the call and stopped in front of a large wooden door. The Succubus gave him a curious look, and thankfully remained silent.

Breathe in. He'll be dead soon. Breathe out. Calm. Bastard little asshole... NO! Breathe. Just breathe. In. Out. Dead. In. Out. Dead.

116

He took a last deep breath before opening the door in front of him and waving the Succubus through. Good. She was the one part of his plan going well. And to make sure she didn't cause trouble, he'd memorized the Red Mist spell.

Clint led her through the building and down a set of stairs, stopping before a large set of double doors. He knocked in a specific pattern Adolfo insisted on. Clint stopped himself from shaking his head. *Secret knocks. How childish!*

The doors swung open on silent hinges, and he stepped through, entering the cavernous meeting room of the Underground. The group gathered on the other side of the altar set in the middle of the floor, mocking the two Elite bound in magical chains. After a quick headcount, he verified that all members of the Underground were present. *They all followed instructions for once.*

Clint gestured for the Succubus to step forward before clearing his throat and demanding their silence. "My friends, may I present Succubus Deidre."

He stepped back as attention turned to her.

In a low tone that reached no further than the Succubus, Clint warned, "Don't fail me. Drain them all, to death."

She nodded once then turned back to the group. He caught a flash of her smile and felt a surge of lust course through him. He tramped it down, snarling at his own reaction.

No! I won't feel lust for her. Elaine help me!

The imaged of Elaine popped into his head. Her blonde hair, pulled into its customary severe bun, and her unsmiling expression. Grief poured through him, muting his reaction to the Succubus.

Clint tilted his head, a subtle gesture for the Elf to join him. He motioned for Antwon to precede him to the door. Clint turned and saw the expressions of naked lust on the faces of Adolfo and his friends. A smile tugged the corners of his lips as they left the Succubus to her entertainments, adjourning to the office a few doors down from the main chamber.

Clint sat in one of the leather chairs, leaned forward with elbows on his knees.

The sweet scent of incense filled the chamber, soothing his temper and clearing his head of the remnants of the Succubus' pheromones.

"Have you heard from Alexi?"

Antwon sat in the chair across a small table and nodded. "The converted humans have Damien Alexander in sight and are about to converge on him. I expect to hear something soon."

Clint nodded and sat back to wait. While he doubted the humans would do any damage to Alexander, the Elite would take care of the half humans for him. And if the converted took out an Elite? It was a win-win situation no matter how he looked at it.

§

Deidre was left alone in the room full of young male Paranormals. She sighed. This would be her trickiest draining yet. She needed to drain them at the same time, otherwise they might be suspicious and call for help. It would be difficult to get the timing right, as the young males wouldn't be able to control themselves.

What to do?

Her gaze locked on the two warriors tied up in the corner. They were on their knees, hands tied behind their backs, gags in their mouths. She could see anger in their expressions as they observed the group.

A jolt of recognition shot through her. The two from yesterday.

One of the benefits of her magic was that after she drained a male, they would remember everything for the first four hours. Then they remembered the pleasure, not the person. That enabled her to feed on the same people and not have to worry about getting caught. It had been useful back when the population was sparse.

Through trial and error, she had learned that in order to drain the Elite, she needed to be in physical contact with them, due to their greater magical resistance. The rest of the group would have to be drained by proximity.

A challenging situation; a challenge she relished.

Deidre grinned. *Let the games begin.*

She walked forward and clapped her hands in front of her chest. Perhaps they'd fall for the ditzy routine. She was the focus of their attention. They ogled her, their gazes roaming over her body. She gave them a coy smile, and batted her eyelashes. "Hello," she breathed.

Glasses fogged, breathing and heart rates increased, and lust rose.

One of them came forward and stretched out his hand. "Hi, I'm Adolfo. You're gorgeous."

She shook his hand, giggled, and twirled a lock of hair between her fingers.

"Thank you! I'm so pleased to be here."

Adolfo's eyes clouded over with lust. "You don't look like a demon."

She ran a finger from his lips down his chest, stopping at his belt buckle. "Have you seen a demon before?"

Adolfo shook his head.

"I feed off sex. I wouldn't be effective if I were ugly now would I?"

His eyes widened as he gulped.

She smiled at him. "Now shall we get this party started?"

He gave her a slow nod, and she clapped her hands again.

"I have an idea! Why don't we take the two who are tied up and put them on the altar? I can fuck them there. That way they can't escape. I know you guys are smart and observant, and they wouldn't get away, but why take any chances? And then when I'm done with them, I can fuck you guys."

Adolfo looked around at the others and grinned at her.

"Can you handle all of us?"

On any day of the week.

But she smiled and added a breathy hitch to her tone. "Oh yes. I'd love to handle each and every one of you."

She paused for a moment. "I do have a question though. Did you want me to take you one at a time or in groups? If I do you one at a time, it could take quite a while, but if I take you in groups of three…"

Deidre trailed off, letting their imaginations fill in the blanks. "Well?"

A shout filled the room. "Groups!"

She bounced on her toes. "Oh good. I just love having multiple partners! Now let me choose the groups."

Deidre turned and looked for the three strongest looking youths.

Twirling a lock of hair around her finger she asked. "When I'm ready could you please lift the captives to the stone table?" They nodded, eager to please.

"Since you're so strong, I choose the three of you to go first after I finish with the prisoners."

She moved to another group, "And then you three, and then you, then you, and finally you."

An expression of anger filled Adolfo's face. She'd put him in the last group and it looked like he was going to make trouble. *I need to stop that before it escalates.*

She sauntered up to him, swaying her hips and gave him a coy look. "You're the leader right?"

He puffed up his chest and smiled at her.

She bent forward, and made sure she flashed a hint of cleavage. "You are so sweet to let the others go first. It shows leadership and strength of character." She leaned against him and rubbed her breasts against his chest. Standing on tiptoe, she breathed into his ear. "Would you like to see me do a strip tease before I fuck those two?"

120

Adolfo's eyes widened and his gulp was audible as he nodded.

Deidre hid a laugh. *Immature and horny, perfect for the plan.* "Shouldn't I get up on the stone bench so that everyone can see?"

He nodded and the others in the room cheered.

Deidre walked over to the altar and gestured to two of the youth waiting. "Can you please help me up?"

They each grabbed an arm and lifted her onto the stone slab. She stood on stiletto heels, and walked from one end of the altar to the other. The surface had looked smooth from a distance, but it was pitted and scarred, an uneven surface for her heels.

A sea of eager faces beamed at her. She held up a finger, curling it toward her, beckoning them closer until they touched the stone.

Sending out a pulse of power, she sighed in relief, they were all in range.

Deidre stroked her hand down her body and eager eyes followed the movement. She took a step and wrinkled her forehead in a frown.

"What's wrong?" one of the young males asked.

"We don't have any music. I always like to dance with music."

One of the others eagerly held up his phone. "I have it!"

She smiled and winked as music filled the room.

Deidre swayed her hips a couple of times before spreading her legs wide and bending at the waist. The medallion hung from around her neck, and she grabbed it with one hand before it hit her in the forehead. She could see the males in front of her focus on her cleavage. And looking between her legs, she saw the males behind her ogle her ass.

Wolf whistles filled the air as she put both hands on one ankle and slid them up her leg.

Standing straight, she pivoted making her skirt flair and sauntered to the other side.

She winked at Adolfo. "Ready for the show?"

He nodded, and the rest of the room cheered.

Deidre turned away from him, tilting her head back and lifting her arms above her head. Her hands clasped the back of her neck, and she gyrated in a slow circle. When she faced Adolfo she raised her hands and lifted her hair, letting it tumble back to her shoulders as she straightened her arms.

Deidre licked her lips. "Now, handsome, is this making you hot?"

He nodded as waves of lust rolled through the crowd; their resounding cheers filled the room. Deidre took a deep breath, inhaling the tendrils. *Good, this shouldn't take long.*

She played with her hair, rubbing it back and forth and leaning her head back, stroked her hands down her face, over her breasts and back again.

She swayed and moved to the beat as the music tempo changed, making each move sensual and erotic.

Deidre made eye contact with her audience as her power moved through the room, reinforcing her sexual hold.

She blew kisses, and they cheered her on.

Deidre faced the wall and rubbed her palms over her hips, up to her waist, and under her shirt. She raised her hands up, caressing her sides, lifting the shirt with her wrists. Turning to face them, she cupped her breasts, making sure to lift and drop the hem of the shirt in a tantalizing peek a boo show.

Deidre stopped and gave them a coy look before turning her body around. She drew the top over her head and handed it to one of the males. "Keep track of this for me."

He gulped and crushed the shirt to his chest, never taking his eyes off her. She smiled and gave him a small wave before sauntering to the other end of the stone slab.

Deidre wiggled her shoulders, and the males surge against the edge of the altar as her breasts jiggled.

Dipping a finger inside her mouth, she removed it slowly, lifted it up and tested the level of sexual energy in the air. It was high, but not enough to trigger a simultaneous release. They needed more stimulation. *On with the show.*

She reached behind her to the button and zipper closure of the skirt. Her back arched, thrusting her breasts forward. She slid the zipper down and eased the material over her hips.

The skirt fell around her ankles, and she stepped from the pooled material, bent over and picked it up. She walked to the edge where she handed it to a different male.

"Can you hang onto this for me?" he nodded, expression eager.

Deidre turned in a slow circle, rubbing her hands up and down her body. "Do you want me?" her voice was soft, sultry.

"Yes!" Their response echoed through the room.

"Everyone please come to this end of the table." She pointed at the far end and stifled her laugh at their eagerness as they followed her instructions.

Deidre got down onto her hands and knees and crawled toward them, lips parted, her tongue licking her lips. She exaggerated the motion; ignoring the rough scrape of stone against her knees, hoping she didn't bleed. She'd hate to ruin the moment by trying to explain the color of her blood.

When she reached the end of the table top, she sat back on her heels and spread her knees wide. As one, all their gazes snapped down to her bare mound. She tilted her hips back so they could get a better view.

She reached down with one hand and spread her nether lips. She brought her other hand to her mouth and sucked on her two fingers, drawing them in and out of her mouth. Moans and groans rose from the group. *Time to turn up the lust.*

She removed her fingers from her mouth and slid them down the front of her body. She stopped to pull on her nipples, leaving them hard and glistening before moving down the rest of the way.

When she reached her core, she paused for effect before plunging her fingers deep inside. She moaned and jolted her hips in feigned pleasure.

The throng pushed forward so much that the ones in front were being squished into the stone, but they didn't seem to mind. She thrust a couple more times before she withdrew her fingers and brought them back up to her mouth. She winked at the males before she began to lick her fingers. A shudder rippled through them.

"Are you ready to see me fucked?"

They nodded and shouted their agreement.

"You can surround the table again."

Deidre stood and picked out the strongest three. She pointed to the bound captives. "Please strip them. Lay the Elf down on his back."

The three were quick to follow her orders. Once in place, she turned and crawled up to straddle his body, rubbing her lower body against his erection and her breasts against his chest. He moaned and thrust his hips, and she moved before he could thrust into her.

She put her fingers against his mouth. "Shhh, not yet. We need to wait for your friend."

His aura was strong for having been drained yesterday. She looked deeper, seeing the energy signature of a healer. That explained the normal levels of energy and the clarity in his gaze. Deidre turned back to the three and motioned for them to bring the Wolf up. "You'll need to release his hands so he can keep his balance."

They lifted him into position behind her.

She looked back over her shoulder at him.

"You're not going to try to escape are you?" She asked in a breathy voice.

"Yeah, but not until we're done. We're going to show you what happens to naughty little girls who tease Elite."

She raised an eyebrow, "Confident, are you?"

124

A smirk twisted his lips. "Of course. Once we take you, we'll head out."

"And what about them?" she motioned to the young males around the table.

"They're harmless."

"But they caught you."

"Did they? Or did we let ourselves be caught?" He gently pushed her forward so that she was on all fours still straddling the Elf below her. She glanced back at the Wolf who stroked his hard erection and stared at her ass. She wiggled it.

The Wolf turned to the audience. "Want to see the bad girl get a spanking?"

The resulting cheer was deafening.

She blinked as he slapped her ass, first one cheek then the other. Her butt warmed as he increased the frequency of the smacks.

She moaned and wiggled with fake delight. "Oooh I've been such a bad girl!"

"Anyone have lube?" His deep voice growled the question.

She turned to see one of the males hand him a small tube. He undid the cap and squirted a generous amount onto his straining penis.

Deidre looked into his eyes as he reached down and stroked his erection until it glistened.

He pressed himself against her bottom and she turned to look down at the Elf who gave her a wicked smile.

The Wolf pressed the head of his erection against her anus and thrust deep.

She gasped and threw her head back, moaning at the sensation.

Around them, the young males cheered, egging the Wolf on. He pulled out slowly and she squeezed him, milking him with her muscles.

"Damn little girl you're good." he huffed.

He thrust again. And again. She looked over her shoulder at him. "Stop for a moment."

He stopped, fully buried to the hilt in her ass.

"Are you ready for me to get fucked by both at the same time?"

They all cheered. It wouldn't be long now.

The Wolf pulled out of her ass so she could mount the Elf. She sat down hard on him, taking him deep with the very first thrust. She shuddered with feigned pleasure. She ground herself down on him a couple of times and he lifted his hips to meet her.

A hand from behind pushed her so that she was laying flat against the Elf.

The Wolf thrust into her, strong and hard.

Deidre clenched her inner muscles, causing both captives to groan. "Now I want you to fuck me hard and fast."

The Wolf grabbed her waist and sank deep.

They alternated thrusting, one drove deep as the other retreated, then reversed.

Deidre let her head loll back as they began to plunge into her at the same time, filling her.

The sexual energy in the room rose.

"Oh please," she begged. "Faster, fuck me faster."

They increased their pace. In and out. Out and in.

She clenched her muscles tight, and could feel the tension in their bodies. They'd come soon.

The sexual energy was building; a smoky haze rose from the group.

Deidre inhaled, pulling the sweet energy into her.

A shout from the Wolf behind her, triggered the Elf's release. A wave of climatic energy crashed through the room.

Grunts and groans filled the area all the males achieved release at the same time. She squeezed her eyes shut, concentrating on absorbing the power.

The Wolf collapsed on top of her, squishing her against the Elf. She wiggled and the Wolf slid from her body, collapsing on his side next to her and the Elf. She placed her hands on their chests and was about to finish them off when the medallion began to glow.

J'kala! She wasn't done yet!

Deidre felt the energy drain from her faster than she absorbed it.

The glow began to fade and she inhaled the last of their energy. She shifted and the Elf opened his eyes. She kissed his cheek. "Thank you."

"Anytime." he exhaled with his final breath.

Deidre slid from the altar and stood on shaky legs and managed to retrieve her clothing. She dressed and stumbled toward the door, weak with hunger.

She turned and looked at the bodies sprawled around the room. A burst of pride filled her at a job well done. The amount of bodies drained was a personal best.

Deidre opened the door and saw Antwon leaning against the wall with his arms folded across his chest.

"Are you finished?" his voice held a trace of wariness.

She fought a smile. "Yes."

Deidre took a few steps toward him. He held his hands up, palms out. "I'm not on the menu."

"But I need energy."

"Didn't you get enough?"

"No, Sir took it all," she huffed out a breath when he continued to back away. "Where is he?"

"Waiting in the office." He motioned her ahead of him and she entered the office to see '*Sir*' resting in a chair with his head leaning against the back of the chair. He opened his eyes at her approach.

"Are they dead?"

"Yes, Sir."

"Excellent, I'll call you later with your next assignment."

She bowed and left the room, careful not to say or do anything that would change his mind. She left the building, stumbling as her drained state made it difficult to walk. She needed energy and fast or she'd never make it home. Ahead of her, a group of humans spilled from the door of a bar. She smiled at a couple of the males and led them to an alley.

§

Cyn looked down from where she was perched on the roof of the building. Nothing was happening in Shadow, so she popped into Real. This intersection in the Tenderloin was the most active when it came to the idiots in the Underground. They hadn't been a real threat until a few months ago. Even the local criminal element had laughed at their efforts.

Something had changed, however, making them dangerous. Her gaze encompassed the intersection, and with a bit of movement, she could see up and down those streets as well.

She cursed under her breath recognizing the black-clad figure walking toward her. *Damned Elite! What the hell is Damien doing here?*

The Elite left this area alone as long as the residents kept to themselves and didn't make trouble elsewhere. The neighborhood attracted the criminal and undesirable elements of the Paranormal races, and it was her self-appointed job to keep things from spilling into other areas. If the Elite realized what she did, she'd be killed at best or reconditioned at worst. Females weren't allowed to do anything that interfered with their ability to breed. If they did, the Council would wipe out their personalities. How she envied human women and the freedom they enjoyed!

He didn't seem to be paying attention to his surroundings, which was odd. From everything her sire, Casimir, said about

Damien, she had expected to see the best of the best. It was obvious he wasn't at his best now.

A movement further up the street captured her attention. She squinted and recognized the auras. A small group of half human males, half Vamps walked down the street. The same kind that had cornered her the other night. They spotted Damien. One pulled out a cell phone and started talking. She'd give them credit, they kept their distance as the Elite crossed the street and continued down the block heading toward her position.

She glanced around and saw movement farther up the intersecting street. *More? Where the hell are these things coming from?*

Fuck! She'd seen this once before. Some idiot was attempting to convert normal humans into Vampires. She'd have to take care of it, before the Elite were called in.

She watched the farce unveiling below her. Three male *things* were coming toward the intersection. One had a cell phone to his ear. She had a bad feeling about this. It looked like a well-planned ambush.

She'd step in and help, but only if he needed it. After all she couldn't let him die. That would bring the other members of the Elite out in force. She sighed once more and brought out her dart gun. The darts were filled with a potent cocktail of ingredients able to kill any Paranormal.

She glanced back at the intersection. Damien and the second group were going to bump into each other right... about... now.

Chaos reigned.

Even with her sharpened senses, the movements on the street below blurred. Fists punched, bodies dropped, and the sound of flesh hitting flesh echoed in the empty streets. *Where are the taunts? The sarcastic comments? The attitudes?*

Bodies littered the ground around Damien. He turned with his hands on his hips and surveyed his surroundings. One of the men on the ground played possum. Cyn watched as he rose and removed a length of pipe from his jacket. He crept up behind Damien and swung at the Elite's head as she fired. His body jerked. Hit! Momentum carried the pipe to Damien's head.

Cyn felt her grin fade as Damien tumbled to the ground.

The half human, half Vamp disintegrated into dust. The others did the same, leaving body-shaped piles of ash.

Cyn rappelled down the side of the building to clean up the mess.

She knelt beside Damien, and put her ear to his chest. His heart beat was slow and faint, but audible. Damn. Now what? She couldn't leave him here; the residents would rob him at best and kill him at worst. She'd take him to Luna Clinic and let Bar'ella deal with him.

Cyn leaned over and with much grunting and cursing heaved him over her shoulder in a fireman's carry. She struggled with his weight even with her greater Vampiric strength.

"Damien, you need to watch your blood intake. You're one heavy son of a bitch."

Cyn staggered down the street to the clinic, aware that she was being watched over the entire way. Hans' network of spies would keep an eye on her until she reached her destination. No one wanted Elite attention in the area.

§

Damien woke to the smell of antiseptic, sensing two people standing a few steps away. He tried to use his psychic abilities to determine who they were, but his head was fuzzy and he couldn't focus enough to get a lock on their identities.

"What do you want me to do when he wakes?" a familiar female voice spoke.

It took him a few moments before he recognized the voice. *Bar'ella? What was she doing here? Where am I?*

130

"Let him go. Why?" The second voice seemed familiar, but he couldn't place it.

"He's going to want to know what happened and who helped him." Bar'ella's voice carried a liquid Southern accent. How had he never noticed *that* before?

"He may not remember what happened. If he does, tell him the truth. You don't know anything." The owner of the second voice continued to elude him. Female, a slight accent, one he'd not heard before. The voices faded, and he realized they were moving away.

He opened his eyes and saw the healer, Bar'ella, standing in the open doorway of the room he occupied. She was facing the other direction, speaking to someone in the hall. A quick look around showed an empty room. *Damn.* He'd missed the chance to see the owner of the second voice.

He was in a hospital bed with bars at the sides, in a room painted apple green. Up in one corner, a television mounted on a bracket hung from the ceiling showed some sort of reality show. In the other corner, he could see the tall back of a chair.

He glanced down and saw an I V with a blood solution entering his arm. His clothes were missing and he wore one of those damned paper dresses that opened in the back exposing his ass to the world. Movement sent pain radiating through his body. *What happened?*

Bar'ella walked into the room.

"Ah I see we're awake. How are you feeling?"

"Fine. Where am I?"

She smiled and picked up his chart at the end of the bed. "Welcome, Detective Alexander, to the Luna Clinic. And you aren't 'fine.' If you need something for the pain, let me know."

"Luna Clinic? How the hell did I get here?"

"Sorry, I'm not able to divulge that information. Your guardian angel wishes to remain anonymous."

"What is it with women and secrecy?" he grumbled.

Bar'ella laughed. "I think it's genetic. Why?"

Damien shook his head and hissed at the sharp pain. "Never mind. When can I leave?"

Her eyebrow arched, and he realized he'd been rude. "Sorry Dr. Bar'ella. When may I leave your fine establishment?"

A grin teased the corners of her mouth.

"Your wounds are healing. Dawn isn't far away. Rest today, and you'll be ready by sunset tonight. Would you like me to call anyone?"

He immediately thought of James. "Yes. If you would be so kind as to contact James Kirk." He rattled off the number.

She left the room, pausing in the doorway.

"The healers here are off limits, in case you weren't aware."

"Yes ma'am."

She left the room, closing the door behind her. He let out a breath in relief. Dragons were very tricky creatures to deal with. If you were stupid enough to offend one, two possible fates awaited you. Barbeque or flambé. He didn't want to extend his stay in this clinic any longer than necessary.

Chapter 9

Clint dressed with great care, after performing the necessary rituals. He arrived at the Library of Magic earlier than required.

He was shown into the Head Librarian's office, glad to see he was not the only early one. Others arrived a few moments later.

Gathered with him were fourteen of the highest level Mages. Pride filled him. These were the brightest and most powerful, and for this task, he was one of their number. They were joined by the Head Librarian and Master Marshal Dean.

The Librarian snapped his fingers and a melodious tone filled the office. All conversation ceased as attention turned to Master Dean, standing in front of the unlit fireplace.

"Thank you for being here today. I don't have to tell you what an honor it is to be chosen as part of this team." He made eye contact with each of the men in the room. "Before we begin, there are a couple of precautions that must be taken. You'll need to ward yourselves well and wear these."

Master Dean motioned to the Librarian, who nodded and approached each person, holding an ornately engraved wooden box. He lifted the lid to reveal several medallions. Handing one to each man, he circled the room.

Clint examined his medallion. It was a powerful charm. The ancient writing on the metal surface revealed the specific Tome it protected against. The Tome of Power. He fought a laugh and glanced around to see if he'd given himself away. The others were examining their own medallions and putting them on. He slid the ribbon over his head, donning the protection.

Head Librarian Roberts addressed the group. "You're now protected from the insidious influence of the Tomes. I don't need to tell you how dangerous they are. Many Mages have perished due to those cursed volumes. Guard your minds well. They'll cajole, promise you riches, fame, fortune, everything you could ever desire."

Master Dean gave them all a stern look. "The punishment for stealing the Tome is dire. You'll be stripped of all Magic and banished into Real Earth for the rest of your life, so think before you risk everything for one of the Tomes."

"Follow me." Master Dean motioned for the Librarian, who tilted a book on the shelf forward. The fireplace slid open revealing a curving stone staircase.

Clint followed the others as they ascended.

Not far from the top, he felt the tingle of magic. Someone was opening the door to the sealed archive.

A shout of disbelief echoed down the stairwell.

Clint shared a confused look with Mage Keith. "What's going on?"

"No idea."

The Mages ahead of him, turned. "Back down to the office."

Clint turned around and headed down the stairs. Entering the office he stood by the door, making room for the others.

Once the fireplace was secure, questions flew.

"What happened?" "What's going on?"

Master Marshal Dean held up his hand and silence followed.

"One of the Forbidden Tomes has been stolen." Gasps of shock filled the room. Clint made sure to mimic the expressions of surprise and outraged, his glamour charm keeping others from sensing his true thoughts and feelings.

134

"Rest assured we'll find the thief who did this. Until then I'm commanding all of you to keep this to yourselves." Master Dean looked at each man. Clint felt the reinforcing push on his mind. He fought a grin; who would he tell?

§

The musical clink of metal had her opening her eyes. J'kala take it, she was bound in chains again!

Deidre gagged at the stench of rotting flesh.

Not again!

Khan rose from his throne and paced around her, his smile sent shivers of through her. Palms sweaty she tried to wipe them on her legs, but her body was held immobile. Panic threatened, but she wouldn't give in.

Khan grabbed her around the throat with one clawed hand and lifted her in the air. Pain stabbed her throat. Wetness dripped from the points his claws pierced her flesh.

"You are mine Deidre." his low whisper was filled with menace.

She knew with unwavering certainty that this time there was no getting out of whatever he had planned.

He carried her through the throne room to a side door, his hooves striking a perfect cadence on the floor.

The only thing her limited view of the room revealed was a table with restraints set at the corners. The table tilted up at an angle, and bits of flesh dangled from the rusted manacles. She tasted bile as fear surged through her. He secured the chains to the table, binding her to it.

A sadistic smile crossed his face and lit his ebony eyes. He ran his claws down her body from throat to the top of her thigh, leaving bloody furrows.

She grimaced at the pain, but didn't cry out, knowing that was the reaction he wanted.

A ringing intruded. Stopping him, making her listen. It sounded like a phone. But what was a cell phone doing in Demoni?

Deidre bolted upright, opening her eyes. It was Cyn's living room. Relief made her sage into the cushions at her back.

Thank Dar'kirm, I'm back on Earth.

The cell on the end table beeped. A message from Cyn. "Meet me at Angelini's tonight."

Deidre untangled herself from the sweat-soaked sheets. It took her a few moments to extract herself from the couch. She walked into the bathroom, stood in front of the mirror, and stared at the image in front of her.

She ran a finger down one of the rapidly healing welts that ran from her throat, over her breast, and down her stomach.

J'kala! What in Dar'kirm was going on? How had Khan reached her? Fear raced through her. Toes and fingers felt cold and she lunged for the shower, needing to wash the feel of Khan from her body and mind.

She stood beneath the pummeling water, letting the heat soak through her pores and into her bones. Her thoughts tumbled around like a hamster in a wheel.

Khan and Damien. What to do? I can't do anything about Khan... he can't reach me here. The marks are gone. It's probably my over-active imagination. But what if it isn't? No don't think about that. It's your imagination. It has to be.

She ignored the niggling little voice in the back of her mind reminding her that Demons didn't have imaginations.

And what about Damien? Do Vampires make slaves or minions or whatever they're called? Could he be influencing me? Aren't Demon's immune to Vampire mind games? I should have asked Bar'ella.

Too many questions without answers ping-ponged through her mind. Deidre finished her shower, dressed and headed out. Perhaps Cyn would have answers.

§

Fifteen minutes after sunset, James walked into Damien's clinic room.

"What the hell happened to you? Don't you know better than to walk in that part of the City alone?"

Damien sighed. James could be such a mother hen at times.

"Get me out of here and I'll tell you."

An assistant healer entered the room and removed the bandages, revealing healthy, healed skin. Thankfully, Damien had been born a Vampire. Most wounds healed over day sleep, and the more serious life threatening ones took no longer than three days to repair, as long as he had a sufficient blood supply handy. He hadn't needed to be admitted to the clinic, but once there, they wouldn't release him until he was fully healed.

Once the discharge paperwork was complete, he was ready to leave.

"Ready to go?"

Damien left the bed and pulled on his clothes. In the hall, he had to shake his head, as James turned on the charm and flustered the young female healer.

Bar'ella came out of her office, a frown on her face. Damien grabbed James' arm and forced him out the front door, before he could offend the Dragon.

Once outside, Damien realized where they were. The worst section of San Francisco in both Shadow and Real Earth. The Tenderloin was not an area to be in after dark, and he'd been stupid to walk there alone at night. Wait... had it been last night?

"What's the date?"

James answered and he sighed in relief. He hadn't been out long.

James interrupted his thoughts. "Boss wants a report. We need to meet with him first. I feel the need for serious caffeine to deal with these situations you're always dragging me into."

137

"Me? That's not the way I remember it. You're the cause of most of our trouble."

James scoffed. "I've heard older Vamps suffer from delusions." He clapped Damien on the shoulder. "Lucky for you, I'm here to keep you in line."

Damien raised an eyebrow. "Don't be so cocky. You're only a couple of years younger than I am."

Before James could respond, Damien opened the door to the office where chaos reigned.

They both stopped in confusion. Two Elite bumped into each other, the papers in their hands fluttering to the floor in a parody of a ticker tape parade. An Elite in the corner was trying to talk on three phones at once, and by the look of consternation on his face, he wasn't succeeding. The room lacked its normal organizational efficiency.

"What the hell is going on?"

"Festival," reported Shifter Jared, on his way to a ringing telephone.

"Ah." That's right. Today was the official start of the Festival of Lern.

A shout from Jor'dan's office silenced the chaos for a moment. "James and Damien. In here."

Damien exchanged a look with James. "What have you done this time?"

"Me? Oh no buddy, this one's all you."

"I'm innocent."

James snorted, "Yeah as innocent as a lamb… chop."

They entered Jor'dan's office to find their boss pacing back and forth in front of the window.

James opened his mouth, and Jor'dan held up a hand stopping him.

Jor'dan took a deep breath and asked in a low tone. "What were you thinking?

138

Damien felt the heat rise to his face. He should have known better than to enter that part of town without full riot gear and plenty of back-up. Thoughts of Deidre distracted him. "I wasn't."

Jor'dan glared at Damien. He drew a deep breath and ran his fingers through already tousled hair.

"What happened last night?"

Damien gave a brief account of his encounter with half-changed humans.

Jor'dan walked behind his desk and sat back in his chair. "And you have no idea who your guardian angel is?"

Damien shook his head. "None, and Healer Bar'ella wouldn't say."

Captain Jor'dan nodded. "I'll talk to her. Meanwhile, Elf Klaus and Wolf Roger are missing. You're to pick up Jared and find out what happened to them."

Damien asked. "What about Randall?" Randall and Jared were partners, and after Jor'dan's strict orders not to separate, Damien wasn't about to get another reaming.

"He's looking into something else."

James frowned. "I thought Klaus and Roger were recovering?"

"So did I." Jor'dan closed his eyes, and Damien could see the clenched muscles of his jaw as the Fae fought to control his temper. "Imagine my surprise when I found out they received a phone call and released themselves from the healer's care. Jared was the last to speak with Klaus.

"The official report came back on Earl. Cause of death, severe energy drain. The same symptoms Klaus and Roger suffered from. Someone is draining the Elite, and until the perp is found, all precautions must be taken. Jared will take you to the scene. Be careful."

He waved them out of the office. "Dismissed."

Damien opened the door and spotted Jared leaning against the opposite wall, arms crossed over his chest.

"Where's Randall?"

Shifter Jared shrugged. "He's with Elliot and Reggie, helping with Festival Security. I'm assigned to you until he's done."

"How long?" Damien asked.

Jared glanced at the clock. "Long enough for me to track your subject."

Damien felt sorry for the Shifter, but was careful to keep those thoughts contained. The man had struggled through more pain and adversity than either he or James had ever known. Shifters were born into their families and clans, but Jared had been created by an experiment. Unlike most Shifters who were predators, Jared had been crossed with a rabbit, making him prey. The Elite had found the renegade Mages who began the experiments, but it had been too late.

The Mages had genetically manipulated a few thousand humans in an attempt to create their own Shifter army. Out of the hundred or so successful experiments, Jared was the only remaining survivor. The others hadn't been able to fully integrate their human and animal halves. If Captain Jor'dan had not tapped into Jared's protective nature, they would have lost him as well.

Mage Randall and Shifter Jared were partners, and Damien could not imagine a more mismatched pair. They were civil to each other and that was it. Whereas Damien trusted James to watch his back, the same could not be said of Randall and Jared. But then again, most of the Elite barely tolerated Jared.

The Shifter held his own against all the Paranormals he'd gone up against, but it made for a lonely existence. The man was a technology genius. That coupled with his extraordinary tracking abilities, made him an asset the others grudgingly tolerated.

"Do you know their last position?" James pulled out his phone and started tapping on the screen as they left the building.

"They were headed toward Folsom, trailing one of the Underground gang."

"James and I investigated the location of the power surge at the warehouse. Do you think the Underground is involved?"

Jared tilted his head. "I don't know...."

At that moment two other Shifters left the building and caught Jared's comment.

One nudged the other with his elbow. "So there _is_ something the great and mighty bunny doesn't know!" They laughed and walked to their car.

Damien reached over and grabbed James arm. His partner looked like he was going to murder the two Shifters. He glanced at Jared to find a blank expression on his face.

"As I was saying. I don't think anyone in the Underground has the necessary power level. Shall we go?" Jared motioned toward the car with forced calm.

"If you're sure you don't want us to knock them down a few pegs?" James' offer was made in a joking tone, yet Damien knew if Jared gave the word, James would take the two offenders out.

"Don't bother."

James got into the driver's seat, and Damien got in the back, leaving the passenger seat to Jared.

James cruised down Folsom at a slow pace, looking for anything out of the ordinary.

Damien watched Jared freeze, and put a hand out to touch James' shoulder. The Vamp pulled over and killed the ignition.

Damien focused on Jared. The Shifter stared out the window at a building halfway down the block.

"Let's go." Damien removed his seat belt.

Jared held up his hand, stopping them. "Not necessary. They arrived here, and left with a group of others to a different location."

Damien and James exchanged a look before Damien asked. "Can you follow them?"

Jared cocked his head to the side. "I'm not sure. Let me check."

He got out of the car and walked toward the building, stopped and tilted his head. A few moments later, his posture relaxed and he turned in a circle studying the area.

James cleared his throat. "What was that about?"

Damien shrugged. "I don't have any idea. I've never seen a Shifter in action, have you?"

James shook his head. "Nope. He's the first who hasn't had that holier than thou attitude."

"Can you track like that?" Damien asked, curious.

"No. I can track your creature because she's an anomaly and I can only track her within a short amount of time. Jared's ability is finer tuned than mine. I can tell you it was a Mage, but he can tell you what School of Magic they practice as well as their power level."

"Can he read a room the way you do?"

"No. To read a room you need the big picture, an overall view. My talent is macro and his is micro."

Jared walked back to the car, opened the door and got in.

James started the car. "Where to now?"

"Head to the ball park. I can get a fix from there."

James put the car in gear and drove east.

"Stop."

James pulled out of traffic, and Jared got out of the car. "There's a faint trail heading west. Drive slowly until I tell you otherwise."

They drove up and down the streets as Jared directed, following a convoluted path. "The others entered this building, but didn't come out. Klaus and Roger continued on with someone different."

James called in the location, while Damien asked, "Who was it?"

"I can't tell, his aura is strange, one I've never seen before."

A sick feeling rose in Damien's gut. "You're sure it's male?"

Jared froze, eyes closed. "Yes, he's male. Don't know what he is though, not sure what his power is."

Damien sat back in relief. He was half afraid that Deidre was behind this, but if a male was with them, she wasn't. He needed to find out what she was and as soon as possible, for his own peace of mind.

The Shifter leaned forward. "Slow down. We're getting close."

A few moments later, Jared stiffened again. "Stop."

Damien scanned the densely wooded area. Nothing was moving among the trees. He turned as James and Jared came to stand next to him. He looked at James. "Can you sense anything?"

The other Vamp closed his eyes and stilled for a moment, then shook his head. "Nothing. No echo or anything. No one has been in that grove."

Jared smiled. "They're in Real."

Damien could feel his jaw drop. "What? How do you know that? Wait.. you can track between Shadow and Real?"

Jared shrugged. "Sometimes. It's something I've been working on. It's hit or miss at the moment. Why didn't Claudius sense this? Or do they not patrol in Real?"

Claudius, a Shifter lion, and his Elf partner, Desmond, were in charge of patrolling Golden Gate Park. It wasn't the biggest patrol, but Damien had to wonder why they hadn't found anything. Klaus and Roger had been missing for more than twenty four hours, and neither Elf nor Wolf were night dwellers. He put a call into Captain Jor'dan to bring him up to date.

Call complete he turned to the others. "Captain says Des & Claude will meet us here in a few minutes. We should investigate before they get here. Which way, Jared?"

Jared motioned toward the west. "We need to get out of sight."

They followed the Shifter deep into the grove of trees, making sure they weren't visible from the road, before popping into Real Earth.

The roar of traffic from the busy streets never failed to jolt Damien. One would think, after more than a century, he'd be used to it by now.

He turned to see James opening his eyes. "It's pointless. Too many humans have been through here to give me an auric fix."

Jared looked off to the right, and assured them in an absent minded tone. "That's all right James. I can find them."

The Shifter led the way through the underbrush, drawing his weapon from its holster as he did so. Damien exchanged a look with James, before he too drew his weapon and followed on soundless feet.

§

Damien couldn't get over the shock of the mutilated bodies they'd found. Klaus, Roger, and an unidentified human. How the human had gotten into Shadow was a mystery. Their faces had been left intact, but all other identifying marks had been removed, including skin. He called it in to the boss.

"We've found them, tortured."

Captain Jor'dan's cursed before taking a breath. "I figured as much when they didn't answer. Are there any clues or leads?"

Damien lowered his voice. "Not anything solid. But I'd like to check up on the psychic anomaly. I'm sure she's hiding something, and I want to find out what it is."

"Very well. Have James and Jared take the bodies to Bar'ella's. Meet with the female."

"Yes sir."

"Oh, and Damien?"

"Yes?"

"Be very, very careful. Your life may depend on it."

144

Chapter 10

The bitter aroma of roasting coffee beans assailed Deidre as she entered the coffee shop. Cyn was seated at the same table as yesterday, away from the others near the back of the café. Standing in line, Deidre tried to remember her order. It had milk and chocolate. Mocha latte. Coffee in hand she walked through the maze of tables and sat across from Cyn.

"Is it always this crowded?" she asked.

Cyn shook her head and leaned toward her. "It's because of Festival."

A group of Fae, dressed in ornate robes, left the cafe. "And none of the humans are suspicious?"

Cyn laughed. "This is San Francisco. Folks are used to strange looking people."

Deidre propped her elbow on the table and rested her chin in the palm of her hand. "I have a question regarding your people."

A gamine grin crossed the Vampire's face. "Go ahead. I like that 'my people' thing."

"Is it easy you to coerce me?"

Cyn thought about that for a moment. "I suppose it depends." A look of concentration crossed her face. Deidre felt a small flutter against her mind. "I can't get through your shields, but my mental powers haven't matured yet."

146

"How long does it take?"

"A couple hundred years or so, why?"

"Do you think he's powerful enough to influence me?"

"Maybe. He who?"

Heat rose in Deidre's cheeks and she twisted the paper sleeve on her coffee cup. "Detective Alexander."

"He's powerful enough, but what makes you think he's messing with your mind?"

"I have strange sensations whenever he's around."

Cyn leaned closer. "Like what?"

"It starts with shortness of breath, increased heart rate, sweaty palms and it feels like small creatures performing a ballet in my stomach."

"Hmmm… anything else?"

"Isn't that enough?" The sleeve slid around the cup, faster. Deidre opened her mouth to speak and then closed it. Better not to share the fact that her power sat up and purred whenever Damien was around.

"What?"

"Nothing."

"You were going to say something."

Deidre gave her a small smile. "Yes but I forgot what it was."

"How do you feel about doctors?" Cyn asked.

Suspicion rose along with Deidre's eyebrow. "Why?"

Cyn leaned back in her chair. "I know someone who may be able to help in case the problem is physical."

Deidre shook her head. "Won't work. Most doctors haven't seen my type of being before, so there's no baseline for normal."

"That could be a problem."

Cyn reached into a pocket and pulled out a card and slit it across the table. "You may want to give her a call anyway."

Deidre picked up the card. Luna Clinic with a picture of a crescent moon with the name Doctor Bar'ella in gold foil.

Laughter bubbled through her as she glanced at Cyn.

"Did she put you up to this?"

Confusion crossed Cyn's face. "Who? Doctor B?"

Deidre nodded. "Meddling dragon."

"Wait, you know Doctor B?"

"Yes. She's been poking and prodding at me since I've known her."

"Well then it shouldn't be a problem then, right?"

"I'll think about it." Deidre put the card in her pocket and took a sip of her latte.

Cyn stilled. "Shit. What the hell is up with those two? If I didn't know better I'd swear they were stalking us."

"They probably are. Let me guess tall dark and vampy?"

"Accompanied by light and dreamy."

"I don't need that kind of attention." Cyn hissed in a whisper as she turned and smiled at them.

Damien and James pulled out two chairs and sat at the table.

"Hello ladies. May we join you?" James asked.

Deidre raised an eyebrow. "Would it help if we said no? And you're already seated, isn't it a bit late to ask?"

A dimpled grin appeared on James' face. "Just being polite. And we'd have joined you anyway." He waved his arm to encompass the crowed café. "There aren't any free seats."

Cyn rolled her eyes. "Don't you have bad guys to apprehend, or something?"

James put his hand over his heart. "We're protecting two beautiful women."

Deidre shook her head and turned to Damien. "You're friend is full of it."

Cyn engaged in conversation with him, leaving her to deal with Detective Alexander.

Damien winked at her. "James enjoys being contrarian."

Deidre tilted her head. "Don't all males?"

Damien shrugged. "I refuse to perjure myself."

148

A strange tune rang out. A bright red hue covered Cyn's face. "Excuse me a moment." Glancing at the phone she cursed. "Fu…dge. I've got to go."

"Anything wrong?" Deidre asked, concerned.

Cyn shook her head. "A friend needs help."

"Anything I can do?"

"Nope, I got it."

Cyn stood and James followed. "I'll assist you."

The Vampire shook her head. "No thank you. It's a delicate situation."

"All the more reason I should help." James insisted.

Cyn put her hands on her hips, arms akimbo. "It's a female problem."

That stopped him for a moment. "Oh."

Cyn leaned over and gave Deidre a hug. "Call me later."

"Are you sure you don't need any help?"

"Positive."

James took Cyn's arm. "At least allow me to escort you to your destination."

Cyn closed her eyes and took a deep breath before removing her arm from his grip. "No, but thank you for the offer."

"I insist."

Cyn turned and walked away. "I decline."

James followed Cyn out of the coffee shop.

Deidre twirled the sleeve of her cup. *Hope Cyn loses her Elite shadow. What will I do with mine?*

"So do you have any urgent business to attend to?" Damien asked.

Deidre thought about it for a moment. "Not off the top of my head, but I'm on call."

Damien took her hand and rubbed small circles on the sensitive flesh of her inner wrist. She tugged her hand, and he tightened his grip. Her power wanted to lure him to her. Better put a lid on that. Concentrating she shoved her power back down, which was difficult when the sensations he was generating, distracted her.

"Is there a problem?" he asked.

"No, why?"

"You seem a bit nervous."

Deidre didn't know what to say to that.

A devils grin crossed his face. "Are you done with your coffee?"

Deidre took the last sip. "Yes."

"Then let's get out of here." Damien used her wrist to pull her to her feet. She took a deep breath. She could handle him right? Right.

He moved his hand from her wrist and intertwined their fingers. "How long will you be in town?"

"For the rest of the week." And if Sir kept his word, she'd be here longer. However, she refused to hope. Promises had been broken before.

"We need to make the most of your time."

"Perhaps."

He led her to a car parked on the street, and held the door for her.

Deidre balked. "I don't think this is a good idea."

"What are you afraid of?"

What am I afraid of? Khan, the Red Mist and you. Isn't that enough?

"I promise you'll be safe tonight."

"What if you're manipulating me into coming with you?" Deidre asked, hesitant to go anywhere with him.

"I'm not." He took both of her hands in his and looked into her eyes. Instead of Cyn's flutter-touch, his mental touch felt like a slice if ice, cold, sharp and deadly. It failed to penetrate her mind. He blinked once. "You have interesting shields."

"Thank you?"

He grinned. "I can't get into your mind. I'm not manipulating you. Come with me and I'll show you the city."

She was seated in the car and they were driving before she realized it. Turning in her seat she faced him, arms crossed over her chest. "I didn't say I would come with you."

He flashed her a grin. "Please?"

Deidre rolled her eyes. "I suppose it's too late to say no?"

Damien's expression turned serious. "If you really mean it, I'll stop the car and let you out."

Deidre turned to face front. "Fine. We can see the sights."

He reached over and gripped her hand, holding it for the rest of the trip. This was the second time he'd held her hand. It was nice.

"Have you been here before?" he asked.

"Yes, a long time ago."

"Then I'll show you the highlights."

"Okay."

They drove through the city, and Damien pointed out a few landmarks. They stopped in a parking lot under a lit suspension bridge.

Deidre stared at it. "When did they build this?"

Damien turned and stared at her. "Just how long ago were you here?"

The fingers of her free hand tapped against her thigh and she tugged on the hand held in his. He tightened his grip and didn't release her. "Why?"

"The Golden Gate bridge was finished in the 1930's."

When had she been here? "It was when the big earthquake happened."

"The one in eighty nine?"

Deidre had to translate eighty nine. Her brain spat out information about the Loma Prieta earthquake. "No, I think it was… sometime in the early nineteen hundreds. My employer was excited about going to see Enrique Caruso. Then the ground danced and the world came crumbling down."

Memories of the destruction flashed before her. The fires, the screams, the absolute terror that pervaded the city. She'd wanted to help, but her Master at the time forbade it. She'd managed to pull two children from the rubble before she was summoned away.

Deidre shook her head, bringing her back to the present. She needed to focus on getting this Vampire out of her system. Spending time with him should help make her immune to his charm.

"Shall we walk?" he asked.

She nodded. "Sure."

Deidre went to open the door. Her skin tingled right before he touched her wrist. "Wait."

She turned to him and tilted her head. *Why?* "Okay."

Damien got out of the car and hurried around the front, opening the door for her.

Deidre tilted her head.

He tried to hide his eye roll, but she caught it.

"Well, come on."

"Oh, that's why you wanted me to wait?"

"Yes." A frown marred his features. "Where have you been that you don't know common courtesy?"

Deidre got out of the car and took a deep breath of the salty ocean air. She looked toward the blurred reflection of the lights on the fast moving water. "I've been shown little consideration, common or otherwise."

Damien stepped in front of her, blocking the view. "But…"

She needed to distract him from her past. She reached out and touched his chest running her hand over the firm layer of muscle.

"Are you sure you want to dwell on that?" her tone lowered.

152

His breathing deepened and eyes dilated.

"What were we talking about?" his voice rasped.

Deidre smiled. "Nothing." She stepped away from him to look at the lit bridge. A dense fog bank moved in creating an otherworldly glow around the lights of the bridge.

A gust of chill wind blew the hair around her head and her skin burst out in bumps.

A frown crossed his face, and he removed his coat, draping it around her shoulders, smoothing his hand down her back.

Startled, she looked at him. What was he doing? Cocking her head to the side, she was about to ask.

"Why don't you have a coat?"

"I..."

"Forgot to pack it?"

Deidre snorted. "You could say that."

"Make sure to get one."

She smirked at him. "Yes, sir."

He took her hand and led her around the path under the bridge. Small creatures jumped and danced in her stomach. She felt, anxious? Afraid? Excited? *Where had that come from? Why should I be excited when I'm with him?*

They stopped before a stone wall. Damien stood at her back, with his arms around her waist. Looking out over the turbulent water, the heat from his body, penetrated the thick layers of his coat, warming her. She shivered, and not because of the cold.

"You're still cold. Let's get back to the car. I know somewhere we can talk."

He led her back to the car, and once again held the door for her, while she got in.

They drove to a heavily wooded park.

"Where are we?" she asked.

"Golden Gate Park."

Though she knew of the park from her previous visit, she'd never been there. He pulled into a deserted parking lot.

Once out of the car, he took her hand and led her toward a large lawn area.

"Where are we going?" Deidre asked.

"A safe place."

They walked through the garden and down stone steps. It looked like a pedestrian tunnel under the roadway. Halfway along, Damien stopped and pressed stones in the wall in a specific pattern. A door swung open and he pulled her inside.

Once the door was closed, pitch black surrounded her. Normally her night vision was excellent, but not in absolute darkness. It reminded her of her travels through the voice, but his hand was the anchor, instead of a spell.

He stepped away and pulled her with him. Their movement triggered a soft glow illuminated the stones at their feet, letting her see the long passageway ahead.

"What is this place?"

They stopped at a steel door with an electronic panel imbedded into the stone wall beside it. She could also see the spell work pulsing in waves over the panel. Damien typed in a code and pressed his hand to the door. It opened with a slight hiss and a pop. "One of our emergency bolt holes."

Deidre stepped into a large room. Fine art hung on the walls, comfortable looking furniture filled the central area, and a small kitchen in the corner gave it a homey look.

Damien closed the door behind her and walked into the kitchen. "Can I get you something to drink?"

"Water please."

A vision, fueled by her growing desire, filled her mind. Damien spread on a bed covered in chocolate. She'd lick her favorite treat from his chest and.... *Wait.. What am I doing? I'm not supposed to be thinking this about him.*

Her body warmed at the images, and she shrugged out of his coat, putting it over one of the couches. Handing her the water, he gestured for her to take a seat.

Damien gave her a smile of pure devilry.

J'kala.

He was potent. Her pussy clenched in anticipation. His grin slid from his face and a tremor of foreboding crept up her spine, causing goose bumps to break out over her skin. She rubbed her hands over her arms to dissipate the sensation. "Am I in trouble?"

He shook his head. "No, but I need information."

"As Bar'ella told you, I can't give you the information you want."

Damien prowled around the living room, a leashed predator. His movements were slow and deliberate. A few feet in front of her, he stopped and gave her a heated look.

Deidre felt like sensual prey, a feast he was eager to devour. He closed the distance between them and reached out to touch her. His gaze locked on hers. He leaned forward, and she knew he was going to kiss her.

She felt the stroke of his finger as it traveled from the outside edge of her eye, down her cheek, and along the jaw. The sensation brought to mind the last time she'd been touched like that. Khan. The touch jolted her. She jumped up, pacing away from him. Her hand brushed her cheek. No blood.

"What's wrong?" He sat on the edge of the couch, one hand on the back, the other on his leg.

"Bad memories." Deidre wrapped her arms around her body, and rocked forward on her toes.

Damien walked over and pulled her into his arms, and rubbed a hand down her spine. The repetitive strokes calmed her racing heart. Slowly she relaxed into his body, letting the scent of male Vampire erase the remembered stench of blood and rotting flesh.

"Better?" his voice was deeper with her ear pressed to his chest.

"Yes."

One hand tilted her chin up and his lips brushed hers. "What are you?" His breath whispered against her lips, a lighter than air caress.

"A woman." Her voice was whisper soft.

His tongue traced the seam of her mouth and he pressed his lips against hers, stealing her breath. She opened her mouth to his questing tongue and reveled in his spicy taste.

Hours or minutes later, she wasn't sure which, he broke the kiss to ask. "Who brought you here?"

He nipped along her jaw, soothing the bites with small kisses to her ear. She tilted her head giving him better access.

"Hmmm?" she was breathless as tingles of pleasure ignited her blood

"What are you? Who brought you here" His tone was low and sexy as he continued his journey down her neck.

"I… I can't tell you."

"Can't or won't?" he breathed into her ear.

Her skin shivered in response, as he nibbled his way down her neck.

"Can't." She felt his teeth prick her neck.

J'kala! Vampire!

Panic gave her the strength she needed to burst from his loose embrace. She fled to the other side of the room, her hand on her neck as she realized he hadn't pierced the skin.

How could I have forgotten he was a Vampire?

Oh yeah, he was trying to seduce her into forgetting herself. Amused that he'd try to use sex and seduction against her, she ignored the fact that he nearly succeeded. The blood thing, that was a no-no. *Who knew what information could be gleaned from a drop of her blood?*

"What the hell?"Confusion crossed his face.

Deidre sighed in relief at the close call, and glared at him.

"I've not given you permission to take my blood, Detective."

Damien shrugged in apparent nonchalance. "That's an easy enough fix."

Deidre shook her head. "No."

"Why not?"

Dar'kirm! I can't tell him about the blood. Another reason... ah! "I never gave you permission, and I'm not interested in becoming your slave."

He lifted an eyebrow. "Are you sure about that?"

Deidre was taken aback by the question. Sure? About not wanting to become his slave? When she was bound to her summoner already? She narrowed her eyes. Oh she was sure. "Positive."

She gave him her best glare, but it didn't appear to have an effect. Hands clenched at her sides, she annunciated every word. "I will *never* be your slave."

He paused a moment as if considering her reaction. "You think my bite will enslave you?"

"Won't it?" her sarcasm was evident.

He shook his head and walked around the loveseat to sit on the couch. He patted the cushion next to him.

"Come here and let me explain."

Deidre shook her head. She had enough problems concentrating on the conversation instead of his bad boy body. Sitting next to him was too dangerous for her piece of mind.

"No thanks, I'm sure I'll be more comfortable over here."

She walked over to the armchair and sat down, each move deliberate and graceful.

He grinned at her and her heart stuttered in her chest at his roguish charm. "My bite won't thrall you unless you're human, and even then the effects wear off after a couple of hours."

"My blood is off limits, Detective."

He shrugged and she didn't know if he accepted her demand, or if he were hoping to catch her off guard. Probably the latter.

Time to get this conversation under my control.

Deidre crossed her legs in a slow deliberate movement, making sure the hem of her short skirt rode high on her thigh. *Let's see how you like being seduced.*

From beneath her lashes she saw his eyes widen and a dark flush rise to his cheeks. He inhaled and she knew he could scent her rising desire.

He stared at her with predatory hunger, and for an uncomfortable moment she knew what it felt like to be prey, the heart-pounding fear as death approached.

Deidre smiled to distract him and concentrated on getting her body back under control. She sat in silence waiting for his next move. It was like playing a game, but the rules of this skirmish weren't clear. She'd just have to adjust the rules to suit her.

"What are you?" The intensity of his gaze didn't diminish.

"And I told you, I'm female." *Mostly.*

He sighed and rested his arm along the back of the couch.

"If you won't tell me what you are, tell me something else."

"Like what?"

"Any old thing that comes to mind. For instance, how old are you?"

She snorted. "Don't you know it's not polite to ask a woman her age?"

He rolled his eyes. "Are there more of your kind around?"

Damien saw the flash of vulnerability in her eyes before she gave him a cocky smile. "Sorry, Detective. I'm one of a kind."

He shifted, trying to ease the denim over his cock to a more comfortable position. He'd been half hard standing in the hallway, and one look at her finished the job. He was hard enough to stake a Vamp. Her little tease had tested his control. He managed to keep the conversation going when all he wanted to do was sink into her soft flesh and savor the taste of her on his tongue.

As a centuries-old Vampire and a cop, he should have more control than this.

158

Shit. Damn. Fuck.

She was getting under his skin, deeper and faster than anyone before. This wasn't good, but like a moth to flame, he couldn't resist her.

Damien wanted her to trust him, to confide in him, to let him take care of her. He wanted to wrap her in his arms and keep her safe.

Whoa. Where the hell had that come from?

She was a suspect, out of bounds for him. But that didn't mean he couldn't seduce her to get the answers he wanted. He'd make sure to keep it light, superficial.

Her little smirk challenged him on a primal level, and it was all he could do to remain seated. He needed information. That was the only thing stopping him from going after her in a lust crazed haze.

"What about your family?" He struggled to get the question out and not focus on her low cut blouse and the soft curves it revealed.

Focus. Play time later.

She cocked her eyebrow and hesitated. "Sorry, I don't have one."

Damien leaned forward bracing his elbows on his knees; the way she responded had his internal instincts blaring.

"What do you mean, you don't have a family? I find that hard to believe."

He stared at her, seeing the vein in her throat pulse faster.

"I have no family," she paused. "No one."

"You were abandoned?"

Her eyes flashed with something he couldn't identify before she lowered her eyelids. "I suppose you could say that."

Her answer raised new questions, and he opened his mouth to ask when he saw a soft smile curved her mouth. Once again his thoughts spiraled into the physical realm, and he realized with a jolt that she was using her sensuality to distract him.

Damn. It was working.

The way to get things back on track was to let her think she'd won, then question her when she was feeling more vulnerable. If he could tear his attention away from her delectable body.

She wasn't helping.

Deidre leaned forward to reach for the glass of water on the coffee table in front of her, flashing a glimpse of cleavage before re-crossing her legs.

Damien felt his control shatter.

He jerked to his feet and stalked toward her. He had to feel her, touch the warmth of her flesh, taste her secrets.

Damien grabbed her wrist and jerked her out of the chair, lifting her into his arms. She gasped in surprise and kicked her feet. Her low sensual laugh made his straining cock harder. He didn't think that was possible.

Damn.

The scent of her filled his head. Flowers with an undertone of sulfur. He felt like consuming her in one. Greedy. Bite.

Control. Stay in control.

Although she made it damned difficult by brushing her breasts against his chest, playing with the hair on the nape of his neck. He stopped walking and enjoyed the sensation. Her soft weigh in his arms made him feel protective, like a conquering hero.

She leaned up and kissed the lobe of his ear, causing shivers of pleasure to race through him.

He walked down the hall, anticipation rushed through him and he had to fight to keep from taking her up against the wall.

Hell, the carpet on the floor looked comfy... but the bed close. If he could hold on that long.

A few steps later and he lowered her on to the silky surface of the bed, following her down, not wanting to lose contact with her soft body.

He kissed her, needing to quench his thirst. "You frustrate me."

160

Her low laugh frayed the remaining threads of his control. "I do my best."

His lips touched hers and she was enveloped in sensation. Firm lips, warm breath, thundering heartbeats. Pleasure, true pleasure, raced through her. She felt strange, giddy, and at the touch of his tongue against hers, her power lay quiescent, a warm curl deep within her. He tasted of chocolate and coffee, a combination that could become addictive.

He broke the kiss. "I need you. Let me have you."

She looked up into his dark eyes and nodded. "No blood."

He frowned down at her. "I can't come without it."

She smiled and traced his lips with her finger. "We'll see. But promise you won't take my blood." She'd make sure he reached release by using her power. No problem.

He nodded. "Okay. I won't take your blood without your permission."

That wasn't quite what she'd said. She wasn't sure she liked his phrasing, but before she could ask, he distracted her by moving his hand over her body, leaving her skin sensitized even through her clothes. His strong hand molded her breasts, stroked down to the curve of her hip and over her legs.

"Tell me what you like." he placed small nips over her collar bone.

"You're doing fine." She arched into his body, pleasure rioting through her. She'd never felt this before, the anticipation, the buildup, the pure sensation. It beckoned; enticed. Deidre had enjoyed her previous sexual encounters, but she'd manipulated her body's responses. The sensations that Damien pulled forth, were richer, deeper than anything she'd ever felt before.

With one hand he ripped her blouse from her body, exposing her lace clad breasts. The sheer dominance of his action ratcheted her pleasure up another step.

161

His forcefulness turned her on. Moisture gathered between her legs.

That wasn't something she'd expected.

He leaned on one arm and with the other, traced the edge of the lace covering her breasts. A frown marred his expression.

"What's wrong?" A host of insecurities assailed her. Had she done something wrong? Did her current form not please him?

Why in Dar'kirm was she thinking these things when she'd never cared before?

With one tip of a finger, he traced the chain of the medallion that rested between her breasts. "What's this?"

The medallion. Relief filled her, that it wasn't anything she'd done, nor her body. This would be so much easier if she used her power, but she didn't, wanting to explore the strange reactions he evoked within her.

Deidre couldn't believe she'd forgotten all about the damned thing. "A necklace."

"Why wear it under your clothes?"

Uncomfortable with the question, she searched her mind for a quick answer that would satisfy his curiosity yet not reveal the truth.

"It has sentimental value." *To Sir.* "And I don't want to attract thieves. It's safer under my clothes."

"Let me remove it."

Damien reached for the necklace.

She had to stop him. Fast. Deidre grabbed his wrist and looked up into his eyes. "Don't worry about it."

To distract him, she reached up and put a hand on either side of his head before pulling his lips to hers. Her mouth opened in a carnal kiss that had them both groaning.

It took seconds for him to wrest control from her. He ate at her mouth igniting a blaze of sensation. He demanded and she was helpless to resist.

Heat. Lust. Passion.

162

A potent mix of urges and desires that overwhelmed her. While she'd been kissed before, no one had taken desire to this level. A place of pure sexual need and she reveled in it.

He tore his mouth from hers and trailed nips and kisses along her collar-bone, down to her breasts.

His tongue ran over the nipple through the peach lace of her bra. His deep suction of her nipple had effervescent bubbles floating through her body. She felt the pleasure deep within her.

Damien released the nipple with a small pop and reached between her breasts to unclasp the bra. When the two halves slid away from her breasts, he stopped moving and gazed at them.

He reached out and traced a nipple with one finger.

"Perfect." He breathed the word, as if in reverence.

He bent his head and began worshiping her breasts with lips and tongue.

He pulled back and waited for her to look him in the eye. He flashed his fangs.

He wasn't going to bite her was he?

Deidre was about to ask when he lowered his head, kept his gaze on hers, and ran a fang over the nipple. Once. Twice. Then bit down hard enough for her to feel, but not enough to draw blood. She gasped as the small hint of pain blended with the pleasure.

Damn, his mouth and fangs, felt wonderful against her flesh. Who knew a simple breast could generate that much sensation? He continued with the other breast until she was reduced to clutching his head against her.

More. She needed more, more sensation, more something. It was there, yet out of reach. If only she could feel it, then she'd understand.

Hold on. This wasn't normal. Something wasn't right. She looked up at him, trying to figure out what was wrong. He was responsible, but how?

The haze of lust receded a bit allowing her to question him.

She looked up at him. "What are you doing to me?"

"Why? Doesn't it feel good?"

He tweaked her nipple again, causing a moan to slip free.

"Feels too good."

"There's no such thing as too good."

"Need to stop."

"Why?" he continued his journey over her heated skin.

"Can't think."

A smile blossomed on his face. "And is thinking important?"

"Yes... not good."

She felt his chest shake before he hugged her to him and laughed out loud.

"Ah sweetheart, if you're not thinking, I'm doing it right."

Deidre shook her head. "Something's wrong."

He stroked his hand over her body. "What?"

"Don't know. Isn't normal."

"Tell me how you feel." His deep tone demanded an answer, but she was drunk on sensation.

"Hot, and achy, empty. Something is missing, but it's more than before."

"Let me try this."

Damien stroked his hand over her heated flesh, marveling at the soft silk of her skin. He wanted to worship her breasts for hours, but that wasn't what she needed now. Later he'd take the time, but now she needed release.

He slid his hand up her leg, past her knee, and to the outside of her thigh. He studied her expression, willing to stop the moment she became uncomfortable. Her eyes fluttered closed as if concentrating on the sensation of skin against skin.

He felt lace beneath his fingertips and he traced the lower edge of her panties, over her thigh and down. She shifted her legs apart, granting him access. He brushed his knuckle against the damp lace, and she jerked.

A promising start.

164

Deidre was the most responsive female he'd ever met and it made the possessive part of him want to roar in triumph. But not yet. Now he ached to feel her hot body sheathing him.

He slid a finger under the material and felt himself seared with the heat of her wetness. His finger explored the flesh, teasing her lips, passing over her clit, with a brief foray into her tight body. He glanced up and saw her head thrown back, eyes clenched tight. Time to take it further.

He removed his hand, and she frowned at him. "Are you done?"

He suppressed a laugh when he realized she was serious. "Done? Not by a long shot."

"What are you doing?"

"Making you comfortable."

The confused expression that crossed her face filled him with tenderness. It was obvious she hadn't had much experience with sex, if she thought he was stopping now. He'd make this special for her, even if it killed him.

He tugged her lace panties down her legs then maneuvered her so that he could remove her skirt, before pulling alongside him. He settled in to explore the delectable flesh spread like a feast before him.

He caressed her body in long, slow strokes, savoring the feel of her. He traced her collar bone, down the center of her chest, tickled her belly button before lightly touching her engorged clit. She arched her back and moaned at the contact. He could hear the blood pumping through her heart, making him thirst. For her passion and her blood.

Now to make her scream.

Deidre struggled to breathe. Pulses of electricity arced between her clit and her nipples, hitting all points in between. A nagging thought intruded. She was supposed to do something wasn't she? But what?

A jolt of sensation seared through her.

What was that?

Damien's finger was pressed against her clit. He flicked and once again she jolted at the touch.

She felt like a spring being wound tighter and tighter.

"What…"

A final caress and the world exploded. Pleasure ripped through her from the soles of her feet to the tips of her fingers. The universe burst behind her eyelids a brilliant display of exploding suns. Her body detonated in a shower of glory. She flew to the stars then drifted back; a feather in a gentle breeze.

Deidre felt a movement on the bed, but was too lethargic to do more than open her eyes.

She saw Damien remove the last of his clothes before crawling on the bed.

"Mmmmm."

He smiled down at her. "I'm glad you approve."

She stretched like a contented cat and saw his gaze flash with lust.

Deidre checked her energy and nearly gasped in surprise.

She was full.

I didn't drain his energy, did I?

He hadn't come yet, so it was improbable that she had.

Strange.

Damien's hands stroked over her sensitized flesh and she wanted to purr.

"Are you ready?" his voice was soft, but she could hear the desire, barely leashed.

Deidre sat up and motioned for him to lie down.

"My turn."

He frowned up at her. "Your turn for what?"

"To touch and investigate your body."

He spread his arms out and cupped his hands behind his head. "Have fun."

166

A chuckle escaped her. "Oh I will."

Deidre wasn't going to miss this opportunity. She could count on one hand the times she'd been able to explore a male body. Her previous explorations had been cut short due to interruptions, circumstance or limited amounts of time. He was her playground to explore and indulge.

She marveled at the differences between them. Her body was soft and rounded, whereas his was hard and muscled. She knelt next to him, and ran her hands over his chest, unmarred by chest hair. Small male nipples beckoned. *Were they as sensitive as hers?*

A flick with her fingernail had him inhaling a sharp breath. *Good to know.*

She leaned over and ran her tongue over the nipple before sucking on it.

"Gods!" his breath exploded from him.

She released the nipple and grinned up at him. "Problem?"

He shook his head, and she bent to give the other nipple the same treatment.

A string of kisses down his ribs caused him to squirm and she didn't think it was with passion. She accidently brushed against his side. His laughter rang through the bedroom.

He's ticklish, how cute.

She placed small nipping bites around his belly button and over each hipbone.

Deidre stroked his straining cock with one fingernail and watched as his erection bobbed up and down. She repeated the caress then used her tongue to lick from the base to the head where she swirled her tongue around the crest.

It appeared to be too much for him as he grabbed her and pulled her on top of him, positioning her legs so she straddled him.

Deidre looked down into his passion-filled gaze, and forced her bottom lip out into a pout. "But I wasn't done yet."

"Explore later. Need you now."

She looked down into his dark eyes, swirling with heat and something else. She felt the broad head of his erection probe her entrance, and in a slow controlled motion, he guided her hips and impaled her on his cock.

Deidre felt full, penetrated.

The sensation was the same. The same as all the other males she'd taken before. It was like being doused in cold water. The strange feelings of pleasure and lust faded away and she was back in control.

Now to give him pleasure.

She rocked her hips back and forth, and was pleased to hear him groan beneath her.

With a sudden surge, he rolled her beneath him. His thrusts becoming faster. This was more like it. The male crazed with lust eager to reach release.

A few moments later however and he hadn't stopped moving.

She noticed him looking down at her and smiled. He slowed to a stop, a frown marring his face.

"What's wrong?" His voice was full of concern.

"Nothing. Why?"

"Aren't you enjoying yourself?"

"Of course, aren't you?" Deidre hid her disappointment behind her smile. It had felt so good before, she'd been expecting something different at his penetration. But it was the same.

Damien struggled to think. She felt so good around him, like hot soft silk. He frowned as he realized that she wasn't responding to him as she had moments ago. Her body yielded to his, but it was if she wasn't taking pleasure in the act. Her heartbeat was at normal levels, and her breathing was steady. She seemed to be on guard. Well there was only one way to get her past her resistance.

He lowered his head and kissed her, pulling out all the stops, as he began his sensual assault. He was determined to make her

168

feel pleasure. His hand stroked over her breasts and down her side to her hip. Tilting her hip, he thrust deep.

No reaction. At least no reaction he was satisfied with.

Perhaps a different position would work better.

He pulled out, regretful at the loss of her softness around him. She frowned up at him, and opened her mouth to speak. Before she could get a word out, he turned her on her side and spooned behind her. He lifted her leg over his and with one thrust felt like he'd come home.

"What are you doing?" Her question startled him.

"Trying something different."

"Why?"

"To see if this works better for you."

"The other way was fine."

He could hear the frown in her tone.

Damien snorted. "Never lie to a Vampire darling. We can tell."

He wrapped his arms around her. One under her neck was able to play with her breasts, and he stroked her stomach with the other. Down through her curls he found her clit and rested his finger on it. And began thrusting.

Damien lowered his head and rested his forehead against her shoulder. She felt so wonderful around him. Hot and tight around his aching erection. He needed to control himself so that he could bring her to orgasm once more.

No way he was going to disappoint her. The good news was that as a Vampire, he had more staying power than human males. The bad thing was he needed blood to come.

She writhed in his embrace, and he could hear her heart beat speed up, as well as her breathing. *About time.*

She felt so good in his arms, warm and female and his. A pulse of pleasure tore through him and he threw his head back and groaned. His hips thrust faster almost without his conscious thought.

The pleasure rose higher, hotter. His hands tightened on her breast and clit and in a few moments he felt the milking of her body trigger his own orgasm.

Impossible.

The pressure built from the back of his spine and became uncontainable. With a shout and a frenzy of thrusting, he emptied himself into her willing body, collapsing behind her.

Deidre smiled as she felt him relax behind her. She'd allowed herself a small release, knowing that he would hold off until she came. She'd been in control enough to manipulate his energy to allow him to come without taking her blood.

His softening cock slipped from her body and she rolled over to face him.

His eyes fluttered open. "Wow."

She smiled and got out of bed. A hand on her wrist stopped her.

"Where are you going?"

"To clean you up."

"That should be my job."

She tilted her head. "Why?"

Damien shrugged. "That's the way I like to do things."

"Please?" she asked. This was disconcerting. Her first Master had made it clear this was a task expected of her. To have him say otherwise, was strange.

Deidre fetched a hand towel and cleaned up. She frowned when he opened his arms to her.

"What?"

"Come here."

She crawled onto the bed and let him pull her down to his side. "What are you doing?" *What ritual was this?*

"I'm snuggling with you."

"Is this a new thing?"

"No, why?"

170

"It's not normal."

His chest moved as he chuckled. "It is for me."

"Oh." *How odd.*

Most males either fell asleep, or left the bed when done. He grabbed her hand and placed it over his heart, her head resting on his shoulder.

Deidre felt safe, sheltered in his embrace. It felt... nice.

Longing filled her and she wanted to stay with him. Which was the last thing she should do. It wouldn't end well. She jerked up and looked around, searching for her clothes.

"Where are you going?" His deep voice almost pulled her back into the warm bed.

Panic, sharp, and stabbing, pierced her heart. This tenderness was wrong; it wasn't for her, no matter how much she longed for it to be.

"I have to go." She jerked on her clothes.

He got out of bed, pulling the sheet around his waist. "I'll give you a ride."

Deidre shook her head. "You can't, it's morning. I can get myself home."

He pressed a scorching kiss to her mouth. "Call me when you get home."

"Is that necessary?"

"If you don't want to be trapped here with me all day, then yes."

Deidre glared at him before finally acquiescing. "Fine, I'll call." She let the lie slip from her lips. Her plan to get him out of her system had failed. She craved his touch, and his tenderness like a junkie.

He walked her to the door, kissing her again as if he couldn't get enough of her.

Deidre escaped, moving quickly as if the hounds of hell were after her. But she couldn't outrun her desire for something more.

Chapter 11

Damien picked up James on his way to Angelini's. He needed to talk to Deidre. While last night had been mind blowing, he hadn't gotten any of the answers he needed. Hell, he hadn't been sure what the questions were.

James' cell phone rang. He looked at the caller id and cursed. "Yes, Captain? We'll be right there."

He put the phone in his pocket, in a deliberate manner.

Damien knew something was wrong, but James, for once, didn't elaborate.

"So what is going on?"

"We've been summoned to the High Chancellor's office."

Damien felt the blood drain from his face. "Shit! Why?"

James shook his head. "The Captain didn't say. We have fifteen minutes."

"Real or Shadow?"

"His office is in Real." James gave him the address.

Damien drove to the heart of the financial district, and into an underground parking garage. They entered the foyer and popped into Real to find Captain Jor'dan waiting for them.

Lines bracketing his mouth and rigid posture were signs the Fae was unhappy about something. And when the Captain was upset, no one was happy. Not even wearing his favorite grey-on-grey formal suit, could lighten his expression.

"I wonder who pissed in the Captain's Wheaties?" James whispered.

Jor'dan glared. "How would you like to be demoted to meter-man?"

James held up his hands, palms out. "Sorry, sir. Just wondering what was going on."

"I don't know. We'll find out soon enough." He led them past the bank of elevators to a single door. A control panel in the wall with enhanced security measures meant fingerprint and retinal scans. The door opened, and they stepped into the elevator.

"Let me do the talking." Jor'dan warned.

Damien exchanged a look with James, who shrugged back. They reached the penthouse a few moments later. The doors opened onto a fancy reception area where a female Elf waited.

Her dark hair was gathered in a bun at the nape of her neck. She wore a navy blue suit with a calf length skirt and white blouse. Dark-framed glasses perched on her nose. Were they for show or did she actually need them?

James gave her a flirtatious smile and a wink. She arched an eyebrow and turned to Captain Jor'dan. "His Grace is expecting you. If you'd be so kind as to follow me?" At the sound of her melodic voice, James turned to him and pantomimed panting.

"Has the other party arrived yet?" Captain Jor'dan asked.

"Yes sir. Master Dean arrived shortly before you did." She stopped at the double doors. "Would you like refreshments?"

"No thank you."

She knocked on the door, opened it, and stepped inside. "Captain Jor'dan, Detective Kirk and Detective Alexander are here to see you, sir."

A deep voice from within the room replied, "Thank you, Denise. Show them in."

Damien followed Jor'dan and James into a luxurious office. Ahead of them, a large mahogany desk sat in front of floor-to-ceiling windows. Off to the right were two comfortable looking chairs with a coffee table in front. At the polished black conference table on the left, two figures waited, a Mage dressed in Council robes and the High Chancellor.

The Elf left the room, closing the doors behind her.

Captain Jor'dan bowed low from the waist, Damien and James did the same.

The High Chancellor, Ashton Octavious Ignatio, the only known Phoenix in existence, rose from his chair at the head of the table. The intimidating man was the pinnacle of Paranormal power. He'd been elected to the position before Damien had been born, and was the ultimate authority in their world.

This was the first time Damien had met the Phoenix in person. According to rumors, his short, light brown hair and hazel eyes had made many women swoon. Damien couldn't see it himself, but there was charismatic presence about the man that made Damien want to please him. He was much taller than media sources had portrayed him, taller than his own six foot six frame.

The Mage came forward and held out his hand. "Captain Dušan, what a pleasure it is to see you again."

Captain Jor'dan shook hands, "It's nice to see you as well, Master Dean. I hope your trip west was uneventful?"

Master Dean shrugged. "You know how it is when mixing with the humans. But the fare in first class, was passable." The twinkle in his eye and the generous smile, invited the others to join him in his amusement.

"Please be seated and we can begin," the High Chancellor motioned to the table.

"Yes, Your Grace."

Damien followed Captain Jor'dan's lead and sat on the opposite side of the table from Master Dean.

Once everyone was seated, His Grace cleared his throat.

"Allow me to introduce you. Master Marshall Dean is the Mages' United States Representative to the High Council. Master Dean, you already know Captain Jor'dan DuŠan. The two Elite with him are, Detective Damien Alexander and Detective James Kirk."

The Mage smiled, but didn't offer to shake hands.

Rude son of a bitch.

Damien saw His Grace's lips twitch, as if he'd heard his comment. He tightened his mental shield so no stray thoughts could escape.

"How may we be of service to you, Master Dean?" Captain Jor'dan asked.

The joviality fell from Dean's face and a fleeting flash of anger crossed his features before they smoothed out into a concerned mask. "The Tome of Power has been stolen."

Shit. Damn. Fuck.

Shock held everyone still.

Master Dean sat back as if pleased with his announcement.

A host of questions jumped into Damien's head, and he had to bite the inside of his lip to keep from asking them.

The Captain pulled out a pen and pad of paper from his jacket pocket. "When did the theft occur?"

"I don't know. The theft was discovered yesterday morning during Retrival."

"Why haven't you reported it before now?"

Master Dean gave the Captain a look. "We've spent the last day performing tracing and tracking spells. The Tome does not want to be found."

"If your spells have failed, how can we help?" Jor'dan asked.

The Mage held out his hands, palms up and shrugged. "We've exhausted our resources and frankly I don't know what else to do."

The Captain made a couple of notes on the page. "Why didn't Master Bernard bring this to our attention? He's the Mage Governor for this region."

176

"Because we don't want panic to spread."

Damien tried to puzzle out the meaning of that.

The High Chancellor spoke up. "If Master Bernard were seen coming to this office, others would think something is wrong. Master Dean's visit is seen as a social call."

"What about those at the retrieval ceremony? Will they spread the tale?"

Master Dean shook his head. "They've all been commanded to silence." He leaned forward palms flat on the table. "We need to find the Tome."

"I'll get my people on it right away." Jor'dan put the pen and paper away. "If there's nothing else?"

The Mage cleared his throat. "There were two other small details Bernard wanted know."

"And they are?"

"First, a few days ago there was a power surge in the City and your offices have not reported their findings. Second there evidence of a new being, what is it, is it harmful and what is being done to contain it?"

"We're still investigating." Jor'dan smiled.

"Is there any information you can give me?"

"Upon arriving at the scene of the power surge, the investigators discovered a containment drawing. We were told that there were no Mages involved in the power surge, yet it is clear from the diagram that a Mage performed a spell summoning the new creature. We've yet to determine the nature of the creature and why it was summoned. The Guild has refused all requests for information and the investigation is low priority."

"You don't think the creature is dangerous?"

Jor'dan shrugged. "Until it harms someone, we don't have the resources to go after every creature that evades a Mage's control, especially when the Guild disavows all knowledge."

"What do you need?" Master Dean asked.

"I need someone to tell me what creature was summoned, where the spell came from and if the identity of the Mage can be determined by his spell-work."

"The spell-work can be narrowed down to a specific School of Magic, but depending on how many practitioners there are in the area, it might be difficult to pin down who the Mage is."

"I'll deal with that dilemma when I get to it."

Master Dean nodded. "I have no idea why the local Guild isn't working with you, but I'll make sure they give you a call tomorrow. Meanwhile, can I rely on you to find the Tome?"

Captain Jor'dan nodded. "I'll get my men on it at once."

Master Dean stood, leaned across the table and shook hands with Captain Jor'dan. "Thank you for your help. If you need anything let me know."

"Thank you, Master Dean, I will."

"Gentleman." Master Dean bowed to the High Chancellor and left the office.

Silence reigned for a few moments. The High Chancellor held up his hand and tilted his head. Damien exchanged puzzled looks with James and Jor'dan. His Grace walked around the table where Master Dean had sat, knelt down and peered under the table.

He stood and held out his hand. In his palm was a small metallic disk. He released a small puff of breath and the disk exploded into bright green flames. The disk became so hot it evaporated, leaving nothing behind.

"There. Now we may converse."

He leaned against the corner of table with arms crossed over his chest.

"Be careful Jor'dan, you've made the Guild look petulant. They'll want revenge."

Captain Jor'dan shrugged. "This wouldn't be the first time, nor do I think it'll be the last."

His Grace nodded. "Now tell me, what the hell is going on?"

178

"Same shit, different day, Ash. The Mages are up to something, and as usual we're two steps behind. Three of my men have been killed investigating suspicious magical activities around the City. Two of them have been tortured. The healer assures me, it's Voglio."

Voglio was a torture method that began in the mid 15th century during the Spanish Inquisition. The knowledge was strictly controlled and forbidden to the general population. Only a handful of people were allowed to study it, and none were allowed to practice it. Damien had wondered about that as a young Vamp. Why study it if you can't use it, he'd asked his teachers Any knowledge, even horrific, was to be saved in case it was needed.

"Do you think the creature is involved?" His Grace asked.

Jor'dan shook his head. "I doubt it. But I won't rule out the possibility."

Is Deidre practicing torture? It didn't seem to fit the little he knew about her. And how would she have learned about it in the first place? No, someone else was doing it and using her arrival to hide their activities.

"Do you have a list of those who've studied it?" Captain Jor'dan asked.

His Grace, walked over to his desk and searched through a drawer, before finding a paper and handing it to Jor'dan. "Here's the list of practitioners of Voglio. I'd concentrate on getting that damned book back first. Whatever is going on, that Tome is dangerous."

"Do you have any idea what the Mages are up to?"

"No. But whatever it is, it's going to coincide with the end of the Festival."

"That's my impression as well. The theft of the Tome makes them look like incompetent asses. They have the highest security around those books. The fact someone was able to bypass it, is an uncomfortable thought."

Damien's mind thought through the puzzle. "What if the thief had inside help?" Everyone looked at him.

"Why do you say that?" Jor'dan narrowed his eyes.

"Look at the facts. A Forbidden Tome is stolen. Why? Someone wants access to the spells within. But how many of the races can do magic? Mages, Dragons, Elves plus a couple of others. But none of them use magic in the same way. The spells that the Elves perform are different than the spells Mages perform. It has to do with the cultural belief of where magic comes from, I think. So the only one able to use a Tome spell is a Mage."

Jor'dan looked at him and smiled, before turning back to His Grace. "Looks like he finally learned his Lore."

His Grace smirked. "It took him long enough. Let me know what you find out."

"Yes, Your Grace." Captain Jor'dan stood and bowed, followed by Damien and James.

They left the office, and Damien couldn't help but stare at his Captain. Once in the elevator, James asked the question.

"How well do you know the High Chancellor?"

Jor'dan smirked at them. "He and I grew up together, and that's all I'm going to say."

Once in the lobby, a partition shielded them from view, and they popped into Shadow.

They reached Jor'dan's office without incident.

"Is your office secure?" Damien glanced around looking for anything that would be obvious as a protective measure.

Jor'dan lifted a snow globe from his desk and shook it. The globe began to glow and a magical hum filled the air. The glow subsided and the snow drifted to the bottom of the globe, signaling they were secure.

He cocked any eye at Damien. "Satisfied?"

Damien and James grinned at each other.

Jor'dan sat behind his desk. "We need to find out who stole the book."

180

"Are there any other teams available to help us?" James leaned against the wall.

Jor'dan shook his head. "My hands have been tied by those damn Mages. Each visiting Councilor is insisting on personal protection, as well as increased patrols around their hotels."

"They're doing this on purpose, trying to get us to stretch our resources so thin that they'll be able to get away with whatever they're planning," Damien commented.

Jor'dan nodded. "Yes, but my hands are tied. The High Chancellor has agreed with the Mages' request for protection. It's up to you two. Now go out and save the world!"

James gave Jor'dan a sour look. "Rah, rah, rah."

Jor'dan sat back in his chair and steepled his fingers. "Now you didn't hear this from me, but I'm assigning two other teams to investigate the Mages. But they are doing it covertly. You my friends, are going to be the visible investigation. You'll meet here at my office first thing each evening and exchange information."

"To start off, Damien, I want you to check out the theft of the book. Contact the Library of Magic and set an appointment."

"What? Why do I have to make an appointment? We're the law."

Jor'dan shook his head. "That's one rule the Mages are insisting remain intact for everyone. Supposedly they don't want to show favoritism. James I want you and Randall to investigate the area down by Folsom, there's been too much Mage activity there for my liking."

"What about Jared?" James asked.

"He's helping out with the Games."

Damien exchanged a concerned look with James. "Isn't that dangerous?" he asked.

Captain Jor'dan grinned. "No, he'll be fine. He's administering the final test to the candidates."

§

Ashton Octavius Ignatio sat back in his chair, a soothing cup of tea on the desk in front of him, and one across from him. His visitor should be arriving any moment.

His assistant poked her head through the door.

"The Oracle is here to see you sir."

"Send her in."

The door opened and Regina entered the room in her signature red power suit. Her brown hair was in loose curls around her shoulders. Her dark eyes scanned the office.

"To what do I owe the honor of your visit?" He cocked an eyebrow at her.

She shrugged and sat in the chair opposite, picking up the cup of tea that had been left for her.

"You have questions, so I'm expediting the process by appearing in person."

"You do enjoy riling Jor'dan, don't you?"

She smirked. "It's not him, per se. It's the Elite as an organization. The fact he is head of the local branch is icing on the cake."

They sipped for a moment, and he became serious. "How will this turn out?"

She put her cup down and cocked her head to the side. "Events are as yet unclear. Too many decisions need to be made that will affect the outcome."

He smiled into his cup. "And how is the creature?"

Regina raised her eyebrow. "Creature? Who the hell called her a creature?"

Ash snorted. "First Dean, then Jor'dan."

"Creature! She'll kick all their asses if they're not careful."

"How is she?"

Regina shrugged. "Fine at the moment, although I don't envy her her dreams."

"Anything we can do to help?"

182

"No. Any interference at this point will change the probable course of events and possibly destroy this reality."

"That's what I thought."

"Events around the bunny are going to get nasty soon."

"I'll try to drop a subtle hint to Jor'dan."

"I've tried, but I end up getting yelled at."

"That's because he knows you like to jerk him around."

She shrugged and managed to keep a straight face for two seconds before succumbing to laughter. "I can't help it, it's too much fun."

"What about the missing Tome?"

Regina cocked her head to the side and looked off into the distance. Her eyes went completely black. Creepy. In a higher voice unlike her normal speaking tone, she spoke, "Events are transpiring as they should. It was time for the Tome to go walkabout."

After a few moments, her entire body shuddered, the black shrank to the center of her eyes, and she took a sip of tea.

"Are you alright?" Concern filled his tone. He'd never seen her go into a vision before.

A smile crossed her lips. "I'm fine. Small seeings don't wipe me out like larger visions." Her watch beeped. "Damn I'm late for an appointment." She put her cup down on the desk and walked to the door. She paused for a moment before turning back. "One more thing. You'll need to instruct the creature on how to cast spell."

Ash frowned. "But…."

"Don't screw up," she said opening the door.

He chuckled. "Yes ma'am."

The door closed softly behind her, and he swiveled his chair to gaze out on the clear moonlit night.

Chapter 12

Clint Douglas picked up the phone on the second ring. "Library of Magic, how may I help you?"

He paused a moment as he heard Detective Alexander's voice on the line. If it weren't for that Vampire Elite, his family would still be alive. The Elite had executed Sienna and Robbie for allegedly attempting to kill Alexander. Heartbroken that her babies were gone, Elaine had joined them in death.

A bubble of anticipation rose. *Finally, I have the Detective right where I want him!*

"Why yes Detective, I'd be happy to give you an appointment. Unfortunately, Master Librarian Roberts won't be able to see you until tomorrow evening... Yes, I'm aware of the urgency, but the Master Librarian is engaged this evening. Eight pm? See you then, Detective." He entered the appointment in the master calendar and hung up the phone.

That gave him twenty four-hours to finalize his plan. *Perfect.*

A knock on the door had him swiveling around. "Enter."

Master Mage Marshall Dean stood in the doorway.

Clint rose from his chair and bowed low before the Mage. "How may I help you, Master?"

"I assume that was one of Jor'dan's lackeys on the phone?"

"Yes, sir. Detective Alexander will meet with Master Roberts tomorrow evening to investigate the theft of the book."

"Tell Roberts he's to cooperate fully. I want the Detective in and out with a minimum of fuss. The Guild will not be accused of standing in the way of their precious investigation."

"Yes, sir."

Master Dean gave him a measuring look sketched a sigil in the air. A bubble formed in front of him and expanded to encompass the entire office. Clint recognized the ward against eavesdroppers via both magical and non-magical means.

Master Dean sat in the chair opposite Clint, leaned back and steepled his fingers.

"The Alliance has heard of your plans."

A shiver of dread raced through Clint. *Damn it.* It looks as if he'd gotten rid of the Underground too soon. They were supposed to have provided a distraction to keep everyone's attention away from him. But too late, now. Perhaps he could fudge his way out of this?

The Alliance, a highly secretive group, worked behind the scenes to establish Mages as the predominate Paranormal Race. The organization had laudable goals, but their methods were enough to give him nightmares.

"What plans?" Clint stalled. What did the Marshall know and more importantly, would the Mage stop him? Was his old friend a member of the Alliance? Clint opened his mouth to ask. Marshall held up a hand stopping him. "No I'm not a part of it, but I do have connections. We'll leave it at that."

Clint nodded. Hopefully they didn't know everything. A sudden determination to make sure they knew as little as possible, filled him. "Why are they interested in my plans?"

Master Dean shook his head. "Don't be stupid. They have eyes and ears everywhere."

Clint remained silent, not sure how to respond.

Master Dean spoke again. "Interesting thing, this Underground. But no one has seen any of the leaders for a while. What happened?"

"Unfortunately, that group of hot-heads outlived their usefulness."

"Just what are you up to?"

Clint stood and walked to the window of his small office at the Library of Magic and stood looking out over the grounds for a long moment.

"I want justice. For my family."

In the reflection of the window, he saw the Mage nod.

"Are you sure this is the best course of action?"

Clint took a deep breath. "It's the only way. Damien Alexander will pay for killing them." He turned to look at the Council Mage. "Surely you, of all people, can understand that?"

Marshall had lost loved ones to Elite investigations. He nodded. "Yes, but beware Clint, the need for revenge can become all consuming."

The Mage stood and snapped his fingers, bursting the bubble before leaving the office.

Clint stared at the door and in a soft tone replied, "It's too late."

§

Deidre arrived at the coffee shop, eager to show off her new wardrobe. It was only one outfit, but it was hers. She'd had fun this afternoon, trying on various clothes at the store. Like any good friend Cyn exclaimed over the short skirt and flirty top. They were just finishing their drinks when Deidre felt them enter the shop. She had to warn Cyn, "Vampires at" she looked at her watch, "Ten o'clock."

Cyn gave her a funny look. "That's not the right way to use that expression."

"Why not?"

Cyn shook her head. "I… " She looked thoughtful for a moment. "You know, I'm not sure where that expression comes from exactly."

Deidre grinned. "Then I could be right, right?"

"I don't think so, but we could always look it up."

Deidre shrugged, then grinned at the Vampire across from her as the female fluffed her hair and ran a hand down the front of her leather suit.

Deidre turned and watched the male Vampires approach. Both had eager grins on their faces.

"Those two are up to something."

Cyn's reply was soft, almost dreamy. "Yeah. Makes a girl wonder what they've got planned."

Deidre turned back to Cyn. "Oh really? And just what happened last night after you left?"

A fine blush rose to Cyn's cheeks and she leaned forward, whispering. "Nothing more than a kiss, so you can get your mind out of the gutter."

"Must have been good to get that dreamy look in your face."

Cyn threw a napkin at her. "Never mind. Oh hi, James."

James grinned down at Cyn. "Hey, Cyn. What are your plans for the evening?"

Deidre missed Cyn's reply as Damien's heat surrounded her. He brushed the nape of her neck, sending tingles of delight through her now sensitized body.

Damien leaned over and whispered in her ear. "Miss me?"

A shudder pulsed through her. "Maybe."

He straightened as James offered. "May we buy you a drink?"

Deidre looked at her empty cup and then at Cyn who shrugged. "Sure why not?" the Vampire said, "Two mocha lattes, please."

Damien and James headed to the back of the long line that formed in front of the ordering station.

"What are you planning?" James whispered.

"Why?" Damien asked, thankful that the noisy crowd around them swallowed the sound of their whispers.

"Because you have that look on your face, one that means you're thinking about doing something stupid."

"Stupid?"

"Yeah. Like the time you decided to petition the Council to marry Sienna."

That had turned into a giant cluster fuck that had nearly resulted in his death. Damien rubbed his hand over his heart, where the bitch had stabbed him with a stiletto. His quick reflexes had been able to stop the blade from completely destroying his heart.

"Yeah, that was a bad idea."

"And?"

"And what?" Damien shrugged. "Deidre's different." The line moved forward two steps.

James shook his head. "And she's been summoned here by a Mage to perpetrate some dastardly deed upon our fair city."

Damien turned back to look at James and raised his eyebrow. "Dastardly deed?" Someone bumped into his back and he turned to a mumbled apology.

A flush rose on James' cheeks. "You know what I mean." He paused for a moment. "So really, what are you planning?"

"I was going to take her back to my place and cook dinner."

James' jaw dropped. It took a few moments for his partner to recover. "Your place? But you never take women home."

"I know." It was a long standing rule, never to invite female company over. He slept better by day knowing no one would stake him to the bed. A rule he was about to break.

"Why this one?"

Damien sighed. He didn't want to delve into the emotional crap for James. "She's different and it feels right." And he prayed his friend wouldn't push further.

188

"I hope you know what the fuck you're doing." James whispered, as he stepped up to the counter to place his order.

So do I.

When the male Vamps walked away, Cyn reached out and grabbed Deidre's arm, leaning forward so their whispers wouldn't be heard. "So you and Damien?"

Heat filled Deidre's face. "How did you know?"

"The chemistry between you two, is hot!"

Deidre looked over her shoulder at tall dark and Vampy. "If he was human the attraction would be over by now."

"So you think because he's a Vamp, he's got what? Extra staying power?"

Deidre turned back. "Something like that. I've never slept with a Vamp before. It's new territory for me."

"Is it scary?" Cyn asked.

Deidre twirled the sleeve on her empty cup. "Very, yet exciting at the same time."

Cyn grinned. "That's how I feel about James. Even though he's a cop."

"Really? But you've been in relationships before right?"

"So? Each one is different in its own way. Scary, exciting, thrilling, nerve-wracking and heart-breaking."

Deidre tilted her head. "Why go through it then?"

"Because the happiness and joy outweigh the pain."

"It won't last."

Cyn reached over and put her hand on top of Deidre's. "It never does. You have to enjoy the ride while it lasts."

"I'll give it one more night."

"Then what?"

"I'll break it off."

"But why?"

Deidre opened her mouth, but how to explain that things with Sir were going to come to a head soon. "Work will keep me too busy."

"Right," Cyn patted her hand and leaned back, a smirk on her lips. "You just keep telling yourself that."

"What's that supposed to mean?"

"It means you're caught, but you don't know it yet."

Deidre shook her head, and the males sat down at their table. Thankfully the conversation was light and relaxing.

Everyone finished and Damien took Deidre's arm and escorted her through the tables and out onto the sidewalk in front of the café. She glanced behind her to see James escorting Cyn.

James spoke from behind her and Damien. "I'll see Cyn home. Have fun at dinner."

Deidre watched them turn away and walk around the corner before turning to Damien.

"What if Cyn weren't going home?

"Then James would take her to wherever she was going."

"And where are we going?"

His quick grin sent a tingle of pleasure through her.

"It's a surprise."

Damien presented his arm in an old world gesture. She took it and allowed him to lead her in the opposite direction. She tried to ignore the rising excitement running through her at the thought of where they'd end the evening. Being with Damien was becoming an addiction she didn't want to give up.

They walked a few blocks before he stopped and turned to her.

"Do you know about Shadow?"

"Yes, why?"

He ignored the question, "Can you enter?"

Deidre was uncertain if she should answer. For many years she'd avoided it, not wanting to run into any Paranormals. Now she was surrounded by them in Real. *Talk about jumping into the fire, from the pan.* "Yes, I can enter."

"Good. Shift into Shadow, we'll get there faster without the crowds."

Damien led her into an alley and popped into Shadow. A few moments later, she popped into phase beside him. Looking at the street and the throngs of people, she raised an eyebrow. "I thought you said it wouldn't be crowded?"

"Sorry, forgot about Festival."

"Is our destination very far?"

"No." He kept his answer vague, not wanting to alarm her or raise her suspicions. He knew exactly how he wanted the evening to end. Him, buried inside her tight body. He'd wondered if last night had been a fluke, brought on by over six months of celibacy. He'd find out tonight.

Thoughts of her distracted him from his job. While James had given a report, he'd been daydreaming about her luscious body.

It had to stop.

He led her toward his apartment. Across the street she stopped. "Where are we going?"

He smiled down at her and tugged on her hand. "We're having dinner at my place."

"Is this one of those, need permission to enter a Vampire's lair, type of situations?"

Damien stopped and looked at her. "Where did you hear that?"

She paused and he was distracted by her white teeth worrying her succulent bottom lip.

"That's a myth. Vampires don't need to be invited into homes. Nor do you need to be invited into mine. Wait. That didn't sound right." She laughed and he shook his head trying to get his brain back on-line and free of its lust-filled cage.

Deidre nodded and he led her into the lobby and to the elevator and when the doors closed, pulled her into his arms. Her body was stiff against his for a long moment before she relaxed into his chest. Contentment filled him at the gesture of trust. If he could manage it, they'd stay like that for longer than it took to get to his floor. The doors opened, and keeping his arm around her shoulders, he led her to his apartment.

Damien paused for a moment. This was it. Inviting her into his home, his sanctuary. What if he'd made a mistake and she wasn't who he thought she was? He was letting James' doubts feed his own. Silencing them, he opened the door and ushered her inside.

Damien removed his boots as was his custom and switched on various lights to give himself something to do while Deidre looked around.

What did she think of it?

He wasn't able to read her expression.

Did she like it?

Deidre looked Damien's apartment. "Incredible."

The expensive leather furniture and quality of his possessions gave her an insight into who he was. He had an appreciation for the finer things from the vases and statuary in niches along one wall, to the museum quality art hanging from the walls.

Tinted floor to ceiling windows looked out over the lights of San Francisco. Hard wood floors were softened by the occasional decorative rug. An open gourmet kitchen gleamed under the bright lights and opposite the kitchen, a hallway led to the rest of the apartment.

Damien walked into the kitchen

"Make yourself comfortable. Would you like something to drink?"

Deidre nodded. "Sure. A glass of wine please."

Sounds came from the kitchen while her gaze was caught by the lights of the city.

Damien held out a glass of white wine. "Give me a moment to get dinner started."

Her head tilted. Puzzled, she asked, "I thought Vampires didn't eat?"

At least according to Cyn... No, wait. The female Vampire had said they didn't feed from humans. It was all so confusing.

He grinned. "Oh we eat. Not very much, though. Food doesn't give us the proper nutrients that blood does."

Damien opened a cupboard and bent over giving Deidre an excellent view of his tight butt. He looked good enough to eat. Her power curled around her warm and soft, and strangely content. It didn't reach out to him, as if it knew she'd be fed well by his energy tonight.

A sudden feeling of dread overtook her. Something was coming, something bad that would destroy this. She needed to make the most of the moment. A snapshot memory to keep her company for the rest of her life. Tonight would be their last, of that she was certain.

Damien stood, turning and winking at her, as if he'd known she'd been ogling his ass. He grabbed the second glass of wine and motioned to the couch.

They sat on the couching and he put his arm around her shoulders, pulling him into his body.

Mouth dry, she took a sip of wine. "You have a beautiful view."

"Thanks, I enjoy it."

She looked up and saw the restrained lust in his gaze. There wasn't any doubt in her mind as to the reason they were eating here instead of a restaurant.

Deidre leaned closer and inhaled the scent of his body. Delicious. She could feel the lust pulsing beneath his skin and her hunger woke, not for food, but for him.

Deidre put her wine glass down on the glass table in front of the couch. She leaned back and whispered into his ear, "So what else did you have planned for the evening Damien?"

He responded with a groan and tilted his head back.

"A little of this; a little of that."

"Something along these lines perhaps?" She placed small bites along the column of his throat before soothing them with a lick.

Deidre flattened her palm against his chest and straddled one of his jean clad thighs. The short skirt she wore rode up, exposing her pink lace panties. The denim felt rough against the soft skin of her inner thigh. Her hips rocked once before he grabbed them, stilling their motion.

She grinned down at him.

"What's wrong?"

What's wrong? Was she kidding? He was about to come at the enticingly erotic picture she made.

God, she felt fabulous. He could smell her arousal and feel the dampness of her body soaking into his jeans. He'd wanted to wait until after dinner, but who was he to argue with her timing. Perhaps a pre dinner appetizer was what they both needed.

"Stand up." He meant it as a request, but even to his own ears it sounded like an order.

She wiggled, and squirmed, slipping off his thigh before standing between his legs. Damien placed his palms on either side of her knees and stroked upward, savoring the feel of her silky soft skin. The flirty little skirt she wore lifted as it bunched up on his wrists. His hands went higher, until they reached her sexy panties. In one smooth motion, he lowered them to her ankles.

"Step out."

One hand rested on his shoulder as she lifted one high heel, then the other. The view he had was enough to make him lose control. Knowing she was bare under the skirt, and in those killer heels made his mouth water and cock ache.

194

He looked up and saw her watching him with an indulgent smile on her face.

"Would you like me to lose the shirt as well?" Her voice was husky, as if she too was turned on by the situation.

Damien leaned forward and placed a quick kiss on her skirt covered abdomen, and with great force of will, sat back and spread his arms out along the back of the couch.

"Make it good."

A smile of pure devilry crossed her face. "If you insist."

She turned and sauntered toward the windows. Because it was dark outside, Damien could see her image reflected in the glass, as if he were looking into a mirror.

Deidre tossed her hair over her shoulder and gave him a coy look through the glass. "Do you have any music to accompany this tease?"

"Of course." He reached for a remote lying on the end table and soft blues music filled the room.

Her body began to sway to the beat. Her hips rocked back and forth showing him a peek of her ass when the skirt flared too high.

Torture; pure torture. His hands gripped the couch to keep him from pouncing on her. His teeth descended and shredded his lip. But even that small pain couldn't stop the lust from rising hard and fast.

Deidre looked over her shoulder at him, before rolling her head back, turning to give him a profile. She arched her back, making her luscious breasts stick out even further. He had to swallow at the drool that pooled in his mouth at the sight.

Another move emphasized her legs. Long legs that looked amazing in heels. He'd imagined those legs wrapped around him as he thrust into her.

The tight denim constricted his dick. He unbuttoned the jeans, eased the zipper down, and freed his cock.

Deidre brought her hand up to her mouth, bent her wrist and bit down on her index finger, slowly pulling her hand away as if taking off an imaginary glove.

Shit. Damn. Fuck. She was hot. Hot enough to incinerate a Vampire. And what a sweet death it would be.

She turned to face the glass, and he saw her lift the hem of her shirt showing off her belly. The shirt rose higher, baring the pink lace cups of her bra. Deidre rested the shirt on her breasts as she swayed her hips, then crouched down with her knees together, balancing on those fuck-me heels.

None of the strippers he'd ever seen could hold a candle to the peek-a-boo move she did next. In a slow movement, she opened her legs and ran her hands up along the inside of her thighs, not quite touching herself. She was covered by her skirt... barely.

He caught tantalizing glimpses of her damp blonde curls and pouty lips.

In a move that seemed to defy the laws of physics, she rolled up until she was standing then stalked toward him in an exaggerated model walk.

A coy grin graced her face as she once again stood between his legs.

"How was that?" she asked, breathless.

"Ni..." He had to clear his throat and try again. "Very nice, except for one problem."

Deidre arched her eyebrow and straddled his lap.

"What's the problem?"

"You still have your shirt on."

"What are you going to do about it?"

He grinned at the challenge in her voice.

"This."

Damien grabbed the hem of her shirt and tugged it up and over her head before throwing it to the floor.

"Much better."

196

"Oh indeed." She agreed as she rocked her damp flesh against his cock.

It was too much.

He needed her.

Now.

Damien grabbed her hips, adjusted his angle and in one smooth stroke, entered her hot body.

Her head fell back and she moaned at his entrance.

A vein throbbed in her neck in time with her heart-beat and he craved her blood. He promised he wouldn't take it without her permission.

To distract himself, Damien pulled her head down to his and gave her a deep tongue tangling kiss, devouring her. The kiss went on and on as he began to thrust into her.

It wasn't enough. He wanted more. To be inside of her as deep as he could go. To imprint himself upon her so that she knew she belonged to him.

Damien broke the kiss and opened his eyes to see an expression of bliss on her face.

In a swift move he rearranged them, bending her over the end of the couch while he knelt behind her.

"What…?"

Her hesitant question became a moan as he entered her in a strong thrust that buried him deep inside.

Her body squeezed around him, causing a groan to slip free.

"Please…" came her breathless plea.

He thrust again, unable to remain still.

"What?"

"Fuck me. Hard."

Control snapped.

Damien pounded into her, harder, faster, using his Vampire strength and speed to fuck her.

And it wasn't enough.

He fought the primitive need to mark her as his. To bite. It was the hardest thing he'd ever done. He gripped her hips hard, knowing he'd leave bruises, and regretting the marring of her pale skin, but he couldn't stop.

Wouldn't stop.

Not until he found heaven within her body.

A flash of heat and his orgasm rose, hotter and more devastating than before. And the impossible happened.

Again.

He threw his head back and shouted his release to the universe. Fire coursed through his veins, and explosions of pleasure wracked his body.

He pumped into her again and again until he was drained dry. There was nothing left. He felt like a dry shell of a Vampire, and yet he couldn't stop the smiling.

A groan from beneath him had him frowning.

Shit. Damn. Fuck.

He'd neglected her pleasure, something he'd never done before with any of his lovers.

He pulled out, moaning at the loss of her heat.

"Damn that felt good." Her voice was filled with satisfaction.

"You came?"

"Oh yeah." She purred. "Wanna do it again?"

Laughter roared through him.

By God she was perfect!

Damien smacked her on one butt cheek and noticed a shiver of pleasure race over her skin. Good to know for future reference. His darling had a kinky streak.

"Come on, let's get cleaned up and eat. We've got plenty of time for fun and games."

Deidre smiled, a delicate shiver raced over her body. "If you insist."

Her limbs weren't working right, and it took her a few tries before she was able to retrieve her panties. She busied herself with putting her on her clothing, not wanting him to see the turmoil. What the hell had just happened? Her body was not under her control. The pleasure had been real, and it scared her down her bones. She'd always been in control of sex, but this time, sex had controlled her. And she didn't like it one bit. But she was beginning to crave it.

She took a step toward the kitchen and wobbled. Her legs felt like they were made out of wet pasta. Deidre sat down hard on the couch. A chuckle from her right and she looked up to see his hand out. "I'll help you to the table."

"Thanks." She placed her hand in his and let him take most of her body weight as he led her to a small table next to the windows. Seating her, he placed plates filled with pasta in front of her. Suddenly ravenous, she ate as if she were starved. Deidre checked her energy levels and she was full. Perhaps there was something to having a Vampire lover.

She looked up to find him watching her, his gaze intense.

Deidre licked her lips and watched his eyes follow the movement. He took a hasty sip of wine. Damien allowed her a few more bites before he pushed back from the table and held out his hand. "Ready for round two?"

She smiled up at him. "Of course." She took his hand and he led her down the hallway to his room.

The room was hot as purgatory, and the pungent scent of incense filled the air. Deidre looked around trying to figure out where she was, but the darkness was complete. A clanking noise had her turning toward the sound. A thin sliver of light grew and she realized she was in a cell of some kind. The minimal light allowed her to see the blood stained walls and floors. Scurrying sounds lifted the hair on the back of her neck at the thought of vermin sharing her space.

She lifted a clawed hand and realized with a jerk that she was in Demoni form.

J'kala! Not again!

Khan strode through the door; his grin of delight frightening.

"Ah my Deidre. So lost I've been without the pleasure of your company."

Terror froze her response in her throat.

The sound of rusted metal grating against stone came as the dim light grew fainter and fainter. She was trapped alone with Khan... and she couldn't see.

His laughter filled the small space and she backed away from the sound.

Stinging pain flashed down her arms and she cried out as his claws pierced her shoulder. He pulled her, and she crashed into his chest.

She sensed his head dip low and felt his tongue bathe the pain on her arm. It felt as if rough sand paper were being used to soothe the cut. Warm wetness trickled down her arm to her wrist.

His claws dug deep into her shoulder and she felt his face near hers. She turned her head to the side and thrashed in his embrace.

"That's it my little captive. Struggle against me. I crave your struggle. Your submission will be all the sweeter."

"No!"

Her scream echoed in the small cell, followed by his triumphant laughter.

Damien was shaken out of his doze by Deidre struggling in his hold. He leaned over her and saw her eyes move back and forth under her closed eyelids. Red marks streaked down her arm, and he frowned. He hadn't put them there had he? Had he been too rough with her?

"No!" Her head rolled back and forth as if trying to escape her dream.

"Deidre! Wake up! It's only a dream." He shook her shoulder, but she didn't awaken. Damien tried again, harder this time. She was still caught in the throes of her dream.

He got out of bed and grabbed a towel, running it under cold water. He'd read somewhere that this was the only way to wake someone caught in a nightmare.

He laid the cool washcloth over her chest and got an immediate reaction.

Deidre let out a small scream and jerked upright, almost hitting him in the nose with her head.

Violet eyes flashed with anger. "What in Dar'kirm...?"

The cold cloth fell to her lap, eliciting more annoyance. "What's this?"

He shrugged, grabbed the washcloth and tossed it onto the nightstand.

"You were having a nightmare."

"Oh." She rubbed her arms then stopped and glanced down at her left arm. A puzzled frown crossed her face. "What...?"

He followed her gaze and watched as the red lines faded into nothing.

"Was I too rough with you?"

She shook her head. "I think that happened in my nightmare."

"Impossible."

She shrugged. "Yeah."

He got back into bed and pulled her into his embrace. "Feeling better?"

"A bit."

He rolled over her and entered her in a long slow thrust. "I want to make you feel one hundred percent better."

She gasped as he pulled out and slid home. "Oh... okay."

He took her on a slow journey to the stars, where every touch and every breath was savored.

Dawn streaked the sky as he rolled to the side and pulled her into his arms.

A warm silence filled the room and Deidre drifted on a wave of lassitude. She'd never felt this… contented before.

Warning bells filled her mind. What the hell was wrong with her? She shouldn't be feeling like this.

His arm tightened around her. "Relax." His tone was soft, soothing.

Her mind started working, plaguing her with doubts. How was Khan able to get into her dreams? Could he kill her in them? And if he did, would her body here, die? Not even the slow stroke of his hand down her spine calmed her. It exacerbated the feeling of being closed in, trapped.

Deidre jerked from his embrace, her momentum taking her out of bed and onto her feet.

"What's wrong?"

She ran a hand through her hair and stared at it.

A human hand. Five fingers. Nails instead of claws.

"I don't know." Deidre hesitated a moment. "I should leave."

Damien reached out and grabbed the same hand she'd been staring at, stopping her from turning to the door.

She looked into his eyes. Tenderness filled his gaze.

"Stay. Please."

Deidre shook her head. "I can't."

"Why not?"

"I have things to do today. Appointments to keep."

Damien held her gaze as if searching for a hidden meaning behind her words. He sighed and got out of bed.

"What are you doing?"

"I'm going to walk you home."

Deidre shook her head again. "You can't."

He glared at her, putting his hands on his hips. "Why not?"

She pointed out the window at the lightening sky. "It's dawn."

"I'll walk you to the door."

Deidre gathered her clothing from the various locations around his living room and dressed. At the door, he pulled her into a kiss that was more soothing than passionate.

"You'll stay next time." There was no mistaking the order in his tone.

She stepped through the door and out into the hall before looking at him over her shoulder. "We'll see."

His dark eyes flashed with temper before he nodded once and closed the door.

Deidre let out the breath she'd been holding and walked to the elevator. On the ride down and the subsequent walk home, her thoughts went around and around like a hamster in a wheel. Too many questions and too few answers.

The thought of not seeing Damien again caused a swift pain to pierce her heart. But she had to do it, had to break this off now before something bad happened.

She arrived at Cyn's, stripped out of her clothes and let the hot water of the shower soothe her muscles.

Deidre curled up on the couch, pulling the blanket up and prepared for sleep. Her cell phone rang.

A quick check of caller-id showed it was Sir.

"Hello?"

His voice sounded terse as he gave her his orders.

"You're to come to this address at midnight tonight."

He rattled off the address and hung up.

"Yes, Sir."

Chapter 13

Damien and James met the other teams in Captain Jor'dan's office to exchange information.

James shuffled the papers in his hands. "What were Klaus and Roger investigating?"

"The rogue Vampire," responded Merrick, one of the Elite Mages.

"And Eric?" James' question met with a sudden silence. Damien saw the others cast suspicious looks at each other.

The Captain entered the room. "Eric was investigating a security leak from within our offices."

Shit! No wonder no one wanted to pick up his investigation. It'd point the finger at one of their own. Damien wanted to ask if the support staff had been investigated. That would be an easier scenario to swallow than one of the Elite selling out their brethren.

Captain Jor'dan cleared his throat as he sat down. "All right, gentlemen. The official word from the healers is that Earl, Klaus, and Roger all experienced severe energy drain before they died. One thing that makes it hard for us to be killed is a higher level of magical force than normal Paranormals possess. Someone or something is draining that energy and allowing the Elite to be easily killed."

"But, I thought they were killed by Voglio?" Damien asked.

"The Healers verified it was administered post mortem." Jor'dan replied. "We still need to find out who did the torturing and bring him in, but that is a lower priority than this new weapon."

One of the others spoke up. "What kind of weapon is it? Do the Tech Mages have something to counteract it?"

Jor'dan held up his hand and all went silent. He looked at each of them. "It's not a weapon per -se. The healers found evidence of sexual activity immediately preceding death."

Damien looked around the room at the cocky expressions of his fellow Elite. "Sex doesn't drain us, sir. Just the opposite."

Ribald comments and snickers filled the room.

Jor'dan smiled, but it failed to reach his eyes. "The healers have checked the records and nothing like this has been seen in the Paranormal community before. But it's been documented in the human population."

A knock on the door heralded the arrival of Healer Bar'ella. Everyone stood until she sat in a chair next to the desk. Others re-took their seats, or stood against the wall.

"What have you found out?" Jor'dan asked.

Bar'ella took a deep breath and one of the Elves spoke up. "I still don't see how something that has been draining the humans can drain the Elite, Sir."

The Healer glared at the Elf. "That's because Paranormals have never seen a Succubus before."

Confused murmurs filled the room. Gene, a Shifter Wolf, cleared his throat. "What's a Succubus?"

"According to human lore, a Succubus is a female demon that drains a man of his semen then turns into an incubus, a male demon, and impregnates the female population." Bar'ella responded.

Damien chuckled. "A Succubus? Aren't they a myth made up by humans?"

Captain Jor'dan gave him a stern look that wiped the humor from his demeanor, and arched an eyebrow. "Are not Vampires, Shifters, and others also myths created by the humans?"

"So you're saying Succubae exist."

Bar'ella shook her head. "No. I'm saying a Succubus exists. To my knowledge there is only one."

Harold, an Elf, spoke up, "But how does that affect us? It's a human myth."

Jor'dan tilted his head. "We don't know anything about this creature, or what she's capable of, other than draining Earl, Klaus, and Roger."

Bar'ella expression blanked for a moment. She knew more than she was letting on, but Damien had no idea how to get the information without becoming barbequed.

"Excuse me, gentlemen, but I must be going." Bar'ella asked.

"Thank you for coming by." Jor'dan escorted her to the door.

"You're welcome." Bar'ella left the office.

A Succubus. A bad feeling crept up Damien's spine. He exchanged a look with James. It couldn't be Deidre, could it? But no, he had spent the last two nights with her engaged in marathon sex, and he was still hale and whole.

"Who's tracking the Succubus down?" Damien asked.

"No one." Captain Jor'dan responded.

"What? Why not?"

Jor'dan gave him a look of disbelief. "This female is extremely dangerous and the only person able to capture her is another woman, which, last time I checked, we don't have."

Merrick scoffed. "We can handle her, sir, no problem." Others in the room nodded in agreement, lascivious grins on many faces.

Jor'dan glared at the Mage. "No. And that is my final word gentleman. I'm taking care of it." He took a deep breath. "Until we can capture this Succubus, be very careful with whom you sleep."

He paused a moment.

"Dismissed."

Damien glanced at his watch. He needed to leave for his appointment with the Head Librarian.

He drove to the Library of Magic, parked and walked up to the building. The hair on the back of his neck rose and he was certain he was being watched. He scanned the area with his psychic senses. Nothing. The watcher was careful. Damien would find the watcher after his appointment. He walked up the steps to the main entrance of the Library.

A junior Mage in a gray robe met him at the door.

"Welcome Detective. You are expected." His speech was formal and held a hint of condescension. Damien didn't want to piss him off, so he gave the man a polite nod.

"Follow me please." Damien crossed into an elaborate foyer. The marble tiles had been patterned in a permanent magical diagram. As he crossed the floor, tingles from a magical barrier crossed his skin.

He kept track of the active security measures he could detect. The cameras in the corners of the ceiling were unobtrusive, yet followed his progress across the foyer. How hard would it be for someone from the outside to break in? Another tingle, another magical barrier.

At the back of the foyer, a grand staircase swept to the right. He followed the Mage up the curving stairs and into a gallery. They turned left into a long wood-paneled hall extended from the top of the stairs and ended at a single door.

Doors on both sides of the hall made him nervous. He kept waiting for someone to jump out. He recognized a couple of the aversion spells in front of the doors. None of them were marked, nor did they have any symbol to identify what the room held. They walked to the end and his guide stopped and knocked on the door.

"Enter" a voice from within ordered.

The Mage opened the door and waved Damien through.

Inside, a Mage sat at a desk in front of a bay window. Damien recognized the furnishings in the room as Victorian; substantial as a twig. Neither of the two chairs in front of the fireplace looked to be able to support his weight. Neither did the two wing back chairs in front of the desk. The wall to his right was lined with bookcases. The wall to his left held a stone lined fireplace. Two sconces with fat candles flanked the mantle. Bookcases filled the area on either side of the stone hearth.

The fire wasn't lit, but the wood was set and ready. Scattered around the room were pedestals with knickknacks and vases, most of which Damien didn't recognize.

Damien approached the desk and executed a low bow. "Good evening, sir."

The Mage before him had white hair, and a lightly wrinkled face. Eyes of indeterminate color, squinted at him from behind a pair of reading glasses perched on the tip of his nose. Ornate embroidery lined the collar of his black robe.

The man did not get up, nor did he extend his hand.

"So you are the Detective Captain Jor'dan sent." His voice was filled with condescension.

"Yes, sir."

Damien gritted his teeth against the urge to correct the Mage's impression of him. *Don't piss him off. I can't investigate if I'm turned into a newt.* The mantra kept repeating through Damien's head as he smiled politely and nodded.

"I'm Head Librarian Master Edward Roberts. How may I help you?"

"My name is Damien Alexander and I've been sent to investigate the theft of one of the Forbidden Tomes. First, I would like to see the room where the Tome was housed. Second, I'd like to look at the log of visitors to the Library in the twenty four hours preceding the discovery of the theft. And finally I need to talk with any staff that worked that day."

"I assure you, Detective, the staff has been spoken to most sternly about allowing this to happen."

Damien shook his head. "That's not the reason I want to speak to them. It could be that someone noticed something out of place, or a little off, or a bit strange, and I would like to follow every lead possible. Which of the five was stolen?"

"What do you know of the Forbidden Tomes?" the Mage asked, the skepticism in his voice matched his condescending manner.

Damien could see the man censoring what he really wanted to say. *Poor egotistical Mage.* Too bad he'd researched what he was investigating.

Damien put his hands behind his back and began to speak, like a little boy reciting his lessons.

"The Forbidden Tomes of Magic hold the spells that the Lern Mages used to create the Shadow Earth. The five are broken into the elements. Earth, Wind, Fire, Air, and Energy or Power. The spells contained within were found to be too powerful for any one Mage to handle, so they were locked into the most formidably protective room that could be devised."

He stopped speaking. It looked like he'd impressed Master Roberts, judging by the shock on his face.

Master Roberts stood behind his desk and went to the fireplace, robes concealing the clothing beneath. Damien glimpsed a pair of black dress shoes before they were hidden by the hem of the robe.

The Mage lifted one of the pillar candles from the sconce, and the room was filled with the sound of a low grinding, like metal on stone. A few moments later and a passage behind the fireplace was revealed.

Damien could almost hear a voice say "Put zee candle back." James would appreciate the humor, although he didn't believe Master Roberts would. He swallowed a smirk and followed the Mage into a small stone landing.

Thank God he wasn't claustrophobic.

The landing was the size of a small closet. On the left, narrow flagstone steps circled upward. Master Roberts waved toward the open door, and the fireplace slid back into position with a heavy thud that echoed up the stairwell. Once the door shut, the landing was plunged into darkness.

Damien heard muttered words and a glow appeared on the outer wall of the staircase. He followed the Librarian up the steps. As they approached, another glowing orb appeared a few steps above the first one. He paused and looked behind him. The orbs extinguished as they passed. It seemed like a waste of power to him, but then he'd known many Mages and as Merrick had once said, "It's all about the image of being powerful. The more power used on seemingly frivolous pursuits, the more others are impressed and the more political power acquired."

Damien wasn't sure how many stairs he'd climbed, nor how many were left. The stairs seemed to go on and on forever. Finally they came to a heavy wooden door.

Master Roberts rummaged in the pockets of his robe and removed an antique-looking key. He inserted it into the lock and stepped back.

The door melted into the stones beneath, like water cascading down a glass window. Damien took a step forward and a robed arm shot out in front of him stopping his progress. "Wait."

In the center of the open doorway, Damien saw a circular pattern of light spiral out. It branched out until it hit the threshold and formed intricate shapes that glowed iridescent. It reminded him of a shimmering spider web. The center glowed silver.

Master Roberts put his hand in front of the silver and spoke three words. An arch opened in the midst of the web and grew to human height.

The Mage turned back to him and warned, "Do not touch the sides when you go through, or you'll be trapped in the magic, stuck like a fly, forever."

Damien nodded and followed the Mage through the hole.

210

Once inside the room, he turned back toward the door, and watched as it un-melted from the floor. The key hole with the key still inside reformed on the inside of the door. He looked around.

The room was dark with only the glow of the Tomes providing illumination. Each glow consisted of a different color. The room was empty save for the five wooden pedestals arranged in a semicircle. All but one of the pedestals held a book, bound to the wood with numerous chains and padlocks keeping them shut.

Damien estimated the books to be about fourteen inches long by twelve inches wide and four inches thick. These were not small books. He turned to Master Roberts.

"How was someone able to steal the Tome and remove it from the premises without being seen?"

Mage Roberts looked at the Tomes before turning back to Damien.

"The Tomes are able to mask their presence when necessary."

Damien frowned at that. "Are they alive?"

"Not really, but there is so much concentrated magic within the pages that they have become semi-sentient."

Every now and again one of the books shifted, testing the strength of its bonds. The middle pedestal stood empty. The chains that had held the Tome of Power lay scattered on the floor around the base.

"Why are they chained?" Damien asked.

The Mage rolled his eyes and motioned to Damien to approach book closest to him. He took two steps toward the pedestal, and the book began to shake, gently at first, and then with more enthusiasm the closer he got. "I wouldn't go much further Detective," the Mage warned.

Damien stopped three feet away from the book. He watched, stunned, as flames burst from the pages toward him. The flames came within inches of his black duster. The book fought against its chains, and the darts of fire became longer and longer. A wave of heat emanated from the book and Damien took a hasty step back.

He'd hate to be flame broiled, although James would get a laugh out of it.

"What's it trying to do, kill me?" Damien asked.

Master Roberts shook his head. "No, it's trying to possess you. If you came within range, it would subvert your will and override your body, setting itself free."

Alarm washed through him. At one point, during Elite training, he'd been subjected to another's will. That training exercise had been brutal. He'd almost killed James, before he'd gotten control of his body. To be possessed like a puppet horrified him, and he'd developed the mental fortitude to resist further attempts. He had a bad feeling all of these books could easily overcome that mental training.

He turned to the middle pedestal and then looked back to Master Roberts. "So you're telling me the Book of Power possessed someone, and that's how it managed to escape?"

The Mage nodded. "Yes. The thief is out there and the Tome is doing what it does best, granting him access to some of the most dangerous spells in existence. Be very careful, Detective, it will try to posses anyone who comes in close contact with it."

Damien ran a hand through his hair. "What protections are used for someone who wants to look at it?"

"No one has ever wanted to look at it, so no protections have been necessary."

Damien looked at the Mage in disbelief. "No one has ever wanted to look at any of these?"

"That's not what I said, Detective. No one has ever petitioned to see the Book of Power. These others have all been looked at, at one time or another. The protections for each book are very different depending on which book you want to look at. For example, the Mage looking at the Book of Fire would need to be in a magical flame-resistant suit, and have the appropriate mind control blocking spells in place."

Damien nodded his understanding. Another problem occurred to him.

"How do we get the book back, without having that person possessed?" he mused aloud.

Master Roberts shrugged. "I don't know Detective. I think he would have to be unpossessable, or a creation of power."

"Is there anything else that you can tell me?" Damien did not look forward to sharing this info with Captain Jor'dan.

"I have a couple of very powerful medallions that may help, but I can't guarantee they would completely block the Tome's influence. I have them in my office, if you're ready?"

Damien took one last look around the room, but couldn't think of anything else he wanted to see.

"How many keys or people have access to this room?"

"I have the only key. The one entrance to this room is through the fireplace in my office, which is locked anytime I'm not in it."

They left the room the same way they entered it, with extreme care.

"Where were you when the book was stolen?" Damien asked, following Master Roberts down the stairs.

"I was out of town on business at a conference in Seattle."

"Did you leave the key with anyone?"

"No, I always keep it on my person. It is too dangerous to be left lying around, where just anyone can get a hold of it."

Damien thought about that. "What would happen if someone needed to access one of the Tomes while you were away?"

Master Roberts stopped and turned, giving him a look of disbelief. "Detective. To gain access to the Tomes is not easily done. There are procedures and steps that take anywhere from months to years before receiving final approval."

"What are those steps?" Damien asked as they continued their descent.

"First, the petitioner would have to submit multiple copies of a thorough application to the Library and the Council. Then he has to give references of a minimum of two higher placed members of the Council not of his race. And it gets more complicated from there."

"I see. I got in today…?"

The Mage turned to frown at him. "You were only allowed to view the room, Detective. Had you wished to open any of the Tomes, or study the spells, you would have had to go through the process."

Damien nodded, filing the information away.

"If someone wanted to unlock the room, does it take the key, or does a specific person have to wield it?"

"I'm not sure I understand the question." Master Roberts admitted.

"If you gave me the key, could I enter on my own?"

The Mage shook his head. "It's not that easy. The person with the key has to know the correct words and be a Mage. As a Vampire, you can't get in unless accompanied by a Mage."

"Does it have to be a Mage or can any magic user enter? Would an Elf or Dragon be able to enter the room without a Mage?"

Master Roberts stopped mid-step. "I-I'm not sure. It has always been assumed that only Mages may enter the room. But I suppose if the magical level of the Elf or Dragon was sufficient, they might be able to enter. If they knew the words of the spell."

"Where is the spell located?"

"In the private memoirs of the Lern Mages. I read them when I assumed the office of Head Librarian."

"Who else has access to these memoirs?" *Would these stairs never end?* Damien was sure they'd walked down many more steps than they walked up.

"I think they might be down in the Level Two Library."

"What are the levels, and what is the security like for each level?

214

"This tower is Level One. It has the highest security, and most difficult and convoluted protection spells. Level Two has slightly less security and the access is open to the top two council members from each Race. Level Three is available to any members of the consular organization. Level Four is open to any of the members of any race, and Level Five is open to everyone including humans. The Public Library system is Level Five."

And finally they were back at the landing. The Mage fiddled with a lever and the fireplace swung out. Damien ducked through the opening in time to see the main door close.

Master Roberts frowned. Damien opened the door and looked out into the hallway. Empty, and all the doors were closed.

He closed the door and went back to the desk where the Mage was rummaging in a desk drawer.

"Hold on a moment." He rummaged some more and brought out a small notebook. He flipped it open to a book marked page, and withdrew a wand from the cup of pens and pencils on his desk, then began to mumble and wave the wand through the air..

Damien wondered if he ever grabbed the wand by mistake and tried to sharpen it in a pencil sharpener.

The Mage brought the wand down in a sharp movement as he uttered the final word. A green glow came from behind one of the books on the fireplace side of the room. The Mage pulled out a book and behind it was a small figurine. The Mage brought it to his desk and set it in the middle of the blotter. He took a large bell jar and set it over the figurine. Once it was secured, he muttered again and a blue glow appeared to surround the figurine within the bell jar.

"Now we can chat." The Mage looked at the figurine. "Interesting that you are investigating the theft and that," he pointed at the small metallic figure, "appears today."

Damien nodded. "What is it?"

"A magical listening device."

"Can you trace who left it?"

Master Roberts frowned at it and shook his head. "No. It's a standard item sold in many magical item shops. The Mage's personal signature is not present, as the activation key is set up during production."

"An interesting puzzle then."

"Indeed."

"Do you have a record of those who entered Level One?"

"Unfortunately there isn't a record, although after this fiasco, you can be sure we'll be creating one."

The Mage got up and went to the book wall opposite the fireplace. He pulled out a couple of books and removed the medallions that were stuck in the secret compartments hidden within.

He handed them over to Damien. "I would suggest you hurry. The Tome is needed for the stabilization spell to be performed at the height of Festival. And the longer the book is out in public, the worse its possession will be."

Master Roberts paused for a moment. "There is one piece of good news though. Most Mages can do one or two of the spells in the book. They don't have enough personal power to activate the higher level spells."

"So why the concern?" Damien was curious. On the one hand, the theft of the Tome was serious business. On the other, it didn't sound like anyone could use the book, so why bother stealing it?

Master Roberts shook his head. "It's not the quantity of the spells that can be cast that I'm worried about. It's what some of the lower power spells can do."

"Like what?"

"One of the spells in that book allows the practitioner to summon demons."

Demon… female demon… Succubus.

"Or perhaps summon a Succubus?"

Master Roberts nodded. "Yes."

Shit. Damn. Fuck.

"I think she's already been summoned."

"What do you mean?"

"The healers have diagnosed at least three cases of magical energy drain."

Master Roberts paled. "Oh this is bad. Very bad."

"Yeah. We know."

The Mage shook his head. "You don't understand the extent of the danger."

"Explain."

"The Succubus is being used to drain magical energy, which can then be stored and used to power higher, more dangerous spells."

"Fuck."

"I completely agree with that sentiment."

Damien thanked Master Roberts for his time and headed for the door.

"One last thing Detective," he called out.

Damien turned back. "Yes?"

"With enough power, it can be used to destroy Shadow Earth."

Damien blanched. *Fuck.* Just what they needed with the Festival of Lern heating up.

A thought crossed his mind.

"Is it possible that something would happen coinciding with the end of the Festival?"

The Mage nodded. "Yes. With the amount of energy generated? That's a given."

Shit. Damn. Fuck.

"Thank you for your time, Head Grand Librarian."

Master Roberts came forward and offered his hand in a polite handshake. "Good luck."

"Thanks." Damien shook his hand and left the room, tucking the two amulets into an interior pocket.

After making arrangements to speak with those working the next evening, he got to the street level door. A young Mage came running up behind him.

"Detective, Detective, wait a moment!"

Damien stopped and turned back to the man.

"Yes?" he asked as the Mage stopped and tried to catch his breath after running.

"The Head Librarian… forgot… to tell you… Master... Clint… Douglas… may be able to… help with the investigation."

Clint Douglas… That name sounded familiar. Now where did he know that name from? Nothing was coming to mind, so he'd deal with it later.

"Do you know where I can find him?" The Mage was still trying to catch his breath. He nodded and thrust a folded paper at Damien, with directions to a home a few blocks away.

Chapter 14

James called Randall on his cell phone, wondering where the Elite Mage was. He was late for their appointment.

It took multiple tries, but James finally reached him. "Where are you? We're supposed to be looking into suspicious activity on Folsom."

"I'm finishing up another assignment. I'll meet you there in a half hour." Dial tone reached James' ear as he was about to respond.

James sighed and shook his head. There was nothing he could do except head toward the rendezvous point and perhaps snoop around.

A few moments later, he parked a couple of blocks away in Shadow. As he moved closer to the building, dread pooled in the pit of his stomach. He wiped clammy palms on his jeans and it felt as if his heart was going to beat out of his chest. The closer he got, the greater the feeling of terror. Maybe it would be better in Real?

Making sure he wasn't seen, he popped into Real Earth.

On a rooftop, hidden from view, Cyn cursed as James appeared. Could it be coincidence that he showed up now, after reports of rogue Vampire activity? She didn't think so. Cyn didn't know where the hybrids were coming from, but she'd narrowed it down to a few blocks in this general vicinity. One thing she knew for certain, James was going be in a world of trouble if she didn't figure out something and fast.

What the hell was he up to? Rappelling down to the street faster than was considered safe, she was thankful for the noise of traffic which covered the sounds of her descent. On the ground she unclipped the rope from her belt and gave it a sharp tug, which sent the line careening up the side of the building.

Cyn walked to the corner and, with her back against the wall, glanced around to make sure James remained oblivious to her presence.

Careful to stick to the shadows and recessed doorways, she followed him into the heart of her neighborhood. He stopped across the street from Hans' warehouse and looked around.

Shit! If Hans caught him, James was dead.

Hans had let it be known throughout the area that he wanted an Elite to practice his latest technique on. As of yet, no one had wanted to take the risk of pissing off the Elite. However if one of them happened to walk into his trap, they were fair game.

And it looked like James was walking straight to his death.

Cyn was too young to be able to influence older Vampires, a lack which she cursed now. There was a slight chance he'd walk past; that he would heed the aversion field around the property to discourage Paranormal visitors, even in Real Earth.

But no, the idiot had to cross the street and walk right up to Hans' front door. *Son of a bitch! What the hell is he doing?*

Like Damien, if anything happened to James, the Elite would descend upon the area like an avenging mob and disrupt the activities and lives of those who resided here. She and Hans kept the area safe without infringing on any private enterprises. She had to prevent anything from happening to James in order to save her neighborhood. Right, save the sexy detective, save the neighborhood. Why, it was her patriotic duty, right? Yep.

Movement out of the corner of her eye had her turning. A dark figure emerged from the shadows. Hans came to investigate what had set off the alarms, and by the gleam in his eye, she could tell he was pleased by the Elite before him. Dressed in dark leather pants and black pirate shirt, Hans looked like a buccaneer. His white hair was tied back at the base of his neck. Damn, James interrupted a session. Time to stop this before James got into trouble.

Making no effort to hide her approach, Cyn walked up to both men as they sized each other up. She stepped close to James and put her arm through his. He glared down at her and she ignored him, focusing on the immediate threat to him.

"Hello Hans, what's up?"

Hans turned and looked at her, the flame in his eyes surged as he recognized her.

"Good evening, Cyn. I'm making the acquaintance of your friend here. I was about to invite him in for a cup of tea and some conversation." She felt the hard flesh beneath her arm jerk at Hans' scratchy voice.

Cyn concentrated at James as hard as she could, thankful for the blood exchange that allowed them telepathic speech. *"Do not answer him, do not interfere. You're in extreme danger."*

James removed her hand from his arm and pushed her behind him.

His voice in her head ordered, *"I'm fine. Stay out of this. It's none of your concern."*

She smiled, ignoring James. "Hans, I really don't think that's a good idea. James here was supposed to meet me later for coffee, and you know how much I hate to be stood up."

"He is important to you?" Hans' tone was deceptively light. *At the moment?* Hell no, but she knew better than to say that.

"In this instance, yes." Cyn stressed her next statement. "We don't want to invite trouble."

Hans nodded his head once, and turned his gaze to James. "Very well. Perhaps some other time."

James chose that time to speak. "Cyn, introduce me to your friend." She felt his compulsion in her head. "*Now*."

Damned, condescending son of a bitch. Her teeth clenched as she struggled not to let her temper get the best of her. Hands fisted at her side, she took a deep breath. *One... two... three... This counting shit doesn't work. Five... ten.*

She felt another mental push. *Damn it.* "Elite James Kirk, allow me to introduce Hans Drebin."

James glanced between the two of them. Now what the hell is he up to?

"Hans Drebin?" She heard the curiosity in James tone.

Hans bowed his head. "At your service."

"The same Hans Drebin who has been missing since the late nineteenth century?"

Cyn saw Han's eyes narrow. Uh-oh, time to get out of here, before Hans changed his mind. She wasn't worried for her safety; they were family. James on the other hand, was in trouble. She could see it in Hans' expression.

She tugged on James' arm. Nothing. He wouldn't budge.

James shrugged her off, reached into his pocket and fiddled with something.

She concentrated at him again. "*We need to go James. Now.*"

James responded in her mind. "*This is part of my investigation. Stay out of it.*"

Son of a bitch! Here she was trying to save his ass, and he treats her like that?

Hans didn't respond. He stood against the wall of his building, an unmoving statue.

Oh shit, this is gonna get messy. Cyn recognized the intense concentration on Hans' face.

"I am not the one you are looking for." Hans' voice lowered even further, indicating the attempted use of mind control.

Cyn could tell that the psychic suggestion failed by James reaction. He stiffened and glared at Hans. "Do *not* try that again."

"I apologize. I've never attempted coercion on such a healthy specimen before. How very interesting."

Cyn moved a few steps away from James. *Men, can't live with them, can't stake them out in the sun.*

The ringing of a phone broke the mounting tension. James excused himself and answered it. "Yes Randall, I'm here. Yes… See you soon."

He tapped his phone, looked up, and smiled. "Hans Drebin, you are under arrest for the forbidden practice of Voglio."

Cyn moved further away from James. *"Don't do this James."*

He turned and glared at her. *"How many times do I have to tell you to stay out of it? I'll deal with you later."*

"He's sent for reinforcements." Hans' voice echoed in her head. *"Hide now."*

Cyn nodded stood next to the wall.

"What about you?" she spoke back to Hans.

"Don't worry. I'll be fine. Your boyfriend needs to work on his social skills."

She sighed. *"He's not my boyfriend."*

Hans stiffened, turned his head, eyes flaring. *"Hurry. They're coming."*

Cyn concentrated and blended with the rough stone façade of the wall behind her, thankful to her sires for teaching her how to hide her physical body with her mind.

A frown crossed James' face as he looked around for her. "Damn it, Cyn, where are you?"

Hans smiled. "I believe she's escaped your trap, Detective."

Four Elite emerged from the foggy darkness, followed by a large black van. One of the Elite pulled Hans' arms around behind him and placed restraints onto his wrists. They led him to the back of the van, and pushed him inside.

James spoke to a couple of the Elite.

She saw a hand flash in the mouth of the alley next to Hans' building. Keeping her back to the wall, she inched toward the figure.

She reached the corner and stepped into the alley, letting her glamour fade.

"Yes, Carlos?" Her voice was whisper soft.

An answering whisper reached her from the shadows behind the dumpster. "Are you just gonna let them take Hans away?"

"I can't do anything about it now. Not without a blood bath. I'll get Hans back, I promise. Tell everyone to lay low. This area will be under a microscope for a few days. The last thing we need is to have the Elite underfoot. Got it?"

"Yeah. I'll spread the word. We're… worried."

She bowed her head. "I know. I'll do what I can. Give me three days. If you don't hear anything from me by then, assume the worst."

"Be careful, Cyn. The Elite… he wants you."

She snorted, a small cynical sound. "I know, but he won't get me." Not after this little stunt.

Cyn looked back and watched the van drive off. James looked around as if searching. "Go, Carlos." The soft sound of cloth was her only indication of movement.

James' voice rang in her head.

"Damn it Cyn, where the hell are you?"

Cyn remained silent, pulling the shadows around her and blending into her surroundings.

A hard pulse of command. *"Cyn, answer me, damn it."*

Right, as if. Cyn made sure to keep that thought tightly locked behind the walls in her mind.

She could see him look around and clench his fists as anger filtered through his mind voice. *"Damn it. Where are you?"*

Cyn felt his frustration mount as he searched the area. She crouched down behind the dumpster and stilled.

After a few minutes, she watched James run a hand through his hair in frustration, before cursing and popping from sight.

If James was in Shadow, Cyn would stay in Real, the better to avoid Elite entanglements. The Elite offices were a bit of a trek from here, but she'd walked further distances. On the way, she tried to plan.

Cyn knew the holding cells under the building housed criminals until trial, but how long would Hans be there? How long did it take to set up a trial? Crap, she had no idea. Would they let her in to see him? It depended on the level of security surrounding him. Well it wouldn't hurt to ask. Mind made up she looked both ways and took a step into the street.

A hand on her arm jerked her around.

Fuck! Who the hell...?

She looked up to see a very angry James.

"What the hell are you doing?" She didn't even try to keep the shock out of her tone.

"Conducting my investigation. That's all you need to know." He glared at her. "And just what the hell are you doing here, and how do you know someone as dangerous as Drebin?"

As if she was going to respond to that question! She let her anger and frustration show in her face, jerked her arm out of his hold, and turned to walk away.

His hand on her wrist stopped her, as he pulled her around to face him.

"How dare you? Come into the most dangerous neighborhood in San Francisco and arrest people willy nilly?" Her free hand swung up to slap him. He grabbed her other wrist in a punishing grip and squeezed.

"It's my job. What the hell were you doing down there?"

"Nothing that concerns you, Detective," Cyn sneered.

She heard the sound of teeth grinding at her sharp reply. A vein at his temple twitched. An indication of his anger perhaps? *The big bad Elite is upset. Poor baby.*

225

"How do you know Hans Drebin?"

She twisted her wrists inward, freeing them from his grip. A look of surprise crossed his face, as if he hadn't been expecting that move. She stepped back out of reach, rubbing the sting from her wrists.

He huffed out a sigh, and the anger drained from his expression.

"You didn't answer me."

She smiled without warmth. "That should've been your first clue, Detective. I don't intend to."

He grinned back at her, but the smile didn't reach his eyes. "Then you leave me no choice, but to do this the hard way."

Before she knew what was happening, she was over his shoulder, her legs down his chest, her head draped down his back. She tried to kick, but he tightened his arm around her legs, stilling her. She pounded his back with her fists, but they merely bounced off.

"What the hell are you doing?" she demanded.

"Taking you into custody for aiding and abetting a criminal." He paused for a beat then continued. "Unless you want to tell me what I want to know?"

She remained silent, fuming.

"I thought not." He tightened his hold, walked across the street and entered Elite headquarters.

James carried her through the reception area, where many of his fellow Elite were gathered. They turned when he entered, and he knew the incessant teasing was about to begin. Questions flew like arrows and he ignored them all. Even Cyn went still as she heard the comments and questions.

"Going caveman on us, James?"

"Is that how you pick up your dates?"

"Hey buddy, try wining and dining them first before you carry them off to bed."

Laughter filled the room at the last comment. James continued past the desk and over to the wall of elevators. Thankfully one of the doors was open. He entered, and pushed the button for the holding area.

Cyn's stillness irritated him for some reason.

"If I put you down, will you try to escape?"

"Isn't that the duty of a prisoner?"

"Just answer the damned question. Will you try to escape?"

He felt her sigh and tried very hard not to stare at her shapely ass, clad in skin tight black leather. He could see her reflection in the mirrors on the doors, normally used to watch perps. His gaze traced her curves, molded by leather. She reminded him of a villainess from an old TV show, but Julie and Eartha had nothing on his Cyn.

How he'd love to make her purr.

When she didn't answer, he stroked her leather clad calf beneath his hand. Her outraged squawk made him grin.

"Stop that!"

"Why?"

He could hear the aggravation and false sincerity in her voice as she responded. "I'll sue you for use of excessive force and sexual harassment."

"I'd be happy to harass you anytime you want."

She stiffened once again. The elevator doors opened and he walked down the corridor to an interrogation room.

"I don't think so, Detective. I've got more important things to do. Like wash my hair."

He stopped in front of the door and put her on her feet, careful to keep vulnerable parts of his body protected.

James couldn't recall a time when bantering with a woman had been so much fun.

He led her into the interrogation room, unsurprised when she moved to the far side of the room and glared at him.

When had she gotten to him? One look at her mulish expression and he was captivated. He'd enjoyed her shy side. But her stubborn aggressive side? Drew him like a moth to flame. He wanted to tease her until she lost control and freed all the pent up passion he could sense within her. She'd be hot and fierce in bed, and he couldn't wait.

But first things first.

He needed to find out how deeply she was involved with Hans' activities. She might be a criminal, and even if she wasn't, she certainly knew them.

She crossed her arms in front of her chest and leaned against the wall in a gesture of controlled nonchalance. He waved toward the table and chairs for her to sit down. She snorted and stayed where she was. He left the room, making sure to lock the door behind him, and flagged down a passing clerk.

"Please tell Captain Jor'dan I have a suspect for questioning."

The clerk nodded and hurried off. James waited outside the door, keeping his ear cocked for sounds from inside. Silence. A twinge of guilt hit him. He should have offered her coffee or something, but knowing his luck she'd have thrown it in his face. He couldn't help but smile at her fiery spirit. Get her mad enough, and she'd revealed her true character.

James leaned against the wall, trying to get his mind off of Cyn's delectable body and into questioning mode, when Captain Jor'dan approached.

"What have you got?"

James gave his boss a summary of events.

"And how do you know the suspect?" Jor'dan gave him a piercing look.

"She is the best friend of Damien's creature, as well as a known acquaintance of Hans Drebin. We've been trying to get to know Cyn and Deidre to learn their secrets."

The Captain nodded and opened the door to the room, leaving James to follow.

228

James closed the door behind him, noticing that Cyn had yet to move from her position.

Captain Jor'dan sat at the desk and motioned for her to have a seat.

James remained standing, sure she'd try his temper.

"Please, sit down. I assure you it's much more comfortable than holding up the wall." Jor'dan's voice was gentle and soothing.

Cyn shook her head. "Thank you, but no. I'd rather stand."

"If you insist. My name is Captain Jor'dan and I believe you already know Detective James Kirk."

She nodded her head once, never taking her eyes off Captain Jor'dan.

"I need to ask a few questions…"

She held up her hand. "Am I being arrested?"

James frowned. "Not at this time."

"Then why am I being held against my will?"

A muscle in James' jaw began to twitch in time with his pulse. "You are a person of interest. If you don't answer the questions to our satisfaction, you'll be arrested."

"On what charge?" She gave him a smirking smile that pushed his buttons.

"Aiding and abetting a criminal, and willful obstruction of the law to start with…"

Captain Jor'dan turned toward him giving him a look, which stopped the words in his throat. Jor'dan turned back to Cyn.

"I apologize for that. Right now we are simply gathering information."

She took a deep breath and bent her knee, resting her foot flush against the wall.

James moved along the wall so he could observe the reaction of his boss when Cyn got insolent.

Jor'dan sent him an amused look and started questioning her.

"How do you know Hans Drebin?"

Cyn shrugged. "He's a friend."

"How long have you known him?"

She frowned. "I'm not sure. It seems like forever."

"Are you aware of his activities?"

James opened his big mouth. "But she couldn't possibly know about his activities."

Cyn lowered her eyes. *Shit,* he gave her an out.

"Is that true?" Jor'dan sent him a look, and James wanted to curse.

A small smile graced her luscious lips, and she parroted, "Yes. I don't know what he does."

Bullshit. She was lying, and they all knew it, but he wouldn't call her on it… yet.

Captain Jor'dan cleared his throat. "Do the names Earl, Klaus, and Roger mean anything to you?"

A puzzled frown crossed her face and James knew that she spoke the truth when she answered, "No."

Jor'dan was about to ask another question when his cell phone beeped. "Excuse me."

James watched Cyn as she watched the Captain. He couldn't read her expression, but the intense way she watched him, meant she knew much more than she was letting on.

A curse from Jor'dan. The Captain gave him a look filled with sympathy, one that left a bad taste in his mouth.

"What is it?"

"Regina says you need to take her and go rescue Damien. He's in trouble."

James shook his head. "She's a person of interest. I can't have her trying to escape while helping Damien."

James' phone beeped and he read the text. "Either Cyn goes or Damien's creature dies, and the world as we know it will end. You decide."

Fuck.

Captain Jor'dan spoke. "By your expression I'm assuming you got the same message?"

230

"Yeah." James balked. He didn't want to do this.

"Remember what happened the last time you ignored the Oracle?" The Captain asked.

Fuck. Damien had almost died as Sienna tried out her own version of open heart surgery.

"Fine. I'll take her. I do this under protest though."

"Noted. Good luck."

James motioned for Cyn to lead the way out of the room. Before he could close the door, Jor'dan cleared his throat. "When you're done, bring her back to my office."

"Yes sir." James growled and slammed the door.

Chapter 15

Damien walked along the sidewalk, looking for the address. Why hadn't Master Roberts told him about Douglas before they'd parted? Something didn't feel right, but damned if he could figure out what it was.

The feeling of being watched resumed as soon as he left the Library grounds.. He stopped and looked around. The fog had rolled in off the ocean creating an eerie effect that impaired his night vision. Damien let his senses fan out over the immediate area.

Nothing. He couldn't sense anyone around him. The watcher was either shielded, or outside of the immediate area.

Damien took a few steps toward the address that had been given to him, and the sensation diminished.

The hair at the back of his neck prickled in warning. Something was wrong. He didn't know, but he'd give James a heads up, just in case.

Damien sent a brief text to James giving his location and the tip he'd been given. He slipped the phone into his pocket and continued walking toward the address.

He approached the fancy house that had seen better times. While it wasn't falling apart, the air of neglect was evident. A few of the shingles were hanging haphazardly from the roof and the yard, was overgrown and choked with weeds.

Damien's coat caught on the brambles as he walked down a paving stone path through the jungle that had started as a neatly manicured yard.

He stopped a few feet from the house, when his senses flared. *Danger. Threat.*

The door opened and a dark, swirling cloud enveloped him in black oily smoke. Incense filled his nose and his eyes burned at the potency of the scent. His felt off balance, dizzy.

The smell invaded his brain and made it hard to concentrate. His feet left the ground and for a moment he wondered if he was hallucinating.

A shadowy figure appeared before him. Damien squinted, trying to see through the roiling clouds of black. The cloud thinned enough to make out the man's face before the miasma pressed closed, coating his entire body with oily black residue.

He tried to move, tried to wipe the oily coating away, but his arms remained limp at his sides.

Shit. Damn. Fuck.

Panic took hold, pumping adrenaline into his system. He struggled trying to get his body to respond. Since he was physically trapped, he tried to use is psychic abilities, but his concentration shattered like glass hitting a stone wall.

His body jerked and he floated forward, through the open door as if being pulled by a rope.

Squinting, he saw the iridescent bands of magic that held his arms to his body. A thin strand connected him to the mysterious Mage in front of him.

The door slammed closed behind him, startling him. A voice echoed through the foyer.

"Welcome, Detective Alexander. I've been dying to meet you in person." Laughter echoed through the room sounding insane and maniacal.

"Who're you?" Damien's voice slurred as he struggled to get his brain to function. The harder he tried to concentrate, the more his thoughts scattered like leaves on the wind.

The Mage in front of him appeared to waver in and out of focus. He couldn't clear his vision enough to identify the man.

"Allow me to introduce myself. My name is Clint Douglas." The Mage bowed at the waist and straightened with a grin. "Don't you recognize me?"

Damien tried to shake his head and couldn't. Now that Clint Douglas had introduced himself, there was something familiar about the Mage, but he couldn't put his finger on what it was.

"Come, come, surely I'm not that forgettable?"

Damien tried to speak but his words still slurred. "Don' know. Can' think of nothin'."

Clint frowned. "I may have overdone it. We'll need to rectify that. Come along."

Clint snapped his fingers and motioned for Damien to follow. The sensation of floating like a boat on the ocean gave Damien a feeling he'd not felt in a long time. His stomach churned and he swallowed bile.

Nausea. Great.

He bobbed up and down, sure he'd be sick at any moment, but unable to articulate his condition.

Damien swallowed again trying to keep the contents of his stomach from making a reappearance. He took deep breaths, which helped. He was able to focus on his surroundings.

Clint led the way through the house, past doors and rooms, and into a portrait gallery. The Mage walked to the end of the gallery and stopped, gazing at the painting on the wall. He sighed then stood beside it with his arms crossed over his chest.

"Recognize her?"

Damien studied the portrait.

A beautiful woman stared back at him. Raven locks framed a pale oval face with ice blue eyes. Her lips held a small smile. His heart beat faster, and he struggled to get his mind working. He knew who she was, yet the name eluded him. "She's pretty."

"Yes, she was."

"Who's she?" Damien winced at his continued slurring.

Clint Douglas clicked his tongue and shook his head. "My, how soon you forget."

Damien tried to defend himself. "Know her, jus' don' 'member her name."

"Ah. Her name is Sienna. My daughter." Clint paused for a moment. "The woman you killed."

Damien felt his forehead crease as he frowned. "I kill'd her? I don' kill females."

The Mage sighed and snapped his fingers.

A small flash of light blinded him for a moment. He blinked and focused on the item… a book… appeared out of thin air.

It looked important, like something he needed to know.

Where had he seen it before? He tried to shake his head, to get his thoughts into some semblance of order, but he couldn't move, couldn't think.

The book was bound in black leather with intricate scrollwork that seemed to move and change as he focused on it. The book popped opened, and the pages flipped by an unseen hand.

"Here we go," Clint muttered under his breath. Words seared through Damien's brain. They were gone before he knew what was happening, although his thought processes cleared. He was now able to recognize the portrait.

Shit. Damn. Fuck.

Sienna. His ex-fiancé. Beautiful, deadly Sienna. The bitch who'd attempted to kill him during day sleep. The scar she'd left on his chest as she stabbed him in the heart, ached with remembered pain. Betrayal left a bitter taste in his mouth. She, along with her brother Ronald, were tried, convicted and executed for conspiring to overthrow the Elite.

At the trial Clint Douglas vowed revenge.

And now Damien was his prisoner.

"Fuck." Damien wasn't able to keep the sentiment to himself.

"An adequate response." Clint sneered.

His face distorted into a mask of rage as he stepped forward.

"You'll pay for what you did to my family, Detective." He gestured and a bolt of energy surged from his fingers to Damien.

Pain.

Damien's body felt like it was being bathed in acid, overwhelming his senses, rendering him deaf, blind, and mute as agony tore through him.

The pain stopped as if a switch had been thrown.

Clint stepped back and raise a shaky hand to his forehead. The Mage took a couple of deep breaths, and the shaking stopped.

Mental note, don't piss off Clint, but it was too late. The Mage blamed Damien for his daughter's death.

Clint gestured to the book, who appeared eager to please. Pages began to turn as Clint stroked the leather with one hand.

The book... the tome... the stolen Tome of Power.

Shit. Damn. Fuck.

Tonight was going from bad to worse. On the positive side, he'd found the Book. On the negative side, it was in the hands of a Mage wanting revenge.

"How did you manage to steal the Tome?" Damien was thankful no hint of the slur remained.

Clint's cold smiled sent a chill down Damien's spine. "Very carefully. Shall we go?"

The Mage turned and walked away. The magic tether that held Damien, pulled him after Clint, and he bobbed along like a boat on the water tied with a string. They passed through the hallways and rooms before coming to a door.

Mr. Douglas opened the door and led Damien down the steps beyond.

Cold. It was the first thing Damien noticed as they descended stairs that seemed to go on forever. His senses told him they were

236

deep beneath the earth, and the chill became more pronounced the deeper they went.

The smell of damp earth permeated the stairs along with the metallic scent of old blood.

Shit. Damn. Fuck.

I've got to get out of here. His mind whirled. *Okay I can deal with this, right? Right.*

First, things first. I need a plan. Damien tried to reach out with his mind. A bright lance of pain shot from the base of his skull and ended behind his eyes. He groaned.

They came to the bottom of the stairs and Clint stopped on the last step and turned back to look at him. The smile he wore was filled with fake sympathy.

"I'm sorry, Detective. I forgot to warn you. The house is warded to block your psychic abilities. But please, feel free to try again." An eerie laugh echoed off the stone walls.

The Mage walked down the corridor stretching in front of them. Sconces on the walls lit at their approach, and winked off after they had passed. Like the lights in the Library.

Clint stopped in front of a heavy wooden door. The book continued to float at his side as he removed a heavy iron key from his robes.

The key glowed blue as it neared the lock. The key and lock had been spelled together. If a different key had been used, an alarm would sound somewhere in the house alerting the owners to unauthorized entry. Most Paranormals used this kind of security in their homes. Clint turned the key in the lock and Damien heard a click as the door swung open.

He entered the room, and Damien floated in behind him.

The Mage left him floating near the door as he moved further into the room.

A flare of light steadied as the Mage set a candle in the sconce by the wall. He continued around the room, lighting the candles.

Through the flickering light, Damien could see a large stone altar in the center of the room and nothing else. The ceiling, walls, and floor were covered in flagstone, except the one part of the floor in front of the altar. A rusty metal grate and the dark streaks that led to it let Damien know this room was used for dark purposes.

Clint motioned with his hand, and Damien floated toward the altar.

Was he going to be sacrificed? Was that Clint's plan? Damien tried to think of the alternatives, but nothing else made sense.

Another gesture and Damien was tilted onto on his back and lowered to the marble table top. He shivered where his body touched the icy stone. His own body was not much warmer, and the stone leached his meager body heat, from him.

Damien saw the Mage walk around the altar looking him over. Clint shook his head and clicked his tongue against his teeth.

"This will never do." He turned to the book and flipped a few pages and muttered the spell he found there.

Damien felt his clothes loosen, before they disintegrated off his body. "What the hell are you doing?" he demanded, his mind thinking of the sick perversions Clint had in store for him.

The Mage grinned. "Preparing you for my revenge. You see, the Succubus likes her men naked."

Succubus? *Shit. Damn. Fuck.*

Captain Jor'dan had warned them. It looked like he was about to meet her in the flesh.

"How is the Succubus draining me going to help your plan?"

The Mage laughed. "Your energy will go toward my final spell."

"Did you kill Mage Earl?"

Clint tilted his head. "Hmm. He was her first meal. A test draining if you will, to make sure the Succubus performed as expected."

How much energy had the Mage drained? Earl, Klaus and Roger, and how many others? There had to be a way to stop Clint. But how?

Healers had verified that there wasn't a way to block the sexual pull of the female demon. Mind shields didn't work, nor did they recommend the use of mind control, uncertain of the mental processes of an unknown demon.

A low whisper signaled the Mage was using another spell. Clint was using more energy than a Mage of his level. He was using spells left and right and didn't seem to be bothered by the normal after spell fatigue.

The bands of magic that held Damien in place, thinned and separated into smoky ropes that wrapped themselves around his wrists and ankles.

At the last word of the spell, the Mage clapped his hands together and the bands pulled Damien's limbs apart. He was now spread-eagle on the marble surface.

"Comfortable?" the Mage's question was ridiculous.

"Why aren't you tired? Aren't these spells above your level?"

Clint grinned. "How perceptive of you, Detective. I have a magical battery so I don't drain my personal reserves." He opened the door and stepped into the hallway, waiting for the Succubus to arrive.

What to do? First thing was to get off the altar. Damien tried to move. Nothing. He was magically bound to the stone and if he squinted, he was able to see the red bands holding onto his ankles and wrists.

Shit. Damn. Fuck.

Since he was going to be drained, he'd imagine Deidre. He closed his eyes and let her image soothe him. Her soft skin, her wicked smile. The way he felt when he was with her. A feeling of peace washed over him.

He could tell by the sounds at the door that the Succubus had arrived. The image in his mind was so vivid he could almost smell her scent; her unique floral fragrance.

Clint's voice was grating as he ordered. "Drain the Elite."

Damien heard a sharp intake of breath from the female. His stomach tightened.

A premonition. No. It couldn't be. Please don't let it be.

He opened his eyes and looked toward the door. He felt it then. A presence he had come to know and love.

Impossible.

Deidre. Looking as shocked as he felt.

"What the fuck are you doing here?" Damien demanded.

The Mage came within his line of sight. "You know each other?" he asked in a syrupy sweet voice. "But maybe you don't know as much about each other as you'd like. Elite Damien Alexander, I would like you to meet Succubus Deidre."

Cling turned to Deidre. "Kill him."

Deidre took two steps forward and stopped at the edge of the altar.

Damien tried to comprehend the enormity of the situation and his mind blanked and he could not process it. "Is it true? You're the Succubus?"

He could see the sheen of tears in her eyes as she nodded. "Why didn't you tell me?"

She shook her head and in a whisper explained, "I can't. I'm bound by the spell."

Deidre reached forward and touched his face. A thrill of energy shot through him. It wasn't any different from their previous interactions.

Faces floated through his mind. Earl, Klaus, and Roger. For a moment he stared at her.

"Did you kill them? My friends? Klaus, Roger, and Earl?"

She sighed and stepped back. "I drained them, yes."

Imagining her having sex with his friends then killing them was the last straw.

"How could you?" Within his chest, Damien felt his heart shatter into a million pieces. He'd thought what they had was special, but apparently he was just another fuck. He closed his eyes against the pain; to avoid looking at her.

The bitter taste of betrayal coated Damien's tongue. He should have known better. He should have stopped the attraction. Should have demanded the answers she'd never given. He'd give her no satisfaction though. He'd fight to the very end.

His voice sounded as broken as he felt. "Get away from me, bitch."

Deidre stepped away from the table. Hurt searing through her at Damien's rejection. She wanted to explain, but knew better. Explanations never got her anywhere. She turned back to her summoner.

"I won't do it."

Sir turned from the door to stare at her.

"What did you say?" His voice was low, menacing.

She took a deep breath. "I won't do it. I won't drain him."

Deidre cared too much for the Vampire. She couldn't allow him to be killed like the others, not if she could help it. Damien had shown her that sex wasn't merely a function of the body, but a sharing of the heart. And she treasured that knowledge more than she thought possible.

Sir's eyes narrowed. "You don't have a choice. Drain him. Now."

She shook her head and glanced at Damien. The emotions she read in his gaze stopped the breath in her lungs.

"I don't need your help, bitch." Damien's anger felt like a dagger thrust into her chest. She looked down, unable to bear the condemnation in his tone.

I thought it would be different with him. Serves me right for believing. But even as Damien hurt her, she couldn't do it. Couldn't end his life. Something in her rebelled, her power retreating deep within.

Sir snapped his fingers bringing her attention back to him. The book hovered near his elbow and the pages flipped open.

"Do it. Now."

Deidre shook her head. Her body jerked toward the altar, pulled there by the summoning spell's compulsion. She clenched her teeth and fought the command of her master's order. Her teeth ground against each other as she locked every muscle fighting the need to obey. Forward movement ceased.

I did it!

The thrill of victory surged through her until a low murmuring of familiar words filled the air.

J'kala! Red mist.

Pain sliced through her feet. The mist began climbing her legs, leaving agony in its wake. Sharp daggers of sensation ripped through her legs and her body as the mist swirled upward, engulfing her in torturous misery. Somewhere close by, someone cried out, but the agony was overwhelming. Deidre couldn't help them, whoever it was.

A single tear escaped and burned down her cheek. The mist entered her mouth, seared her lungs.

Damien's rejection sapped her will to fight. She might die, but she wouldn't take him with her. For the first time, she allowed herself to succumb to the darkness that promised oblivion.

Damien saw Deidre cry out with pain as her body was enveloped in a red haze. She twitched and shook as if she were having a seizure. Part of him wanted to leap from the table and stop her pain; protect her. The other part of him was cold, logical. This was nothing more than she deserved.

He hardened his heart against her. He had a job to do, and he couldn't be crippled by the emotion tearing him apart.

She'd tricked him. Made him care. All for Mage Douglas' revenge. A niggling thought in the back of his brain pointed out that he'd not been drained when they'd been together, but it was drowned out by the knowledge that she'd fucked and killed his fellow Elite. She'd used him to get to the others, to drain them of their energy for the Mage's purpose.

He buried the hurt searing through his chest at the thought of her betrayal and turned it into anger.

She deserved what she got. How many times had she laughed at him? The pathetic Vampire falling for a Succubus.

He took refuge in an icy calm as he refused to let her and the Mage manipulate him. This was a ploy to get him to defend her. A modified "good cop, bad cop" routine. He wasn't falling for it.

Deidre fell to the floor in a heap, and Damien closed his eyes to the sight, fighting the urge to save her.

A noise jerked his eyes open again, and he turned his head toward the door, looking past the Mage yelling at the fallen Succubus. He heard it again. The faint pounding of footsteps growing louder.

"You'll not fail me, bitch," Clint yelled at the unconscious Succubus on the floor. White foam formed at the corners of Clint's mouth as he ranted at the still twitching demon. His eyes narrowed and next to him, the book's pages flipped in a flurry of speed, mirroring the Mage's anger.

The door burst open, and rescue arrived.

The Mage turned at the intrusion. One punch from James and Clint fell back against the wall, sliding down in a heap on the floor. He didn't move, knocked out cold.

Cyn rushed to Deidre as James came to release him.

James looked over Damien. "You and Deidre getting kinky on me here pal?"

Damien glared at him. "Get me out of here."

James looked over to the fallen Mage then back to Damien. "I don't see any bonds, are you sure you can't move?"

Damien squinted and could no longer see the magical bonds that held him immobile. He moved his arms and legs and sat up. The magic stopped when Mr. Douglas lost consciousness.

"Thanks for the rescue."

"Anytime." James smirked. "That's another one you owe me."

"Weren't we even by now?"

James shook his head. "Nope."

Damien jumped off the table and donned the duster James held out to him. When sufficiently covered, he walked over to the still convulsing Succubus.

Cyn looked up from her position at the female's side. "Help me!"

Damien gritted his teeth against the urge to help as a strong tremor wracked the Succubus' body. "Let her die."

"You son of a bitch! How the fuck can you say that?" Cyn demanded.

James grabbed Damien's arm. "Whoa! What the hell happened?"

Damien waved to the writhing body on the floor. "Meet Deidre. The Succubus. Who has been draining the Elite and feeding that energy to Mage Douglas, allowing him to use the spells in the Tome of Power."

"Holy Fuck!"

Cyn shook her head. "You don't understand."

"I don't need to," Damien snarled at Cyn.

Cyn looked up at him, trying to contain the convulsions, tears streaming down her face. "Why won't the spell stop? What the fuck have you done to her, you bastard?"

"I didn't do anything. Her pal, Mage Douglas, is to blame."

James held up a hand. "Wait a minute. You're saying Douglas cast this spell on her?"

When Damien nodded he continued. "Then why the hell is she still under the spell? It should have been broken when he lost consciousness."

Damien shrugged. "I don't know. I'm not a Mage."

Cyn wrestled with the writhing Succubus.

"You son of a bitch! How the fuck can you say that?" Cyn demanded.

James smiled as Cyn cursed them under her breath. "Damned arrogant Elite bastards. Think they know everything, but they haven't got a clue. How the hell am I supposed to help you, Deidre?"

Damien masked his expression as he watched the severe convulsions bow the Succubus's body off the floor.

He turned away and looked at James. "Call this in. And get me a spare set of clothes while you're at it."

James pulled out his cell and placed the call. "A team is on the way."

Damien saw Cyn on the phone, asking for help. "I can't rouse her. Shit... there she goes again... Hold on..." Cyn was knocked back on her ass as a wild swing from the Succubus's arm hit her. She sat back up and reported, "She's bleeding... green... Okay." She disconnected the call and glared up at Damien. "Fuck you, Detective."

The coppery scent of fresh blood filled the room, overriding damp smell of mildew. A rumble of hunger in his stomach reminded him he hadn't eaten anything in hours.

Shit. Damn. Fuck.

Deidre, no, the Succubus, was bleeding. Dark green fluid leaked from her ears and nose. A trace of it dribbled from the corner of her lips. He forced himself to stay where he was and not rush to her aid. The fact he wanted to, made him angry. Damien clenched his fists and ground his teeth to keep from going to her. He took a deep breath to steady himself, and looked at James. "Arrest her."

James gave him an incredulous look. "What are the charges?"

"Murder. She killed Earl, Klaus, and Roger, and she's a criminal partner to Mage Douglas." His voice and tone were bitter, something he didn't try to hide from his partner.

James face paled as he looked to the two females and back to Damien.

"Shit. Damn. Fuck."

Damien couldn't agree more. "Exactly." He turned away from the two females. "Help me search for the Tome."

James nodded and they quartered the room. "You realized this case is almost wrapped up?"

Damien turned to look at his partner. "How so?"

James explained about finding Hans, the torturer.

No trace of the book could be found. *Damn it.* The bloody thing had been here with the Mage. Unless he'd done something to make it disappear?

Damien was careful to avoid the still convulsing demon. Cyn's voice carried through the small chamber, concern and frustration evident.

From the noises in the hallway, it sounded like back-up had arrived. A group of Elite entered the room, followed by Bar'ella. Jared threw a bundle of clothes at Damien and knelt next to Cyn, adding his strength to keep the female on the floor from hurting herself or Cyn.

Damien watched James kneel down next to Cyn and add his strength to the others. He turned away and supervised as the others lifted Clint and prepped him for transport.

"Take him back to the Office. He's under arrest for theft of the Forbidden Tome of Power, three counts of murder, attempted murder, illegal use of magic, and a few more charges I'm unable to think of at the moment."

He turned back to watch the healer deal with the Succubus.

Bar'ella reached into her bag gave Cyn a cloth. The female Vamp tried to mop up the blood, but it appeared faster that she could clean it. Cyn gave a helpless look to Bar'ella.

"I can't stop the bleeding."

"All right. Jared, you and James lean on her legs and lower body. Cyn I need you to hold her shoulders down, but whatever you do, stay as far away from her face as you can. Here this should help."

"Why didn't the spell stop when the Mage lost consciousness?" Cyn asked.

"Because of the type of spell it is. It will keep going until the counter spell is given. But I think I can short circuit it."

From out of her bag, Bar'ella produced magically enhanced face-masks. She gave one to each of them and donned her own. She removed a large pair of leather gloves and a black lacquered box. Bar'ella placed the box carefully next to the Succubus' head and donned the heavy gloves. Pulling a small jar from the box, she uncapped it and waved it once under the Succubus' nose. Replacing the lid, she put the jar back in the box and the box back into her bag.

The shudders and convulsions slowed both in duration and in strength. The red mist turned pink before dissipating into nothing. The healer peeled back Deidre's eyelids and looked critically at the pupils.

She removed a wooden fan from her bag, and waved it over the Succubus's face.

Damien walked over. "What did you do?"

Bar'ella looked up at him. "I had to treat her with Anti-magic." Cyn and the others gasped and pulled back in shock.

Anti-magic was used on criminals to ensure they never used magic again, as it cut off the part of the brain that utilized magical force.

"You should have waited for the trial before administering it."

Bar'ella shook her head. "I didn't give it to her as a punishment. It's the only known method of breaking the Red Mist spell without using the counter-spell. I only gave her enough to break the spell," She turned back to her patient. "I don't think there's enough Anti-magic to kill her magic."

Cyn spoke up. "Why couldn't you use the counter-spell?"

Bar'ella shook her head. "Two reasons. One, it's located in the Tome of Power which is I believe is still missing?" She looked at him and he nodded his confirmation.

"And two, only the Mage who summoned the Red Mist, can use the counter-spell."

"That sucks." Cyn replied.

Bar'ella nodded in agreement. "It does indeed." She paused for a moment "Now that she's still, I need to get her to the clinic."

Damien shook his head. "Excuse me, Dr. Bar'ella. She's under arrest. You'll have to treat her at the Elite Offices where she'll be held until her trial."

Bar'ella looked up at him, a frown crossing her features. "What's the charge?"

"Murder."

Chapter 16

The scent of rotting flesh filled her nose and dread pooled thick in the pit of her stomach. She looked around and instantly recognized the decaying heads that graced the walls of Khan's throne room.

Dar'kirm, not again! How does Khan find me?

A movement on the throne sent terror shivering down her spine. Looking around she realized they were alone. He stood tall before his throne, a barbed whip in one hand. The other gripped an object on a chain hanging around his throat. He saw her, smiled and released a golden locket in the shape of a flame, that fell to his chest.

On the floor before the dais a brazier stood burning merrily away. Two rods stuck out of the flames, and she had a really bad feeling that they were meant for her.

"I've missed you, my beautiful Deidre."

He stalked down the steps and stopped next to the brazier.

An unseen force propelled her forward until she stood inches in front of him. She couldn't move, and it wasn't until she looked down that she realized why. Brightly colored bands of magic circled her body, holding her prisoner.

Deidre shook her head in denial and raven locks flowed over her shoulder.

She was in Demoni form. At least this body could take more abuse than her human one could.

Khan grinned, and it sent terror pulsing through her. She knew, with every fiber of her being, there was no escape for her.

Khan circled her again. "I have you now, Deidre. And no one will save you this time."

He turned and lifted the iron, tip glowing red with the heat. Deidre watched as the iron approached her breast. The iron stopped a few centimeters away from her skin. Hot, searing, blistering pain. The skin of her chest formed blisters. Agony like she'd never known before inundated her cells. A cry of pain escaped her and he smiled, leaning forward to lick her skin. His sand-papery tongue abraded her abused flesh. She clenched her teeth to stop from making a sound, but couldn't stop the moisture leaking from her eyes.

The iron lost its glow, and he shoved it back into the fire. With a flick of his wrist, a whip uncoiled. It was comprised of three strands that ended in barbed hooks. He circled her once, and stopped outside of her line of vision. A claw slid through the skin at the nape of her neck, drew her hair aside and draped it in front of her shoulder, the soft hair rasped her burnt flesh.

He ran his tongue over the nape of her neck and the sweat beaded there.

Then nothing. No heat, no touch.

She heard the sound of the whip crack as she felt the flesh of her back, part. It took a moment to register the pain, and when it did, she fought to keep her cries contained. Wet heat ran down her back as the coppery scent of blood filled the air. Crack! Her flesh was ripped from her body with every stroke, every touch of the barbs.

"Deidre!"

A voice called to her, but the agony flooding her mind overrode the voice.

"Damn it, Deidre! Wake up!"

Another crack. This time she saw the blur of a whip on her shoulder. Green blood welled in the wake of the barb, running in rivulets down her body.

Crack!

The hook caught the tip of her nipple and sliced away the sensitive flesh. She screamed, no longer able to contain the pain.

Khan drew close behind her, his tongue rough as he licked the blood from her shoulder. "Music to my ears." His laughter filled the throne room.

"Deidre, wake up, *now!*"

The power-filled voice would not be denied. She jerked in her invisible bonds and felt herself race through an alien landscape. Darkness closed in from every direction, smothering her. She gasped, jerked up-right and opened her eyes to find Bar'ella leaning over her, concern and anxiety on her face.

"What.." her voice was hoarse as if from screaming. She cleared her throat and tried again. "What happened?"

"How are you feeling?" Bar'ella asked.

Deidre frowned. What an odd question. She tried to shrug and fire raced across her back. A chill raced over her naked skin as she started to shiver. She took a couple of shallow breaths and was able to move past the pain. Deidre looked at Bar'ella through watery eyes.

"What in Dar'kirm?"

Bar'ella leaned forward and took her hand, gaze intent. "Tell me what happened."

"I don't know."

The door slammed open, and Deidre looked over to see Cyn jerking her arm from James' grip. "Let me go, you son of a bitch!"

"You have five minutes." James warned before he turned left the room, closing the door.

"Cyn? What are you doing here?" Deidre asked.

Cyn glared at the door. "Making sure you're all right." The Vamp's eyes widened. "Holy shit, what the hell happened to you?"

"Huh?"

Deidre looked down at herself. The skin of her chest was blistered and leaking pus. She glanced at her shoulder and the angry red lines that crisscrossed her flesh.

The sour bile of fear filled her mouth and she closed her eyes, not willing to look at the rest. "It was only a nightmare, wasn't it? Bar'ella?"

"Have you ever entered the dreamscape?" Bar'ella's voice was soft.

Deidre opened her eyes and looked at the healer who reached down and brought a jar of cream from her bag. She opened it, and with Cyn's help, started covering the wounds. Deidre was turned on her stomach and she felt them apply the cool, soothing cream all over her back.

Deidre shook her head. "No. I can't. Demons don't dream. Nightmares yes, dreams no."

"Congratulations. It appears you do."

Khan's voice echoed in her head with smug satisfaction. *"I'm anxious to finish where we left off."*

Deidre jerked up onto her elbows, gasping in pain, as she looked around the room for Khan. Her heart pounded in her ears as she searched for the threat, but there was nothing there.

It was all in her head, wasn't it?

Hands smoothed the tense muscles of her back. Ever so slowly, the tension holding her began to unravel.

She tried to focus on what Bar'ella had said. "Wait a minute. What's the dreamscape?"

Bar'ella finished smoothing the soothing cream over her cuts, then positioned her on her left side so as not to irritate the abused skin.

"No one knows for sure. All I know is that it's where the spirit goes while the body is asleep."

"Why are we discussing it then?"

"Because your nightmare left scars on your spirit body that translated to marks on your corporeal body."

"You mean it was real?" Deidre felt the blood drain from her face. If it was real, Khan had found a way to torture her. *J'akala.* "Can someone be trapped in the dreamscape?"

"I don't know. Not much research has been done. It's possible I suppose."

"He can kill me then." She said to herself as she tried to think things through. Cyn and Bar'ella helped her up into a sitting position, and she was careful not to lean against the wall.

Cyn and Bar'ella exchanged a look.

"Who can kill you dear?"

"Khan." She could tell by their expressions they wanted further explanation. "My previous, ah, assignment."

To distract herself, she looked around. She sat on a bed in a small room made of white cinder-block walls. A steel door with a small mesh window in the top, had a narrow slot halfway down the door.

Cyn sat on the edge of her bed; Bar'ella sat on the only other furniture in the room, a chair. A toilet and sink sat against one wall, and there wasn't much room between them and the other wall.

She turned to Cyn. "Where are we? The Clinic?"

Cyn scowled. "No. Don't you remember what happened?"

Deidre shook her head. With the dream fresh in her mind, everything else had faded into the background.

Bar'ella remained quiet as Cyn explained.

"I'm not sure what exactly happened, but James and I found Damien bound on a stone altar and you writhing on the floor covered by a red mist."

Orders to kill Damien. Her refusal. Red Mist.

Damien's look of hatred as he wished her to die. Pain lanced her heart. She bowed her head, ignoring the pull of her tortured skin. She should have known better than to trust Damien, or any male for that matter. They had brought her nothing but trouble. "I remember."

Cyn nodded. "Well, after James arrested Mage Clint Douglas, Damien arrested you for murder. We're in the holding cells under the Elite offices."

"Until when?"

Bar'ella spoke up. "Until your trial."

"Can you spring me?"

The Dragon healer shook her head. "I'm sorry, I can't."

James entered the cell. "Good to see you're doing better."

Deidre tilted her head. "Better than what? I'm in jail."

A boyish grin crossed his face. "Better than before." He turned to Cyn. "Are you finished?"

"Wait. Where are you taking her?"

"Not far. She'll be your next door neighbor."

"Cyn are you in trouble for helping me?"

The Vamp shook her head. "Nah. Apparently I'm an accessory as well." Cyn took her hands and gave them a squeeze. "We'll figure something out."

James escorted Cyn from the room and close the door with a loud clang behind him. Deidre heard another door along the corridor open and close.

Dizziness took her by surprise as she toppled into Bar'ella.

"What's wrong?" Bar'ella narrowed her eyes.

Deidre felt funny, not nauseated, but not well. "Don't know."

"How's your energy?"

She checked her levels. They were low, dangerously low. Lower than after a transition.

"Not good."

"Can you use me for energy?"

Deidre shook her head. "No. Male energy only."

Bar'ella helped her to sit upright, leaning her against the cool wall. "What is that necklace you're wearing?"

"An energy sink of some kind."

"You've not worn it before."

"This time only."

Bar'ella leaned closer. "May I remove it?"

Deidre shook her head. "Only summoner."

Bar'ella sat back and nodded her head. "One of those. Is he using it to drain you further?"

Deidre concentrated on the medallion. There was a faint hum of energy, but it wasn't doing anything to her at the moment.

"Not active."

"Well that's one good thing."

Deidre was about to respond when the sound of metal on metal interrupted her.

A small group entered the cell, all male. From their auras, there were two Mages and the Fae, Captain Jor'dan. The two Mages stood at attention close to the door, and Captain Jor'dan approached.

Bar'ella stood. "Good morning Captain Jor'dan."

"Good morning Bar'ella. May I speak with the prisoner?"

Bar'ella turned to the side and gestured toward Deidre.

A frown crossed his face. "What's wrong with you?"

"Captain, Deidre needs energy to fully heal." Bar'ella answered.

A dubious look crossed his face. "What kind of energy?"

"Sexual," Deidre responded.

The two guards jerked, expressions of horror flitted across their faces. There wasn't going to be energy forthcoming, and she knew it. She tried to catch Bar'ella's eye, but the healer was going toe to toe with the Captain.

"I won't risk my men, Bar'ella."

Bar'ella spoke softly. "She can't heal without energy."

He shook his head and was about to speak when Deidre interrupted him.

"Bar'ella. Don't."

Bar'ella turned to her, a furious expression on her face. "Don't what?"

Deidre fought a smile. "Don't bother. They're planning on killing me anyway. What difference does it make if I die now or later?"

"You're not going to die!" Bar'ella shouted. The Healer stopped and took a deep breath. "I didn't save you from the Mist for you to die now."

"You're not going to die." The Captain chimed in.

"Really?" Deidre nodded toward the two guards. "They're already convinced I'm guilty. It's the nature of males to jump to conclusions, and no amount of facts or arguments will sway them."

"But that's not how the justice system works."

"That's how it has always worked. You've been too blind to see."

While the Captain was sputtering, Deidre caught Bar'ella's hand and gave it a squeeze. "Let me go, old friend."

Steam escaped the Dragon's nose. "No! I won't have it! You're not going to die you bitch demon!"

Bar'ella was beyond pissed, when she brought out the curse words. Deidre closed her eyes with a small smile. "As you command, oh Scaly One."

Two hands were placed on her head, and a wave of Dragon healing magic swirled within her. While it didn't take away the hunger, it allowed her body to conserve what little energy it had. Her wounds closed, Deidre felt better. Except for the gnawing emptiness in her belly. The hands were removed, clothing whispered, and the cell door closed. *Alone at last.*

Conversation flowed from the hall, but she was too tired, too lethargic to care.

"He does care, you know."

She opened her eyes to see the Captain leaning against the far wall, arms folded across his chest.

She snorted. "You're lying, but it doesn't matter."

256

"Why not?"

"Regardless of what Bar'ella believes, I'm dying." She could feel death hovering on the periphery of her senses, waiting for the time to strike. Deidre was so drained that not even her automatic defense system was working. She closed her eyes again too weary to keep them open.

"Tell me something." His soft voice sounded loud in the barren cell. "If I were to arrange to give you energy, would you kill the donor?"

"Probably."

"Why? Would you make him suffer for the sins of others?"

She shook her head. "I need too much."

"I see."

A movement of the bed had her opening her eyes to see him sitting in the place Cyn had occupied. His actions didn't make sense to her.

"What do you want?" Suspicion filled her.

He leaned back against the wall. "Many things, Justice for crimes committed; the end of this damned Festival; return of the Tome of Power and," he paused, his features softened in sympathy as he looked at her. "to save the female Damien loves."

She snorted. "He doesn't love me, Captain."

"Are you sure?"

"Yes."

"How do you know?"

"When he told me to "die, bitch." And besides, I'm a demon."

"And that makes you unlovable?" His question struck too close to home. She struggled with the pain surrounding her heart and fought to keep her tone even.

"Demon's don't love."

"Tell me, are you not willing to try? To forgive him for his knee jerk reaction?"

She shook her head and stared at the far wall. "What is the expression? Been there, done that?"

He stood and walked to the door. "If you change your mind, let me know." He looked back at her, tilted his head and paused a moment before speaking. "I didn't think you were a coward."

Her body felt like lead, and she slumped over to lie down on the bed. The door opened and closed again leaving her alone with her thoughts.

She wasn't a coward, but she wasn't stupid either. She wouldn't fight for something she could never have. For a moment in time, she'd allowed herself to hope, to believe there was something more for her. But Damien had proven to her that love, that tender emotion, could never be for her. She was a demon, not worthy of the emotions of other beings. It was a lesson she'd forgotten. One that had been beaten into her many times before.

She paid no attention to the tears dampening her cheeks.

§

Damien woke early, a half hour before the sunset, feeling like shit. A lead weight centered in his chest. If only he could forget about her and how she'd led him along, but that wasn't possible.

It looked like the Succubus was the key to the investigation. It was too bad the resources of the department were stretched so thin, or he'd have asked to be transferred to a different case.

Anything else would be preferable; hell, even protecting those condescending Mages would be an improvement over this, this agony. He sat on his couch staring out the window waiting for James to get up.

Through the specially protected glass, he saw the ocean swallow the sun. He could hear James moving around in the guest room. He got a couple of bottles of blood from the fridge and resumed his seat facing the glass wall. James appeared well rested, the bastard. "Hey."

James handed over a fancy envelope. Damien handed over a bottle of blood and sipped his own. "This was in your mailbox."

258

Damien winced. *Fuck.* He'd forgotten about that. James sank down into the chair next to him, popped the top and took a swig.

"What is it?"

"A foolish mistake."

James looked puzzled, then opened the envelope and withdrew an ornately decorated sheet of paper. He began to read.

"The Council has approved Vampire Damien Alexander's request to begin the process of filing for a marital exception on the condition he and his chosen mate present themselves before the Council for reproductive assessment."

James looked up from the letter. "What the fuck is this?"

Damien looked out at the lights of the city. "I wanted to marry Sienna and settle down."

"But she died over a year ago."

"I know. I'd forgotten about it until the Captain brought it up a couple of days ago."

"And you didn't cancel it?"

Damien turned to his partner and friend. "I'd met her and thought she'd be perfect."

"Fuck."

"Yeah."

"So now what?"

A shrug lifted his shoulders. On one hand, he was desperate to believe her innocence. But his mind kept insisting she was well aware of her role and that she took pleasure in fooling him.

"After the fiasco with Sienna, I was immune to females. But when she hit town, it was different. She made me believe again." He snorted and continued in a soft whisper. "But it was just her Succubus tricks convincing me I was interested."

"Are you going to cancel this?"

"Yeah."

James shook his head. "Tell you what. We'll solve the case, and then head out to somewhere fun for the weekend. Get drunk and swear off women forever."

Damien's lip twitched in a small smile. "I thought we'd already sworn off all women."

James nodded. "We did, but now we need to re-enforce that decision. Damn their sweet hides, lead us around by the short and curlies and expect us to look the other way when they trample all over us."

Damien looked at James and raised an eyebrow. "Trouble in paradise with Cyn?"

James nodded. "Yeah, you were right. She knows much more than she lets on, and she's a close friend of our torturer, Hans Drebin."

Damien choked on his sip of blood. "Excuse me?"

"She knows him."

Damien shook his head. "As in dating, or just good friends?"

James took a swig. "From what I could determine, they're close friends. But that raises even more questions."

"Yeah, like who and what else does she know?"

James nodded. "At that leads me to wonder how and why she knows him. And if she's involved in some way."

Damien shook his head. "Shit. Damn. Fuck. What the hell else can go wrong?" James hissed, and Damien realized what he said. "Fuck! I cursed us now, didn't I?"

James nodded. "Man, you know better than that."

"Sorry."

James finished his bottle and got up. "We need to get to headquarters and check in with the Captain."

§

Captain Jor'dan sat in his chair. *What am I going to do?* It was obvious the Succubus loved Damien, and that Damien returned the sentiment. Hell everyone in the office knew it. Damien had followed the stretcher into the cell block and lifted Deidre to the bed with tender care. After covering her with a blanket, he snarled, fleeing the scene as if running from the sun.

A knock on his door drew him from his thoughts. "Come in."

Mage Merrick entered the office. "Sorry to disturb you, sir, but there's a problem with the Succubus."

Damien and James entered, and by the expressions on their faces, they'd heard what the Mage had said.

"What's the problem?"

"She won't sleep, sir. After you left, she stumbled out of bed and started pacing. She hasn't stopped all day."

"Let me see."

Merrick went to the computer and pulled up the live video feed to the cells below, typing in his code.

And there she was, as Merrick had stated, pacing back and forth in a slow stumbling gait. Periodically she would rub her hands up and down her arms. When she turned to face the camera, Jor'dan heard gasps of dismay behind him and fought to stop his own reaction.

Her eyes were sunken, and the skin over her cheek bones taut. He could see each of her ribs. She looked like a walking skeleton, as if she was starving to death, and Jor'dan realized with a jolt that she was.

"Shit. Damn. Fuck. What have you done to her?" Damien demanded. "And why the hell is she still naked? Didn't you give her any clothes?"

"Bar'ella left scrubs for her, but she won't wear them." Jor'dan's voice was gentle, not knowing how to soften the blow. "Deidre's starving."

"What the fuck? Didn't you feed her?" Damien pounded the desk-top before straightening and taking a deep breath.

Jor'dan turned to him with a frown. "What the hell did you want me to do, Damien? Have her kill someone to give her the energy she lives on?"

James spoke up. "Why is she pacing? Shouldn't she be conserving her energy?"

Merrick spoke. "We have no idea. When she was first brought in, she appeared unconscious. Subject then began thrashing around on the bed and screaming. Bar'ella was able to bring her back to consciousness, so we didn't think it was anything out of the ordinary."

Jor'dan turned from the macabre sight on the monitor to see Damien run a hand through his hair in frustration. He bit back a smile.

"At least give her something to make her sleep. That pacing can't be good for her."

Jor'dan narrowed his gaze. "And you would care, why?"

James and Merrick lunged to grab Damien's arms before he could attack Jor'dan.

Jor'dan smiled. "I'll go down and speak to her."

He left the room trying not to grin as Damien actually growled at him. Calling the healer on the way down, he said. "I need you to check Deidre."

The healer's voice filled with concern. "What have you done to her, now?"

"Nothing. She didn't sleep today and has been pacing the floor like a caged animal. Damn it Bar'ella! She looks like an ad for famine relief."

"I'll be there in ten."

"Oh, and bring a sedative with you. She needs to sleep." He paused. "Wait, does she sleep?"

Bar'ella sighed. "Yes, Jor'dan, she does sleep, just like everyone else."

"Well, she's the first demon I've ever met."

"She's technically not a demon."

"What?"

"I'll explain later. I'm on my way." Bar'ella hung up as Jor'dan reached Deidre's cell.

He used his key to open the door and enter the room, aware that Merrick, Damien and James were watching via the live feed.

Her appearance looked worse than before. She looked at him with haunted eyes, before getting control of her emotions and smoothing her features.

"What's wrong?" He kept his voice soothing.

She snorted. "Nothing." Her voice a mere whisper of sound compared to a few short hours ago.

"Why haven't you slept?"

The haunted look appeared in her eyes once again. "I… can't." She looked down and continued to shamble and stagger back and forth in front of the bed.

"Perhaps you can sit down and tell me about it?"

She shook her head. "If I sit, I'll relax and then… no. I can't."

"Why?"

She paused for a moment, titling her head. Her face drained of the little color it had and she jerked to the wall away from him, eyes wild.

"Shhhh. It's okay. Tell me what's wrong."

In a tormented whisper she responded. "He's coming for me. He's going to torture me."

Jor'dan took a step toward her, but she cringed away from him. It tore at him that she flinched. He didn't harm women, he protected them.

A knock on the door had him turning and admitting Bar'ella, who rushed over to Deidre, put her arm around the Succubus, and led her to the bed.

The Succubus held herself stiff in the healer's hold. Bar'ella sent him a look.

"What's going on here?" Her voice was soft so as not to alarm Deidre.

"She hasn't eaten, she hasn't slept. Something is wrong. Do you have a sedative?" he asked.

"Don't do it, Bar'ella." Deidre's voice was so soft and agonized that the healer paused a moment.

"Why not?"

She shook her head not answering.

"What's wrong with her?" Jor'dan ran a hand through his hair. Deidre looked up at him. "Nothing."

He shook his head. "The health of prisoners is important. The fact that you aren't eating or sleeping is cause for concern."

"Deidre, why aren't you eating?"

A sarcastic laugh was her answer. "They're trying to kill me too. Why should I make it easy on them?"

Jor'dan and Bar'ella exchanged a look.

Bar'ella patted Deidre's hand. "I don't understand."

Deidre bowed her head and whispered. "Poison."

"What?!?" Jor'dan's eyes narrowed. "What makes you think that?"

Deidre waved to the tray that sat untouched on the chair.

Jor'dan looked over the food with a critical eye. Bar'ella stood and did the same. She lifted a cup of coffee from the tray and wafted her hand over it. A grimace crossed her careworn face and she put it down again. "Anti-Magic."

The healer frowned. "What the hell is going on, Jor'dan?"

"I don't know, but I'm going to find out." How dare one of his people take the law into his own hands? He sent a mental request to the Tech Mages to have them secure the video footage from the food prep area as well as this cell.

Deidre's thin voice startled him out of his anger. "Dead if I do, dead if I don't."

Jor'dan watched the healer's eyes fill with tears. "Deidre, that's not a foregone conclusion. See if you can get her to sleep."

Bar'ella nodded and reached into her coat pocket. She produced a full syringe and an alcohol wipe. She prepped Deidre's arm and gave her a shot.

264

This roused Deidre out of her stupor. She glared at the healer. "Bar'ella. What have you done?"

"Made it so you can sleep."

Deidre grabbed her arm. "No you don unnerstan.. He'll get me inna dream worl'" She slumped over in medicated slumber.

Jor'dan moved forward to help the healer position Deidre on the bed more comfortably before covering her naked form with a blanket.

He turned to the healer. "I forgot to ask. What is this?" He pointed to the medallion around her neck.

Bar'ella shook her head. "A power sink."

Jor'dan touched the worked metal and received a jolt that jerked Deidre. He rubbed his hand, staring at the slight energy burn where his fingers made contact.

"What do you mean?"

Bar'ella grabbed his hand and soothed the burn of his fingers. "She's a slave. Killing and fucking when ordered to. Her master is using the medallion to siphon the energy she gains for his evil deeds."

Jor'dan narrowed his gaze. "Why wasn't I told this?"

The healer shrugged. "I don't think anyone in your department has all the facts." She turned toward the bed and reached for the necklace.

"Careful," Jor'dan warned, "It packs quite a punch."

But instead of grabbing it, Bar'ella held her hand over it. "Unfortunately only her master can remove it."

"And do we know who that is?"

Bar'ella shook her head. "I believe it was Master Douglas, since he Misted her."

Jor'dan helped the healer to her feet and escorted her to the door.

"Come upstairs and have a cup of tea. You look like you could use it."

Bar'ella smiled at the offer. "Thanks."

As they walked up to his office, he asked. "So who is Deidre?"

He opened the door for her, relieved to find it empty. James, Damien and Merrick must have gone back to their offices.

Bar'ella shrugged. "I don't know for sure. The first time I met her was a few hundred years ago. Everything I've learned since then has led me to certain conclusions."

Jor'dan waved her to a chair and sat behind his desk. He leaned forward, elbows on his desk, hands together. "Give me what you have."

A knock on his door heralded a tea tray.

Bar'ella took a sip of hot tea, leaned back in her chair and sighed.

"Deidre is old. I don't know how old, but I do know she wasn't created a slave. She was a free individual until she became cursed. I don't know all the particulars, only that it was a Mage who cursed her. She's been avoiding Paranormals ever since."

"Does she always kill her... prey?"

The healer shook her head. "No. She told me once it's like humans not killing the cow that gives the milk. She doesn't need that much energy at a given time, and when she is low, it's easier to get it from more than one source."

The phone on his desk rang. "Excuse me a moment."

Bar'ella nodded.

"Yes?"

"Merrick here sir. It's the Succubus again."

"Thanks."

Jor'dan hung up the phone and clicked on the icon that brought up the security camera.

The image showed the Succubus's cell, red lines erupted over her arms, neck and face.

"Where the hell is she getting those wounds?" His mutter caused a curse from the healer as she came forward to look at the monitor.

"We need to get down there now!" Bar'ella bolted from the room.

He ran after her, down to the holding area and into the Succubus's cell.

Purple welts covered Deidre's face, and green blood flowed from rips on her body.

Bar'ella knelt by the cot and put her hands on either side of the Succubus's head.

"Shit! He's got her!" Bar'ella removed her hands and snapped her fingers. Her medical bag appeared on the floor beside her. She began digging through it, muttering to herself.

Jor'dan felt the frown crease his forehead. "Who has her? What are you going to do?"

"The sedative should have kept her from dreaming, but it looks like he found her anyway."

"Who?"

"Khan. He tortured her before. I need to wake her up."

Bar'ella dug out a syringe and a glass vial, and prepared the shot.

"Why?"

She swabbed Deidre's arm and administered the injection while answering his question.

"She's being hunted in the dreamscape. Khan is torturing her." She pointed to a wicked looking cut that appeared on the Succubus' face.

Bar'ella began to smear white cream on the cuts, but they were appearing faster than she could heal them. "Shit! She's not waking up! We need help. Get Damien in here now!"

The cell door burst open and James and Damien ran into the room.

Bar'ella motioned for Damien. "Come here, hold her head, and command her to wake up." When he didn't respond, Bar'ella tuned and glared at him. "Now, Damien!"

Jor'dan reinforced the command, "Do it."

Damien sat on the bed and pulled Deidre's head into his lap, hands on her head trying to keep her still. Her body twisted as if trying to escape from the pain of the marks forming all over her body. He brushed a sweat soaked lock of hair from her forehead. She didn't deserve this, whatever the hell it was. He looked at the healer.

"What do I do?"

"Call her back."

"How?"

She glared at him. "I don't know. Just do it!" She turned and began ordering James and Jor'dan to hold onto Deidre's limbs.

He nodded, closed his eyes and concentrated on Deidre. Using all of the psychic power at his command, he called her.

"*Deidre come to me.*"

Nothing. He tried again, harder. "*Come to me.*"

An image bloomed in his mind, and he was transported to a gray barren wasteland. On the horizon he could see a flicker. In the twinkling of a thought he was there. "*Deidre. Come to me. Now.*"

Still no response.

A flashing violet sphere of energy floated before him. Within the globe he saw an amazing scene. An alien world inhabited by devil looking creatures.

One of the creatures held a wicked looking whip, while the other was tied to a table. The devil with the whip would alternate whipping and running his sharp talons down the prisoner's flesh.

With a jolt he realized the prisoner was Deidre, and the globe was her connection to her physical body. The sphere throbbed deep red with each lash and he felt her physical body jerk at every pulse.

He reached out with both hands to grab the orb, and was stunned by an electric jolt.

The globe flared before its glow weakened. Somehow he knew that if the sphere lost its glow, he'd lose Deidre as well.

A voice spoke in his head. "*Trust your heart.*"

268

What the hell did that mean?

He looked around and didn't see who or what was talking to him.

The voice spoke again. *"Hurry."*

"Who are you?" he sent his thoughts out.

Silence.

Inspiration hit.

In this landscape anything was possible. He imagined himself as thin as a sheet of paper, his body malleable. He surrounded the sphere. With a push, he forced energy into the sphere, breaking the hold of the devil who'd captured Deidre. He reached into the sphere and tugged her away from the horrific scene. The bubble encapsulated her as they moved away from the fissure that held the entrance to the devil world.

An arrow of pain shot through him as his shield was attacked by external energy. The devil was trying to get her back. Psychic power strengthened his shield, and he withstood increasingly powerful attacks. Within his bubble, he made sure to cradle her in warmth and comfort.

The attacks grew weaker and further apart. After many minutes without an attack, he reformed into his physical self.

"Come with me, love. You don't belong here."

His mind touched hers and he sent her the strength she needed to escape the dreamscape.

Her flicker strengthened and with a jolt he opened his eyes and saw the white walls of the cell. He looked down at her face. Her violet eyes opened and the desolation in her gaze tore at his soul. She lowered her lashes and turned her head away. Her rejection hurt, but it was no less than he deserved.

He watched Bar'ella rush to heal the wounds and welts. At her nod, he stood up, and with great care, placed her back on the bed. "I'll be in my office."

Damien heard the door of the office open behind him. He leaned over the desk head bowed.

"Hey Damien." James paused to clear his throat. "Ah, Deidre's doing better. Not looking as anorexic. How are you?"

Damien lifted his head and sank down into his chair, tilting his head against the back.

"Fucked up. I still want her. I want to believe this was all some mixed up misunderstanding. But a part wants her to die a slow painful death for what she did. What do I do?"

James sat across the desk from him. "I don't know. But here's something to keep in mind. The Captain and Bar'ella are convinced that someone else is pulling her strings. You've got two choices. You either forgive her, take her back, and make her yours. Or let her go."

"I should let her go."

"You could, but how will that affect you? Knowing she's out there draining other males, being tortured. And most of all, believing she's unlovable."

Damien lifted his head at that. "What the fuck? Where the hell did you come up with that drivel?"

"Straight from the Succubus' mouth."

Chapter 17

Clint Douglas sat on the narrow cot with his back against the wall, his arms resting on a bent knee.

If those Elite fools thought this cell could hold him they were sorely mistaken. Putting him in a magic dampening cell was fine, but they failed to realize that his spells had been prepared and cast in advance and as the recipient of the magic, he need not exert any power here.

If only that bitch of a Succubus hadn't balked at the last minute. Why she failed to follow his command? If she thought he'd free her, she was mistaken. Then again, he'd never planned on freeing her anyway. She'd be another source of energy for his spell. And since she was still wearing the Tap Medallion, he'd draw her power at will.

He'd kill Damien Alexander, avenging the death of his baby girl.

A tingle of magic at the base of his brain made his vision blur. His mind's eye was drawn to the preparations to power the Crystal Orb. Antwon and Alexi finished keying the Orb to him and he felt the stray bits of energy the Crystal absorbed.

The Orb sat on a stand covered with crimson velvet. The excitement of the ritual participants grew, feeding the Crystal.

It wasn't much at the moment, but once the orgy began, he'd have enough power to complete the final spell; the one that would destroy the Council and the Elite.

Energy tantalized him. A weak amount now, but as the Crystal absorbed the energy, it'd be channeled to him. Unlike the Tap Medallion, which only drew energy from one being, the Orb was able to draw from a whole group at once.

A few moments later the ritual began.

Excellent! This was the first piece of good news since the Succubus had failed him.

For a moment, he'd thought all his plans were in ruins after he'd been arrested. But he was still in possession of the Tome of Magic. And that gave him an advantage.

He'd been careful during their questioning, oh so careful. As much as he wanted revenge now, he'd force himself to wait.

Patience. No need to rush.

Clint heard a noise from the hall outside of his cell. Four Elite entered the cell. All were familiar to him.

Clint summoned a frown and glared at Captain Jor'dan. Vengeance would be his, but they mustn't find out. He needed to act normal. *Normal.*

Captain Jor'dan spoke. "Your trial is about to commence. Please accompany us."

How polite.

Elite Mage Randall came forward and bound his hands in front of him with anti-magic wrist cuffs.

Clint fought hard to keep his amusement contained. Energy flowed to him. *These paltry restraints can't hold me!*

He, who had more power in his little finger than most of the traitorous Mages who worked for the Elite, especially Elite Mage Merrick, who jerked Clint to his feet. *They'd get their comeuppance!*

Soon Clint would have more power than the High Chancellor himself!

272

Elite Shifter Jared stepped behind him, blindfolding Clint.

Clint let him, making no move to escape. He'd go along with them... for now.

His arms were held, and he was led out of the room.

As if he couldn't tell where they were taking him. *Fools!* Did they really think he couldn't tell one room from another just by listening?

An echo-y sound followed by running water? They thought they were so smart to conceal the portal to the Council Chambers in a restroom.

The Council Chambers... A small smile broke free. What better place to release his revenge than in the seat of power? Being arrested had worked to his advantage in ways he'd never thought. No one destroyed his family and got away with it.

He'd show them. He'd show them all.

§

Damien found Randall waiting for him and James at Elite HQ.

"James, the Captain wants you to get him the file on Demon Hans Drebin."

James arched an eyebrow. "I gave it to him yesterday."

Randall shrugged and held up his hands. "Hey, I'm just passing along the message."

James sighed and left the room to get the requested file.

Randall turned to Damien. "I'm glad you're here. I heard the trial for the Succubus is going to take place tonight."

"Yeah." Damien's fists clenched. She deserved whatever they did to her. *But hadn't she suffered enough?* He banished his doubts.

"I'm glad she's going to pay. She killed our brothers. The bitch must die."

Damien frowned. "But I'd been told she was a slave, acting under another's orders."

Randall laughed. "Really?" He leaned forward, an earnest expression on his face. "If she were a slave, would she enjoy herself as much as she does? Seems to me, she'd hate sex, not enjoy it."

"Hmmm…"

"A group of twenty dead men were discovered in a warehouse. They were drained of energy, and the healers confirmed it. How many females can fuck a group of guys like that without tiring?"

"None."

"My point exactly." Randall smiled and clapped a hand on Damien's shoulder. "Don't worry, I'm sure the Council will find a fitting punishment for her crimes."

Randall left the office.

What the hell? On the one hand he desperately wanted to believe that she was a victim in all this. On the other hand, he remembered Klaus and Roger and how much they had enjoyed her attentions. Even though they hadn't remembered her, they remembered the way she'd fucked like a dream.

James walked back into the room shaking his head. "Idiot Randall. Captain Jor'dan already has the file."

The Captain's voice spoke in his head. *"Damien, you and James collect Vampire Cyn and Succubus Deidre."*

"Why us?"

Captain Jor'dan's voice became soft. *"Are you questioning my orders?"*

Damien shook his head. *"No sir…."*

"You have one hour to get to the Council Chambers, I suggest you hurry."

Damien glanced at James. "Did you get the message?

James grimaced. "Yeah, I'm not looking forward to this."

"Neither am I."

Damien and James arrived in holding to see the cells that had housed Hans and Clint empty.

James looked in each cell. "Why didn't they transport them at the same time?"

"Too risky." Damien replied. "They'd over power the guards and escape."

"You think so?"

Damien gave him a look. "With the Succubus a walking advertisement for sex?"

"Right, forgot about that. You want to get Deidre or Cyn?" James looked away.

Damien didn't want to see Deidre, let alone touch her, but he didn't trust that she wouldn't try to work her wiles on James.

"I'll take Deidre."

James nodded. "Leaving Cyn for me. Thanks."

Damien paused outside the door and looked through the little window. She sat naked against the wall, with her legs stretched out along the bed, hands on her thighs. The sight of her stilled the breath in his lungs. She looked much better today than she had last night. Dark rings still circled her eyes, and it looked like she hadn't slept. Her flesh had filled in and her coloring wasn't as pale. An insidious thought filled him. Who had she fucked to get the energy she needed? Which of his friends had found heaven between her silky thighs?

He took a deep breath, then another, trying to calm the jealousy boiling within. A measure of calm descended. None of his Elite brethren would have volunteered; they were all aware of the consequences of fucking her. Though why he'd been spared was another question he buried in the back of his mind. Thinking about that would lead questions he wasn't ready to face.

He hated to see her in pain, and yet… and yet nothing. Had all the marks from her body healed? Was she still in pain? From this distance he couldn't tell.

Entering the cell, he leaned against the door and crossed his arms over his chest.

"Who did you fuck? Where did you get the energy?" Shit that wasn't what he wanted to ask, but he didn't take back the questions.

"Huh?" Her look of confusion gave way to flashing eyes. "You."

"What? When?" What the hell was she talking about? The last time they'd had sex was a few days ago.

"Yesterday, when you freed me, you sent me enough energy to get me through the day."

Relief filled him. There wasn't anyone else. Randall's accusation replayed in his head. "Tell me something. Do you enjoy sex?"

A frown marred her lovely forehead. "Where the hell did that come from?"

He shrugged not answering her question. "Did you enjoy draining those poor, defenseless men?"

A flash of anger sparked in her gaze before she lowered her eyelids. "Tell me, Detective, do you enjoy feeding?"

"What does that have to do with anything?"

She glared at him. "Do you enjoy seducing your victims, sinking your teeth into their soft flesh while fucking them to death?"

He shifted at the image that popped into his mind. Him, fucking and feeding from Deidre instead of another female. "I don't need to answer that."

"And neither do I."

Deidre flinched at the mistrust and anger in his eyes. She averted her gaze to stare at the wall beyond his shoulder. His disbelief and accusations hurt. What did he expect, that she'd give up feeding for him? If asked, she knew he'd not give up feeding for her.

She rubbed her chest, wondering how long this malady, this heartbreak, lasted. Bar'ella might know.

276

He cleared his throat. "Did you sleep?"

She looked at his face, trying to imbue a haughty disregard for him into her tone. "Does it matter?"

She watched as the muscles in his jaw tightened, then released.

"The well being of the prisoners is important. I'd… we'd hate for you to become ill during your stay."

"How reassuring. Don't worry, I'll take care of myself." Deidre paused a moment. "What do you want, Detective?"

His hands clenched into fists as if restraining himself from throttling her. *Well isn't that too damn bad.*

He took a deep breath and unclenched his hands. "You've been summoned to stand trial before the Council."

She gave him an insincere smile. "Sorry to disappoint them, but," she held her arms out to the side, "I simply don't have a thing to wear."

Damien's eyes roamed her body. "They cut the clothes from your body when you went into convulsions."

Deidre shrugged. Being naked wasn't a problem for her. She'd spent most of her life naked and was comfortable in her skin. And if the high and mighty Council didn't like it? Tough.

"I have a follow up appointment with Bar'ella." The healer had requested her presence and received an okay from the Captain, before they'd left yesterday evening.

He gave her a smile that didn't reach his eyes.

"It's been cancelled." He tossed a bundle of clothes at her. "Get dressed and let's go."

"Thank you but no. I'm comfortable as I am."

Damien's head cocked to the side as if he was listening for something; his gaze unfocused. He turned back to her. "Shit, there's no time."

Damien took two steps to the bed, grabbed her wrist and yanked Deidre to her feet. Within a heartbeat, her hands were manacled in front of her, his coat was draped over her shoulders

277

and she was plopped down over his shoulder like a sack of potatoes.

Deidre's head hung down his back and her legs were held in a grip that limited her movement. His shoulder dug into her stomach as he opened the door and stepped into the corridor outside her cell.

"Bastard son of J'kala! May the Hounds of Dar'kirm feast upon your genitals! Put. Me Down!"

Her cry was echoed from down the hall. "Put me down!"

Deidre craned her neck around and saw James walking toward them with Cyn draped over his shoulder.

She smiled at James. "What's with the caveman routine?"

James didn't smile back, ignoring her. Another pain in her heart. It looked as if James believed the worst about her as well.

Deidre propped her elbow on Damien's back and braced her chin on her palm to keep the medallion from banging against her head. She tried to get comfortable, but it was difficult.

The two Vampires started walking.

Deidre exchanged an angry look with Cyn.

"Where the hell are you taking us you bloody bastards?" Cyn demanded, wiggling on James' shoulder.

James answered. "You've got an appointment before the Council."

Cyn went still, and Deidre could see the color drain from the Vamp's face.

"We are in so much trouble." Cyn's whisper sounded strained.

Deidre whispered back, "Why?

"The Council is the ruling body of the Paranormal Races. To my knowledge no female has ever gone before them."

"There aren't any female criminals in your Shadow world?"

"Oh there are, but they don't rate going before the Council. They're Reconditioned. Their personalities are removed making them perfect breeders."

Deidre snorted. "And you think *my* actions are horrific? How the hell can you justify wiping women's minds?"

"It's all in the name of keeping control of the breeding population."

"Barbaric."

Cyn's face paled and she rolled her bottom lip between her teeth. "Though we'll probably be Reconditioned after standing trial."

Deidre tried to think of something to ease Cyn's panic. Keeping her tone light and amused, Deidre winked. "I say we give them something to remember us by."

"Like what?"

"I'll think of something, but it should be memorable, don't you think?"

A smile bloomed on Cyn's face. "I like the way you think."

Deidre thought for a moment. "Wait a minute... What are you doing here?"

Cyn sighed and rested her chin on her hand mimicking Deidre's position. "I've been arrested."

"What for?"

Cyn poked James in the back of the head with her elbow. "What were the charges again, Mr. Elite Detective?"

"Aiding and abetting a criminal, obstruction of justice, and assaulting an officer." James sounded smug as he answered.

Deidre grinned at Cyn. "Wow. I'm impressed. Am I the criminal you aided?"

Cyn shook her head, and expression of anger crossed her face. "I have no idea."

James snorted. "Bullshit. You know exactly who and what Hans is."

Deidre grinned. "And what is he?"

Cyn rolled her eyes. "He's a fellow member of the neighborhood watch."

Deidre shook her head. "What is this world coming to? Peaceful members of the neighborhood watch, harassed by the police and getting arrested."

She clicked her tongue on her teeth and shared an amused look with Cyn.

After a moment Cyn turned to her, a puzzled looked crossing the Vamp's face. "Why are you wearing the Detective's coat?"

"*Someone* put this on me before hauling me out of my cell like a demented caveman."

"I know what you mean. I hadn't even eaten when…"

Damien jostled Deidre, stabbing his shoulder further into her stomach. "We're right here you know. And can hear every word you say."

Deidre was quick to reply. "Ask us if we care."

They came to a stop, and Deidre craned her neck around to see where they were. A familiar sign on the door confused her.

"You've got to be kidding me. The men's restroom?"

Cyn laughed. "Need to take care of personal business?"

Neither James nor Damien responded.

James led the way into a restroom. "I'm not looking forward to this."

Damien taunted him. "What's wrong agent TP six? Having problems with claustrophobia?" Deidre felt the laughter through his shoulder.

James defended. "Go on, laugh it up. Just remember, I'll get my revenge. Count on it."

Cyn cleared her throat. "Oh look, one-upmanship, how juvenile."

In the mirror, Cyn was jostled, biting her lip as he opened the door and entered the handicapped stall. He shut and locked the door behind him.

Damien called out. "Don't forget to flush, James."

Cyn's voice floated over the door. "This is disgusting."

A few seconds later, Deidre heard Cyn's squawk of outrage. "Get your hand off my ass you pervert!"

The flushing sound of water running echoed through the room. A click and the door unlocked, allowing Damien to enter the same stall.

"Where did they go?" Deidre asked as she saw the now empty stall.

"You'll see."

He closed and locked the door. A glance at the mucky floor made her glad she was being carried. Talk about ick factor.

Damien put out one hand and leaned against the wall. One of his legs disappeared from view. The sound of running water focused her attention. He stood up straight and turned to face the stall door.

Blue mist rose to envelope them. A tingle of magic swept her skin. Once the water stopped running the mist faded. Damien opened the door.

Deidre glanced around and saw they were still in a restroom. A label on each of the stalls gave a location within San Francisco. On the wall opposite the stalls was a long mirror, with pedestal sinks beneath it. Near the door, mounted on the wall, was an automatic hand drier.

James and Cyn were waiting.

Deidre glanced down and saw squares of toilet paper trailing off the back of James' shoe. She chuckled and met Cyn's amused gaze.

"I won't tell if you won't." Cyn winked.

"Deal."

James looked down and shook his head.

"Damn it! Not again."

He rubbed his foot against the ground and the toilet paper refused to come loose. James walked over to the door stop and was able to dislodge the six squares of toilet paper from his shoe.

"Please tell me they use other access points besides toilets?" Damien asked.

James opened the door and shook his head. "No. They're all johns."

"Why?"

"I think it has to do with the availability of public toilets in most cities."

"How do they keep humans out?"

"A really good spell I imagine."

Cyn rolled her eyes and mimicked talking. Deidre had to look away in order to suppress her laugh.

They emerged into a round cul-de-sac with other doors. Over each door, a sign declared the major city the portal served.

They turned down a long hallway. Damien and James stopped and before Deidre could look around, a thin red band of light scanned them from head to toe. A loud noise echoed down the hall. It sounded like metal sliding on metal.

Damien and James started walking again, and when they passed through the doorway, a large metal door descended from the ceiling.

They stopped again. A greenish light scan and another security check point. This time the doors closed from either side.

"What's with all the security?" Deidre asked, not really expecting a response.

Cyn shook her head. "I think they're paranoid."

"It's to keep the women out." James quipped.

"It's to keep out any who would harm the Councilors." Damien explained.

Deidre responded. "Yeah right. No female in her right mind would be caught in that awful restroom to begin with. This is overkill."

She could hear the frown in Damien's voice. "What's wrong with the restroom?"

Cyn wrinkled her nose. "Ew, gross. Does anyone ever go in and clean the thing?"

"No idea."

"Well there's your answer." Cyn replied.

More light beams, and more doors, all closing in a different manner. One rose from the ground, one descended from the corners of the doorframe, and the last one swirled closed.

Deidre counted seven doors and scans in all.

She turned to Cyn. "The seven levels of hell, or merely Control?"

Cyn shook her head. "No, Kaos. Definitely Kaos."

The final door opened, and they entered a room that looked like a formal receiving room.

Damien turned and closed the door behind them. Deidre saw the Captain pacing in front of an ornate door.

His eyebrow went up as looked at them. "Problems, gentlemen?" An amused smile bloomed on his face.

"Nothing we can't handle, thanks," Damien replied.

"You might like to put them down before we go before the Council."

Deidre was glad to be put on her feet. A wave of dizziness assailed her as the blood rushed from her head.

She leaned against the wall; Cyn was propped up next to her.

Deidre leaned over and whispered, "You're right. This can't be Control. There's no phone booth."

Cyn burst out laughing and received a repressive stare from James. "Thanks. I needed that."

Two ornate double doors stood opposite of the door they'd entered. The room was decorated in deep ruby with gold accents. The plush carpet was soft beneath her bare feet.

The chairs Damien and James sat in looked comfortable and inviting. Priceless art graced the walls and figures stood on lit pedestals in shallow nooks.

Captain Jor'dan was dressed as fancy as the room, with charcoal tailored slacks, dress shoes, and a sweater one shade lighter than his pants. He glanced at his wrist. "You're cutting close." He admonished the Vamps.

Damien motioned to her and Cyn. "Unavoidable trouble with the prisoners."

Captain Jor'dan raised an eyebrow.

A soft chime sounded, and the double doors opened. Damien and James stood.

A short male entered, and by his aura Deidre could tell he was another Fae like the Captain.

Deidre frowned at the way he was dressed. He wore black tights, a red doublet with gored sleeves inset with gold, and an ornate hat.

The Captain bowed, as did Damien and James.

"Who is that?" Deidre's whisper didn't go past Cyn.

"The Sentinel for the Council."

"Is he supposed to look like that?"

Cyn nodded. "It's considered bad form to ridicule him."

"Thanks for the warning."

The Council Sentinel came forward and stopped, mouth popping open at the sight of her and Cyn against the wall.

Captain Jor'dan cleared his throat, catching the Sentinel's attention. "Perhaps you should let them know we're all here?"

Deidre tried not to smile as the male's eyes kept coming back to her.

"What?" the Sentinel asked.

Damien turned to her, his face full of anger. "Stop it!"

Deidre smiled at the Sentinel and raised her cuffed wrists, giving the Fae a little wave with the tips of her fingers.

"Stop what, Detective?" She made sure to make her tone mild, knowing it would piss him off, but not caring.

"Stop using your power to seduce the poor man."

284

Deidre held out her manacled wrists in front of her. "But you forgot Detective, I can't use my power. I'm nothing more than a helpless female." She fluttered her eye lashes at him.

Damien snorted. "You've never been helpless in your life. I doubt you know the meaning of the word."

Deidre closed her eyes for a brief moment. If only he knew how helpless she felt at times, including now. But she wasn't going to let him know.

Her eyes opened and she stared at him. "What's wrong Detective, afraid of a female?"

Captain Jor'dan coughed into his hand and Deidre could see the amusement in his eyes.

Damien took a step forward, anger flashing in his eyes.

"Enough." the Captain grabbed Damien's arm and turned toward the Sentinel. "I assume they're ready for us?"

The Sentinel jerked, and turned to look at Jor'dan. "Yes, Captain, but they," he waved his hand toward Deidre and Cyn, "...are not allowed."

Deidre rolled her eyes at Cyn, and tilted her head toward the exit. Cyn nodded.

"Well gentlemen, thank you for the interesting time, but since we're not expected, Cyn and I will wait out there." Deidre waved her hands toward the hallway of doors.

Damien shook his head and went to stand in front of the exit door. He leaned back against the door and crossed his arms in front of his chest.

"Bastard son of J'kala," Deidre muttered under her breath.

The Captain protested in a low tone. The Sentinel held up a hand, cocking his head, and rushed back through the double doors.

A short time later, he reappeared, bowed to the group and waved them through the doors into the main chamber.

"I'm impressed. Really." Deidre nodded. "But I don't think I need to see anything more. Visions of fat old guys running around naked are not something I'd like to subject myself to. I think it is against a Geneva Convention or something."

Damien sighed and pointed toward the open double doors.

Deidre leaned over to Cyn, and in a soft whisper, warned, "Don't say anything."

Cyn nodded as they entered the room.

Chapter 18

The Sentinel led Deidre and Cyn before a judicial-style bench. Seated at the bench was an aura Deidre had never encountered before. A vivid picture flashed in her mind

A fiery bird rising from ashes.

Ah, so this was the illustrious Phoenix. He was dressed in black robes with a raised hood covering his head. An ornate half mask covered his face, obscuring all but his lips.

The Sentinel bowed, straightened, and intoned, "Sir, the females you requested."

Cyn curtsied before the bench.

Deidre shrugged mentally. When in Demoni, and all that.

Damien's coat dragged on the floor behind her and with her hands chained in front of her, she couldn't move the material out of the way for a proper curtsey. Her foot caught on the hem, and when she straightened, the coat slid off her shoulders pooling at her feet.

Deidre saw the Phoenix smile before the scandalized whispers blanked his expression. Gasps and outraged murmurings filled the room. One voice stood out among the others.

"Female! How dare you appear before the Court naked?"

The voice then addressed the bench. "Your Grace, I demand this female be removed from the premises and punished for her disrespect."

Mr. Phoenix held up his hand, and the scandalized whispers gave way to silence as everyone awaited his pronouncement.

The mask smiled. "Your name?"

"Deidre, Mr. Phoenix." More scandalized whispers started. She caught Cyn's grin before the Vamp bowed her head.

Now what did I do?

"Deidre, please explain your state of undress."

She shrugged, unconcerned with her nudity. "It's my natural state."

Behind her she could hear Damien's soft curses.

Mr. Phoenix cleared his throat. "I see. Detective Alexander? Please cover Ms Deidre with the coat so we can proceed."

Deidre took a step away from the material at her feet so as not to get tangled in it when he lifted the coat back over her shoulders.

Mr. Phoenix addressed them. "Ladies, please stand next to Mage Clint Douglas and Demon Hans Drebin."

Hans. That must be Cyn's friend.

Deidre looked around and saw Sir and another male standing off to the side, two Elite guards stood behind each prisoner.

The second male's aura proclaimed him a half-human, half-demon. He was thin with shoulder length white hair coming from the sides of his bald head. Black eyes flashed red when they rested on her.

Deidre and Cyn were led to the small space between the other prisoners. She stood close to the Mage, while Cyn stood next to her friend.

Deidre stepped away from the shimmering bell jar of energy surrounded Sir. She glanced down and saw he stood within a circle of containment, similar to the one at her summoning.

Hans was also surrounded by a shimmery wall of energy. But his jar pulsed erratically. Instead of the smooth, even surface, the

288

force appeared sporadic. Large holes appeared and disappeared in the swirling power. Glancing at his feet, she understood.

The circle of containment under Sir was set into the tiles of the floor. It was permanent. The other one appeared to have been drawn with haste, as one of the lines was a millimeter out of position. To release the male, all one would have to do is rub out the section where the two lines touched.

The Sentinel called the Council to order using a long flowery speech that had Deidre tuning out.

Deidre cleared her throat and caught Cyn's glance. Deidre nodded her head toward the floor beneath the second prisoner. Cyn looked down and frowned, before turning a puzzled gaze toward her. Deidre glanced straight down and mimicked putting out a cigarette with her foot.

Cyn's eyes got big and she nodded once. *Good, the Vamp got it.*

Sir cleared his throat, and she looked at him. "You are not to speak." He hissed in a low tone, his instruction masked by the speech of the Sentinel.

She felt compulsion shimmer through her.

Dar'kirm take him!

Because it was a function of the spell that summoned her, a spell that was already in place, the containment field didn't inhibit the command from taking effect.

The Sentinel wound down and called the court to order.

"The Council of Paranormal Races is now in session. Before this august assemblage, we have four beings requiring judgment for crimes committed against the Races."

Murmurs filled the room.

The Sentinel cleared his throat and pulled a scroll from his pocket.

Deidre frowned. Why did this seem familiar? *Oh right. I was tried in my last incarnation as well. Demoni justice. I wonder if Paranormal justice is any better?*

Unrolling the scroll, he read in an imperious voice.

"The charges are as follows. Mage Clint Douglas has been charged with the theft of the Forbidden Tome of Magic, use of the aforementioned Tome; attempted murder; and plotting to overthrow the Elite.

Demon Hans Drebin has been charged with the use of the forbidden practice of Voglio.

Vampire Cyn has been charged with aiding and abetting a murderer.

Succubus Deidre has been charged with murder of Elite personnel, aiding and abetting Mage Clint Douglas, and attempted murder."

"Succubus Deidre, please approach the bench."

She exchanged glances with Cyn then went to stand before Mr. Phoenix.

The Sentinel gave specifics. "You are charged with the deaths of three Elite warriors: Mage Earl Davenport, Elf Klaus Christianson and Shifter Lupine Roger Thorn; the mass murder of male Paranormals of mixed Races, and attempted murder of Vampire Damien Alexander."

The Sentinel came forward and put a file on the bench. The Phoenix reached forward and opened the file. The Sentinel recited to the rest of the auditorium the contents of the file.

"Inside is the official autopsy report on the aforementioned Elite warriors as well as the young men. The Mage Earl Davenport was drained of magical energy and stabbed through the heart. The Elf and Shifter Lupine were drained of energy and then tortured to death. The Elite offices request the maximum punishment for the murder of its members. Death by anti-magic."

A smug grin crossed Sir's face. His eyes were lit by an unsavory glint that caused a shiver of dread to tingle down her spine.

Damien's expression was closed as he stood with his arms crossed over his chest. He nodded as the request for punishment was read. A small frown marred his brow and when he looked at her, anger flashed in his eyes.

Deidre averted her gaze, studying her bound hands, despair taking root in her heart.

He didn't understand… but then again, no one did.

With her inability to talk, they'd assume guilt. She took a deep breath and put her shoulders back. It had always been this way and always would. There wasn't anything she could do about it. She couldn't count on a new summoning; it was too soon.

A single tear escaped her eye and she brushed it away. She'd not appear weak before these males.

"How do you plead?"

She jerked as she realized the question had been addressed to her. Deidre opened and closed her mouth, trying to speak. Nothing.

Damien's voice came from right behind her and she jumped, startled to find him so close. "Aren't you going to answer the question?"

Deidre met his gaze, a wistful sigh escaping at the anger and revulsion she could see in his eyes.

She shook her head once and bowed her head, focusing on the elaborate stone floor, not seeing the design through watery eyes.

A chuckle from Sir drew her attention. He was grinning, looking cheerful. She squinted through her tears and saw a soft copper glow surround him.

How could he be glowing?

From what she knew, that only happened when he was absorbing the energy from the medallion. The metal around her neck remained dormant. It hadn't activated. So where was Sir getting the energy from?

No one else in the room noticed the glow, or if they did they didn't comment.

"Answer the question." A voice startled her from her musings.

Deidre looked around. She stumbled on the hem of Damien's coat. The sudden grip on her arm stopped her from falling.

J'kala. She hated being in front of an audience. Nervousness should be the least of her worries.

Deidre looked up at Mr. Phoenix's mask. An angry expression crossed the dark features of the material.

"Why are you not answering the charges?"

Deidre opened her mouth and tried to speak, but no sound emerged.

"Are you trying to be amusing?"

She shook her head. *Not at all.*

The Phoenix tilted his head to the side and his lips curved down.

She heard his voice in her head. *"What seems to be the problem?"*

Deidre jolted at the sound. It went against everything she knew to answer the question, but she couldn't help responding to his voice. *"Compulsion of silence."*

"Who did this?"

She hesitated, unsure of her answer. Unsure if she should even answer.

Phoenix's voice rang in her head. *"Why don't you respond?"*

Deidre shrugged. *"What would be the point?"*

"Justice being served."

"Justice? Justice for whom?"

"For those who've died and their families. Justice for everyone here."

Deidre snorted and shook her head. *"Ha! There is no justice. Not for me. There is only justice for those in power, those who can pay. Those who believe themselves above the law. Not for the innocent."*

"That's a cynical view. And you're wrong. There is justice, even for you. Now who commanded you to silence?"

She glanced at Sir and back down to her bound hands.

"I see." His voice paused a moment. *"How do you plead?"*

292

She glanced at Damien, seeing the condemnation in his gaze; the anger and the disdain of her for what he believed she'd done and who he believed she was. Her heart sank heavy with depression.

With a heavy sigh she gave him her answer. *"I drained the males in question."*

Mr. Phoenix cleared his throat and to speak, when maniacal laughter rang out through the silent court.

Deidre turned and looked at Sir.

His head was thrown back as laughter consumed him. The glow surrounding him strengthened until it was visible by all in the room.

Gasps and shouts echoed in the chamber. Movement from the members of the audience as they stood, and some entered the circle of light in the center of the room.

They rushed to Sir, coming to a stop when the sound of a gavel striking wood froze them in their tracks.

Mr. Phoenix spoke. "Councilors please, return to your seats."

They grumbled and left the flagstone floor for the darkness beyond. The mumbling and gasps stopped to be replaced by the same voice that had wanted her to be removed from the court.

"Your Grace. The accused is glowing. Something he should not be able to do within that containment circle. What is going on?"

The mask's eyes flashed with anger as he turned toward the speaker.

"My Lord Maye. I am as in the dark about what is happening as you are. However if you will allow me to proceed without interruption, I'm sure we can get to the bottom of the situation."

The speaker, Lord Maye, grumbled "Certainly, Your Grace." And Deidre didn't hear a peep from him after that.

Mr. Phoenix addressed Sir. "Mage Clint Douglas, do you have anything to say?"

The gleam in Sir's eyes sent icy tendrils of dread through her blood. There wasn't a single trace of sanity left in his face. Power arced in the depths of his gaze and his laughter came to an abrupt halt as if someone had thrown a switch.

His lips twisted in a grimace of a smile. "Say? Oh yes. You and your precious Council of Elders and those trained dogs you call Elite are nothing. Nothing! You, who sit upon your chair and decide the fate of innocents. Well I'm not innocent, and I'll show you the power of the mistake you made by messing with my family!"

He took two steps and left the containment drawing.

Sir snapped his fingers and a small puff of smoke revealed a book hovering open at chest height.

More gasps could be heard and one of the Mages from the audience came forward.

"The stolen Tome of Magic!"

Ah. So that's what the book was.

The pages flipped by an unseen hand and Sir began chanting. A golden glow rose around him. Energy splashed against his shield and fell away like water on glass. She assumed they were spells trying to stop or contain him.

Nothing worked.

He paced, the attempts to contain him, failing.

Damien and James rushed forward. He pointed at them and Deidre could see a pale trace of magic extend from his finger to encircle the two Elite warriors.

He lifted the two into the air and, with a casual flick of his wrist, sent them sailing into the darkened audience.

Deidre heard a cacophony of noise as the two crashed into the seats and the Council members who sat there. Shouted curses and spells added to the noise of the chamber.

Deidre stepped out of the way, moving toward the door as four more Elite rushed toward Sir.

He laughed and sent them hurtling out into the darkness.

"Enough of this foolishness! You'll pay for your crimes!" Sir's shout stilled the noise in the room for a moment.

The scent of sulfur filled the air as he began to speak the words of a new spell. A premonition of danger had her backing away from him and whatever he was about to unleash.

Damien staggered in from the audience, his lip bleeding and a nasty bruise forming on his forehead.

She heard a voice inside her head. *"Stop him from completing that spell!"*

Deidre turned to find Mr. Phoenix staring at her. *"Why?"*

"To save the lives of those in this room. He's summoning a creature to destroy the Council."

Cynicism filled her, and she chuckled. *"Like they would do the same for me. I'm treated like so much filth under their expensive shoes. They deserve whatever Sir is going to do to them."*

An eyebrow rose on the mask. *"And what about Cyn and Bar'ella? Do they not deserve to be saved?"*

"Yes, but Bar'ella isn't here."

He shook his head. *"And don't think for one moment that whatever he is bringing here will be contained by this room. It will escape and will destroy not only Paranormals, but humans as well."*

Deidre remained silent, not sure what to say, and hating the fact that part of her wanted to help. His voice continued, *"And what about the Elite, James, Jor'dan and Damien. Don't they deserve to be saved?"*

She glared at him. *"They can save themselves."*

He shook his head. *"Whatever is being summoned is too powerful for them. Not even I can defeat what Mage Douglas is summoning."*

"Then how do you expect me to help?"

"By doing something only you can do."

With that cryptic statement, he turned around and walked toward the battle.

She wasn't a Mage; she was only a Succubus who could... drain... energy.

The Medallion!

She reached up and grabbed it in her hand. She tried to concentrate. How had she pushed the magic to him before? A pulse beneath her hand had her opening her eyes. She could see the smoky trail that led from Sir to the medallion.

Deidre smiled. Now to pull the energy from him.

She focused on her magic, treating the medallion like one of her donors. She inhaled the smoky tendrils of energy. It fought her, resisting her call. She closed her eyes, and the noise in the room faded as her concentration became complete.

Reaching out with her power, she caught a tendril of energy and pulled.

There! A small trickle, but energy nonetheless. She opened her eyes.

Sir was reading the spell and didn't notice what she was doing.

The thin smoky trickle, strengthened as she pulled.

As she absorbed the energy, it became harder to keep the flow coming.

Sir looked up from the book, and glared at her. He snapped his fingers and a wave of premonition seized her.

He was going to punish her. She felt the familiar slicing pain on her feet glanced down.

J'kala! Not the Red Mist again.

How could he do two spells at once? Her concentration slipped and the energy stopped. *Shit!* It wasn't important right now.

She needed to focus. Concentrate on pulling the energy. She tried to ignore the slices of agony moving up her legs. Sweat rolled down her cheek as she fought to keep the power flowing into her.

A movement behind Sir nearly broke her concentration. Cyn freed her friend amid the confusion, looked around, and grabbed an object from the floor and lobbed it toward Sir.

The sound of a bell rang through the room as the object hit the floor. It distracted him long enough that he forgot to concentrate on his spell.

Deidre pulled, absorbing as much as she could.

It wasn't enough. Where had he gotten this much energy, this much power?

There was enough to finish the spell. She'd need to be careful; her life depended on drawing enough energy to stop the spell and not enough to kill him.

The copper glow surrounding him dimmed.

Dar'kirm take it, she needed to draw more.

Deidre had never absorbed this much energy before. She felt light headed, dizzy. The one good thing was that it also dulled the sharp pain of the mist to a tolerable level.

She inhaled more of the smoky tendrils until she felt full to bursting, but it wasn't enough to stop him. She drew more and more again. Nothing else registered; nothing else mattered.

The scent of burning leather assailed her nose, but her concentration didn't break. She barely felt Damien's coat being ripped from her body. One small part of her mind registered the fact that someone had doused her with water and that steam rose from the hissing drops touching her skin. The same part of her mind registered the blinding pain that came from her chest. And then she was beyond pain, beyond sensation.

She existed as pure energy, pure power. And was consumed by it.

Damien ran toward Deidre as the duster began to smoke. *What the hell was she doing?*

He tried to rip the smoking leather off her, but couldn't get close enough; the heat rolling off her was too intense.

"Here let me. Take care of Mage Clint." His Grace pushed him toward the Mage.

Damien watched out of the corner of his eye as His Grace removed the burning leather from her body, then doused her with water. Steam hissed as it rose from her and he lost sight of her face. When it cleared, reddish blue flames broke out along her skin before flickering out. *What the hell was going on?*

Maniacal laughter erupted from Mage Douglas. Damien motioned to James and they circled Clint, who was still speaking the words of the spell, though at a much slower pace than before. He finished the spell and clapped his hands.

Damien tensed, preparing himself for whatever the Mage had done.

Nothing happened.

A look of intense frustration crossed Clint's face, before he turned toward Deidre. "Bitch! I'll teach you to drain my energy!"

He took a step toward her, and Damien stepped into his path.

Clint's eyes lit in feral glee. "Finally, Alexander you'll pay for killing my baby girl."

The Mage snapped his fingers, and a long thin blade appeared in his hand.

Damien turned looking for a weapon, any weapon.

"Damien!" He turned at James' shout and caught the blade his partner tossed to him, and turned in time to block Clint's swing. He didn't even question where James found a sword.

"You are going to die, Alexander!"

Clint raised the sword above his head and slashed downward with all his strength. Damien used his Vampiric speed to thrust his blade into the Mage's heart before he completed his stroke.

Clint gazed at him, wide eyed as he looked down.

"Bastard…" he whispered before toppling over.

Damien approached and checked his pulse.

Mage Clint Douglas was dead.

A horrific scream behind him, and he whirled around in time to see Deidre collapse to the floor surrounded by a blue nimbus of flame.

"No!" Damien ran toward her, his heart in his throat as he watched her writhe within the hottest part of the flame. An arm shot out and stopped him before he got close.

"Stop! She'll incinerate you!" His Grace commanded.

Damien turned his gaze to the High Chancellor, who had removed his mask.

"What's happening?" Damien couldn't hide the anguish in his voice.

His Grace shook his head. "She drew more energy than her body could hold. It was the only way to stop Mage Douglas from completing the spell." He paused for a moment. "She saved us."

Devastation crushed his chest as Damien watched the macabre scene before him. Deidre arched her back and opened her mouth in a silent scream before her body went still and the flames died. The scent of burnt skin filled his lungs as her charred body lay on the stone floor.

High Chancellor Ignatio knelt next to her, putting his hand on her throat, checking for a pulse.

Damien knelt across from him, ignoring the intense heat radiating from her skin, hoping that she'd be alright. He looked at the Phoenix as the male drew back and moved his hand over Deidre's face, closing her sightless, violet eyes.

She was gone.

It was then he realized everything she meant to him, how important she'd become. She'd save them, him, twice. The true measure of character was in a person's actions. He'd forgotten that as he'd let other opinions destroy what had been growing between them. Now he'd never get the chance to fix things between them. No more late night chats over coffee. No more mischievous smiles or teasing glances. No more passionate embraces. No more of what made her, made them, special.

His heart felt dead in his chest, as if it had died with her.

He felt a hand clasp his shoulder and turned to look up at His Grace, through watery vision. Sorrow filled the Phoenix's expression. "I'm sorry, Damien."

§

Cyn led Hans to the red and gold waiting room. Ten Elite were scattered around the room, waiting.

"Hurry! Mage Douglas is out of control! He's destroying the Council!"

The Elite rushed into the room leaving the exit clear. As they ran into the hall of doors, Hans grabbed her arm stopping her. "Hold on. Don't rush. The doors may be warded."

Cyn waited. Heart pounding, it felt like they'd be recaptured at any moment.

Hans shook his head. "Sloppy."

"What?"

He gestured to the doors. "The spells are one way."

"So only authorized people in, but anyone can get out?" At his nod, she grinned. "Then let's get the hell out of here."

They ran down the corridor, each door opening at their approach. At the cul-de-sac, Cyn stopped. "Use that door."

Hans grabbed her arm before she could turn back. "Where are you going?"

"I've got to help Deidre."

"You can't. She's surrounded by Elite and you can't get back through the doors."

Cyn glanced back to the first door, hearing a muffled scream. "She'll be okay, right?"

"I don't know. Warn the healer."

"Good idea."

They escaped through the men's room and Cyn was sure they'd get caught as they sneaked through the Elite offices. But no one approached or questioned them. Exiting the double doors and into the fog-shrouded night, Cyn took a deep breath.

They walked blocks toward Hans' warehouse. On one of the corners he stopped. "Go warn the healer."

"Are you sure you'll be safe getting home?"

He smiled, putting his hands on her shoulders and pulling her into him. He placed a kiss on her forehead. "Child, I've been at this much longer than you have. Now go, if I need help, I'll call."

"Yes, Hans."

Cyn jogged to the Luna Clinic. The receptionist was on the phone and waved her through to the back.

Cyn knocked on Bar'ella's door, and it opened before she could grasp the door handle.

Bar'ella grabbed her arm and pulled her into the office, pushing her into the chair in front of the desk.

The healer held a phone between her shoulder and head as she began to make tea.

Cyn didn't say anything, unsure of her friend's mood.

The healer's face drained of color. Cyn saw the shocked expression on her face before Bar'ella dropped the receiver of the phone on the desk.

Cyn jumped up and caught Bar'ella as she collapsed, and helped the healer to sit in her chair. Cyn reached over and hung up the phone.

"What happened?"

Tears leaked from the healer's eyes as Cyn met her devastated gaze. "Deidre's dead."

Chapter 19

Captain Jor'dan accompanied Deidre's charred corpse into the Luna Clinic.

Bar'ella met them, with puffy eyes and tears streaming down her face. Sniffling, she tried to keep her emotions in check, but burst into tears when Jor'dan opened his arms. He gave her a comforting hug. Taking a deep breath, she regained control and stepped away. "Bring her here."

She led the way down the hall through a set of double doors. The gurney with the body bag was pushed into the room. The attendants moved the black bag onto the stainless steel table.

Bar'ella turned to the deep sink and washed her hands before donning gloves and a mask. She unzipped the bag and motioned for him to remove it. "Strange."

"What?" Jor'dan demanded.

Bar'ella shook her head. "Visual inspection reveals severe burns on one hundred percent of her body. Hair burnt to stubble. No pulse, no signs of respiratory activity, and yet..."

She reached out and brushed the charred flesh. Skin flaked off, and she frowned.

Pink skin appeared under the burnt epidermis.

Bar'ella took a stethoscope and placed the diaphragm on Deidre's chest. Nothing.

No sign of life that she could see, or hear, but the dim purple glow of Deidre's aura was still visible.

She stood and turned to the Captain. "She's not dead, at least, not yet."

"What?! Are you certain?" His incredulousness was evident.

Joy filled her heart, and she could feel the smile on her face. "Yes, I'm sure. Her aura is weak, but there."

Jor'dan narrowed his gaze and after a few minutes spoke. "I can't see any auric signature. Are you sure?"

Bar'ella nodded. "Yes. I'm familiar with her signature. It's faint, but it's there."

Stepping into the hall she summoned to assistant healers. "Please see to it that the patient is bathed and taken to a room."

They bowed. "Right away, Healer Bar'ella."

She turned into the room to see Jor'dan frowning down at Deidre.

"What's going on?" Jor'dan looked puzzled, as if he didn't trust Bar'ella's statement. "I can't think of anyone who'd be able to survive what she did, except maybe Ash."

"Come to my office and you can tell me what happened." Bar'ella made a soothing blend of tea, offering him a cup. His bloodshot eyes and deeper lines around his mouth concerned her. "When did you last sleep?"

"A couple of days ago." He took the cup and sighed as he sipped the hot liquid. "I promise I'll take a couple of days off after Festival."

Bar'ella sighed. "You know better than to exhaust yourself."

"Yes, but it's necessary."

"Take a few moments and relax," she instructed.

Jor'dan nodded and they chatted about inconsequential things while finishing the tea. He put the cup down and related the disastrous events of the previous evening.

"It sounds like shock; her body couldn't handle the amount of energy, and it was released as heat, causing severe burns. She was connected to Mage Clint Douglas when he died, probably suffering from backlash."

"What would that do?"

Bar'ella shook her head. "I'm not quite sure. I can base my theory off of what happens to others. If the relationship is close, she'd have followed him into death, but since he was her master, I'm not sure."

"Wait, what do you mean, he was her master?"

"I told you she was a slave. Mage Douglas was the one who summoned her. There's a severe punishment if she tried to harm her master, but I have no idea what happens if he dies."

"So you're saying she didn't kill my men on her own?"

Bar'ella shook her head. "No. She doesn't kill, not of her own volition."

"Why didn't she just say so when asked?"

Bar'ella cocked an eyebrow. "First, the spell that holds her prohibits her from saying anything about it, and second, who would believe her?"

Jor'dan frowned. "What do you mean?"

She sighed. "Look at this from her point of view. She's arrested for murder, sent to trial with everyone assuming her guilt and no one bothering to find a motive. Why would she drain anyone to death, when men are more useful to her alive?"

"I... I never thought of that." Jor'dan admitted.

"I know. And everyone in your office immediately assumed guilt and that was that."

The Fae squirmed in his seat. "We failed her."

Bar'ella was interrupted by the ringing of her phone. "Yes?"

"The patient is ready. Her color is better."

"Thank you." Bar'ella looked at Jor'dan. "Shall we go?"

He stood and held the door for her. She nodded and led the way to Deidre's room.

A much different looking Deidre rested on the bed. Instead of blackened skin, she was now light pink.

Jor'dan stood at the foot of the bed while Bar'ella looked for any vital signs. Still nothing. If it weren't for the aura, she'd be convinced Deidre was dead.

"How soon will she wake?" he asked.

Bar'ella shrugged. "I don't know."

"Why not?"

She looked at him, exasperation in her tone, hand on her hips. "Jor'dan, I don't exactly know what's wrong with her." Bar'ella held up her hand, stopping him. "If there was a way to contact her brother, he might know."

Placing her hands on either side of Deidre's head, she focused on the Succubus' vital signs. No heartbeat, weak aura and energy levels very low.

"She has a brother?"

"Yes. And she needs energy."

"Can he give it to her?"

"I don't know."

Jor'dan spoke. "Why does she need energy? I thought too much energy did this to her?"

Bar'ella sighed. "Yes, it did. Think of it like eating a year's worth of food all at one sitting. You'd get a tremendous stomachache and be very ill until your body was able to process the food. Same situation applies here. She lives off sexual energy. She has a mechanism to take what she needs, but I don't know how she does it."

Bar'ella looked at Deidre. Something about her was different, what was it? Ah.. She turned to Jor'dan. "What happened to the medallion?"

He reached into his pocket, pulled out the disc and handed it to her. "It's dead."

Bar'ella looked at it and could feel none of the magic that had imbued it before. "Did you remove it?"

305

Jor'dan shook his head. "It fell off when they put her in the bag."

Bar'ella put it on the bedside table.

Damien woke to a despair so profound he didn't know how he'd survive. His girl was gone. Charred to cinders before they could reconcile, before he told her what was in his heart. He heard James moving around but couldn't summon the energy to care. Nothing mattered now that she was dead.

"Hey buddy. Want a bottle?" James tone was soft.

Damien shook his head. "Nah. Not hungry."

"I know. But you need to eat. We've got a shitload of cleanup to do tonight."

"All right." But his heart wasn't in it.

Damien heard James rustle around in the kitchen when the other Vamp's cell phone rang. Not even the Star Trek ring tone could bring a smile to Damien's face.

"Holy Fuck!"

James ran in from the kitchen and tossed the bottle of blood to Damien.

"Come on buddy we've got to roll."

Damien popped the top and downed the bottle in one gulp. "What's going on?"

"You're not going to believe this, but according to Bar'ella, Deidre's alive."

"What?" Damien's world shifted again. "Are you sure?" Disbelief warred with hope. *Please let it be true.*

James nodded. "Bar'ella thinks she's alive."

Hope. Love. Joy. "Let's go." He sprinted down the hall of his apartment building. "Elevator's too slow, let's hit the stairs."

He and James hit the lobby and were out the front door in seconds, upsetting another resident who'd entered the building.

James drove, and they reached the clinic in record time.

When the receptionist at the clinic saw them come through the door, she immediately got on the phone. In under a minute the door was open and an assistant healer motioned to them.

"Come on back."

She turned and led the way to a treatment room. Damien felt like a little kid, nervous with anticipation.

"Are you sure she's alive?"

The healer stopped in front of a closed door. "Healer Bar'ella is certain." She knocked once and opened the door.

Damien entered the room and rushed to her side. She was still as death. But she wasn't dead. The healers confirmed it. He reached down and stroked the skin of her cheek with the back of his hand.

"Why won't she wake up?" his voice soft as he looked his fill.

"She's in an energy deficient coma." Bar'ella answered. "Take her hand, Damien."

Damien took her hand in a gentle grip, palm against palm.

Bar'ella placed her hand on top of theirs. "Good, you're giving her energy by touching her, but it's not enough."

"How do you know?"

"I can sense her levels, and they're very low."

"So what are we going to do?"

"You need to give her more energy."

"How?"

"How did you give it to her before?"

Heat filled Damien's face. "Um.." Did she really mean? "Wait, you want me to have sex with her, when she's like this?"

"No, that wouldn't work. You need to achieve release and give her the energy."

Damien looked down at Deidre's pale face. "Let me try something."

He closed his eyes and pushed energy toward her. Her body absorbed the gift like sand soaking up water. Damien opened his eyes to see her draw a single breath. Her body still on exhalation.

Bar'ella placed a hand on his arm. "It's not enough. She needs the energy of your orgasm."

Damien hesitated a moment. "You're familiar with Vampire physiology, right?"

"Yes. What does that have to do with anything?"

"I need blood to come, and I promised her I wouldn't take her blood without permission. And since her blood is different…"

Bar'ella paused a moment. "Hmm. Let me check something."

She picked up and needle and pricked Deidre's finger. A drop of green blood welled and the healer collected it onto a tongue depressor.

"Here, taste."

Damien frowned. "Are you sure?"

Bar'ella sighed. "Damien Alexander, I'm right here monitoring your reactions. Should it be poisonous, you're in the best place to find out."

"All right."

He licked the drop off the tongue depressor and the taste of her blood detonated on his tongue like hundred proof alcohol, a fiery bite with a hint of spice. His head arched back and he struggled for control. Raw lust raced through him and only through sheer will was he able to stop himself from coming in his jeans. A few deep breaths later he managed to open his eyes.

Shit. Damn. Fuck. What a taste!

"Well?" Bar'ella's eyebrow shot up and she tried to hide her smirk.

"She's potent." His hoarse tone surprised him.

"That's what I thought. Take no more than a single sip."

"Yes, ma'am."

The healer turned and ushered everyone from the room. "We'll be waiting for you in my office when you're done."

"Thank you."

Damien removed his hand from Deidre's and looked in the bedside table. He found hand lotion that he could use as lubrication. He pulled it out, and put it within easy reach before turning back to the bed.

He reached down and stroked her warm skin, an indication of life, even though she'd taken a single breath. Damien removed his clothes and shifted her over on the mattress.

He frowned at her slight weight. She felt insubstantial in his arms, as if she were drifting away from him. His heart clenched. He'd bring her back.

Damien climbed onto the bed, settled down beside her, and threaded his fingers through hers.

He grabbed the bottle and squirted a dollop of lotion into his hand. Closing his eyes, he imagined himself in a scenario that would entail him masturbating in front of the woman he loved. They'd indulge in a romantic evening of extended foreplay.

In his mind's eye, a vision blossomed.

A lit fireplace provided the only illumination in the room. He and Deidre sat across from each other Indian style. Both wearing short black silk robes parted over their thighs. Deidre's wavy blond hair was loose flowing over the collar of the robe. A fluffy rug near the hearth protected them from the cool wooden floor below. A bottle of champagne sat off to the side, chilling in a bucket of ice.

Her voice purred at him. "Are you sure you're up to this?"

Damien parted his robe, showing off his stiff cock. "What do you think?"

Her teasing laugh delighted him. "I think you enjoy showing off."

"What can I say, you inspire me."

"I need a closer look." Deidre crawled on her hands and knees toward him, a sensual predator ready to devour. Leaning up she placed a quick bite on his lower lip. The small sting revved his lust into overdrive, and it was all he could do to stay seated and not take her to the floor and fuck her senseless.

"Impressive. Now what?"

"According to the healer, I'm supposed to achieve orgasm and feed you."

Deidre arched an eyebrow. "Really? Is that what they're calling it now?"

"I don't mean oral sex, I meant energy."

She leaned forward and licked his lips before settling on her stomach on the large pillow that appeared beneath her. Her elbows were propped on the floor, and she rested her chin in her hands. Her feet lifted into the air as she swung them back and forth. "Very well Vampire. Show me what you've got."

Eyes locked on hers, he shrugged out of the silk and leaned back against a pillow, one leg stretched to one side of her, the other bent in front.

Deidre was close enough that he felt her breath against his cock when she sighed. "Well? Are you going to get on with it?" she asked her voice husky with passion.

He grinned at her. "Like what you see?"

She licked her lips, "What do you think?"

He put his hand at the base of his erection and fondled his balls, rolling them and kneading them with his fingers. She leaned forward, reaching out to help him.

He leaned back out of her reach, enjoying her frustrated pouting.

"This is a solo effort, darling."

Damien fisted the base of his cock and drew his hand slowly up the shaft. When he reached the tip, he rubbed it with his thumb. Her gaze was locked on his lap and she licked her lips, as if she wanted to suck him deep into her mouth.

Keeping his eyes on her face, he stroked his cock, covering it with the lotion on his palm. God that felt so damned good.

The interest in her gaze heightened his lust, but he wanted to draw this out, wanted to make it last. He stroked slow, up and down. "Like what you see?"

She licked her lips and nodded, reaching out to him, enfolding his hand in hers. Together they stroked him. He removed his hand, letting her do the work. A swift tight stroke had him gritting his teeth. Not yet.

"What about you?" His question stopped her hand.

Her head tilted to the side. "I thought this was about you?"

Damien shook his head. "It's about us both. Let's do it like this."

He released his shaft and arranged them in one of his favorite sixty nine positions.

"Why this way?" Her husky voice filled sounded intrigued.

"I need blood to come."

"But it's poison."

Damien disagreed. "It's not. Trust me. I'll be fine. Now, where were we?"

"I thought you were supposed to do it yourself?"

"I am, but while I'm doing, I want to watch you pleasure yourself."

Between their bodies, he saw her bite her lip. "But it doesn't work for me like that."

Damien sat up. "What do you mean?"

Deidre shrugged. "I don't feel pleasure masturbating."

"I have an idea. Are you willing to try?"

"Okay."

He lay back down and grabbed her hands. One hand, he guided to his aching cock. The other he threaded their fingers together and began touching her body. He tried to ignore the grip on his dick while paying attention to what her body was telling him.

Circling her clit with fingers didn't elicit any reaction. Clitoral stimulation wasn't working for her. Time to try her g-spot. He circled and teased, letting the wetness of her body ease the way for their fingers. A quick delve into her sheath made her gasp for breath. Easing back he circled and did it again, this time pushing

311

deeper. With his middle finger, he found the spot and pressed her fingers against it.

She cried out and clenched her thighs around both of their hands. The grip on his cock became erratic as he heard her breathing fracture. Perfect.

Again and again he returned to the area, sometimes pressing, sometimes stroking. Soon her body clenched so hard it was difficult to move. Her grip on him tightened and he was close, so close.

Removing their hands from her body, he brought her fingers to his mouth, sucking her flavor from her finger. With one tooth he nipped her finger. The explosion of taste over his tongue blinded him to everything but the electric pleasure coursing through him. He was the heart of the starburst, the heat of the explosion and his world fractured.

His cock exploded with hot jets of semen that seemed to go on forever. He slumped to the side and opened his eyes to see Deidre's body splattered with come. Primal satisfaction coursed through him. He'd marked his woman; she was his forever.

She crawled over to him and he rolled on his back with his arm out. She snuggled into his embrace. He hugged her to him and closed his eyes for a moment, content and comfortable.

A few moments later she sighed, breath moving across his chest. He stroked a hand down her back. "How are you feeling?"

"Okay. Why?"

"Do you have enough energy or do you need more?"

Deidre was quiet for a moment. "I need more." Her hand roamed over his chest and his deflated cock surged back to life. Thank God he was a Vampire. He could go all night and still be ready for more.

"What would you like to do now?" he asked, his voice deepening as she rolled onto her side, exposing her delicious front to his gaze.

"I want to feel you deep inside me, all the way up to my throat." She straddled his body and raked her nails down his chest. The sharp sting of pain had his breath stilling in his lung. She was perfect.

"I want you so deep inside, neither of us will know where one ends and the other begins. I want us merged so tightly together we become one. I want to feel you pulsing inside me, filling me with yourself. I want you to fuck me into oblivion."

His cock pounded to the beat of his pulse, her words and the feelings they conveyed were more arousing than he would have ever thought possible.

"Well then let's get on with it shall we?" he smiled at her as she licked her lips.

She leaned over, putting her breasts at mouth level and teased him by grabbing one rubbing the nipple across the seam of his lips. His tongue darted out to taste.

Damien opened his mouth and sucked the nipple into his mouth between his fangs. She gasped and let her head fall back. He sucked and released; sucked and released. Her fingers dug into his shoulders, and she arched back. *"Oh yes!"*

He grabbed her waist, and drew her down hard onto his straining cock. They both groaned at the penetration. He released her breast with a pop, and she gazed down into his eyes.

"Are you going to move?" he asked, flexing his dick inside her.

Deidre tightened her inner muscles, caressing him from the inside.

"How's that?" she asked with a twinkle in her eye.

"Not enough," he groaned.

She lifted off him just a tiny bit and slammed back down hard.

"How was that?" she asked, breathless.

"Okay," he gasped.

"Just okay? Not good enough." She did it again, combining the drop with the fluttering of her internal muscles.

313

"Better. Much better," he managed to gasp out between drops.

God, she was going to kill him with pleasure, but what a way to go. He'd die happy.

Deidre tilted her hips back and dropped again. He felt something. Her body tightened in a delicious grip before she released. He thrust again, hitting her spot. Her reaction was the same, but lasted longer. "I've got you now." He grinned and lifted her enough to thrust deep, hitting her g-spot each time. She clenched around him, a soft sensual fist, as she screamed her release.

She became boneless in his embrace, slumping down so her head rested on his shoulder.

After a few moments, she lifted her head and frowned. "You didn't come."

"I need blood, darling."

She tilted her head to the side. "Are you okay from the blood you took before?"

He nodded. "I'm not dead, if that's what you're worried about."

Deidre bit her lip. "Okay then." Her lashes lowered, hiding her eyes. A teasing grin flirted on her lips. "Bite me. I dare ya."

"Are you sure?" he asked, aroused beyond thought.

She leaned down, tilting her head to give him access to her throat. He bit her neck and her taste sizzled through his blood, energizing and invigorating.

She clenched around him, as his bite seemed to send her over the edge of another orgasm. He followed, his grip tightening on her hips as he slammed them together. Damien felt blissfully drained as he pumped himself dry.

Deidre looked at him, her face soft with a smile. "That was wonderful."

He couldn't help but smile up at her. His erection was still a hard pulsing length inside her.

314

"Are you ready for the next round?" he asked.

"Whenever you are." She responded, removing her body from his.

"Oh yeah," Deidre gave him a Cheshire cat grin, and flipped herself around so her head was at his groin as she lay on her side.

He rolled onto his side, facing her belly.

She opened her mouth and took him inside. He groaned at the feel of her tongue cleaning off his cock of their combined juices.

He lifted her left leg over his chest, bending her leg and securing it with his arm. His head was pillowed on her soft inner thigh. Their combined scent filled his nose. It spoke to something primitive within him. Another level of marking her as his.

He leaned forward and licked her from vagina to anus and back again. She tasted divine, with a hint of his essence. He groaned and pulled back a bit as her tongue found a sensitive spot on his shaft. His tongue teased her clit and he rimmed the opening of her vaginal entrance.

Her hips thrust forward toward his tongue, and he stroked his tongue deep into her channel, savoring the taste of her and the feeling of her closing around him. He rubbed his chin against her, knowing his stubble would further stimulate her sensitive flesh. He felt her moan around his shaft.

Shit. Damn. Fuck. That felt great.

He was rewarded by another vibrating moan on his straining cock.

Let's make things more interesting.

Damien used the fingers of his right hand to tease the rose of her anus.

She groaned again, pushed, and his finger slid deep into her dark hole. The possibilities bloomed in his mind. Strong suction on his cock recalled him to the job at hand. He swirled his tongue around her clit, while pumping one, then two fingers into her ass.

She released his erection from her mouth and moaned encouragement at him, while continuing on with a hand job.

"Oh yes. Harder, please harder."

Her hips were moving back and forth, her orgasm getting closer and closer. He could feel the contractions of her orgasm on his tongue and around his fingers. She threw back her head and screamed in completion.

He was almost there himself, when she once again drew his penis deep into her mouth and swallowed it. His hips began thrusting faster and faster as she sucked harder and harder. The fluttering of her throat as she swallowed pushed him over the edge.

She grabbed his ass with both hands and pulled him into her face so far that her nose was right up against his balls. He bit the inside of her thigh, and he felt himself pulse down her throat as she swallowed his semen over and over again. The pleasure was so intense, he nearly lost consciousness. It was the most intense orgasm he'd ever had.

Once he stopped pumping his seed down her throat, she eased back and gave his penis a tender tongue bath making sure to clean up every drop of his semen.

He glanced down at her and saw her licking her lips to catch every last drop of his essence. "Your taste is addicting. I love it."

He flipped onto his back, and she came to rest within his embrace. They snuggled together for a few moments while their heart rates returned to normal.

"How are you feeling?" he asked, a little concerned for the rough way he had used her.

"That was wonderful." She purred, sounding content.

She turned her head and looked him in the eye.

"That was the best I have ever had, thank you."

Damien blinked, drawn out of the fantasy.

He opened his eyes and found the four walls of the clinic surrounding them. He rested on the bed with her snuggled up against him. He heard her heart beat, and felt her breath on his chest as she inhaled and exhaled. He hugged her to him and glanced at the clock on the wall.

What the hell? Where had the time gone?

It was almost dawn. He'd have to leave soon.

She moaned and wiggled against him. In a soft voice that was more asleep than awake she said, "I mean it, Damien, best I have ever had."

He leaned over and called her name.

"Deidre?"

Damien disengaged from her sleeping form, smiling at the pout that graced her face. He brushed a lock of hair away from her face, marveling at the softness of her skin. Turning toward the bathroom, he cleaned himself up as best he could without a shower and pressed the call button.

"Yes, Damien?" Bar'ella asked.

"I think it worked."

"I'll be right there."

Bar'ella hurried into the room followed by Captain Jor'dan, and checked Deidre's vital signs. She turned and beamed at him. "Thank you Damien. It worked."

She narrowed her eyes at him. "How are you feeling?"

Damien frowned at the question. "I feel fine."

"You're not feeling drained?" Jor'dan asked.

Damien shook his head. "I'm a little tired, but no more so than normal before dawn. Why do you ask?"

Jor'dan exchanged a look with Bar'ella. "No reason, just curious. It's almost dawn. Go home and get some sleep."

"Yes sir."

Damien leaned down gave Deidre a brief kiss. "I'll be back later tonight, love."

He turned and nodded to the healer and his boss before heading home.

Jor'dan turned to see Bar'ella making notes on a chart.

"So why isn't Damien drained like the others?"

Bar'ella shrugged. "I don't know for sure, but I think it has something to do with the emotional bond between the two."

"When will she wake?"

Bar'ella gave him a stern look. "It will probably be a few hours. Why?"

"There are questions that need to be asked, the sooner the better."

"Come back at dusk. She should be fully rested by then."

He turned to leave the room.

"Jor'dan? What sort of question remains?"

Jor'dan looked back over his shoulder at her. "The Forbidden Tome of Magic is still missing. And today is the last day of the Festival. If we don't get the book back, the Shadow Earth spell cannot be renewed."

Jor'dan saw the color drain from the healer's face as she realized the implications. "Oh shit."

He couldn't have said it better himself.

Chapter 20

Deidre sat up in the clinic bed, dressed in a sheet with arm holes. The material was scratchy, not what she was used to. Her physical discomfort allowed her to ignore the small crowd arranged at the foot of the bed. Captain Jor'dan, James, and Damien had entered the room a few moments before and their unwavering scrutiny made her uncomfortable. She kept her head lowered so as not to witness the condemnation she was certain was in their expressions.

She plucked at the sheet to hide her nerves.

The door opened and she glanced at the new comers before once again lowering her gaze.

A striking male with the face of an angel entered the room. His light brown hair was slicked back, accentuating the sculpted planes of his face. She recognized him by his aura. Crap, it was Mr. Phoenix. This was not going to end well for her.

There were too many high-ranking males in the room all focused on her.

Damien walked over to the side of the bed, pulled up a chair, sat down, and reached for her hand. The heat and warmth of him had her biting her lip. Her dream had seemed so real, she could almost feel the contentment that had radiated from him. Too bad it had only been a dream. She tried to pull away, but he held on tight, squeezing as if in reassurance.

Deidre resumed her study of the ugly floral pattern on the blanket. Let them make the first move.

The door opened again, and Bar'ella entered the room. Deidre smiled, glad to see the healer as she checked vital signs. When done, Bar'ella cleared her throat causing Deidre to look up at her. "Very well, gentlemen, she's recovered enough. You may ask your questions."

Captain Jor'dan cleared his throat. "Succubus Deidre, were you aware of any of Mage Clint Douglas's plans?"

Deidre froze. *Dar'kirm take it. Another inquisition.*

She remained silent, taking a small measure of comfort from the familiar action.

Damien leaned forward and whispered. "Answer the question, love."

Deidre jolted. Love? What the hell did he mean by that?

Captain Jor'dan sighed and continued, "You don't know, or you won't answer?"

She looked up into his eyes. "Yes."

"Please cooperate."

"Why?"

Bar'ella sat down in a chair by the window and snorted at the question.

Captain Jor'dan glared at her. "Don't encourage her."

Bar'ella smiled. "I don't have to. Captain Jor'dan, in all the years I've known her, Deidre doesn't answer questions, nor gives up information easily."

Captain Jor'dan turned back to her. "Why not?"

Deidre shrugged. *No one believes me anyway. Why should I bother?*

A smothered snort came from Mr. Phoenix, but when Deidre glanced at him, his expression was serene.

Captain Jor'dan ran a hand through his hair, tousling the neatly combed locks. "Can't you simply answer the question?"

Deidre shook her head and looked at Bar'ella, willing the healer to explain.

Bar'ella sighed. "Captain Jor'dan, I told you before, the original spell that cursed Deidre prohibits her from revealing any information about her summoner."

"But her master is dead."

"That doesn't cancel this spell."

"Why not? I've never heard of a spell outliving its caster."

Bar'ella took a deep breath. "Non-magical humans can cast this spell. That means?"

"That means that the power is from within the spell itself and not dependent upon the practitioner."

"Right. It also why she wasn't able to revert to her natural form."

Everyone in the room stared at Deidre, who picked at the threads in the blanket pooled in her lap.

"So what does she really look like, and where does she get her looks?" James asked.

"I have no idea, her true form." Bar'ella admitted. "Her packaging comes from her Mage Douglas."

Captain Jor'dan frowned. "But she doesn't look that much like Elaine Douglas."

Bar'ella let out a loud breath. "Jor'dan, she's the ideal, of what Elaine looked like."

"Why not an exact copy?"

"Because it's part of her natural defense mechanism. She looks enough like her summoner's ideal to get what she needs before she moves on."

Everyone remained silent while they absorbed the information. Deidre slanted Bar'ella a look. The healer didn't have to give away all her secrets, did she?

"So how the hell do I find out the truth? Spell her?"

Deidre rolled her eyes. *Another freaking spell. Lovely.*

Damien squeezed her hand again, and as much as she hated to admit it, she was comforted by the gesture.

Bar'ella shook her head. "Truth spells won't work on her. I tried it the first time I met her. Try asking simpler questions."

Captain Jor'dan took a deep breath and held it before blowing it out slowly. He did this twice more.

She didn't mean to be difficult, it came naturally.

"Very well. Let's try it this way. Succubus Deidre, do you know where he got a Crystal Orb?"

What in Dar'kirm was a Crystal Orb? "What's that?"

Mr. Phoenix interrupted. "It's a globe that allows for the storage of power, to be released when the Mage requires it."

"Oh. No. I don't know where he got it."

Head bowed, she asked a question before he could ask the next question. "Am I under arrest, sentenced to be killed or…?"

She studied their reactions by looking through her eyelashes.

Mr. Phoenix raised an eyebrow. He held up his hand and stopped Captain Jor'dan who had his mouth open, ready to speak.

"Miss Deidre. There are too many things that we don't know about the entire situation. It would help us greatly if you would cooperate. Once we have the information required, we can proceed."

Which meant she wasn't going to get an answer to her question. The threat was subtle. Either she cooperate or… what? She couldn't tell. It didn't give her a reason to cooperate, that's for sure.

Captain Jor'dan continued with his questions.

"Do you know how many members are in the Underground?"

"I don't know what that is."

James answered her. "It's the organization that Mr. Douglas ran."

She gave him a small smile before turning back to Captain Jor'dan. "I don't know.

322

"Why not?"

Deidre sighed. "He didn't share his plans with me."

"All right. That's all the questions I have for now."

Oh good. We're done.

Mr. Phoenix stepped closer to the bed. "Perhaps there *is* something you know."

There are many things I know…. But I don't think that's what you mean.

Her tone was hesitant as she asked, "Like what?"

Mr. Phoenix paused for a moment. "Where is the book?"

Deidre wrinkled her nose. "Book? What book?"

Mr. Phoenix cleared his throat. "The forbidden Tome of Power that Clint Douglas stole."

How did she know what happened to the bloody thing? The last thing she remembered was Sir using it. She'd drained him and then… nothing.

"I don't know where it is. Why would I?"

Mr. Phoenix shook his head. "When Clint Douglas died, the Tome disappeared. The Council believes you have it. You were linked to him at the time of his death. We think the book followed the bond and attached itself to you."

She shook her head and released Damien's hand. She spread her arms wide. "As you can see I don't have it on me."

Mr. Phoenix smiled at her. "I would like to find out for sure."

Deidre dropped her arms, and Damien immediately reclaimed her hand.

"How?"

"Humor me. Call the book to you."

Oh-kay, Mr. Phoenix was short a few brain cells if he thought that would work, but she mentally shrugged. *What the hell. It couldn't hurt, right?* She closed her eyes. As if she could do magic… not!

"Oh Book of Magic, Tome of Power, I summon you to me."
She heard a snicker from Bar'ella. The healer had caught the
sarcasm in her tone.

Warmth spread over her face and arms, like she was being
bathed in sunshine. She opened her eyes. There in front of her,
floating at chest height, was the book.

"Well, son of J'kala." She looked at Mr. Phoenix, whom along
with the others took a large step back. Damien dropped her hand,
got out of the chair, and backed toward the wall.

"Now what?"

"Please take a hold of the book."

Damien took a step forward. "Wait!"

Deidre stopped mid-reach and frowned at him. "What?"

He turned and narrowed his gaze at Mr. Phoenix. "What if it
tries to take her over?"

Mr. Phoenix shook his head. "I don't believe it will."

Deidre looked around at everyone standing along the walls.
"The book is dangerous?"

Everyone nodded. It wasn't that bad. She reached out and took
a hold of it with both hands. The leather felt warm and
comfortable; soothing.

What was all the fuss about?

Bar'ella smiled as the males in the room took a step back even
further.

"How do you feel?" Mr. Phoenix asked.

What a strange question. Deidre shrugged. "Fine."

"Do you feel the need to use the Book for anything?"

She shook her head and patted the book. It rumbled at her, the
sound resembling a papery purr. She smiled in delight, stroking the
book again.

Mr. Phoenix studied her a moment before turning to Bar'ella.
"How much longer will she be here?"

"Her vitals are within normal range. I'd like to keep her
another day for observation. Why?"

He turned back to Deidre. "I need a favor."

She looked at Bar'ella and saw the healer nod. "All right."

"Please return the book to the Library of Magic. Detective Damien will accompany you."

That sounded easy enough. "Okay."

Music filled the room. "I fell into a Burning Ring of Fire…"

Deidre shared a glance with Bar'ella, who looked confused.

"Ah, that's mine." Mr. Phoenix flushed and pulled out his cell phone. He excused himself and went into the hallway.

A moment later he re-entered the room and looked at Captain Jor'dan.

"Captain, there's trouble. A few moments ago, devils appeared in Shadow Earth." He turned to give Deidre a look. "The leader is demanding someone named Deidre."

Deidre gasped and felt the blood drain from her face. "Devils?"

She shook her head as her heart-beat pounded in her ears. She gripped the book so tight, her knuckles turned white. Her breathing sped up as panic gripped her.

The Tome moved toward her rumbling, as if trying to sooth. But not even the papery purr could still the dread that filled her.

Damien took a step forward when James caught his arm and pulled him back. "What's wrong, honey?"

Deidre looked at Mr. Phoenix. "What do they look like?"

Mr. Phoenix opened the cell phone. "Here's a picture."

He turned the phone toward her, and there on the screen was her nightmare come to life. He had found her somehow.

Khan.

If he got his claws on her, there'd be no escape.

Damien leaned forward and frowned. "What do you know of these devils?"

"They're not devils. They're Demoni."

"You know them?" James tone was filled with incredulousness.

Deidre nodded.

Jor'dan spoke up. "How can we stop them? Guns?"

Deidre shook her head. "No, but swords might slow them down, if you were to strike in the exposed joints. Nothing on earth will kill them."

Mr. Phoenix cleared his throat. "How do you know?"

Deidre sighed. "It's hard to explain. I… think I retain some memories of when I was in their realm. They need to be sent back to their home dimension."

"With magic?" Mr. Phoenix clarified.

Deidre nodded. "It's the only way."

"How did they get here?" Bar'ella asked. "And why are they speaking English?"

Deidre had no idea about how they got here, but she could answer the language problem. "Translation is inherent in the summoning spell. So while they're speaking their native language, we're hearing English."

"Can you speak this language?" Bar'ella asked, interest lighting her expression.

Deidre nodded.

"Is there a chance Mage Douglas completed the spell?" James asked. They all turned to Deidre.

"I don't know. I just pulled the energy, I have no idea if he succeeded or not."

A picture flashed in her mind. Khan fondling a locket. A locket that held a piece of her hair. She closed her eyes and let her head fall back.

Dar'kirm take her! She'd led him here. *Think!*

He had a piece of her hair that had allowed him to track her through dimensions. That coupled with Sir's spell, had given him a gateway to Earth.

The only way to get rid of him was to banish him. But how?

A rumbling noise came to her at the same time the book butted against her chest. She opened her eyes and looked at it. The book flipped open, the pages turning by themselves until they stopped at a particular page. She looked down at the unfamiliar scribbles that danced across the paper.

A throat cleared, and she looked up to see Mr. Phoenix watching her.

"What are you doing?" his tone emphatic.

She shook her head. "Nothing. The book's doing it."

He nodded and considered her for a moment. "Can you read the words?"

She looked down. "No... Oh wait." The strange markings rearranged themselves into symbols that were familiar to her.

"What?"

"I couldn't read it before, but now... huh." She looked up at Mr. Phoenix. "It's a reverse summoning spell."

James piped up. "Who can we get to perform the spell? It has to be someone that won't be taken over by the book."

Deidre didn't like the smile that crossed Mr. Phoenix's face. She knew what he was going to say before he opened his mouth. She shook her head.

"Deidre's going to perform the spell."

Expressions of disbelief filled the room. "What?" "Impossible!" "No."

Deidre met Mr. Phoenix's gaze and didn't look away. "I can't do that. I'm not a Mage. I just got over a massive drain. Even if I knew how, I wouldn't have enough power to summon a toad."

Mr. Phoenix held up a hand, stopping her from speaking further. "The book will lend you the power to send the Demoni home."

She shook her head. "I don't know anything about magic."

He raised an eyebrow.

"Fine. I know a little, but only in regards to the spell that binds me. A Mage would be better."

He shook his head. "No. For some reason the book is not able to assert its influence on you. There isn't a single Mage who would be able to use the Tome and not be overwhelmed by it."

"Wait. Why am I not overwhelmed by it?"

Mr. Phoenix smiled again. "It's because you're magic, created out of the same stuff as the Tomes."

"That doesn't allow me to work it though."

Deidre looked down at the book trying to find inspiration.

If I do the spell here, then Khan and the Demoni will be sent home, and I won't have to see him again. Wait. What in Dar'kirm am I thinking? I can't use magic!

A section of words flickered. Compelled, she read them out loud. "In order to reverse a summoning, the practitioner must be in visual contact of that which was summoned."

Bastard son J'kala, Dar'kirm curse it!

Seeing Khan again was the last thing she wanted to do!

Deidre shook her head. "I can't."

Mr. Phoenix walked toward the head of the bed. "I can help if you'd allow it."

She frowned at him. "How?"

He approached the bed. "May I touch you?"

What the hell? Since when had anyone asked to touch her? She bit her lip and nodded.

His words echoed in her mind. *"Since I respect you as a magic being."*

She met his gaze as he reached out and clasped her head in his hands, palms on her temples.

"What…"

She jolted, her body convulsing as she fell into the flames in his eyes. She couldn't see anything but the dancing fire which pulled her into the deep recesses of his mind.

She floated in inky blackness, and saw… things. Flashes illuminated and went dark before she could identify them. It was like looking through a dark museum where the only source of illumination was from a slow strobe light.

"Concentrate." His voice surrounded her, became a part of her

"On what?"

"This."

It felt like she was in transition, but without the pain. Knowledge flooded her mind and she saw the key to utilizing the physical force known as magic.

As swift as a hummingbird, her mind darted back and reconnected with her body. She opened her eyes.

Everything looked normal, except the book was gone. She frowned and realized it was still with her, but hiding itself until she called.

Her head rested against a strong chest. Deidre inhaled Damien's masculine scent. For a moment she allowed herself to find comfort in his tight embrace, then sat up and pulled away from him. He tightened his arms around her as if he didn't want to let go, but finally released her.

"Anything else?" Bar'ella asked.

Mr. Phoenix shook his head. "No. That's everything."

He faced Deidre. "I'll leave you in Detective Alexander's protective custody."

He motioned for James and Jor'dan to accompany him into the hall.

Bar'ella glared at Damien. "She needs to get dressed."

"Yes, mother. I'll let you baby your little chick." Damien sounded more amused than anything. "We'll talk later." He placed a gentle kiss on her forehead and got up from the bed. He started to leave the room before glancing back to Bar'ella.

"I'm petitioning the Council for permission, and I would like you to testify on my behalf."

"It's about time. I'd be honored Damien Alexander." She placed her hand over her heart and bowed her head.

Damien smiled at Bar'ella then winked at Deidre and left the room, closing the door behind him.

Deidre felt a frown mar her forehead. "What was that all about? Permission from the Council for what?"

Bar'ella merely smiled and shook her head. "I'll let him explain it to you later."

Deidre sighed. "What's going to happen to me, Bar'ella?"

"What do you mean?"

"Am I still in trouble? I know I'm in Detective Alexander's protective custody, but what does that mean?"

Bar'ella opened the cabinet under the nightstand and pulled out a bundle of cloth.

"I suggest you not worry about it now. Things will work out. You'll see."

"Yeah right. Things always work out for the best for me. That's why I'm always in trouble."

"You do have a knack for it don't you? Here."

Bar'ella handed the black cloth to Deidre.

"What's this?"

"Cyn left it for you."

"Where is she? Did she get away? Is she still in custody?"

"She's on the lam, I'm afraid. But she did stop by to give you this as well as to say thanks for everything."

Deidre shrugged, uncomfortable with the thanks.

Bar'ella pulled out a pair of stiletto heeled boots. "She also left these for you."

Deidre's eyes opened wide. "Excellent!"

"Cyn asked that you call her once you were free of," Bar'ella held up her hands to make air quotes. "those Elite parasites.'"

Deidre chuckled and pushed the covers back and got out of bed.

Bar'ella came forward and helped her into the skin-tight body suit.

As she dressed, she noticed the weight from around her neck was missing.

"What happened to the medallion?"

Bar'ella smiled. "It's there on the bedside table. Don't worry, it's powerless."

"How did that happen?"

"I'm not sure if it was Mage Douglas' death that did it or if it was when you were on fire."

"Wait... I was on fire?" Deidre shook her head. "I'm glad I don't remember that. Fire isn't fun."

Bar'ella cleared her throat. "Does this mean you're free?"

Deidre sighed. "No. As long as the drawing is still intact, I'm still..."

"A slave." Bar'ella finished for her.

"Yes."

"How long until you're summoned again?"

Deidre tilted her head in thought. "I think I have a couple of weeks."

"Is there anything I can do?"

Deidre shook her head. "No. The one to erase the drawing has to be male."

"Perhaps I'll drop a word in a certain Detective's ear..."

Deidre grabbed Bar'ella's arm. "No. Don't."

"Why not?"

Deidre pulled on the stiletto-heeled boots. "I can't explain in a way you'd understand." She looked up at the healer from her seated position on the bed. "Just please, don't say anything."

Bar'ella frowned. "You have got to be the single most stubborn being I've ever run across!"

Deidre smiled. "That's why we get along so well."

"Harrumph."

Deidre walked over to the bathroom mirror and looked at her reflection. "Cyn has excellent taste."

Bar'ella leaned against the door. "And I'm sure the Detective will swallow his tongue when he sees you in it."

The smile faded from Deidre's expression. Bar'ella came forward, concern etched on her feature. "What's wrong? It can't be Damien?"

Deidre shrugged. "He likes me for now. But what happens when he remembers who and what I am?"

"He's gotten past that, Deidre. He was devastated when he thought you were dead." The healer put her hand on Deidre's cheek. "Have faith in your Vampire and the love he bears you."

Deidre sighed. "Faith. Ha. I'm not sure I believe in that anymore."

A knock on the window. Bar'ella turned "What in the world?" She walked to the window and opened it. "Who are you?"

"Come in Tomás." Deidre grinned.

"Pardon the intrusion, but I need to reassure myself my sister is okay."

Once he climbed through the window, Deidre ran into his open arms. "Oh how I've missed you!"

His arms closed tight around her, filling her with a sense of safety.

"What are you doing here?"

Tomás pulled back. "I felt your pain. I had to make sure you were okay."

"I am, now."

Deidre watched as her charming brother turned the full force of his smile on the healer. "Thank you for saving my stubborn sister."

Bar'ella blushed bright red. "I had little to do with it." She narrowed her eyes. "Wait a minute. Aren't you that actor who played the trickster god?"

He bowed his head once. "I am."

The healer's mouth hung open and Deidre giggled.

Tomás turned her, looking more serious than she'd ever seen him. "What the bloody hell happened?"

"An incarnation gone bad."

"That's putting it mildly," Bar'ella muttered. "She was barbequed."

"What?!"

"But as you can see, brother dear, I'm fine, now."

He pulled her into his body, hugging her tight.

"Are you in trouble? Do I need to get you away?"

Deidre shook her head. "Not yet. I have to take care of a problem first."

They turned at a knock on the outer door. Jor'dan's voice demanded. "Are you done yet? Those demons are destroying the city!"

Tomás released her and headed out the window. "I'll check on you later."

"Alright."

Deidre waited until her brother left before she opened the door and stepped out into the corridor followed by Bar'ella.

Damien groaned when he saw her.

She lifted an eyebrow. "Is something wrong, Detective?"

He shook his head. "Not if you intended to stop every male thought process within a twenty mile radius."

"It's part of my charm. Shall we go?"

Damien held out his arm, and when she took it, led her to the street door.

She glanced behind them and noticed James and Captain Jor'dan still staring at her in the hallway. Certain they were ogling her ass, she chuckled.

Damien turned to her "What's so funny?"

"Your friends."

He looked back. "Stop staring," he ordered. "We don't have time for this shit."

A car waited on the curb outside the clinic and Damien got into the driver's seat. They others clambered in. Tires squealed on the pavement as Damien raced away.

Chapter 21

They arrived at the point of invasion a few minutes later. Deidre shivered in dread.

There, in front of a group of lesser Demoni, stood Khan, dressed in full battle armor, his sword at the ready. A few of the Elite stood in a line in front of him, and it was unclear what was going on.

Captain Jor'dan spoke up from the back seat. "He's demanding we turn over Deidre to him."

Deidre sighed. "That's me."

Damien clenched his hands on the steering wheel before throwing the car in park and jerking the keys from the ignition.

"How do you know? Is it possible he referring to someone else?"

Deidre shook her head. "No. I'm the one he wants."

"How do you know?"

She gave him a look. "He was my last assignment before being summoned to Earth."

"Well he's not going to get you."

She put her hand on his arm, feeling the tension that invaded his body. "You may not have a choice."

He turned and glared at her. "Giving you up is not an option! So get that thought out of your head right now!"

They exited the car, and the Elite moved around her, enveloping her in a circle of protection.

Khan's voice rang out. "Bring me Deidre!"

Deidre saw a Mage step forward and confront Khan. "We don't know who this Deidre is."

Khan motioned to one of his troops who came forward with an etching.

Damien glanced back and pulled Deidre into the shadow of the building. "Start your spell from here. Do not engage him. Do you understand?"

She nodded, and he leaned down and gave her a scorching hot kiss.

He looked into her eyes and ran a hand through the hair at her temples. "Please. Be safe."

Deidre nodded again. "I'll be fine."

Damien took two steps away from her, turned and pulled her into a searing kiss that heated her from the inside out.

He turned and ran to the other Elite as Khan's forces attacked.

Deidre turned her attention away from the bloody fight and called the book.

"Hey, Book of Power I need you." A small flash and it appeared before her, flipping open to the spell.

She lowered her head, took a deep breath, and began reading the words off the page.

"Tragunita, Alehambrine, Mecaloyteas, Tecoriumate, Ladianis, Zeloralum…"

A deep voice interrupted her recital.

"Deidre. You've been a very bad girl."

Fear trickled down her spine as she looked up into Khan's black gaze.

A black-clawed hand reached for her throat and was stopped by a sword.

"Back away from her. Now!" Damien's voice commanded. "Deidre, finish it!"

She glanced down and recited the words. Khan's form became more insubstantial the further she read.

Khan knocked the sword away from Damien and lashed out at the Vamp. Deidre saw him take the blow that knocked him back into a brick wall. He slid down the wall, dazed.

A clawed hand around her throat halted her chanting. Khan's claws pierced her flesh as he tightened his grip. Wetness trickled down her neck as he shook her like a rag doll.

"Your pitiful little world is perfect for our invasion force, but I've got the real prize."

She looked down at the book still hovering in front of her and a glint of metal caught her eye. The locket with her hair. The means he'd used to track her down.

Damien chose that moment to attack, distracting Khan. Reaching forward she gripped the metal in her hand and in one move, ripped it from his belt and throwing it as far away as possible.

"Book, help me." Her voice came out weak and she began to have trouble breathing as fluid filled her lungs.

Khan's grip tightened while he fought off Damien and the other Elite, cutting off what air she had.

Pain created an unreal haze and the words on the page seemed to waver. The words on the page appeared larger, clearer. Gasping for breath, Deidre recited the last two words and the closing of the spell. "Grandamelia, Sharvonakdli. I repel you, creature, back to the dimension from which you came. Never set foot in this world again!"

Screams inundated her brain and Earth faded from view.

The world materialized around Deidre. *What happened? Where am I?* The overpowering smell of rotting flesh made her gag.

Deidre grabbed Khan's wrist, with both hands, trying to stop his choking grip. Her five-fingered, human hands were pale against the deep ruby of Khan's skin

"Magician!" His yell echoed off the stone walls and made her fragile ears ring.

A Demoni scurried into the throne room. A colorful band was the only adornment on his naked body.

J'kala, she was back on the Demoni home world. *Shit. Damn. Fuck. As Damien would say.*

"Y-yes. Your Merciless?"

She felt herself flying through the air. Agony seared her as she crashed onto the polished stone floor at the foot of the summoned Demoni.

"Change her to a pleasing form."

Deidre looked up at the magician and saw his red skin pale to pink. "Yes, Great Khan."

He stooped to grab her arm and yank her up. A growl stopped him in mid grab.

"No one is allowed to touch her."

"As you wish Sire. I need to fetch my tools."

Khan waved his hand in dismissal, and the magician fled the room.

Khan stalked up the stone dais steps and sat on his throne, a look of determination on his face.

"Change, Deidre."

She shook her head, coughing up blood as her body rushed to repair itself. Her energy was dwindling at a rapid rate, and she felt herself become weaker as blood left her body.

A sound came from the back of the throne, and the Grand Vizier stepped out from behind it.

"Your Merciless! Why have you returned so soon?"

Khan gestured toward her. "Deidre spelled us back."

The Vizier looked at her and stepped back in revulsion. "That's Deidre?"

Khan nodded. "She refuses to change form."

Khan reached for the locket, and a look of consternation crossed his face, quickly replaced by anger.

"Deidre! What have you done with the talisman?"

Deidre struggled to her feet, loss of blood making her dizzy. She tried to speak, but human throats weren't meant to reproduce the guttural speech of the Demoni. So she shrugged and responded in English. "I threw it away."

The Vizier stalked down the steps. "What noises are these?"

Khan followed. "It's how the creatures communicate."

The Vizier stepped closer to her. "Can it understand us?"

Khan growled. "Yes."

"But how do you know, Sire?"

"Deidre, can you understand?"

Deidre debated for a moment, but seething anger in Khan's eyes changed her mind. She nodded her head once.

The Vizier stalked around her in a circle, making sure to keep his distance.

"How hideous these Earthers are! Weak, pale skin and bleached hair. Are you sure this is the same female?"

"Yes."

"How do you know, Sire? Perhaps this is a trap?"

"The talisman led me to her. This is the correct female."

A whisper came from the side of the room, and the Vizier went to investigate. A few moments later, he returned.

"I have bad news, Sire. The magicians have tried every invocation and spell they know. They're unable to return her to Demoni form."

Steam escape Khan's horns. "Leave us!"

The magicians and the Vizier rushed to obey his command.

§

Damien looked up to see Khan and Deidre slowly fade from view. He jumped up and ran to her, his hand passing through her transparent form before she disappeared completely.

He looked around to see all the devils gone.

"No!"

The fight went out of him as he sank to his knees.

His Deidre was gone, captured by the King of the Demoni. She was gone, again.

How was he going to get her back? His mind was blank; he didn't know where to begin.

A small female hand patted his shoulder. He turned to see the Oracle, Regina. "She's not gone forever."

He looked up, hope rising in his heart. "Where is she?"

The Oracle shook her head. "If you love her, set her free."

Anger pulsed through him. "What the hell does that mean?"

"Just what it says." She turned, took two steps, turned and paused, holding out a locket on a chain.

"This may help."

He held out his hand and she dropped the necklace into it. As soon as the metal hit his palm a connection with Deidre snapped into place. And his woman was in a great deal of pain.

"Wait! How do I…"

Regina walked away. "Go to where it began."

He jumped to his feet, clenching the locket in his fist, and ran toward the car, ignoring the shouted questions directed at him.

Damien made it to the warehouse in record time, breaking a few traffic laws along the way. But he didn't care about that now. He needed to get Deidre back.

He pulled the car over and popped into Real Earth, heedless of the two homeless men who saw him. He ran to the backdoor, and forced his way into the machine-littered room.

Damien let his Vampire senses flair out. He was alone. *Good.* Running, he jumped down the stairs three at a time. He reached the room and looked in. The darkness was such that even with his

340

enhanced vision, he could barely make out the shape of the table within.

He pulled a small flashlight from his pocket and illuminated the room. The only part he was interested in was the drawing on the floor. Still intact. Good.

Now what the hell should he do? He paced from the door to the wall and back again.

How do I summon a Succubus?

A small flash of light and a scroll appeared, floating to the floor.

Damien picked up the scroll. "How to Summon a Succubus."

Perfect.

His phone chirped at him. James had left dozens of messages. He called his partner.

"Where the hell are you?" James asked.

"At the warehouse. I'm going to summon Deidre home."

"How?"

I'll do anything to get her back, including making a deal with the devil, if I have to. "A scroll appeared detailing how to do it."

"Isn't that a bit convenient?"

"You think?"

"Don't use it. It could be a trap."

"I have to. It may be the only way to save her."

"Then wait for me. I'm on my way."

"I can't. I have to do this now. She's hurt."

"Okay. Do you need anything?"

Damien glanced down at the paper. "According to this I need the summoning circle, which is still here, candles and the will to summon a demon. Looks like everything is here."

Damien skimmed through the spell and realized he wouldn't be able to perform it now. Dawn was approaching and day sleep would claim him before he finished.

"Can you bring me some blood tonight? I'll attempt it then."

"Are you headed home?"

"No, I'll spend the day here."

"Got it. See you tonight."

He shrugged out of his coat and laid it on the cold stone floor, and tried to make himself comfortable. Exhaustion pulled at him. He looked around, his body telling him that dawn was near. Damien clenched the locket in his hand and let the day sleep claim him.

§

Deidre needed to think and fast.

How in Dar'kirm was she going to get out of this?

She couldn't fight Khan physically, not in her human form. And she didn't know how to change into a stronger being.

Think! How can I defeat him? And the answer came to her in a brilliant flash. *Of course!*

Khan stalked toward her, grabbing her by the throat again. His claws pierced her newly healed skin as he lifted her from the floor.

Being grabbed by the throat was getting old, fast. She grabbed his arm.

What have I got to lose other than my life? Nothing.

Deidre sent her power rushing through him, concentrating on connecting with his energy.

For a single moment, nothing happened.

Her human pheromones were incompatible with Demoni physiology. She'd have to try something else. What if she used her power directly on him, rather than using pheromones?

Deidre sent a pulse of head straight into his mind and encountered an unexpected barrier. *Must be due to incompatible forms.* She pushed hard against the fluid shield, able to move through it slowly. Like swimming through setting gelatin.

She crafted an image, of them intimately intertwined, with her in her Demoni form. His breathing increased, and so did his energy. She pulled at it but it slipped through her metaphysical

342

fingers. Deidre tried again, this time cupping her mental fingers and dipping them into the pool of his essence.

Searing, stabbing pain burned her as she sipped his essence. Demoni power was incompatible with her human form, and it blazed. A red tendril rose from him and she inhaled his power, searing her lungs and sending fire throughout her body.

But she had to keep going, had to pull enough to weaken him.

He appeared to be intent on the images she was projecting into his brain. He didn't realize when his grip loosened, and his arm shook.

Khan shook his head. "What have you done?" His once strong voice had weakened to a whisper. He tried to tug his arm away from her, but she held onto him easily with her meager human strength.

Just a few tendrils more.

Khan collapsed to the ground in front of her, limbs flopping on the floor like a rag doll.

His eyes fluttered closed. "I... own... you," he gasped.

She stopped drawing his energy the moment before his death. He gasped for breath, struggling to regain his feet.

Khan's final breath rattled in his lungs and he stilled.

Looking around, Deidre spotted a jeweled dagger. She had to make sure the bastard stayed dead. Plunging the hard metal into his chest, she twisted it several times, ensuring his magicians could not reanimate him.

Once that was done, she sat on his bed. Now what the hell was she going to do? As soon as he was discovered, she'd be dead. Fleeing and hiding was impossible; her human form was noticeably different.

A soft familiar glow lit the bed beneath her.

Summoned again.

Transition hurt like a bitch. *Where to this time?*

The glowing thread appeared, pulling her to her next master. She'd thought about Cyn, and Bar'ella. *Would she see them again?* And Damien, she'd never forget him. He'd probably forget about her by the time she got back to Earth. It would hurt to see him happily settled with someone else. How she'd deal with uninteresting, anonymous sex, she didn't know. Mentally taking a deep breath, she put that aside and concentrated on her new incarnation.

Her attention turned to her new location and something strange happened. Unlike all the other times, she received no data regarding her new home. Nothing. She poked at the thread, but no information was forthcoming. *Odd.*

The thread encapsulated her. The light faded to a dim glow before winking out.

Once again her vision blurred and jumped. Another candle filled room, another stone lined room. And look, a grate in the floor.

Medieval dungeon? Check.

Containment drawing? Check.

New master? Che… What in Dar'kirm?

"Damien?"

Her mind blanked and she felt her jaw drop. *What the hell was he doing?*

Her handsome Vampire winked at her, glanced down at the paper, and brought his hands together in a clap. "I name you, Deidre."

"What in the name of Dar'kirm are you doing?"

A wide grin split his face. "I'm getting my woman back."

Damien flipped the paper over, frowned for a moment, then looked at the floor. He stepped from the summoner's position and held out his hand. She placed her hand in his and a jolt of energy sparked through her. Tugging on her hand, he pulled her from the drawing, and into his chest.

A soft kiss brushed her lips. "I, Damien Alexander, Summoner of Deidre, hereby free her from the spell."

His foot scraped across the floor, and when she looked down, she saw the containment drawing broken.

A dark, whirling vortex arose from the drawing. A voice from her past, one she hoped she'd never hear again, spoke. "To free the Succubus you must sacrifice that which you hold most dear... your life."

The vortex split in two. One encircled Damien and ripped him from her grip. The second surrounded her. A short time later and hers evaporated, dropping her to the cool stone floor.

A horrific scream echoed through the chamber, followed by a gurgling sound. Deidre reached for Damien, ignoring the sparks of energy that burned her skin. As she touched him, the vortex died, leaving his body hovering over the floor. A moment later he fell.

Deidre rushed to his side, checking for pulse, for breathing, for any sign of life. *Damn it, how was she to tell if he was dead or sleeping?*

Sightless eyes looked at her. She reached out and closed them.

Deidre shook his shoulder. "Damien, wake up."

No response.

Sitting back on her heels, she huffed out a breath. What to do? He'd saved her at great cost to himself. But how to tell?

Leaning over, moving her brown hair out of the way, she kissed his mouth, licking the seam of his lips. Her tongue caught on an incisor and her blood smeared his lip. He jolted then settled.

Could that be it?

Deidre searched his pockets... Where was it? She pulled the small knife from the sheath on his belt and made a small cut on her wrist, placing it over his mouth.

Please let this work!

For a long moment, nothing happened. Deidre thought her heart would stop.

Jagged pain ripped through her wrist as his fangs sung deep. Relief drowned out everything else.

A couple of swallows and his eyes popped open. The seductive glide of his tongue over the cut caused her body to melt with heat.

He moved her arm away. "Thank you."

Deidre nodded her head. "You're welcome."

Using her wrist, he pulled her down on top of him, and pulled her head to his, kissing her long and deep. When he pulled back, she could see love and something else in his eyes.

"I'm sorry."

Confusion filled her. "For what?"

"For not believing in you."

Deidre pulled away and sat back. Drawing up her knees, she wrapped her arms around them. "It's okay."

He sat up. "No, it's not. I let circumstances spoil us. And for that I'm sorry."

"But I did kill your friends."

"Yes, but that wasn't by choice, was it?"

Deidre bit her lip. "No."

"Would you have killed them if you'd had the choice?"

She shook her head. "I don't kill, well, not normally."

Damien narrowed his eyes. "Who did you kill?"

"I had to kill Khan. It was either him or me."

Damien stroked her arm, sparks of sensation following the trail of hand. "That's okay then. Please forgive me?"

Deidre took a deep breath. "I guess." After all he'd gone through a great deal to not only summoner her back to earth, but to free her from the spell which could have cost him his life. "I forgive you."

Damien pulled her down to him and nibbled on her lips, then moved to her jaw. He wanted to show her his love, so he took his time worshipping her. Sipping at her lips, licking and nibbling her breasts, stroking her stomach and inner thighs. When he thought she couldn't take any more, he settled himself between her legs and slowly pushed inside her.

He groaned as his length filled her, stretched her, made her his.

He rocked his hips with gentle power and soon they were headed toward the crest together. This was what he had been searching for all his life, a true mate, the partner of his soul.

The climax was devastating in its softness. A gentle tumble from the heights. She sighed and gazed at him with love-filled eyes.

"That was nice," she whispered. Her eyes took on a mischievous twinkle, "Can we play rough now?"

He laughed, still pulsing within her. "That's my girl, insatiable to the end."

She used his inattention to roll him onto his back where she proceeded to take him hard and fast… her way.

A long time later she was resting against him, both naked on his trench coat.

"So why did you change your hair?" he asked, running fingers through the long strands.

"What do you mean?"

Damien showed her a hank of her hair. It was reddish brown rather than blond. Deidre reached out and touched it. "I forgot," her voice was soft.

"Forgot what?"

"This is my real hair." She sat up and looked around. "Do you have a mirror?"

"Why?"

"I want to see what I look like."

"Don't you remember?"

She looked down at him. "No. I've not seen the original me in a very long time."

He pulled her down and whispered, "Look later," against her lips.

"Why weren't you killed?" she asked, tracing random drawings on his chest.

"Maybe the Mage didn't take into account the Elite's higher magical resistance. I'd have been okay, but your blood sped the healing process."

A ring from his phone brought their pleasurable interlude to an end.

He answered the phone. "Yes? It worked... yeah, me too. Okay, we'll be right there." Finishing the call he closed his eyes and sighed. "We've got to go."

"Where?"

"You need to return the Tome of Power to the Library of Magic."

"Oh. I forgot about that." But wait. Did she still have the book? "Tome of Power, are you still with me?"

The book popped into existence beside her. Grinning, she reached out and patted it. "Good."

Damien rose and got dressed. "We have to hurry, the Mages are frantic."

Deidre sighed and rose from the makeshift pallet. "Do you have clothes for me?"

He nodded and threw her a bundle. "From Cyn, via Bar'ella."

She pulled on the skin-tight leather mini skirt, lacy top, and heeled ankle boots. Cyn had excellent taste.

Damien caught her around the wrist and pulled her to him. Her soft body yielded against his hard frame. "You look hot enough to eat."

She smirked up at him. "What are you going to do about it?"

His firm lips crushed hers, and a part of her thrilled that she was able to unleash his aggressive nature.

Damien sighed and pulled away from her. "Stop distracting me. We have to get that damned Tome back where it belongs."

A short trip later, they arrived at the Library. The Mages wouldn't let her in to see the Head Librarian, insisting she hand the book over to one of the junior Mages.

Beside her, she felt Damien tense.

"What the hell do you mean she can't go up? She's the one with the damned book."

The Mage in front of them cowered for a moment and Deidre thought Damien had succeeding in cowing him, until he spoke. "Be that as it may, no female is allowed access to the third or higher level."

"Even with permission?" Damien's jaw clenched

The Mage shook his head. "No female is given permission… ever."

"Call the Head Librarian."

When the Mage in front of him hesitated, he growled and showed his fangs in a parody of a smile. "Now."

Deidre hid her grin as the Mage scurried away into an office and picked up the phone.

"This is bullshit."

Deidre shrugged. "I guess they don't want the book back badly enough. Shall we go?"

Damien shook his head. "I've got another idea. If it doesn't work, we'll leave." He pulled out his phone and hit a button. "They're blocking us." His low tone sent shivers along her spine.

"Well now what?" she asked.

He smiled down at her. "We see what they do next and then play it by ear."

"Alright."

The Mage strutted back. "I'm sorry, the Head Librarian is in a high level meeting and can't be disturbed. If you'll be good enough to leave the Tome with me, I'll be sure to return it to the Tower."

"No." Damien took a hold of Deidre's elbow and turned to lead her through the doors outside.

"Wait!"

Deidre looked over her shoulder at the panic in the Mage's face. It took all her skill to keep from laughing.

Damien stopped. "Yes?"

"You forgot to leave the Tome."

Damien tilted his head down and looked over his sunglasses at the Mage. "I'm sorry did I not make myself clear? We'll only deliver it to the Tower, not into the hands of a flunky with more hair than brains with a trumped up sense of superiority."

The Mage's jaw dropped in shock.

Deidre could see him floundering when a deep voice interrupted.

"Is there a problem here, Detective Alexander?"

Damien pulled her around again and Mr. Phoenix was standing in the rotunda with them. *Where did he come from?*

Damien bowed, and nudged Deidre, who remembered to curtsy.

He straightened and smiled. "Not at all, Your Grace. In order to return the Tome of Power, we need to see the Head Librarian."

Mr. Phoenix frowned. "And where is he?"

The Mage spoke up. "He's in a meeting and can't be disturbed."

"I see." Mr. Phoenix tilted his head for a moment. "Detective, Miss Deidre, if you would come with me?"

Damien nodded and motioned for Deidre to precede him, and they followed Mr. Phoenix up the circular staircase.

"Wait!"

Deidre turned to see the Mage scamper after them. "You can't go in there. She's not allowed in there!"

Mr. Phoenix stopped and crossed his arms over his chest. "She has my permission. Have I made myself clear?"

"Y-y-yes sir."

350

"Good. You may go now."

They watched as the Mage left, running to the nearest office.

A sigh drew her attention back to Mr. Phoenix. "He's probably calling security. Shall we go?"

Deidre followed Mr. Phoenix until they reached the Head Librarian's office. They entered and Mr. Phoenix locked the door behind them, and turned with arms crossed over his chest. "I assume you know how to get to the Tower?"

Damien nodded and went over to the fireplace, removing the correct candle from its holder. The fireplace popped open and he led the way inside. Up the stairs they climbed, Deidre following Damien and Mr. Phoenix following her.

When they arrived at the landing before the door, Damien cleared his throat. "According to Master Roberts, only a Mage can get into the room."

Mr. Phoenix smiled. "This goes no further than the three of us." Mr. Phoenix leaned forward and whispered, "He's wrong."

He turned to Deidre. "Please return the Tome to its proper place."

"Yes, Mr. Phoenix." Deidre paused for a moment. "Book, I need you."

She felt a soft caress and the Tome appeared, floating before her. "Come on, Tome, we're going to put you back where you belong."

Deidre turned to Mr. Phoenix. "In there?"

He nodded.

She walked to the door and reached for the handle at the same time Damien shouted. "Stop!"

Deidre looked over her shoulder at him. Mr. Phoenix moved to Damien's side and put a hand on his shoulder.

Mr. Phoenix nodded. "It's okay Miss Deidre. Continue."

"But…" Damien's protest was forgotten as she approached the door.

She grabbed the door-knob, and it warmed under her hand. Turning the knob, she opened the door and entered the room. Deidre looked back to see Damien's mouth hanging open in surprise.

She shook her head with a smile and approached the empty pedestal in front of her. She reached out and grasped the Book, placing it on the pedestal. Reluctance came from the Tome and she petted the ornate cover in sympathy. "I know you don't want to be here, but this is where you belong until you're needed again."

Resignation emanated from the Tome, and it shuddered once as she attached the chains and padlocks. She leaned down and whispered. "And who knows, maybe we can have some fun again in the future."

A wave of acceptance and promise came from the Book, and Deidre knew the next time it was free, it would find her.

She gave it one last pat and turned to leave the room. Deidre felt a sense of anticipation from the other Tomes and smiled. "Power will tell you all about its adventures."

A commotion at the door had her stopping in her tracks.

"What is the meaning of this outrage!" an angry voice demanded.

Deidre turned to look through the door and saw five Mages with Damien and Mr. Phoenix.

"She's returning the Tome of Power," Mr. Phoenix answered.

"But that's impossible. No female is allowed in this room, much less one who is not a Mage." The speaker turned to her, glaring. "Remove yourself from the room at once, female."

Behind her. Power bristled in its chains, and the others followed suit. She touched each leather cover, calming the Tomes. "There's no need to get upset on my behalf."

One of the Mages took a step toward the door. A wall of flame appeared on the outside of the door. Gasps came from those on the landing. The flames died, and a wall of ice appeared, followed by gale-force winds, then a wall of marble, and lastly a swirling void.

Once the doorway cleared, she could see the shocked expressions on everyone's face.

"What in the world was that?" asked a Mage, his tone pompous and condescending.

"It appears, Master Dean, that the Tomes are protective of Miss Deidre."

In response, each of the Books glowed.

Deidre turned back to them. "Aren't you the sweetest? Thank you for your support." A sigh left her. "As much as I'd love to stay and chat, you're needed for the ceremony."

A sense of resolve filled the room, and after giving each Tome one last pat, she left the room, pulling the wooden door closed behind her.

She looked at the shocked faces of the Mages in front of her. "What? How?" they sputtered.

Mr. Phoenix smiled. "It's nothing to be concerned about." He turned and gave her a stern look. "This is a onetime occurrence. You are not to visit this room again without going through the proper channels first."

Deidre bowed her head. "Yes Mr. Phoenix."

She led the way down the stairs, leaving the Mages to do whatever it was they were going to do.

Leaving the building, Damien turned to Mr. Phoenix. "Your Grace, how was Deidre able enter the tower room without the spells?"

Mr. Phoenix grinned. "Miss Deidre is a creature of power, formed of the same stuff housed in the Tomes. That's why their magic held no allure for her. The wards on the door are of a younger magic which recognized hers as being more powerful. Simple really."

They parted ways in front of the Library.

Damien took her back to his apartment.

Deidre tapped her fingers together, nerves jumping. "So what happens now?"

Damien too her hand and led her to the armchair. He sat down and pulled her into his lap. "I want you to stay here, with me."

"Why?"

He tilted her face up so their eyes met. "I love you. I want you in my life, by my side, forever. You're already in my heart."

Deidre wet her lips. "But what if you remember…"

"How wonderfully stubborn you are?"

She glared at him. "That's not what I meant."

"I know."

He brought their entwined hands up to his mouth and placed a kiss on the back of her hand. "You still have doubts."

Deidre nodded. "I can't help it."

"Will you at least try?"

"What would that entail?"

"You'll move in with me and we see how it goes."

It was a big step for her, but with all that had happened in the past few days she realized this was exactly where she wanted to be.

"Okay."

Damien leaned down and kissed her, letting the love in his heart infuse the meeting of their lips. He stood and carried her into his room, and spent the rest of the night convincing her to stay.

§

In a board room, high above the streets of San Francisco, a high level meeting was taking place.

"So you're telling me the Succubus was able to enter and leave the Tower room at will?"

"Yes, sir."

"Very interesting. I'd like to have a chat with this Succubus."

The Chairman waved his hand. "Yes, yes, but on your own time. How are the experiments coming along?"

The End